Oh, thank you, God!

I am wrapped in my own rapture of thankfulness and relief as the hateful rope is taken from my neck and I am taken down and tossed into a rough woodshed. I hit the earthen floor and hear a bolt being thrown.

My hands still bound, I wriggle about the floor, searching desperately for some way out, but find none. Then, on the breeze that blows in through the cracks in the door, I smell a wood fire being started. *Could they mean to burn me?* I wonder with renewed dread.

Then I hear the squawks of chickens being chased and then the thump of ax on chopping block and then I hear the squawks no more. *Could it be that they are preparing dinner and have forgotten about me for the moment?*

Oh, no, that is not it at all.

For then I breathe in the unmistakable smell of hot tar.

L. A. MEYER

Mississippi Jack

Being an Account of
the Further Waterborne Adventures
of Jacky Faber, Midshipman,
Fine Lady, and the Lily of the West

GRAPHIA

Houghton Mifflin Harcourt
Boston New York

www.graphiabooks.com

The Library of Congress has catalogued the hardcover edition as follows:
Meyer, L. A. (Louis A.), 1942–
Mississippi Jack: being an account of the further waterborne adventures
of Jacky Faber, midshipman, fine lady, and the Lily of the West/L. A. Meyer.
p. cm.—(A Bloody Jack adventure)
Summary: In 1806, the exploits of Jacky Faber continue as she
heads west to avoid capture by the British and discovers adventure
aboard a keelboat on the mighty Mississippi River.
[1. Voyages and travels—Fiction. 2. River boats—Fiction. 3. Orphans—
Fiction. 4. Mississippi River—History—19th century—Fiction.] I. Title.
PZ7.M57172Mi 2007
[Fic]—dc22 2006034709
HC ISBN-13: 978-0-15-206003-9
PA ISBN-13: 978-0-15-206632-1

Text set in Minion
Display set in Pabst
Designed by Cathy Riggs

Printed in the United States of America
QUM 10 9 8 7 6 5 4 3 2 1

As always, for Annetje…
as well as for the Meyer and Lawrence families
and for Team Gayle, too

Mississippi Jack

Prologue

Yes, we sailed into Boston Harbor on that glorious day, all of us up on the deck of the *Juno,* we, the students of the Lawson Peabody School for Young Girls, having recently delivered ourselves from confinement most cruel on the vile slaver *Bloodhound.*

And yes, it was an absolutely perfect day—the sun was shining, the breeze was cool and light, and the sky was a brilliant blue. As we stood into the harbor, we were met by a multitude of small boats, all within them *halloo*ing and waving and blowing horns. Fireworks were set off and brightly colored smoke bombs were exploded. We could hear bands playing on every jetty that we passed, the city having already received word of our salvation and imminent arrival. All flags were out and flying.

As we approached Long Wharf, for that was plainly our destination, Dolley, Clarissa, and I stood together, back from the others. We had decided that our last act as Division Officers would be to designate ourselves as the last ones off. It suited Dolley's sense of rightness, Clarissa's sense of aristocratic privilege, and my sense of the dramatic.

1

Dolley, like the others, was in school dress, the clothing in which we all were captured. Clarissa, having no dress, or any other clothing for that matter, it having been left on the deck of the *Bloodhound*, was dressed in my maroon riding habit. She looked splendid, and how could I deny her? It is her way, I know that now, and I know we could not have gotten through what we did without her. So, let her preen, for she had earned it. I had thought of wearing another of my fine outfits that were stuffed down in my seabag, but, no, best to remain modest for a change. I was wearing my school dress, too, newly cleaned and pressed as best HMS *Juno* could do it.

Yes, my wound had healed up quite nicely and now hardly bothered me at all, which is remarkable since I'd almost died from it all those weeks ago. And yes, my worries that the officers and men on this British ship would discover my true identity gradually fell away as our journey continued and I was treated with the utmost courtesy.

Yes, all is well, I reflected, as I looked around at the happy scene on the deck of the *Juno*. I knew Captain Rutherford couldn't wait to get rid of us. He had bent on all sail to get the last bit of speed he could, to get us up here as fast as the ship would go, both on our voyage from the middle of the Atlantic, where we had been rescued from our tiny lifeboat, to New York, and hence here to Boston. Discipline on his ship, as far as the midshipmen and junior officers were concerned, had gone completely to hell—many of our girls had been flirting outright with the young men, and the young men, astounded at their luck to find thirty or so young women in various states of undress in the middle of the ocean, were certainly easy prey for their charms. I'm sure many pledges of undying love and devotion were exchanged, and, who knows, maybe some of them might turn out to be true. Even little Rebecca's thirteen-year-old self had found a midshipman her own age, and they had been holding hands and making cow eyes at each other these past precious days.

I looked upon my dear Sisters and reflected that many of the parents of these girls would be surprised in these daughters who have been so miraculously returned to them, as they are not the same girls who gaily left on that fateful day. Yes, they have been through much, but they survived through their own strength of will and, because of that, may very well not be as accepting of the manners and roles that were formerly assigned to them by their families and by society. They might very well be trouble, and yes, you may mark me on that.

The instant the *Juno* was warped to the pier and the first line thrown over, a flag was hoisted on the masthead of the Customs House and immediately every church bell in the city started to peal out, and they did not stop.

The gangway was lowered without great ceremony, and the girls swarmed off the *Juno,* having been formed up in their last muster of Sin-Kay's alphabetical line. They did not mind, for it gave them great joy to see little Rebecca run first down the gangway and into the arms of her family, then Ruth, then Sally, then all the rest.

Now there goes Annie and Helen and Dorothea and... *There's Higgins!*

Oh, my God, *Higgins,* and Peg and Mistress beside him... and now Connie and Martha go down and... *There's Amy and Ezra!*

And there…*No, it can't be.* There, next to Higgins. *Oh, Lord, it's Jaimy*…Good God, it's really Jaimy, standing there smiling up at me and reaching up his hand, and the tears pour out of my eyes and down my face and they are tears of absolute joy.

My happiness is complete.

Dimly, I sense Clarissa, who still stands next to me. "So that's him, eh? Well, he looks presentable…Good chest… fine leg…," she says. "Well, even though I owe you one in that regard, I might let you keep him." And with that, she turns and follows Dolley down the gangway, head up, the Look in place, to the cheers of her Sisters.

It is now my turn to go. I have not been able to take my eyes off Jaimy's as I float, as if in a dream, to the gangway. I put my foot on it, and then…

And then two bayonets cross in front of my chest and I hear the Captain intone, "Miss Faber, by order of His Majesty, King George the Third, you are under arrest on the charge of Piracy!"

PART I

Chapter 1

⚓ My name is spoken and the damning words are pronounced and I see the bayonets cross my chest, and all the fond hopes that were rising within that chest die. *I am found out.*

I drop my seabag. *Maybe I can make it over the side and into the water,* I think desperately and lunge for the side, but then two hard, heavy hands grasp each of my upper arms and I am held fast and then pulled back from the gangway, back from Jaimy and all my friends, and back to what I know will be my doom.

After my years of military service, it is my instinct to obey the authority vested in a British captain and yield myself up, but, *No!* Not this time, not with Jaimy not fifty feet away. *No!* No more Good Soldier Jacky, no more Obedient Midshipman Faber! I twist my head to the side, thinking to bite the hand that holds my right arm, and so be able to draw my shiv from its sheath hidden in my left sleeve, but it is all in vain—the marine senses my intention and pulls his hand out of range of my teeth by hauling my arm behind my back. *Ow! Damn!*

I squeal and squall and struggle and squirm and curse them all to Hell and back, ten times over, and while I try to bring my heel up into the left marine's crotch, he is too tall for that, and the two just hold me all the tighter. All I can do now is watch as this all plays out around me, and cry out in total frustration and rage. *So close. Oh, Jaimy, so close...*

A stunned silence falls over the formerly festive crowd. *What? What is going on?* I dimly hear a parent say. *Who? What? Piracy?* I hear from another dumbfounded onlooker. *She's just a girl! Why are they holding her? How could—?*

Clarissa Howe, being the last one down the gangway, is the first to react to my arrest. She turns and charges back up, crying, "Like hell she is! Run, Jacky! Run!" and she launches herself at Captain Rutherford, as it was he who uttered those damning words.

The crowd is now roaring its disapproval, and others come storming up the gangway.

"Get her off me, dammit!" shouts the Captain, flailing his arms against Clarissa's onslaught of fists, fingernails, and teeth.

"Let her go, you!" snarls Clarissa, baring her teeth for an assault on Captain Rutherford's defenseless nose. His nose, however, is spared that grisly fate as the arm of a burly Bo'sun's Mate encircles her about the waist and hauls her to the rail.

"But what do I do with her, Sir?" bleats the obviously overmatched Bo'sun, as he endures a torrent of blows and curses from the struggling form he holds.

"Throw her overboard, that's what you do!" roars Captain Rutherford, outraged at this unlooked-for chaos on his holy quarterdeck. "And pull up the gangway!"

Clarissa shrieks as she is tossed over the rail, a shriek that is cut short as she hits the water.

If the sound of the splash as Clarissa Worthington Howe enters the chill waters of Boston Harbor gave the Captain any cheer, that cheer would have been quickly dampened by the grim sight of Chrissy, Rose, Hermione, and Minerva, who had wrested themselves from their parents' joyous embraces to string their bows at Katy Deere's command of "Dianas! To me!" and now followed her up the not-yet-pulled gangway, arrows nocked and looking for targets.

I can see Katy's eyes narrow as she sizes up the situation and pulls back and lets fly her arrow, which wings across the quarterdeck and thuds into the chest of the marine at my right hand. I expect him to drop my arm and fall to the deck, but he does not, for Katy's aim was true, too true—it hit him directly in the middle of his chest where his two white leather belts cross on his breastbone. I doubt the arrow, which had a crude nail as an arrowhead, even pierced his skin. Even so, he stares down at the arrow in horror. I try to jerk free again, but his grip is still strong in spite of his amazement at the thing sticking out of his chest.

Chrissy King pulls and aims and lets fly at Captain Rutherford's neck, but her father, charging up the gangway, shouting, *"Christina! Whatever are you doing?"* manages to jostle her enough to spoil her aim, and her arrow buries itself in the mast a scant few inches from the Captain's outraged face. I know that this is a man who has faced murderous cannon fire, cruel clouds of flying splinters, and the peppering of bullets from enemy sharpshooters, but I know also that he has faced nothing like this.

"Cut the gangway!" he screams, and two men run up

with knives and cut the ropes, sacrificing the *Juno*'s gangway to the riot. The gangway crashes down to the water, spilling the rest of the Dianas into the harbor and preventing any more arrows from being loosed in the direction of the *Juno.* Chrissy's father, Mr. King, also joins his daughter and her friends in the muddy water.

Pandemonium rules on the dock. The rest of my Sisters, denied access to the ship, grab fruit and other things from the vendors on the wharf and wing them toward the officers on the deck of the *Juno,* often with great effect. But not, however, on my two restraining marines, who continue to hold me in an iron grip. I try stomping on their feet, but though they grunt, they do not let go.

"Arrest them!" shouts the Captain, rushing to the rail and shaking his fist at the crowd. "You, there! Constable! Do your duty," he orders the confused Constable Wiggins, "or, by God, I'll blockade this godforsaken harbor and starve you all to death!" The Captain then takes a well-thrown fish to his face and staggers back, his great dignity gone, and he is reduced to wiping the fish slime out of his eye and cursing the fact he ever picked up this pack of goddamned Amazons from the middle of the goddamned ocean.

I see Wiggins furrow his brow over his piggy little eyes, and I know he is thinking: *The female in question, that Jacky Faber: bad. Authority in the person of the British Captain: good.* He nods, then blows his whistle, and he and his henchmen wade into the crowd, swinging their rods.

"Get her below!" yells Captain Rutherford. "Put her in the brig! And keep watch on her. *Yeow!* Damn!" He ducks as another arrow whizzes by his head. It appears that not all of the Dianas went down with the gangway.

I had seen Jaimy try to struggle up the gangway. *Oh, Jaimy! Don't! It won't work! Go back!* But with the crush of girls and parents, he could not gain the quarterdeck, and now with the gangway fallen, there is no hope of him boarding. *Could I not have spoken to him, embraced him, been with him, if even for a moment? Oh, why am I denied even that?* I slump down, defeated, in the hands of my captors, who begin to drag me to a hatchway.

As I am pulled back from the rail, I lose sight of the people on the wharf, but I can see fish and vegetables and various animal parts continue to rain down on the formerly spotless deck, and I can hear the howls of rage and the curses that continue unabated from the crowd. A bucket arcs through the air and hits the deck, spilling bloody chicken heads across the booted toes of the still-lined-up officers. And above it all, there's Wiggins, sounding like an enraged bull as he bellows orders to his men, who attempt to control the mob.

One of the marines kicks open the hatch, and I am shoved toward the hole, but then I hear: *"Release her or I'll kill you where you stand!"*

I snap my head around and see that Jaimy has managed to get on deck and is facing Captain Rutherford. He must have crawled up Two Line, just like when he was a ship's boy, and now he's red in the face with fury and he is drawing his sword. *No, Jaimy, don't. There's too many of them!*

Captain Rutherford puffs up, his face as angry and red as Jaimy's, as he pulls his own sword and roars, "A boy dares come aboard my ship, dressed in the uniform of my service, and addresses me thus? I fear it shall be you, Sir, who is killed, not me!" I see him nod at officers who stand behind

Jaimy, but Jaimy does not. A large man pins Jaimy's arms to his sides before he can get his sword even halfway out of its scabbard.

Jaimy sputters in helpless rage, "God damn you to Hell! Get them off me! Stand and fight me like a man!"

Captain Rutherford calmly puts the point of his sword at Jaimy's throat and demands, "Just who the hell are you and what is your concern in all this?" The sharp point pricks Jaimy's neck and a bright spot of blood appears and runs several inches down the blade.

Don't tell them, Jaimy! I silently mouth and shake my head. *No, they'll take you, too!*

But to no avail, no, as Jaimy is angry beyond all reason. He puffs up and shouts in the Captain's face, "I am Lieutenant James Emerson Fletcher of His Majesty's Royal Navy, I am affianced to this girl, and I demand satisfaction of you!"

"You shall have neither the girl nor the satisfaction that you crave," replies Captain Rutherford, smiling slyly. He withdraws the point of his sword from Jaimy's neck and wipes the blood from it on the arm of Jaimy's coat and then sheathes his sword. "I have need of a junior lieutenant. Mr. Henshaw, see that Mr. Fletcher's name is entered into the log of the ship's company." An officer next to the Captain nods. The Captain goes on. "You are now under my command. I am now your Captain. Reach for your sword again or utter one more threat against me and you are a dead man. Hanged from that yardarm, as per Navy Regulations. Understood?"

Jaimy strains against the arms that hold him, never taking his eyes off those of the Captain. He is beyond coherent speech, but the Captain is not. "You, Sir, have been read into the ship's company and you will go back to England with us! Your apparent interest and past association with this criminal female will be viewed as quite suspect! I may tell you that, Sir! Quite suspect and with the greatest suspicion!"

Just then I see the head of little Rebecca Adams appearing above the *Juno*'s rail. Having seen Jaimy climb the rope, she must have figured she could do the same, and she was right. 'Tis plain that she slipped out of her school dress and did the climbing in her undershirt and drawers, our old fighting costume on the *Bloodhound*. Then Caroline Thwackham's head appears at the rail, then Beatrice's, then Annie is over, and then...

And then they're *all* over the ship and up in its rigging.

"God damn it! God damn it to Hell!" screams Captain Rutherford, upon seeing this. "Get them down! Get them off my ship!"

Rebecca, before she heads up the ratlines, plucks a few belaying pins from their rack along the rail and begins flinging them at those who would pursue her. Yelps are heard from those sailors who get too close to her. Having fended them off, she sticks a few more pins in the waistband of her drawers and climbs aloft.

The attempts of Jaimy and my Sisters to rescue me renew my spirit and I jerk my arms suddenly and, *yes!* I manage to get away from the marines for just a second and I head for the side. *If I can just get over! If I can just...*

But, no. An arm gets me around the waist just as I am about to launch myself over to freedom, and I am pinioned again. This time I am thrown facedown on the deck, with heavy feet grinding me down. I see belaying pins, hurled from above, hitting the deck and bouncing. Over there a sailor kneels and holds his head. *Good shot, Rebecca!*

Then I look up to see a now belaying-pin-less Rebecca being grappled by her former midshipman sweetheart. "Please, Becky, dear!" he cries plaintively, but the fiercely struggling form he can barely contain in his arms bears very little resemblance to the dear girl with whom he kept such fond company on the voyage here.

Then I am roughly hoisted up and hauled below and I see no more of this battle. The dark hatchway swallows me up and I am tumbled down stairs, across a deck, and into the brig. While I see no more of the tumult, the noise of it goes on for what seems a very long time. Then, gradually, all grows quiet, and once again, in yet another jail cell, I am left alone with my thoughts.

Home again, girl.

In deep despair, I sit on the bench in the brig and reflect on the past few weeks. It is plain to me now that they knew all along about the warrant for the arrest of the female pirate Jacky Faber. The discovery was undoubtedly made by the *Juno*'s doctor as I lay unconscious from the effects of my wounded leg. He would have spied my tattoo and known instantly that I was the one the Admiralty was looking for. I can well imagine his excitement as he went and got the Captain, then, upon his arrival at my bedside, whipped back the sheet from my oblivious form lying there naked except for the bandage on my thigh. He would have pointed to the damning mark and congratulated the Captain on his great good luck. Throwing the sheet back over my inert self, they would then have gone for a celebratory drink over their discovery.

They kept it a secret during the voyage from the Sargasso Sea to here, I suppose, to keep the other girls calm. Well, they sure had me fooled. What an idiot I was to think that I might one day be happy. I squeeze out a few tears of self-pity and then wipe them off and review my situation. I look about my cell, which I realize will be my home for the next month or so. It is very similar to other cells I have known—bunk, chamber pot, and bars. Maybe if I give my word and promise not to try to escape, they'll let me out for the voyage. Then I'd get to see Jaimy, at least, for this one last time. Nay, they won't do it. They'd accept word-of-honor from a fellow officer like Jaimy, but not from me.... Being a flighty female, I might do something stupid like jump overboard to cheat the hangman and deny Captain Rutherford his reward.

Funny to think of this now, but I sit here and regret the loss of my maroon riding habit, the one that Amy had given me that Christmas and that Clarissa was wearing when she was thrown overboard. I had to lend her something from my seabag—count on her to take the best. Ah, well, the least of my worries. And besides, where would I wear it now? On the gallows? I'd look elegant, but it's tradition that the hangman gets to keep the clothes of those he hangs, and I wouldn't want the blackguard to get that outfit. Nay, I'll probably just wear my Lawson Peabody black dress. I hear they put a strap around your knees to keep the dress from billowing up when you are dropped. For modesty's sake... *Stop that, you. Enough of that.*

I look out through the bars. Once again a marine is posted to guard me. He is standing at Attention. I suppose he will be there around the clock. I still have my shiv up my sleeve...At least there's that. They didn't think to search me for weapons. After all, I am just a girl.

Funny, I think, *but when I was being taken, I looked over the rioting crowd for Higgins, as I have come to depend on him for so much, but he was nowhere to be seen.* I mean, I surely didn't expect him to come charging up the side to try to save me like Jaimy did, for that is not his way. But still, strange...

Strange, too, to think that Jaimy is right here on this ship. Probably not fifty feet away from me. Ah, well, it might as well be fifty miles, or fifty thousand miles, for all the good it will do us. *Oh, Jaimy, we were so close, so close to finally coming together at last!*

I squeeze out a few more tears on that.

Oh, well, I've got my shiv and I've still got my wits and I'm not dead yet, so a couple more tears of self-pity and then let's get on with it. I take a breath and begin: "And what is your name, Corporal, if I might ask?...Michael Kelley, is it? And a fine, proud Irish name it is. I must say you were most gallant in the performance of your duties this day, Corporal Kelley. To have taken an arrow in the chest and still stand your ground. *Tsk,* such bravery, I can scarce imagine it. I'm sure your sweetheart back home must be very proud of you. What might her name be, could you tell me please, as stories of young love do cheer me in my dark hours, and a dark hour this is for me, indeed...Ah, 'Maureen.' What a lovely name, and she is already wife to you?... What a fine thing...And do you have wee ones? And what are their names, then..."

Night comes. I am given some food and water, and then all is silence.

Chapter 2

I did not think that I would sleep, but I did. When I awoke the next morning to the ringing of the ship's bell, I thought for a moment that I was back on the *Bloodhound*, and I lifted my head from the hard bench to look about for my Sisters, but no such luck—the events of yesterday came flooding back, and I sat up and buried my face in my hands. It had been a long night and the bench was hard, but harder still is the sure knowledge that all my dreams are now dust.

Nevertheless I arose and did the necessaries and groomed myself as best I could, having neither wash water nor soap. I was given a breakfast of tea and burgoo and I ate it. Then I asked my marine if he would get my comb out of my seabag and he did, and I combed my hair and waited.

Now I have not only myself to worry about, but also Jaimy. What will they do to him because of me and what I have done? I burn with indignation. It's not fair, for he had nothing to do with any of it. All he had been guilty of was being steadfast and true to my errant self. *Oh, I am so very hard on my friends...*

In the midst of these dark thoughts, I hear a whistle and commands shouted from outside the hull. What is this? They do not sound like naval commands, what with stomping of boots and clatter of arms. My marine looks curiously out of the hatch.

"What is it, Michael?" I ask, standing and grasping the bars and straining to look up what little I can see of the hatch.

"It's a troop of soldiers, Miss," he says. "British Regulars, it looks like. Where they come from, I ain't got the foggiest. Down from Canada, maybe?"

What the hell?

"There's a full colonel being piped aboard now, and the Captain and himself is takin' off their hats and bowin' at each other like a pair o' bloody peacocks. Damn peculiar it is, Miss. I ain't seen no Redcoat Regulars since we left England, I haven't."

Hmmmm.

My Corporal Kelley continues to listen to the goings-on outside. Then he suddenly lurches back to his station and hits a brace—musket at Parade Rest, chest out, chin in, back straight as a ramrod. The reason for this is quickly apparent.

"Corporal! Bind the prisoner and bring her up!" shouts down someone, who I suspect is the senior marine officer on board.

Corporal Kelley loses not a second.

"Yes, Sir!" he cries and reaches for the cell key, which I had previously noted was hung on a hook next to the hatchway. "Sorry, Miss, we must take you up."

He crams the key into the lock, turns it, and the door to my cage swings open. I step out. "It is all right, Michael. I place myself in your care. Will you take up my bag, please?"

18

I put my hands before me and they are bound. Gently and lightly bound, to be sure, but bound nonetheless.

I put on the Look, and then we go up the hatchway stairs and emerge into the light.

I blink, and when my eyes adjust to the brightness, I see that Captain Rutherford stands next to an officer, a British colonel in full regimental rig. There are other army officers on the quarterdeck as well, arrayed in all their red-coated splendor behind their leader. The colonel, wearing a conical high hat, scarlet coat with a bit of ribbon in his lapel, white trousers, and shiny black boots, is, I believe, in the uniform of the Royal Dragoons. His hair is powdered, and in his hand is a fancy handkerchief. He affects a look of high hauteur as he says, "You will see the papers are in order, Captain. It is a simple matter of prisoner transferal. His Majesty's intelligence operatives in New York wish to question her before she's sent over to face justice." He glances over at me.

"Ah, so this is the valuable piece of baggage, then?" he asks, contemptuously, looking me up and down with great disdain. "Hardly remarkable looking."

Captain Rutherford reads the document in his hands, and while he does that, I look about. The *Juno*'s officers are all on deck, as well, and down on the dock is a small squad of Regulars standing at Attention behind a coach-and-two. I had seen Jaimy as soon as I came out of the hatch, but upon seeing the Colonel and casing out the situation, I determined not to look at him, though I could feel his hot eyes burning into me as I was brought up before the two commanding officers. Jaimy is not bound, but he is between two very large lieutenants. No, I keep the Look on my face and wait to see just how this thing will play out.

"But this is highly irregular, my dear Colonel Swithin...,"
says the Captain, continuing to scan the paper, great doubt
plain on his face. He shakes his head. "...and the matter of
the reward..."

"Put your mind at rest, my dear Sir," says Colonel Swithin,
a slight smile playing about his rouged lips, "all is in order."
He gestures to one of his junior officers behind him, who
steps forward bearing a heavy sack in his hands. Captain
Rutherford's eyes go wide.

"I think you'll be delighted to learn, Captain," continues
the Colonel, "that the reward had been increased to a full
three hundred pounds. I congratulate you on your fine prize."

I know that swept any remaining doubts from Captain
Rutherford's greedy head. A fine prize, indeed—more than
three times his annual salary as Post Captain—enough to
buy a small estate, even.

"Very well," he manages to say, ill concealing his joy, "if
you will leave with me a signed transfer document..."

"Of course, my dear Captain," says Colonel Swithin with
a slight bow. "But first, a mere formality. Would you bring the
female over to me so that I might be sure of her identity?"

"Bring her here," barks Captain Rutherford, and I am
dragged up before Swithin.

He puts his perfumed handkerchief up to cover his nose,
as if to prevent any foul smell from entering it that might be
coming from me. He reaches out his other hand and puts
his palm on my forehead and shoves my head back so as to
peer at my damning white eyebrow.

I bristle at this. "I am not used to being handled so by
one to whom I have not been properly introduced. You will
take your hand from my person," I hiss from beneath his

grasp. I sense a rustle of discontent from the naval officers behind me at this display of maltreatment of one whom they had come to know with some fondness on the voyage here. I cannot see Jaimy, but I imagine he is being restrained.

The Colonel does not answer me but instead runs his thumb over my eyebrow, apparently convinced of its genuineness. He drops his hand and says, "Men of my station are not introduced to harlots. Lift up your dress."

"What? Am I to be made a spectacle of, then, here before any who care to gaze upon me as I am shamed by you?" I ask, outraged. I shake off his hand.

"Hold her," orders Colonel Swithin, and poor Corporal Kelley, who I know wants no part of this, has to grasp me tightly by the upper arms and hold me steady. "I must protest this," I hear one of the officers of HMS *Juno* say, and there are echoing calls for the stopping of this outrage upon my person, but they are silenced with a hard look from their captain. *Shame on you, Captain Rutherford, for allowing this outrage to happen on your ship.*

"Talbot. Jameson. Lift up her skirt and hold her."

The two Redcoat officers advance on me. They lift my skirt and petticoats up to my waist, and they wait, the cloth wadded up in their fists, my lower undergarments exposed to the light of day and the scrutiny of all. I do not squeal or struggle in protest. Instead I fix this despicable colonel with the proudest Look I can manage and remain rigid as they hold me thus.

Colonel Swithin, his kerchief still held to his nose, reaches out one finger and pulls the waistband of my drawers down over my right hipbone. I feel the cool of the air hit my skin and hear a gasp from the crew of the *Juno*, some of whom are my friends. Is that a *hmmmmm* of protest starting up? *Thanks, mates, but I know you can do nothing . . .*

"Ah. Just where it is supposed to be," says the Colonel, referring to my damning tattoo. He withdraws his finger but not his handkerchief. "All is in order. You may cover her. Mr. Hale, step forward."

At that, the officers Talbot and Jameson release my skirts, which fall back down to my ankles. The officer holding the bag of reward money steps forward. If Captain Rutherford had been trying to resist licking his lips in anticipation, he failed in the attempt. It is not a pleasant sight to see, and so I look away. Neither do I look at Jaimy, oh, no. Instead I fix my gaze upon the face of the Colonel of Dragoons. His cheek is powdered and rouged, I notice, and a small black beauty mark is affixed on his right cheekbone. A curious fashion, I reflect, what they call *macaroni,* the high style, and curious indeed to find it here in the States.

"Captain Rutherford, have you a secretary with quill and ink so that we might sign the necessary papers?" he asks, apparently satisfied that I am indeed the Dread Pyrate Jacky Faber, Scourge of the Caribbean and the Normandy Coast, Misappropriator of His Majesty's Property—to wit, the brigantine bark *Emerald*—and, as such, properly despised by all good Britons.

"Smithers!" barks the Captain, and the ship's purser dives below, to reemerge with a small table and pen and ink, which he sets up very quickly in front of Colonel Swithin, who takes the pen from Smithers's quivering hand, dips it in the inkwell, and scratches his signature on the Letter of Prisoner Transferal, then hands the paper to Captain Rutherford.

"And now if you will just sign this receipt for the reward

money, we shall be on our way, a good day's business having been concluded," says Swithin.

Captain Rutherford takes the pen, but he does not sign. At a nod from Colonel Swithin, the bag of money is placed in the hands of the purser Smithers, who takes the bag and disappears below. There is a pause as Captain Rutherford continues to examine the receipt form, until Smithers reappears and nods at the Captain. At this, Captain Rutherford beams, dips the pen, and signs the receipt. He hands it to Colonel Swithin, who passes it to his subordinate.

"All is concluded, then. I must take this creature back to New York, where, I assure you, she is most eagerly awaited. Put her in—"

"I assume I am to go with this female, as you put it, to face whatever charges are against my good name," I hear Jaimy call out.

"What is this?" asks Colonel Swithin. "Is there no discipline on this ship?"

Captain Rutherford reddens and says, "This man, Lieutenant Fletcher, has made it known that he is romantically attached to the Faber girl. I intended to take him with her back to London, to see if he had committed any crimes against the Crown in that regard."

"Charges against my good name have been lodged by Captain Rutherford because of my connection to this woman. I demand that I be allowed to be taken with her so as to be able to clear those charges against me." I still do not look in his direction.

"Well, then, perhaps we should take him with us. For interrogation," says Colonel Swithin, appearing to consider this option.

"Nay," says Captain Rutherford. "There is no warrant or reward out for him. He shall remain with us. I'll take him back to London and turn him over to the authorities." He turns to Jaimy. "No, sir, you shall come with us. You can see your lady love in London when they bring her out to the gallows! Perhaps you will even join her there!" He barks a laugh at his own wit.

At this, my heart dies within me.

"And what do you have to say about this young swain, then, Miss? He seems to hold you in some regard," sneers Colonel Swithin in my direction.

What can I do? I'm going to have to deny him to save him. With the Look in place, I turn to face Jaimy. "This boy?" I say, my voice dripping with contempt. "Why, he is absolutely nothing to me. It is true we shared a friendship when we were children on the *Dolphin*, but since then he has turned against me in every instance of our meeting."

Strong hands now hold Jaimy back. His eyes burn into mine, but I hood my own eyes and go on. "What would I say about such a boy? That he proved untrue with another girl, that he sank my ship, an action which resulted in my capture, that he is member of a service that has vowed to bring me low, as low as you see me here. Nay, he is less than nothing to me. Let us be off. I hope the accommodations and the company in New York are better than what I have found here."

"Take her. I've had enough of her twaddle," says Captain Rutherford. Lieutenants Talbot and Jameson come up and take me by my arms. I give Michael Kelley's hand a final squeeze as he releases me. Lieutenant Hale takes up my seabag and I am led off the ship.

"Adieu, my good Captain," I hear Colonel Swithin say behind me. I assume there is much bowing and many compliments as he leaves. No compliments for me, though, as I am hustled down the gangway, across the wharf, and thrown roughly into the carriage. Lieutenants Talbot and Jameson are on each side of me. I sit there and fume.

In a few moments, the door opens again and Colonel Swithin heaves his bulk into the carriage. "Driver! Go!" he roars out the window, and we clatter off.

We sit there in silence for a moment, and then the Colonel says, "Well played, Miss."

And I say, "Well played, Higgins, but we must go back and get Jaimy, we must—"

"We must be calm and carefully plan out our next move. Mr. Fletcher is in no danger, believe me."

I put my face to the window and look up at the rail of the *Juno*. Is that Jaimy? *Oh, Jaimy, I didn't mean any of what I said, no I didn't, but...*

"Miss, you must get back from the window. Here, let me undo your wrists." My hands were still bound but I didn't notice, as I am so often bound and confined.

"Oh, yes, very well played by all," chortles Mr. Bean, formerly Lieutenant Talbot, who sits on my right, "but I must especially compliment you, Mr. Fennel, on your portrayal of Officer Jameson—you were the very picture of a British junior officer—just the right amount of officiousness, bluster, and complete asininity."

Both Mr. Fennel and Mr. Bean begin hurrying out of their uniforms, showing that particular lack of modesty common to the theatrical world. It is not an easy thing, as the carriage is rocking wildly back and forth. I noticed when

I boarded that the driver was Ed Strout, the same member of the acting troupe who worked in the daytime as a hack driver and had been the one to help me haul poor Jim Tanner off for repair after he had been badly beaten by those rotters Beadle and Strunk those long months ago.

The carriage careens around a corner, and our escort squad disappears—I know they will have slipped into the side entrance of the theater to doff their costumes and slip back into anonymity. *Thanks, mates.*

"Thank you, Mr. Bean, and I must say I found your performance to be equally above reproach." Mr. Fennel struggles out of his striped regimental trousers and reaches into a bag concealed under the seat and pulls out a pair of workman's overalls. He tosses a similar pair to Mr. Bean. "But I do think the highest accolades belong to our Mr. Higgins."

"Oh, without a doubt, Sir!" exults Mr. Bean, as he worms himself into his overalls. "Such carriage, such easy elegance, such a fine turn of leg!"

"Yes, surely you must return someday to our stage!" says Mr. Fennel. "What a Caesar you would make with that fine brow and that noble nose! Or Marc Antony! Can you see it, Mr. Bean?"

"Oh, yes, Mr. Fennel. Hamlet, even."

Higgins, for his part, merely smiles and doffs his helmet and red coat, then puts on his fawn and white suit coat, pulling his white trousers out of his boot tops so that the cuffs fall about his ankles. Higgins pulls off the beauty mark from his cheek and flings it away and then takes out a handkerchief and wipes the powder from his face. A matching fawn top hat, and he is once again the civilized civilian that he so very much is.

"You flatter me, gentlemen, and I do look forward to returning to your stage. However, we do have our young charge to consider." Higgins adjusts his cravat. "And was not her performance something for the ages?"

It is all too much for their young charge—coming into port in high triumph at our victory over the *Bloodhound*, seeing Jaimy, and then being taken and losing Jaimy once more, and then my sudden deliverance from a certain death sentence to where I now sit. The tears spill out of my eyes and over my cheeks.

"Her selfless denial of her young lover to save him from durance vile, the self-sacrifice, oh, the dramatic possibilities. Can you not see it as a play? Why, there would not be a dry eye in the house."

"I shall get out pen and paper immediately upon our return to the theater. I can see the program notes: The story of a young maiden forced to renounce her own true love for the sake of his own dear safety. We shall call it *She Gave All for Love, or, Love's Favor Lost*... Why, my dear, what ever is the matter?"

I wrap an arm around each of the actors' shoulders and plant a wet, tear-mingled kiss on their cheeks. "That you should risk all—your freedom, your reputations, your very lives—to save me in my moment of peril, I cannot tell you—"

"Tut-tut, my dear. Do you think we would leave our own Puck, our own Ophelia, our own Portia, to languish in the cruel clutches of a heartless enemy? Nay, never! Excelsior. What? Into the fray, that's the ticket!" says Mr. Fennel.

"All that and more, but now we must *Exeunt* Stage Right, Miss," says Mr. Bean, his hand on the door latch. "Come back to us soon. You must finally consent to play Cordelia! You must!"

They each don a workman's cap, stick a foul pipe into their mouths, and, as the carriage pulls to a prearranged stop, they are out the door and onto the street, just two doughty yeomen heading home after a day's honest labor.

"We will be debarking soon, so you must make yourself ready," says Higgins. "Your Jim Tanner will be at the bridge to Cambridge with horses to take us into the interior until we can decide what to do."

"Higgins." I sniffle. "I thank you from the bottom of my heart for my rescue, but still I worry about Jaimy. What will they do to him?" I wring my hands in despair. Poor Jaimy, to have to stand there and watch the rescue attempt and not say anything. He would have recognized Higgins right off but was condemned to stand there and let everything play out, for fear of messing things up. *I am so very hard on my friends.*

"I think you can put your mind to rest on that, Miss," says Higgins. "No harm will come to your Mr. Fletcher, trust me. As you so plainly said for all to hear, he did sink your ship which resulted in your capture, and besides, he has done nothing to aid you in your supposed crimes against the Crown. He did not assist you or hide you or do anything in that regard."

"I suppose," I say, chewing worriedly on a knuckle. "Still, I am not at ease."

"You denied him so utterly, and so convincingly, I might add—a nice touch, that. Very quick thinking, under the circumstances. You do continue to amaze me."

"It was not an easy role to play, believe me. Poor Jaimy."

"I fear that for the moment, at least, the pangs of young love must yield to the cold scrutiny of painful reality. It is *you* they mean to hang, not Mr. Fletcher. Keep that in mind."

We rattle on some more, and I look out at my beloved Boston, a place I had so looked forward to seeing again, a place I know I must now leave.

"Where did you get the money, Higgins?" I ask. "Three hundred pounds is a lot of money. I know Faber Shipping, Worldwide did not have anywhere near that sum in its coffers."

"Oh, yes, a lot of money, indeed," says Higgins, smiling. "I'm sure Captain Rutherford is in the highest of spirits right now. However, I wonder just how high his spirits will be when his superiors find out he let the notorious Jacky Faber slip through his fingers, and confront him with that distressing fact."

"The money, Higgins?"

"Oh, yes. Well, you'll be cheered to know it was collected from your sisters of the Lawson Peabody. The coffers of Faber Shipping are indeed light, but what there is, I safely tucked here in my breast pocket." He peeks out the side curtain. "We are approaching our rendezvous."

"Those girls? They're upper-class, they never handle money. How could they come up with that amount?"

"Well, it came mostly from Mademoiselle de Lise and Miss Clarissa Howe. They were the two who had ready money on hand."

Clarissa Worthington Howe bailing Jacky Faber's tail out of jail. Now, if that ain't the world turned upside down, I don't know what is.

My eyes, which have been none too dry this entire ride, moisten up yet again. I shake my head in wonder at it all. *Such good friends to come to me in my hour of need.*

"We'll be there in five minutes, I believe," says Higgins, with another look out the window, and that brings me out of my reverie. I certainly can't ride in this school dress.

"Unbutton me, Higgins," I say, turning so he can get at the row of buttons on the back of my school dress. "I've got to get into my serving-girl rig."

He does it, and as I'm slipping off the dress and the petticoats and the chemise that go with it, Higgins goes into my seabag and comes up with the proper garb. Off with my white stockings and on with the black, then on with the blousy white shirt, the black skirt, and finally the black lace-up vest. I put my riding boots on my feet, my shiv in my vest, and my cloak about my shoulders, with its hood upon my head. I am ready to ride.

Higgins expertly folds my clothes as I take them off, and he neatly tucks them into my seabag.

"Where are we going?" I ask, when I am done messing with my clothes. It is good to get back into this tight-fitting rig.

"Out to the West for a bit till we can figure out our next move. We need some breathing room."

"Aye on that, Higgins, but could we not merely have gone to Dovecote and hid out there till things calm down?"

"Ahem. I'm afraid not," says Higgins. "During our time on the *Emerald*, Miss Amy Trevelyne finished and published her second book concerning your travels and exploits, titled, I believe, *The Curse of the Blue Tattoo*. It has received wide circulation locally and is about to be published in London.

So everyone will know of your connection to the Dovecote estate. It is the first place that pursuers would look."

Damn! Thanks, Amy, once again.

"Never trust someone with a pen in their hands," I say ruefully.

"True, but then again, Miss Amy, at the time, figured your adventuring days were over," says Higgins in a soothing voice, "and besides, all proceeds from the sale of the books go to your Home for Little Wanderers in London."

Well, there's that, I suppose. Fair trade. "But won't they think me safely captured, at least for a little while? Doesn't that give us some time?"

"*Hmmm,* I don't know. Our little ruse might yet be discovered—there are communications twixt Boston and New York. It was really the money that effected your release, not the artfulness of our performance."

I take in this information and I begin to think. And to plan. We cannot go to New York, or Philadelphia, or to any of the Yankee towns. We cannot take passage from any port, for I may be recognized. I cannot go north to Canada, nor east to England. Very well, west it must be. I think back to what Katy Deere told me of the West when we talked those long hours on the *Bloodhound*...how the rivers out there joined together, how the Allegheny flowed together with the Monongahela to form the Ohio, and how the Ohio flowed on to the—

"We are here, Miss. Let us debark."

The carriage rattles to a stop and I jump out of the coach. There at the foot of the bridge over to Cambridge stands my good coxswain Jim, holding three horses by their reins.

"Jim Tanner! Oh, well met, Jim!" And I rush over and wrap my arms around the boy. He returns my embrace ardently. *Hmmm. Very* ardently. It seems the boy has grown some since last we parted.

"It is good to see you, too, Missy. We feared you lost for so long a time." I swear I see a mist in his eye, too.

"Well," I say, wiping a tear from my own eye, "you can see that I have a way of popping back up, against all odds."

"Yes, Miss, and for that I am very glad. Up with you, now. Mr. Higgins, the toll has been paid and we are free to cross."

He holds the stirrup steady, and I put my foot in it and swing myself up. *Oh...oh, it is so good to feel a stout horse between my legs again.* He passes me the reins and throws my seabag up behind me and straps it down.

"Three horses, young Jim?" I ask, as Higgins mounts his own, much larger horse. I know he suppresses a groan, for I also know that my stalwart Higgins is not overly fond of riding.

"Yes, Missy, I am going with you."

"But what of the *Star*? Our traps? Faber Shipping, Worldwide?"

"The *Star* has been hauled out at Dovecote for safekeeping. Faber Shipping shall have to watch out for its own self for a while as Constable Wiggins has a warrant out for me, since I winged a rock at his fat head during the fight on Long Wharf when you were taken. So I must hide out, too."

"*Hmmm.* Very well, Jim. Your company will be welcome. Are we ready? Then, let us go." I dig my heels into my mount's flanks and he leaps forward across the bridge.

And with a whoop, I call out, "Steer westward, on a course of 290 degrees, march!"

And westward we do thunder. We ride down Cambridge Street, past the college where only a few months ago my fellow students and I serenaded the Harvard boys, and onto the Boston Post Road, heading west, ever west, away from the dangers of the coast. It is not like me to shy away from the sea, but there is water where I am headed, and I am told there is lots of it, so it will be all right.

We make a good twenty miles on what is left of this day and pull up for the night at Howe's Tavern in Sudbury for the night. *How many Howes are there in this world,* I ask myself, thinking of Clarissa Worthington Howe, my sometime enemy, my sometime Sister-in-arms.

Tomorrow we push on to Worcester, the route that Ezra Pickering planned out for the conspirators to escape west. But that is the extent of Ezra's knowledge of the frontier, and we will be on our own after that. Just head west is my thought—I've got my compass—and ask directions as we go. Shouldn't be that hard to find the Allegheny River, should it?

Howe's Tavern—a house of entertainment, it calls itself—turns out to be quite a lively place. I wish I could take out my sweet Lady Gay, my fine fiddle—*Thanks, Higgins, for remembering to bring her along*—and add to the merriment in the room, but alas, I cannot, for safety's sake. Maybe when we get farther inland I can start doing some sets again. After all, we are going to need money.

We take a room, Higgins and I, me being presented as his

daughter, and Jim will sleep in the barn, to watch over the horses. We must conserve our coin, and even in the span of this day's ride, the countryside has grown decidedly wilder. At least to this city girl's eyes.

We take our dinner together in the Great Room of the tavern, and I find the dinner tastes wondrous good to me after all that awful burgoo on the *Bloodhound,* the standard ship's rations on the *Juno,* and then back to burgoo when I was confined. I'm afraid I disappointed Higgins with the licking of my chops as well as my greasy fingers. Don't care. It's been a long time. I'll be a lady tomorrow.

We go to our room, and a bath is ordered up and a tub is brought to our room and filled with steaming hot water. I disrobe and crawl in and give a great sigh of pure sinful delight as I sink up to my neck in the suds.

"Oh, Higgins, you cannot know, it has been so long since I have had a true bath, ohhhhhh..." I sigh and close my eyes as I lean my shoulders against the high back of the tub. Higgins takes up a small pail and dips it twixt my knees to fill it with water, and that water he pours over my head, and it courses down over my face. I feel a bar of soap put into my hand and I take it and wash my face and neck and shoulders and armpits and then lean back down, to feel Higgins's expert fingers begin to work the soap into my hair.

"I suspect that it feels quite good, Miss, considering what you have recently been through. Although Sylvie was quite expressive in her description of the horrid conditions on the *Bloodhound,* still, I cannot imagine it. And what are you smiling at, if I may ask?"

I smile to think on Sylvia Rossio, my good and dear but generally quite shy and quiet friend and fellow captive, as well as fellow serving girl at one time, joyously meeting up with her own true love Henry Hoffman there in New York Harbor and then riding with him up to Boston to bring the glad tidings of the deliverance from slavery of the girls of the Lawson Peabody to the once bereft and grief-stricken parents and friends. *Just how was your journey from New York to Boston, Sylvie,* hmmm? I think, wickedly.

"Oh, nothing," I say. "Just my sinful pleasure at this bath, and in your own sweet company. I'm sure Annie and Betsey would say I'd just bought myself a lot more time in purgatory because of it, but I don't care. I shall offer up some sacrifice on my part in the future to make up for it."

"You have a curious theology, Miss. Here, please lean forward so that I might rinse."

When I lean back again, my hair lank about my face, I ask, "How much money do we have, Higgins?"

"Not a large amount, I'm afraid. Most of the money available from your friends in Boston went to fund your reward. Faber Shipping had twenty-four dollars in its coffers due to Jim Tanner's exertions with the *Morning Star*'s traps. I have one hundred and fifty-five dollars left from the money I got from the sale of the jewel you slipped into my hand when you were confined on board the *Wolverine.* You will recall that I tendered the bulk of the sale of that jewel to your London Home for Little Wanderers for their continued maintenance, retaining only enough to maintain myself until such time as you were back on your moneymaking feet again, as it were. And Ezra Pickering pressed another hundred dollars on me, begging me to tell you that Miss Amy Trevelyne considered it a small advance on her second book, the one detailing your early adventures in the New World."

This gets another sigh from me, this one not of pure pleasure. "Am I not famous enough, Higgins?"

"Ahem. I believe she has even started on the third."

Oh, Lord! Is there not a single part of me that will remain unexamined? Will none of my depredations against good manners and good order and propriety in all their unseemly tawdriness be kept from the world's curious eye?

I sink under the water in despair.

"A false suicide attempt will avail you nothing," I hear Higgins say. He reaches down and pulls my head from the water, and piles my hair on top of that same head. "Besides, you and your Home need the money, and Miss Amy is most discreet in her revelations, as far as I can discern."

"She wasn't all that *discreet* in the first one, as I recall. Can you imagine being mercilessly teased by your fellow midshipmen over something written about you and a boy being snugged up for weeks in a hammock on a British war-ship, a penny-dreadful book that—"

There is a knock on the door and Higgins says, "Who?" and Jim Tanner from outside the door says, "The pallet you ordered, Mr. Higgins."

"Come in, Jim," says Higgins, casting me a glance. Although my back is to the door, I cross my arms before my chest and sink further down into the now soap-clouded water.

Jim comes in, bearing the narrow straw-filled mattress. I had told Higgins that he should sleep with me in the big bed, that I wanted him to sleep with me, as it would give me comfort, but he would have none of it—he felt it wasn't proper, considering.

Considering what? I'm thinking, but I let it go. I turn my head to look at Jim, and he stands there looking over at me, astounded. I imagine the warmth and steam of the room has something to do with that look—the smell of the soaps, the smell of the shampoo, and, possibly, the smell of well-toasted female.

"Here, Jim, let me help you with that," says Higgins, leaving the side of my tub.

While the two of them are setting up the pallet, I splash about a bit and then call over to Jim, "I have just heard that your efforts with the *Star* in my absence have put a fine twenty-four dollars into our coffers. I am most proud and gratified that my early trust in you has proved most true."

With a very deft move, Jim dodges Higgins's restraining hand and appears at my side. He looks down and stammers, "I-I wish it could have been more. I wish we could've gone fishin' together like we used to do, Missy. I wish—"

Whatever Jim Tanner wishes is cut short as Higgins collars him and tosses him out the door. My trusty wedges are set, and that door will not open again till morning.

I rise and towel off and Higgins gets me my nightdress and cap and I sinfully revel in his attention and then crawl into the bed and sink into the feather mattress with a heartfelt groan of more pure pleasure. I close my eyes and offer up yet another heartfelt prayer for Jaimy Fletcher's safety, and I do it quickly, for I know sleep is coming on fast. Tomorrow I shall think and plot and plan, but for now...

Ah, sweet sleep...

Chapter 3

The next morning, we're up with the dawn. We will have breakfast, then the horses will be saddled and we will be off again.

At breakfast Higgins and I have some time to talk.

"So the plan is to go to this Allegheny River, which you have on good information flows into the Ohio and hence into the Mississippi, and we pay for passage downriver to New Orleans, and then book passage on a ship bound for God-knows-where?" asks Higgins, with not a little doubt in his voice.

"Aye. We'll decide in New Orleans what our next move will be. At least we'll be safe there, as it is a French port. Or a Spanish port. I forget which."

"Ah, Miss. I'm afraid you're mistaken. It is now an American port. Their President Jefferson has recently bought it from our old friend Monsieur Napoléon."

"Indeed? When did that happen?"

"About three years ago. It was called the Louisiana Purchase."

"How much did he pay for it?"

"About three cents an acre, I hear."

"Ah, these sharp Yankee traders," I say, patting my lips with my napkin, a lady again. "Still, they bear no special love for the British, so I should be safe there."

I recalled Amy Trevelyne saying something about all that when we were up on the widow's walk at the school, enjoying the spring air before the disastrous outing that resulted in all us girls (except Amy) getting nabbed by that slaver. At the time, when she said it was an enormous amount of land and a grand and great thing, I came back at her to ask, "Ain't you Yankees got enough land, for God's sake?" and she said that it's more about national borders and protection from foreign invasion than being just about land. She said the President had sent out an expedition to chart the new lands and it was due back this summer. I said, "Oh, Amy, wouldn't you just love to have gone along on that expedition?" and she looked at me as if I had lost my senses and said, "Certainly not, how could you ever think that?" "All those new places and wonders to see," I said back at her, and she said, "All those bugs and red savages and wild animals, you mean. How could you want that, Sister? I swear, had I not seen you *déshabillé* on many—in fact, too many—occasions, I would suspect that you were not even of the gentle sex." Though she and I are the very best of friends, we are cut from different cloth, I guess.

"And what, Miss, of the Brothers Lafitte, when we get to New Orleans?" asks Higgins.

"I thought of that, Higgins, and I think it would be well that we enter that city in disguise."

"In *very* deep disguise, I should think, Miss," retorts Higgins. "I well remember Jean Lafitte shaking his fist at us standing at the rail of the *Emerald* as we parted from him, and vowing eternal revenge on you for the theft of, what, four hundred and fifty slaves?"

"*Hmmm.* I think that was the number. I recall that his threats were rather colorful. Especially when he described what he planned to do to me and various of my parts."

"Yes, Miss. But perhaps you should not have laughed at him and taunted him so."

"Aye, but I do hate a slaver," says I, patting lips with napkin and rising. "Let us be off."

Higgins, the imperturbable Higgins, gives a small groan as we rise from the table to begin the day's ride. When we get to the barn, I note that young Jim doesn't look too steady on his pins, either, and I know the cause: Although your feet sit in stirrups when riding a horse, you actually stay on the beast's back by squeezing your legs together, which puts great strain on the inner thigh muscles, and if those muscles are not used to the strain, they'll cramp and they will hurt, especially the next day. I well remember the morning after the first riding session I had at the Lawson Peabody, when I rose from bed and fell to my knees with the pain. But I got over it and so will my fellow fugitives.

We saddle up and head out.

It is a glorious morning, and I, for one, exult in being completely free for the first time in almost a year. I hoot and shout and sing and ride high in the stirrups and goad my poor suffering friends unmercifully.

I'm sorry, Jaimy, but I am so very glad to be free!

The road grows ever narrower as we press on. We stop for refreshment at noon at another tavern, one that is not nearly as grand as Howe's. I suspect pickings will get leaner and leaner as we head into the wilderness.

When we go back out to our mounts, Higgins begs us to wait a moment as he opens one of his saddlebags.

"I know you will not like this, Miss, but I thought it wise." He reaches in and withdraws two fine pistols and puts them in my own saddlebag. I can see that they are of the brand-new percussion-cap design, murderous things, made never to misfire as the old flintlocks had. He knows me well. I don't like them, but he is right. We are headed into uncharted territory and must be ready for anything.

"I have two of my own, as well as holsters for all, but I don't think we need to attach them to our persons just yet, for this is still considered civilized territory."

I agree and we mount up and push on.

Somewhat later, as I rise in my stirrups to pluck an apple from an overhanging branch, I catch a glimpse of someone, something, up around the bend in the road, flitting furtively into the bushes.

"Hold!" I say, reining in. "There's someone in the brush. Get back." Both Higgins and I reach for our guns, as our horses dance about, confused. When we both have them in hand, I shout, "You, there! Show yourself! If you are a high-wayman, you should know we are well armed, and mark me, we are not shy about using our weapons!"

"Don't shoot, Jacky," I hear a low female voice say, and out from the woods steps Katy Deere, her bow slung over her shoulder.

"Katy!" I exclaim, jumping off my horse to embrace her. "How do you come to be here?" Embracing Katy Deere is very much like embracing a wooden Indian, the kind that stand outside tobacco shops.

"I'm powerful glad to see you, Jacky," she says. "I thought you was wrapped up for good and ever by them on that boat. Sorry that me and my girls couldn't do more for you in the fight, but we'd used up most of our arrows on that little boat, shooting fish."

"And they couldn't have been better spent," says I, beaming at Katy's long, dour face, "for they kept us alive till we were rescued." I plant a kiss on her brow.

"I reckon you are hard to hold, for sure," she says, turning her face away and looking over the treetops.

"But what brings you here? In the middle of the wilderness?"

"Huh!" she says. "We ain't in the middle of no wilderness, you city girl, you. This is farm country—this hain't no wilderness. And this is the only road west from Boston, so—"

"But still…"

"Figured there was nothin' for me in that town. I know I'm too…raw for them that's there. Figured there warn't nothing for me in any of the cities out east, them bein' all the same. So after that fight on the dock, when I knew I couldn't do nothin' more for you and I didn't want to end up in no Boston jail, no sir—which is where they was takin' all the other girls—I ducked back and lit out."

All my dear Sisters arrested by the vile Wiggins? Oh, poor, poor girls! What your families must think!

"I figures to go back West, where I knowed some things, at least."

"Go back and do what?" I ask, still holding on to her shoulders and trying to look into her dark eyes, eyes that won't take mine.

42

"Go back and kill my uncle and take back the land that was my momma and daddy's. Ain't afraid of my uncle no more, no, I ain't," she says, fingering her strung but arrowless bow.

Her uncle's as good as dead right now, and that's all right considerin' what he done to her, I'm thinking.

I release her and climb back up on my horse. "Here. Get up behind me. We're going to the Allegheny River. You can show us the way. Then you can go kill your uncle. All right?"

She thinks, then nods, and hops up behind me, without using the stirrups or anyone's helping hand. It's those long, lean legs, I suppose.

"So how far is it, then?" I ask as we start off at a walk.

"'Bout three hundred miles," she says.

There are heartfelt groans of despair from both Higgins and Jim.

"Huh!" she says from behind me. "Distance don't mean nothin' out where we're goin'. Three hundred miles? *Pshaw!* We do thirty miles a day on these nags and we're there in ten, maybe twelve, days."

I think on this as we come up to a brisk trot. *Three hundred miles! I know from looking at my charts on the* Emerald, *that's the same as the width of England, herself, at her widest part!* Katy's strong arm encircles my waist so as to steady herself, and she goes on, "Make that twelve or fourteen, 'cause the roads is about to get a whole lot worse than this."

More groans from my two male companions as we kick up to an easy, mile-devouring canter.

Westward, ho, indeed.

Chapter 4

Ezra Pickering, Esquire
Attorney at Law
Offices at 38 Union Street
Boston, Massachusetts
July 7, 1806

Miss Jacky Faber
Chief Executive Officer
Faber Shipping, Worldwide
Somewhere out West, USA

My Dear Miss Faber,

I wish you the joy of your newfound freedom and your reunion with your young man.

I am sending this letter with that selfsame Mr. Fletcher, who is hot to get off on your trail, and I do believe that "hot" is the proper word, however indiscreet.

I was as astounded today, as you are right now, without doubt, to find him standing before me in my office, dripping wet and looking very bedraggled and muddy. Apparently he waited till the *Juno* cast off her lines today and was well under way before leaping overboard—it seems his regard for you is greater than his love of the Royal Navy. Not surprising, considering his ill-use by that service recently.

You will hear from him (as soon as you climb down off of him) an account of how we got your young lieutenant cleaned up and how we reclaimed his gear from his lodgings, procured a horse from Mistress Pimm's school stable, and sent him on his way, so I will write no more about that. As he is only two days behind you, he should catch up with you soon, and though he is a seaman and not used to the land, he shan't get lost, as there is only one road west. Besides, he will be able to easily follow the path of destruction you usually leave in your wake.

I will, however, relate to you with extreme relish the happenings that occurred after your unfortunate arrest, the chief of which was the Battle of Long Wharf and the arrest of the entire student body of the Lawson Peabody School for Young Girls on a charge of Inciting to Riot. Oh, if you could have but seen it, Jacky, knowing, as I do, how you love a good dustup! The girls were shouting and throwing things and screeching like any band of angry red Indians, and many of the townspeople, sympathetic to your cause, joined in as well. You may be quite sure that Wiggins and his minions had their hands full with this mob.

The large jail coach was brought down from the courthouse and the police began throwing the girls very unceremoniously into it. A girl would be tossed in, the outside latch thrown, and the officer would go seek out another victim. Mistress Pimm, herself, was arrested for attempting to brain Wiggins for putting his hands about the throat of Julia Winslow and likewise abusing others of her girls.

And, yes, even Miss Amy Wemple Trevelyne was destined to see the inside of Boston's fine jail that day. And that night. She was apprehended for beating her delicate little fists on the broad back of an officer who was dragging a squalling Annie Byrnes off to the hack.

What, you fault me for allowing Miss Amy to be hauled away on the shoulder of a brute without a fight? Well, maybe you might, but, no, I stepped aside, disdaining false heroics, knowing I would be needed later in my official capacity and would not be effective from the inside of a cell. Actually, I found the sight of the usually very reserved Miss Trevelyne upended, with limbs kicking and petticoats all ahoo, to be quite a delightful sight. Yes, indeed.

Ah, I digress. Back to the account: I went to the jail in my official capacity as Officer of the Court and viewed the pandemonium. All the girls were thrown into that very cell where I first laid eyes upon your own very scared self in the riotous company of Mrs. Bodeen's girls those several years ago.

I must say that Mrs. Bodeen's girls had nothing on the girls of the Lawson Peabody in the way of riot—they immediately set up a chant of "Free Jacky! Free Jacky! Free Jacky!" punctuated by loud clangs of the cell's metal water dipper against the bars of the cage, wielded by the very wet and muddy Miss Clarissa Worthington Howe. The chant was peppered with some very vivid language from Miss Howe, as well. Wherever did she learn those words? Not from you, I should hope.

Goody Wiggins, wife to our Head Constable, marched her considerable bulk up to the bars and demanded that they all "shut up and be quiet or I'll come in there and whip the daylights out of ye little hussies!" The ranks of the girls parted as Goody approached the bars, but not out of fear, it seems. No, they parted to allow Rose Crawford to advance with the cell's bucket of drinking water and to throw it over the redoubtable Mrs. Wiggins, soaking her to the skin. Goody screeched out her dismay at this watery blow to both her pride and her status as matron of the jail, and she demanded that Constable Wiggins himself enter the cage and thrash the evil little harlots. But he shook his pink jowls in absolute refusal, he having looked at the claws and teeth awaiting him in there, and apparently deciding that the scorn of a wife was far better than the wrath of the furies contained therein.

I did manage to sidle up to the bars, a bit away from the main action, and reassure Miss Amy that all would be well. She reached through the bars and held my hand, and I assured her I'd have her out in the morning, after Judge Thwackham's court convened. Though somewhat distraught, she was bearing up well, and we did hold hands and converse until Wiggins spotted me and shouted, "You, Lawyer Pickering, out! Out till tomorrow morning!" I think it was his vain way of trying to reestablish his authority in his own prison. I made so bold as to raise Amy's hand to my lips before I turned and left. On my way out I heard Miss Constance Howell lead all the girls in a fervent prayer, not for their deliverance, but yours, a prayer we now know has been answered. They then returned to their chanting, and I am informed that they kept it up till dawn.

———

In the morning, I was readmitted to the cell area to find the girls, no less subdued now than when I left, in the process of being bound in a line to be taken to court. Curiously, they insisted that they get in line in a certain order, or there would be trouble. Wiggins, wanting no further trouble, agreed, and as each came up, she allowed her left wrist to be bound to a long rope. The line, which I heard referred to as "Sin-Kay's Line," was headed by Rebecca Adams, the youngest of the Societé de Bloodhound, and, oh joy, just wait till Old Revolutionary John, down there in Quincy and retired from the Presidency these past five years, hears of this. It will be "Abigail! Abigail! Saddle up my fastest horse! We must ride to her aid!" And she'll call him a dear old fool and order him to let the lawyers handle it, to which I would agree. Only Clarissa Howe would not submit to the binding of wrists and so was bound and gagged and carried to the courtroom.

But I digress again: After the girls were led in and arrayed against the far rail, Mistress Pimm was brought in from the separate cell, where she had been confined for the night, and placed in the dock. I stood next to her as her attorney. Then the call of "All rise" was heard, and a very grumpy Judge Thwackham, garbed in his usual judicial finery, entered the room and plunked himself down in his chair high above. He slammed down his gavel to start the proceedings and growled, "All right, be seated, the whole miserable lot of you. What's on for today, then, Mr. Cross? I count on it being some extremely annoying bother, accomplishing nothing except disturbing an honest man's digestion of his breakfast. Harrumph. Who's first?"

The Clerk of Courts, Mr. Cross, stood up and said,

"Commonwealth of Massachusetts, City of Boston, against one Miranda Pimm, female, Headmistress of the Lawson Peabody School for Young Girls, on a charge of Aggravated Assault on a Police Officer, to wit: Constable John Wiggins."

Now that woke up the old buzzard. The Lawson Peabody? Can it be? Can it be that he had not yet heard of yesterday's riot down at the docks? Apparently so. He shook his copious jowls and glared at Mistress Pimm standing ramrod straight in the dock. He then peered incredulously at the line of girls awaiting his stern judgement at the back of his courtroom.

"What is this, then?" he growled at Mistress Pimm.

She lifted her chin, her face immobile in what I believe you Lawson Peabody girls call "the Look," and said, in a strong, clear voice, "Sir, I was apprehended in the performance of my duty in trying to protect one of my girls from brutal treatment at the hands of one of your court-appointed thugs. I should think you would applaud my action, considering that your granddaughter Caroline is one of my charges as well and I would do the same for her at any time. I saw it as my duty yesterday, and I will see it as my duty tomorrow, Sir, whether my girls and I are back in the safety of our school or remain here in your foul prison! Arrogant authority stole one of my babes yesterday, but by the God who protects the weak, by the God who protects innocent young women, by the God that smites the wicked, by that same all-seeing and loving God, they shall get no other!"

The galleries, of course, were packed, with more people cramming into the outside hall and spilling into the street, and this bit of impassioned oration brought forth a roar of approbation: "Hear, hear!" and "Huzzah, huzzah!"

The judge, who obviously had not been apprised of this entire situation, not even of his granddaughter's incarceration (I mean, who would have had the nerve to tell the old warhorse?), turned a vivid shade of red as he cast his gimlet eye across the line of accused females arrayed below him, to pick her out. Miss Caroline, upon seeing her grandpapa's face turn from red to purple upon spotting her, lifted up her unbound right fist and shouted out, *"Sic semper tyrannis!"* This brought another thunderous acclamation from the crowd, a crowd that was in danger of fast becoming a howling mob.

The temper of the Court was not helped when Mademoiselle Lissette de Lise, the very elegant daughter of the French Consul, a bloodstained bandage wrapped very fashionably around her noble brow, raised her own fist and intoned with Gallic fire, *"À bas la monarchie d'Angleterre! À bas le roi George! Vive la Révolution américaine! Vive l'école Law-sahn Pee-bod-dee! Vive Ja-kee Fay-bear! À les Barricades!"* giving the whole affair a certain international flair. Her father, the Comte de Lise, was in attendance and was not at all pleased when she was finally brought down and subdued. There were mumbles of withdrawing the French Embassy, thereby creating a political crisis of the first order.

Judge Thwackham's main role in all this was pounding his gavel and vainly calling for "Order! Order! By God, I'll have you all whipped! Order! Order in my courtroom!"

The explosiveness of the situation was not helped when Colonel Howe burst into the proceedings, fresh from riding up from the South to reclaim his daughter, only to find her bound and gagged and on her knees in a Yankee courtroom, wearing only very damp undergarments. He threatened to call up a regiment of Virginia Regulars and start a civil war if he did not receive immediate satisfaction. He was joined in this sentiment by Amy's father, Colonel Trevelyne. We were indeed lucky that her brother and your ardent admirer, Randall Trevelyne, had been sent off on a horse-buying errand to Philadelphia, else real blood would have been spilled by that hothead, had he been at the Battle of Long Wharf, and the legal cleanup would have been much messier. And much costlier. I know that Randall will be furious to have missed it all. I do hope I am there to see his face when he receives the news.

But with cooler heads prevailing, mine not the least of them, God save the mark, things were finally sorted out and peace was restored in the City of Boston, Commonwealth of Massachusetts.

I made it a special project to gain Miss Amy's release first of the girls, she being not as battle-hardened as the others, the veterans of the *Bloodhound*. When I stood up in court and successfully pleaded her case and delivered her to the arms of her parents, I received a squeeze of my hand and what I took to be a very warm and heartfelt look.

All in all, it was one of the greatest days in my life so far.

I was able to bill out many hours of legal assistance to some of the most prominent families in Boston. In short, I prospered, and I made some very good contacts, you may be sure.

All is well now and all have been released. Oh, some fines (read that "bribes") will have to be paid, and some apologies (written, formal, but not spoken) will have to be made, but all will return to normal eventually.

Now let me tell you of more prosaic but equally happy

things. I believe you'll be most pleased to hear that the marriage of Sylvia Rossio and Henry Hoffman will occur next week at the Church of the Holy Cross on School Street, Signore Rossio and Herr Hoffman having finally given their permission for the match. I believe both papas concluded that the two young people in question had probably already made their marriage vows to some Reverend Bedpost in a room in some wayside inn on the way up from New York to bear the news of the salvation of the girls of the Lawson Peabody, so something had better be done and the sooner the better.

But, of course, you will already know of this because you will hear it from Mr. Fletcher, who stands impatiently before me. His horse is outside, saddled, packed, and ready, and Mr. Fletcher is most anxious to be off. Again, I wish you the joy of your reunion.

I will add only that Miss Amy sends her regards. She has made arrangements for your *Morning Star* to be taken to Dovecote for storage until your most heartily wished-for return. She is still too unnerved to write, but wishes me to quote her: "My dearest friend: I am filled with joy at your deliverance, and with sadness at our continuing separation. How you do try me, Sister. I fear I shall expire of emotional exhaustion, but God be with you, in spite of it all."

Lieutenant James Fletcher opens his vest to stuff this letter in, and he will brook no further wait, and so I conclude by saying that I am,

Yr Most Devoted Friend,

Ezra

Chapter 5

Up in the morning and back on horse. It is the fourth day out and we have turned, at Katy's direction, from the Boston Post Road, which I know from asking our last innkeeper would have led us to New York City, a town I mean to visit someday, but not just yet. This road immediately gets narrower and rougher, but I believe my male companions are bearing up better, now that they've had some time to shake off the kinks of easy city living.

The road widens, so I pull up next to Higgins, and we ride knee to knee, each of us lost in thought. After a bit, I say, "I want to thank you again for my rescue, Higgins. It was a very fine thing."

"Thanks are not necessary, except perhaps to God. It was very lucky that the Fennel and Bean Nonesuch Players were doing *Fanny, the Pride of the Regiment,* so that we had the proper British uniforms for our little deception."

I consider this, then I reply, "Yes, I have had a great amount of luck in this life, and not all of it was bad. But I have enjoyed the greatest of good luck in having the love and protection of my friends."

"Well said, Miss."

"Well, I try. But what is this 'Fanny' play?"

"It was penned by Messrs. Bean and Fennel themselves. It is short on substance but high on wild plot twists, risqué antics, and outrageous theatricals. Much like your own life to date, Miss."

"Higgins, you wound me."

"I was merely making a jest, Miss."

"*Hmmm...*"

"One thing, though, that has me mystified. Messrs. Fennel and Bean have reported to me that you have often been offered the role of Cordelia in *Lear* and have always absolutely refused to do it. This strikes me as peculiar when in fact you have done other doomed heroines—Ophelia, Lady Macduff, even Lady Macbeth, herself, once, and thought nothing of it. Why is that?"

"It's 'cause Cordelia gets hanged at the end, and the Nonesuch Players have got that grisly scene down pat, believe me—the noosing, the kicked-out chair, Cordelia's vain struggles—and I've got a thing about that...like I still have the feeling that I'm going to end up that way. Dangling at the end of a rope."

Higgins considers this for a while, then says, "Well, considering your lifestyle, that's not an implausible fear. However, could not living, as a child, in the shadow of Newgate Prison have something to do with that fear?"

"I don't know," says I, wanting to change the subject. I turn back to Katy, behind me. "What's the chance of us finding a good inn?"

"Pretty good. There's one 'bout fifteen miles up ahead, at a fork in the road. Prolly the last one like it 'fore we hit the frontier. Then things get right meager in that way. We'll prolly be sleepin' out some. Prolly a lot."

That doesn't rile Jim Tanner, but it sure raises one of Higgins's eyebrows.

"Then I intend to enjoy my last night as a civilized human," says he, "before I turn into a red savage."

The inn, the Martin in the Maples in the town of Port Jervis, turns out to be in New York State, and seems to be snug and comfortable, and I arrange to play a set that night in return for tips. I tried to wrangle lodging, but it was no go. *Damn cheap Yankees.* After we were settled in, I sent Jim to try to round up an audience, but he found slim pickings out there, that's for sure. Still, we had a small crowd of about fifteen people that night, mostly horse traders and plowboys, and farmers come into the town to sell their produce, and they were jolly enough. I began with "In the Good Old Colony Times" and followed that with "Springfield Mountain"—no singing, just the fiddle—and topped it off with a Scottish dance. I told some stories and some jokes and then played some more tunes. The pennywhistle was new to many of them, they being mostly of Dutch stock, but they loved my fiddle and were astounded by my dancing. Nothing they'd ever let their daughters do, but still fun to watch. The tips made it worthwhile, and I did love getting back into performance.

It was the first time Jim had seen me do my full act, and I think he was charmed. Katy, too, shook her head and said in wonder, "If that don't just beat all," as I dipped and took my final bows.

After all is done and the place is closed, we all go to bed. An extra mattress not being available in this place, Higgins is in a chair, with feet propped up and pistols in his lap, facing the door. Katy is in bed to my right, and Jim Tanner is out with the horses. Rather reluctantly with the horses, I think. From the ardent glances he cast my way as I was performing, I think he'd rather have Higgins out in the barn and himself in here between Katy and me, but, no, that is not to be, young Jim.

Before I sleep this night, though, I cannot help but think back on the events of the last week, and tears trickle down my cheeks and onto the pillowcase.

Oh, Jaimy, for you to have had to stand there and not say a word as I was stood up and shamed and then taken off the Juno, knowing, as you did, that if you raised too much of a fuss, Higgins's charade would have been uncovered and all would have been lost. I am so very hard on my friends.

And now, Jaimy, you are being taken back to England, once again half a world away from me. I do hope that no harm comes to you because of my actions, and while Higgins tells me not to worry in that regard, still I worry. I don't know...So many things can go wrong in this world, and things generally do go wrong.

Aye, maybe it would be best if you found another girl when you get back to England, for as you know, I am nothing but trouble and grief. And one of these days my luck has got to run out, virtuewise. Will you still want me then? I don't know. I don't know anything. But I know I will always love you, Jaimy, no matter what you do, and where you go. I want you to know that, Jaimy.

G'night, now...

I give a sniffle and maybe a slight sob and Higgins's hand reaches out in the darkness and gives my shoulder a comforting pat. *Good Higgins—you always know, don't you...*

Chapter 6

Ex-Lieutenant James Emerson Fletcher
Howe's Tavern on the Post Road
Massachusetts, USA

Miss Jacky Faber
Somewhere up ahead of me on the road west
In the wilderness, Massachusetts, USA

My Dearest Jacky,

   Again I write to your absent self, but this time I am com-pletely confident that we will very shortly be united for good and ever.

   I am here at the very same lodging that you stayed in a scant two days ago. I swear I can smell your scent on the breeze, I am getting that close! It is with the utmost regret that I stop for the night in my pursuit of you, but I feel that I must, for safety's sake and for the sake of sleep. And so, by lamplight, I sit here and pen this letter, in hopes that you (or our children, should we be so blessed) will read it and be entertained.

I found, upon closely questioning the landlord here at Howe's Tavern, that your own dear self and those of your party had been here and left the next day intending to head for the Allegheny River. (I know that Higgins and Jim Tanner are with you, and for that I thank God, but who is the other girl? Never mind, all shall soon be plain.)

After finding out, upon further inquiry, into what other river the Allegheny flows, I believe I now know your mind on where you plan to go and how you plan to get there. I chuckle to think that it is so much like you to seek out open water when you are on the run, or otherwise in trouble, which is, of course, virtually all of the time. I have been chuckling a lot for the past day, knowing that I will soon have you in my arms, from which embrace I vow you shall never again escape.

I hope you are not dismayed, given your deep sense of loyalty to our Service, to find that I have left the Royal Navy, and I left it quite abruptly, having dived overboard as the *Juno* was being warped out of Boston Harbor. I don't care. If a career in the Naval Service means the loss of you, then the hell with it. I'll find something else to do. Maybe join the Hottentot Navy, eh, what? It was reassuring to me, though, to find out that I could indeed swim, as I had not tried before.

But all of that is of no matter, as I am sure to catch up with you the day after tomorrow, at the very latest, and we shall have a leisurely cruise down these American rivers to wherever they may take us, in, I hope, a state of wedded bliss. On that, I can but hope, but I have lingering doubts, to wit: I know that you have been on the stage, and while I know that you are an accomplished actress, still, when you stood on the deck of the *Juno* and denied me so convincingly, so chillingly convincingly, well, I don't know what to think. I am but a poor fool when it comes to understanding you, Jacky. But I trust that all will be resolved when we meet.

I have been provided with ample money from our friends in Boston, especially from Miss Trevelyne, Miss Howe, and Mademoiselle de Lise. Such fine friends you have, Jacky. I have directed Ezra Pickering, another invaluable friend to both of us, as I do not need to tell you, to contact my father in London for restitution of these funds, which, incidentally, I keep safe upon my person. Restitution will be quickly made, I am sure, since Fletcher & Sons Wine Merchants has prospered since we recovered the losses we incurred from the depredations of a certain female pirate...ahem, excuse me, *privateer*. Don't worry, you will make it up to me, oh, count on that, but not in monetary ways. Oh, no. I have many other, much more pleasant things in mind.

Your Mistress Pimm, upon presenting me with a fine horse from her school stables, said to me, "Go, young man, and find her and bring our lost sheep back to us. As I perceive you to be a gentleman, I trust you will treat her honorably."

I nodded at that and said I would, but I spoke the truth only up to a certain point. Actually, upon finding you, I intend, honorably, to haul you up in front of the nearest preacher, or what passes for a preacher out in this godforsaken wilderness, say the words, and then find a bed or convenient patch of grass, strip you of your garments, lay you down on your back, and again, honorably, finally and completely consummate our union. I have waited and suffered long enough.

That is sufficient for now. Suffice to say, there will be portions of this letter that will not be read to the children. Especially to the girls.

I have made the acquaintance this evening of two fine gentlemen who are traveling the same road as I, who pronounce themselves knowledgeable in the highways and byways of this region, and tomorrow we shall travel together. I took dinner with them, actually, and they proved most amiable. They are a Mr. McCoy and a Mr. Beatty. I am sure they will be pleasant and informative company as I continue on my journey.

Till we meet again in joyous congress, I am,

Your Most Obedient and etc.,

Jaimy

Chapter 7

Once again we saddle up for another day of travel. As Katy settles in behind me, I ask, "Your uncle. On your farm. Should you not approach that very carefully? After all, it could be dangerous, and while we are well armed, well…"

"Don't worry, Jacky, I'll scout it out some, believe me."

"Maybe instead of killing him outright, maybe you could bring him up on charges? Get him sent to prison or something?"

"Ain't the way it's done out here. Ain't much law out where we're headed, and what there is of it tends to hang around the towns. 'Sides, he'd have the law on his side, him bein' a man with property and me bein' a penniless girl. Huh! Ain't no prisons, neither. If you're guilty of something', it's either the noose or whippin' or banishment, and that's it."

She settles into the rhythm of the ride, satisfied with her lot for now. She has fashioned a quiver out of the leftover leather and she wears it over her right shoulder so that her new arrows are right at her command should she need them. She still wears her white headband.

We stop at noon for what we think will be refreshment at a very small wayside general store, hardly more than a hovel that has a porch with some barrels on it, but we can find no one there. Mystified and somewhat disappointed, we push wearily on.

"Jim," I say. "Ride up ahead and see what awaits us."

Jim eagerly puts his heels to his horse and leaves the rest of us sluggards in the dust. I would join him, but we cannot push these two horses too hard, since they bear heavier loads than does Jim's lucky nag.

We grumble along a bit more, saddle sore and hungry, for an hour or so, when Jim comes pounding back.

"Missy! There's a big tent in the middle of a field up ahead and to the right! And there's tons of people there!"

We spur on our reluctant mounts and eventually come to the spot Jim described.

Katy takes one look and says, "Huh! Revival meetin'."

We gaze down on the spectacle. The huge tent has its front and side flaps open, the weather being mild and the crowd being big. I'm amazed to see so many people, since we have spied so few on our way here.

Inside the tent I can see a stage, and on it is a preacher shaking his fist and roaring at the congregation. I cannot make out his words, but I can surely pick up on the religious fervor with which he delivers them. So can the crowd. They sway back and forth like people in a trance, like people transported to another realm.

"He's pretty good," says Katy, plainly familiar with such revival meetings. "I ain't seen him before, but he's good. He's got 'em goin'."

"Let's rest here," I say, dismounting by throwing my leg over the horse's neck, Katy being behind me. We all slide off and go to sit in the shade of a tree to watch.

The preacher has slipped from his harangue into a hymn, and the crowd picks up on it with fervor.

> *Oh come, Angel Band,*
> *Come and around me stand,*
> *Bear me away on your Silver Wings*
> *To my Eternal Home.*

I'm surprised to hear the normally quiet Katy humming along with the tune as it goes into the next verse.

> *I'm going there to meet my mother,*
> *She'll meet me on the way,*
> *To take me up on Silver Wings,*
> *To my Eternal Home.*

They go back to the first verse and then do the second one, except they substitute "father" for "mother." And so on, through "brother" and "sister." I'm surprised that they don't go all the way through "friend," or "nephew" or "cousin" or even "mother-in-law," but they don't. They eventually bring it to a halt, and the preacher is right on top of them with more preachin,' and I see the collection plates goin' out. *Aha!*

Every fiber of my being wants to be down there working that crowd with any of at least ten scams that I know, but instead I say, "Let's head off. Night's comin' on."

We leave and press onward, but I am glad we stopped. I learned a lot from that man.

Another mean tavern tonight, but we are grateful for what comfort it offers. Horses are put up, dinner is downed, and so to bed.

Good night, Jaimy. I hope and pray that all is well with you.

Chapter 8

Good-bye forever, Jacky,

No, I will not catch up with you on this day, nor the next, nor the one after. I will never catch up with you, because I am a fool. This will be my last spiritual message to you, as I will be dead very shortly.

No, I am not writing this down on paper, as I have none. I have no paper and no hope. In fact, I have very little sense left to me. No, I am composing this in what is left of my mind, in order to preserve what scraps of consciousness and sanity I may have left in this world before I depart for another.

I try to rise to my knees but am unable to do so, since one of them clubs me back down. I am dimly aware that my clothing is being stripped from me, but I cannot stop them. I swim in and out of consciousness, but in one moment of clarity I hear "Someone's coming. Finish him off."

I sense one of them straddling me and I hear the cocking of a pistol's hammer.

Good-bye, Jacky. You are the very best of girls and I wish you the best of lives, I'm sorry, I—

I hear the explosion of the pistol and feel a deep burning in my head and then I know... nothing.

PART II

Chapter 9

And so we traveled across this American landscape—climbing up mountains and down into lush valleys, fording streams that we were told flowed into the Allegheny, fighting off the fearsome mosquitoes—on roads that grew ever narrower and rougher. The towns became villages, then hamlets, then clusters of forlorn buildings at crosses in the road. The inns petered out and lodgings became what we could find in the common dwellings of the people, those who would take us in and feed and shelter us in exchange for what we could give. We paid in kind, what money we could spare, but we were getting out to places where money was less common than barter, so I bartered some musical entertainment on my part, playing fiddle, pennywhistle, and concertina, with funny songs and storytelling for the kids. "Froggy Went a-Courtin'" was always a hit. There were many warm evenings spent around a family's table in a simple but friendly home.

I also did miniature portrait paintings—stern chin-whiskered fathers, more gentle mothers, rambunctious kids, young lovers—I did them all, and all pronounced themselves satisfied with my skill. And yes, I did some mourning portraits, too, those of young children who had died and who were dressed up in their best clothes so that I could come with my paints and ivory disks to paint them, so that the grieving parents would have something to remember their beloved child by, after they put them in the ground. It seemed the children, so perfect and quiet, were merely sleeping, but I knew they were not. Most often it was the poor young mother who had to comfort me, rather than the other way around, so as to get me in shape to do the work. It was sad, but I always got it done. Once, we lost a day's travel when I was begged to visit a house in a small village, far up a side road, to paint the portrait of a bride who had died the night before her wedding. She was laid out in her bridal gown and turned slightly to the side in her coffin so as to look more natural for me to paint. I, of course, was shattered, but managed to paint the portrait for the sake of the bride-groom, who sat by her side the whole time I painted.

So we paid our way west as best we could.

The stores began to get farther and farther between as well, so we got what we could get when we could get it. We bought a tent and blankets. We loaded up on powder, balls, and caps. We bought a small-bore rifle, a German-made carbine, for Jim, of which he is most proud. He has practiced and become quite accurate with it. Katy was offered a similar one but declined, preferring her simple bow, which had proved so deadly on the *Bloodhound*. She, however, did accept a gift of a fine knife. Upon seeing me disrobe that first night, and spying my leather arm sheath that held my shiv under my sleeve, there for ready use, she opined that it was a fine thing, and so we also bought some leather and an awl and some waxed cord, and soon she had a rig similar to mine under her own sleeve. She has used the knife to begin fashioning more arrows for her newly made leather quiver.

As we crossed into Pennsylvania, with night coming on, we pitched the tent and made camp. Higgins, bless him, has grown very proficient in setting up the damned thing, which fought us every step of the way when we first tried to set it up in a pouring rain.

Jim's rifle brought us two brace of fat squirrels, and we skinned and roasted them over an open campfire. We ate them with some bread we had left over from our last stay at a farmhouse, and it was good. Could have done with a spot of wine, though. *Now, girl, come on. You've gotten too soft with all that high living on the* Bloodhound, *it seems. Toughen up, now.*

Higgins has adapted to this rough life in fine form, managing to make a meal of roasted squirrel seem like something served in the finest houses.

Tomorrow we will get to the vicinity of Katy's farm and we will have to see how things work out there. Killing her uncle and all. We'll see.

When it came time for sleep, all of us crawled into the tent and got under the blankets. Higgins tried to keep order, but in the morning, Jim Tanner somehow ended up with his nose in my neck hair and his arm about my waist.

I don't mind, though. I hate sleeping alone.

Chapter 10

James Fletcher, Idiot & Fool
Naked & facedown in the dirt
Somewhere in the American Wilderness

My Dearest Jacky,

It is well said that we sailors have no business on land, as we are easy prey to the designs of landsmen, curse them all to Hell, and I am afraid I proved myself easier prey than you—despite your diminutive size and gentle nature—ever did.

I do not remember much about that day, but I do remember setting out—full of hope, in anticipation of our imminent reunion—with Mr. McCoy and Mr. Beatty, who represented themselves as honest merchants dealing in dry goods and notions, and who turned out to be dealing in something else entirely.

As we rode along, I talked freely and ardently about you and your party up ahead, and they jollied me along, getting all the information they could out of me, assuring me that we should come upon you at any moment. After we traveled some miles through the forest, we stopped by a clear stream to water our horses and refresh ourselves. As I knelt by the stream to cup some water to drink, I felt a shadow fall upon me, and then that's all I clearly sensed for a long, long time. I know now that either McCoy or Beatty had come up behind me and brought a bludgeon down on the back of my head.

I fell face-first into the stream, instantly and totally senseless. I suspect that the shock of the cold water brought me partially back to my senses, for at least I could tell that my clothes were being stripped from me, although I could not prevent it. I tried to rise to my knees but was unable to do so, as one of them clubbed me back down.

I was rolled over, I suppose to make it easier for them to remove my boots and trousers, then rolled facedown again such that my face was in the mud.

It was not long after that I sensed they took alarm from a sound in the brush and quickly gathered the horses to make their escape. Then I heard those chilling words "Someone's coming. Finish him off" and the report of the pistol above my head. Then nothing but darkness.

I came back into this world, with the taste of mud and leaves and dirt in my mouth and, strangely, the feel of a cool cloth pressed against my face. My eyes opened and tried to focus and... *the pain, oh, the pain!* My head felt as though it would explode. When the blows had been dealt, they felt nothing like this. Then it was more like pure shock rather than pure pain, but this, *oh, God, the pain!* I groaned and twisted with the throb in my head and I heard someone say,

"Now, now, boy, lie back. Easy now. They're gone, don't worry. You'll be all right, you'll see. Easy, now. Roll over on your back. That's it."

I managed to crack open an eyelid to peer at the one who knelt above me. "What...who...?"

The face of a girl swam into my vision. She had straight corn-colored hair and a very freckled face. The cool cloth that wiped the blood from my face turned out to be the wet hem of her simple shift, held in her right hand. Then there was quiet. She must have gone back to the stream to rinse the mess from her skirt, and then she came back and sat down next to me.

She ran her fingers lightly over my bare chest and said, "My name is Clementine Jukes, and you are one very pretty boy."

Chapter 11

"We're in Armstrong County now," says Katy, sounding a little worried there behind me. "We're gettin' close to the river."

"Don't worry, Katy," I say, patting her knee. "We'll take it slow."

We have, in the past days, crossed some seriously high mountains, and while the views were breathtaking and the weather generally good, I am glad we are getting close to the water. We grow ever more weary of riding, of bedding down in strange houses or in the tent by the wayside, of trying to find grain for the horses, of this whole landlocked journey. Oh, how I yearn for some open water, some far vistas where not everything is trees, trees, and more trees. I am sick of green and yearn for blue. I want a proper bath. Note to self: *Stop whining*. Still, it's the truth.

I'm beginning to wonder if this idea of mine was a good one—this country is just so damned *huge*.

We are down from the last mountain and have come into a river valley. The forest finally begins to thin out and farmland reappears. I can sense the usually unshakable Katy growing more and more nervous. I guess she's wondering what she's gonna do when she gets to her old place. I think I know what she's thinking: *Will he still be there? Will he try to come at me to dirty on me ag'in? Did he tell the folks hereabouts that I'd whacked him in the head with a shovel and then run away, leaving him out cold in the dirt?*

Katy has kept her bow strung this day, and the new leather quiver that hangs on her back contains an even dozen good, straight arrows. These arrows, unlike the ones she fashioned on the *Bloodhound,* have well-shaped flint arrowheads, the edges of which are sharp as razors. Not that the ones she had made on that vile slaver were not deadly, oh, no. They proved quite deadly, as many, many rats, including those human rats Bo'sun Chubbuck and First Mate Dunphy, found out to their infinite sorrow. No, it's just that on the ship, she had to make do with nails for arrowheads and split wooden battens for the shafts. And I don't think we could have done without her, no, I don't.

The road takes a turn and I spy a girl coming across a field, leading a lowing cow. It looks like she means to lead it back to the barn, the top of which we can see over the next small hill. Katy spies the girl, too.

"Hold up here," she says. We do and she calls out, "Gert! Gertrude Mueller!"

The girl's head jerks around and she looks like she's about to fly away in fear.

I feel Katy slip off the horse, behind me. She walks over to the edge of the field and stands there, straight. "Wait, Gertie. It's me, Katy Deere."

The girl stops, then leads the cow over in our direction.

"Katy Deere," says the girl, wide-eyed, when she is close enough. But not too close, I notice. There are the other three strangers on these horses, and I do not blame her for being careful.

"Where you been, Katy?"

"'Round the world and back again, I reckon," says Katy.

"Huh!" says Gertie.

"Our old place. Our farm. My uncle. He still there?"

"Sorry, Katy, t' tell you, but he's dead and laid in the grave."

"Huh! How'd he die?"

"Took some infection from a cut on the back o' his head, near as folks could tell when they found him. He was lying there dead fer a good long spell."

"How'd he git the cut on the back of his head?"

"Dunno. He warn't around no more t' tell it."

"Anybody there now?"

"Don't think so."

"What about me?"

"Ever'one thought some Injuns come and took ya."

"Huh!"

"What you gonna do, Katy?"

"Go on up t' our farm, I reckon. These here are my friends."

Gertrude Mueller looks at us as if we were creatures from another world, us bristling with pistols and rifles and strange clothing and all.

"Uh-huh," she says doubtfully.

Katy comes back and swings up behind me again. "Good seein' you, Gertie. Give my respects t' yer ma and pa."

"I will, Katy."

And with that, we are off again at a slow walk.

I sense a much more relaxed Katy Deere behind me now.

"Looks like you already killed him," says I.

"Uh-huh...Glad of it, too," says Katy.

"Where away, Katy?" I ask.

"Up ahead, there'll be a fork to the right. Take it."

And we do.

We dismount and lead the horses through the last half mile to the place that was all the home that Katy Deere ever knew.

We come at last to a crude gate and Katy goes up and throws back the bar and we go through into the farmyard.

"Hard t' believe it's only been a year. Not even that," says Katy, all quiet, looking around at how overgrown with weeds the place has become. "Poor Mama, she was always so particular 'bout how her front yard looked. In case anyone should come visit and all." She leans down and picks up a small branch that had fallen from the tree that looms overhead, then she tosses it into the bushes. "Don't mean nuthin' now, that's fer sure."

Higgins and Jim and I know to be real silent now as Katy walks across the yard. It's strange to see her dressed in the uniform of a Lawson Peabody serving girl out here on the frontier: white blouse and black vest and black skirt and stockings and all. Certainly ain't the way they dress around here. Around here, seems like most of the girls' clothes are made from feed sacks. But who am I, child of the London slum streets, to say nay to that?

There's a house, sort of, made of rough planks that look like they've been split off of rough logs with wedge and ax, the bark still clinging to the edges. There is mud and clay crammed into the spaces between. There are two wooden steps up to a door. The roof is made of rough shakes, like shingles split off a short log.

There's a barn, with a door barely hanging on its leather hinges, and Jim goes to take the horses there, as we know we will spend the night here, but Katy says, "Let 'em graze out here for a while, Jim, as they ain't gonna find no hay nor oats in there now, that's fer sure."

Jim nods, then takes the packs and the saddles off the horses. He puts a rope hobble around each horse's front ankles so's they can't run off, but the horses don't seem to mind. No, they heave great horsey sighs of relief at having us off their poor backs and they settle into pulling at and chewing the abundant grasses.

Katy doesn't go right into the house. No, instead she walks over to the side of the yard, her arms crossed on her chest. She stops and stares down and I walk over next to her. I see that she is gazing down at three graves. There's a wooden slab at the head of each, but there ain't no writing on them. I don't say anything.

"That's Father over there, 'cause he went first. Then Mama. Then *him*." Saying that she kicks over her uncle's marker and sends it flying into the weeds. "I wisht I could dig him up and feed what's left of him to the pigs. But I guess there ain't no good in that."

She turns and goes back toward the house. "Just don't like the idea of him layin' close to Mama and Father, is all." She goes up the few steps and pushes the door open all the way. She goes in and I follow. Jim starts to come with us, but I see Higgins's gentle restraint on his arm and he stops, and they both remain outside. Though Katy shows not the slightest bit of emotion, Higgins knows that this is hard on her.

She walks through the front room, a simple room with a table and some chairs made from black birch saplings. It looks like small animals have been here—and maybe some large animals as well, because there seems to be nothing of value left in the place. There is a cloth strung across a doorway, and she pulls it to the side and looks in. I see that it is a small room with only enough space for a bed, a bed that still has its mattress.

"I was born in that bed. My father died in that bed. My mama died in that bed…"

"And you and I shall sleep in that same bed tonight, Katy Deere, and take comfort in each other's presence," says I, grabbing her by her shoulders and turning her around to face me. "What do you mean to do here, Katy?"

She looks away. "I dunno. It's early enough to get a crop in. Prolly ask some neighbors for help. Maybe find the best man I can around here and marry up with him so I can get some constant help. Prolly—"

"Is that what you want, Katy, in your heart? Is that what you really want?" I have to stand on my tippy-toes to look into her eyes. Still she shies away and looks down.

"No, I reckon I don't," she says quietly. "Ain't nothin' fer me here, neither, ain't nothin' fer me."

"Then come with us, Katy, and see what lies ahead. Will you do that? I need you, as I ain't got no notion of this great land, and you can help." I give her shoulders a shake.

She stands deep in thought for a while. Then she straightens up and shakes off my hands, and says, "Yeah, I reckon I'll go with you. See what's out there, anyways."

"Good girl," I say, leaning up and putting a kiss on her forehead. "Now let's get settled for the night. Higgins. Jim. Come on in. Tomorrow, the river!"

Chapter 12

Jaimy Fletcher
Brought low
Somewhere in godforsaken America

Dear Jacky,

The girl Clementine got me unsteadily to my feet, saying, "We've got to get you away from here. They might come back to finish you off."

I reeled and staggered my way out of that clearing next to the stream, leaning on the thin shoulders of that young girl, the one who had found me and who had, probably, saved my life. I was still confused, with my thoughts running about my head like wild things. With each upright step, though, my mind cleared some, and soon I was able to take stock of my situation: I was stark naked, with not a thing to my name—no money, no horse, no clothes, no personal belongings, not even a ribbon to bind back my hair, which fell lankly about my face as I struggled on. *Those brigands even took the ribbon from my hair,* I thought, vowing eternal revenge. *I'll get you, you bastards, and you'll regret the*

day you ever thought to get the best of Jaimy Fletcher, by God,
but then my head starts to spin and I sag against a tree. Even
I know that to be an idle threat. I am such an utter fool....

"Here. Come on, a little farther and you'll be safe. There.
Sit down. Rest now." She propped me against a tree trunk
and lifted the cool, wet cloth of her skirt once again to my
forehead.

"Looks like they tried to shoot you, boy," she said, dab-
bing away at the wound on my head, "but they missed. The
bullet went alongside your head but not in it, thank goodness. Here, lean against me till you feel better," and her arms
encircled me as she pressed my head against her breast, and
I did feel better for it. So much so that when I relaxed and
started to slip from consciousness once again, I thought I
heard her say, "Thank you, God, for answering my prayers.
He's just what I wanted. Thank you, thank you. Amen."

When I awoke, she was again pulling me to my feet.
"Come on, boy, we've got to get you back to our place 'fore
dark 'cause you gonna get mighty cold out here, considerin'
you ain't got no clothes on you. Here, give me your hand."

As we stumbled along, my head began to clear, and it
cleared enough for me to realize that I was walking through
deep woods with a girl whilst stark naked.

"Where are we going?" I asked.

"Gonna try to get you to our barn 'fore Pap sees you, so's
you can rest up and get better. Don't worry, I'm gon take
real good care o' you...What's your name?"

"James...Jaimy Fletcher."

"Jaimy...that's a real nice name. Y'know, Jaimy," she
said, trying out my name, rolling it around on her tongue as
if savoring the sound of it, "I prayed to God for Him to

send me a boy to love and for Him to take me away and take care of me, and He sent me you. It's amazin'...that He delivered you naked and all, just like a newborn babe, sent from Heaven above."

"Well, actually I came from across the ocean, from England, uh, Clementine, is it?" I said, somewhat doubtfully.

She turned her head and smiled at me, and amidst my pain and humiliation, I saw that, despite her flimsy dress, once-white apron, and bare feet, she really was quite pretty— straight hair the color of corn silk, good straight teeth, slim frame, and the bluest eyes I had ever seen. She looked to be about fifteen or sixteen.

"Uh-huh," she said, squeezing my hand. "I gotta admit I used to doubt things about God, seein' as how He put me on this earth in a miserable place, without a mama, just mean ol' Pap to kick me around, but He's made ever'thin' right now, that's for sure."

"Um," I said, feeling somewhat less than Heaven-sent, "Clementine, if you could see your way clear to give me the loan of your apron, I would feel much more comfortable."

We stopped walking and she put her hands behind herself to loosen the apron strings. She dipped her head and took off the garment. "You sure do talk funny, don't you?" she said, grinning. I do not believe she has stopped grinning since I arrived on the scene. "I like you just fine the way you are, but, here, turn around."

I did so and she reached around my waist and tied the apron strings, at my back. I could feel her fingers working back there, and it seemed to take longer than really necessary. She was good in that she did not put the neck thing over my head, which would have made me look even more foolish, but instead folded the apron over so that it performed its function of covering my manhood without making me look like I wore part of a dress.

"There," she said, "now you look jest like a real pale Injun."

A flush went to my cheeks as she lightly patted my buttocks when she finished the job, then whispered, "Oh, thank you, God," yet again.

We continued on through what I considered a trackless wilderness, but Clementine seemed to know where she was going, so I followed meekly behind.

"So far from your home," I asked during our trek, "what were you doing by that stream?"

"I go there sometimes to...well, to get away...to dream and hope about things. Maybe you could call it prayin', I don' know..."

Eventually, we came to a cleared bit of land and she bade me crouch down and be quiet.

"If we have any luck, Pap'll already have passed out from the drink and we'll be able to git you into the barn for the night."

I looked out across the clearing and made out what looked like a large rough lean-to. A barn, hardly, but what did I know of this barbarous land? I kept my mouth shut, putting my trust in my guide.

"Shush, now," she said, rising up. "Looks good. Come on. Quick!"

I rose up, too, and together we ran across the open space to the door of the barn. Clementine lifted the bar and the door swung open.

"In here! Quick! We'll get you into the loft and I'll be back later. I'll bring you some food. I'll—"

"Yew'll what?" growled a low voice behind me. "Yew'll what? What the hell's goin' on here? And jus' who the hell are yew, anyway?"

I turned around to discover that I was looking down the barrel of a very long rifle. Behind the rifle stood a very large and very dirty-looking man, unshaven and clad only in a pair of stained overalls, with one broken shoulder strap dangling from a hairy shoulder. His unkempt lank hair hung in his eyes. It was plain that he had been drinking, as he was unsteady on his feet and weaved about as he spoke.

"Please, Pap," said Clementine. She wrung her hands piteously. "He's a boy what God give to me and I mean to keep him. Can I, Pap, please?"

"I asked who the hell are yew?" said this creature to me, his deep-set eyes drilling into mine, the gun's barrel not wavering an inch from a spot between my eyes, in spite of its owner's drunken condition.

"My name is James Emerson Fletcher and I am—"

"Yew am in a ton of trouble, boy! Clemmie! Yew been out there in the wood ruttin' with this boy? Answer me true now."

"No, Pap, I ain't, I . . . ," she wailed.

"Lift up yer dress, let me see yer drawers. Let me smell yew, so's I know what yew been doin', to see if'n his stink is on you, 'fore I kills this boy!"

In spite of looking down the barrel of that gun, I gradually gathered my courage and found my voice. "Sir, I assure you that nothing of that sort has transpired. Your daughter did nothing but help a poor waylaid traveler in distress!"

"That so?" He looked at me and lowered the barrel. He poked me in the shoulder with it. "Turn around, boy." I sensed the barrel being brought up to the back of my head and I did it.

"Why, this boy is butt-nekkid! Yew tellin' me yew ain't been up to somethin' nasty, Clemmie? Shame on yew!"

With that, he took a hand from his rifle and backhanded his daughter across her face, and she went down, sprawled in the dirt. Still keeping the gun trained on me, he pulled up her skirt and peered under. Then, apparently finding nothing damning about the condition of her undergarments, he pulled the dress back down and said, "Both of you'uns. Get inside. C'mon, pretty boy, move it!"

We went into the cabin. There was a fireplace, with several embers glowing in it, and a table on which rested an earthenware jug.

"Yew. Stand over there where I can see yew," said this Mr. Jukes to me, gesturing with the barrel of the gun. "Clemmie. Make up the fire and git me somethin' t' eat."

The girl, no longer the happy, free wood sprite I met in the forest, slumped over to throw some pieces of wood into the fireplace. She took down a pot from a hook overhead and spooned what I took to be cornmeal into it. Then she ladled in some water from a nearby bucket. Her face was now dead, a mask, totally devoid of expression. It was then that I noticed the bruises on her arms, neck, and lower legs. In my own pain and torment, I had not previously seen those very plain marks of pain and abuse upon her, more shame on me.

The demeanor of the father, upon entering the cabin, completely changed from that of threatening bully to that of sneering, snickering bully. I wondered at it but figured that he perceived that I, barely half his size, was no physical threat to him, and so he could in all ease put aside the gun and lift the jug of spirits to his lips. He could not have known that I had been an officer in His Majesty's Royal Navy and, as such, trained in many ways of death-dealing, none of which, I had to admit, seemed to apply here, as I had no cannon, no pistol, no sword.

"Yew look right pretty in that little apron, pretty boy, oh yes, yew do." He giggled, having yet another hit at the jug. "Whyn't yew come over here now and share a drink with me, *hmmm*?"

"Sir, I would rather retire for the night, as I have had a very trying day. You and your daughter have been most gracious to me in my hour of need, but I am now in great need of sleep and would consider it most kind of you to let me gain that rest."

"My, yew sure do talk funny," said Jukes, rising from the table. "But come with me and we shall put yew to bed, oh, yes."

He took up his gun again and led me out into the farmyard and to the barn. On the way out, I caught Clementine's eye, but she gave a quick shake of her head in a warning way. I took the warning to heart.

"Git in there, pretty boy, and up into the hayloft. In the mornin' we'll put yew to some work in payment fer yer lodging." He chuckled again. "And maybe even before then."

I went in at the point of the barrel. There was a stall, with a very large plow horse in it, and a ladder up to the hayloft.

"Up there, boy. That's it. G'night, now."

With that, the barn door closed and I heard the locking bar fall down in place.

I waited a long time, savoring the quiet and peace. Then I felt my way to the door and tried to figure out how to jimmy up the bar from inside. I am sure, Jacky, that you would have been out of this place in a minute and on your way, knowing your skill at escaping confinement, but I, alas, was found wanting, and the bar stayed in place and my attempt at fleeing this madhouse was thwarted. This whole country is a madhouse, as far as I am concerned, and I am sick of it.

Bone tired, I crawled up the ladder and burrowed into the straw and fell instantly asleep.

My sleep, however, was not to be undisturbed.

I do not know how long I had been there when I felt her slip in beside me. When I started, she put her hand on my lips and said, "Shush, Jaimy, quiet now. Pap's passed out asleep, but still, it's best we be quiet, just in case."

She wriggled around and her head came to rest on my shoulder and her arm draped around my chest. I felt her skin warm against mine. I did not feel any clothing and I knew that she wore none.

"Ain't this nice, Jaimy? I kin feel your heart beatin' there under my hand. *Mmmmm...*"

I was quite sure it was beating much faster now than it was before Miss Clementine Jukes's arrival. I could not protest, as that would raise an alarm and she would be in trouble with her father, and no telling what he would do to me.

No, there was nothing for me to do but remain as I was, and forgive me, Jacky, but I did not find it the most unpleasant thing that happened to me on this day....

Chapter 13

I could smell the river way before we actually got there. While it lacks the salty tang of the ocean, smelling more of dark pools and grassy banks and fish, it was a most welcome aroma.

We had spent the last night at Katy's place, getting as comfortable as we could on the few straw pallets that were left in the house. It was plain that someone had gone through the cabin during its time of abandonment and taken all of value. We did, however, manage to find a few saucepans and a banged-up old teapot, which Higgins judged could come in handy later, and Jim added them to our packs.

Higgins has become quite lean and craggy-looking during these past few weeks on the road—the rough life is good for him physically, though it certainly doesn't suit his refined temperament. Still, he does not complain, and he maintains his good humor.

Before we left, Katy asked me to rummage in my seabag for quill and ink so I could write a note on a fairly clean cedar shake she had found:

*This here farm belongs
to Katherine Deere
and I will come back
to claim it someday
so stay off it*

I wrote it down just as she said it, and we nailed it to the front door. Then we climbed on the horses and rode off. Though Katy was behind me and I could not see her, I sensed that she did not look back.

"There it is!" shouts I, standing up in the stirrups and pointing to the gleaming ribbon of river lying in the valley down below. "The Allegheny River, at last."

"Yes, and a most welcome sight it is, Miss," says Higgins, with feeling. "Although this stoic beast has been very accommodating of my bulk these past weeks, still, if I never again see him or any of his brethren, I shall be content."

"Don't be expectin' too much down there, Jacky," warns Katy into my left ear. "East Hickory's only a little itty-bitty town."

"I'm sure it will serve, dear, for all we will need is to find us a boat to take us down the river," says I, full of hope and anticipation. "Let's go!" And we pound down into the river valley.

"Itty-bitty" is an understatement. East Hickory consists of a general store that, as a matter of fact, doesn't seem to have much in it, a stable containing a few dispirited swaybacked nags, a smelly tannery, and a rickety dock sticking out into the flowing stream—a very swiftly moving stream, I note. The Allegheny, being about a quarter-mile wide at this point, has a *lot* of water moving downstream. *And this is the littlest of the rivers we will ride?* I wonder.

It turns out that the man who runs the general store—a fat, fussy little man with a squeaky voice—also runs the stables and the commercial dock, at which, I notice with dismay, no boats are tied.

We dismount at the foot of the dock, and the little man hurries up to us.

"Welcome to East Hickory," he squeaks. "My name is Enos Tweedie. What will be your pleasure? We have the finest of whiskey and some very good beer." There is a board balanced on sawhorses at the dock's entrance, and Mr. Tweedie lays out several bottles and glasses thereon, then peers at us expectantly. This, apparently, is what passes for a tavern in East Hickory, Pennsylvania, in the United States of America.

I decide that the Fine Lady persona will serve us best here, so I put on the Lawson Peabody Look and say, "Mr. Higgins will have a whiskey, and Miss Deere and I will each have a glass of wine. And a beer for young Master Tanner, if you please, Landlord Tweedie." I pull up the small purse that hangs at my waist.

I can see that he is pleased to be addressed as such, and extremely pleased by the sight of my purse.

"Yes, oh, yes," he chortles, and he goes to pour some whiskey into a glass for Higgins.

"Wait," says Higgins, as he takes the empty glass from Mr. Tweedie's hand, holds it up to the light, frowns, pulls out a spotless handkerchief, and proceeds to polish it. Then

91

again he holds up the glass to the light. "Ah. That is much better. We wouldn't want to sully the taste of your finest of whiskeys with a less-than-clean glass, now, would we?"

Mr. Tweedie, somewhat amazed, takes the glass back and fills it with brown liquid and places it in front of Higgins, then says, "Sorry, Miss, but no wine until the elderberries get ripe."

"A beer, then," I say, and a foaming tankard is put in front of me. I stick my nose in it and drink. It is very poor. *Very* poor. I look over at a silo that stands next to the tannery and suspect that there is a spigot at the bottom of it. The silage is soaked from the rain leaking in at the top, and the so-called beer comes out the bottom. But I drink it, anyway, as I cannot offend my host, from whom I will want to get some information.

"You got any birch beer?" asks Katy.

"Oh, yes, Miss, right down here." He stoops down and picks up another jug.

"Good. One for me and one for the boy."

Jim tastes his and his eyes open. "Oh, that's good," he says.

"Thought it might be," says Katy, tasting hers. She looks at me over the top of her glass, and I think she's saying silently to me, *Y'oughta check with what the locals are gettin' 'fore you plunge ahead, girl.*

I take that silent advice to heart. I push my very sorry beer to the side and say, "I'll try some of that."

Another glass is put in front of me, and I look at the clear liquid and then I taste it. *My, that is good!* It reminds me a bit of the sassafras root beer that Amy had at Dovecote.

Anticipating my question, Katy says, "You peel up a bunch of black birch twigs, then you soak 'em for a long time. Later you add sugar and yeast, and there you go."

Hmmmm. Good to know, I think, quaffing the rest of mine down.

"Actually, this is quite good," says Higgins, rolling the whiskey around on his tongue.

"Only the finest barrels of Kentucky bourbon come up this river, Sir," explains Mr. Tweedie with satisfaction. "Only the finest. The crowned heads of Europe have not tasted finer."

"Amazingly, I can agree with that," says Higgins, finishing off his glass.

All right. Down to business, I'm thinking.

"Landlord Tweedie, we desire to book passage downriver, but I see no boats moored at your dock. Why is that?" I ask.

"Ah, Miss, all the boats have gone downriver with loads of logs for Pittsburgh, they havin' used all theirs up in their furnaces for makin' glass and suchlike. They'll be polin' back up in a couple of weeks."

A couple of weeks! We can't wait that long!

I stand and think on this: Our horses are about shot—they need rest and food and shelter, things we cannot give them. The roads out here grow worse and worse—soon we will be leading the horses, rather than riding them. *Damn!*

"Maybe we could build a raft, Jim?" I ask of my coxswain.

"Yes, we could, Missy, but we'd need seasoned lumber and tools, neither of which we have," he says, but then, like any true can-do sailor, he goes on to say, "but maybe we could find a good stand of straight timber, cut 'em down, and bind 'em together with rope and…"

"WEEEEEEEE…OOOOOOOOP! WEEEEEEE-OOOOOOP! GET OUT OF MY WAY! BY GOD, GET OUT OF MY WAY OR GET CHEWED RIGHT ON UP! WEEEEEĖEEE…OOOOP!"

Shocked, I look upriver and see a boat coming down. It's about forty feet long, got a cabin, no sails, and a long, long sweep of an oar out the back to which clings a huge solitary figure. *Is it man or ape?* I wonder.

"Christ. It's Fink," curses Mr. Tweedie. He hurriedly scoops the bottles from the board and hurries them inside his general store, which he then locks securely.

I walk out on the dock to study this "Fink," angling its way to the dock with great swipes of its sweep.

It turns out to be a man, after all, a man about six and a half feet tall, chest like a barrel, arms like eighteen-pound cannons each, legs like hogsheads of molasses, and, perched above it all, a head that is mostly hair and beard and beady eyes, all crowned with a round, flat-brimmed black hat.

"Is he drunk?" I ask the scurrying Mr. Tweedie.

"No, only about a quarter drunk, I'd say, 'cause you can still understand what he's sayin'," says Tweedie. "Half drunk he talks to the angels, three-quarters he talks to God, and full drunk he shouts with Satan. Least that's what he says, and when he's full drunk, it's best to believe him."

Hmmmm…I decide the waif approach would be the best. I go to the end of the dock, fold my hands before me, and cast down my eyes, all girlish and respectful-like in front of the big, bad man who's coming on in, his head back and shoutin'.

"WEEEEEEEEE...OOOOOP! LOOK AT ME! WEEEEE...
OOOOP!! LOOK AT ME! I'M A RING-TAILED ROARER! I'M THE
ORIGINAL IRON-JAWED, BRASS-MOUNTED, COPPER-BELLIED
CORPSE MAKER FROM THE WILDS OF ARKANSAS! I'M HALF
HORSE AND HALF ALLIGATOR! I WAS BORN IN A CANEBRAKE
AND SUCKLED BY A MOUNTAIN LION! CAST YOUR EYES ON ME,
AND LAY LOW AND HOLD YOUR BREATH, FOR I'M ABOUT TO
TURN MYSELF LOOSE. WEEEEE...OOOOP! WEEEE...OOOOP!"

I stand and wait for his boat to land. Quarter drunk or
not, he brings his boat expertly into the dock, roaring out
one last blast.

"WEEEE...OOOOP! LOOK AT ME! I CAN SPIT FARTHER, PISS
HIGHER, AND FART LOUDER THAN ANY MAN JACK ON THIS
RIVER! WEEEE...OOOOOP!"

"I am sure those are all admirable traits and abilities, Mr.
Fink," I say, demurely. "Jim, will you attend to the gentleman's lines?" Jim Tanner jumps in the boat, grabs the stern
line, and secures it to the butt on the dock. Then he does the
same with the bowline. "Now, Mr. Fink, if you would give
me and my friends a ride down to Pittsburgh, I would indeed count you a man among men."

A look of low cunning comes over what I can see of the
man's face. "Hey, girly-girl. Didn't see you standin' there, or
I would've—"

"You would have had perhaps a gentler speech of introduction to your splendid self?" I ask.

"Hell, no," he says, hands on hips and grinning hugely.
"I would've bragged more about my legendary prowess in
splittin' sheets and tearin' up mattresses with pretty little
things like yourself! Ha!"

"Be that as it may, Mr. Fink, will you carry us down to Pittsburgh?"

He casts an eye on our party. "Four of you, hey? Hmmm...All right, twenty-five bucks apiece—a hundred dollars even."

"I perceive that you are not only a man of great renown, Mr. Fink, but also a thief who preys on the misfortunes of poor young girls," says I, batting the eyes.

"You're breakin' my heart, girly-girl," says Fink. "A hundred dollars or you swim it."

Higgins comes up next to me and whispers, "That's half our current fiscal holdings, Miss!"

"I know, Higgins. Go and sell the horses and let's get on board," I whisper back at him. "Think of it not as fare money, but as the purchase price of this fine, fine boat."

Higgins looks at me sharply. "While there is a price on your head in Britain, there are no charges against you in this land. It may be well to keep it that way, Miss."

"Don't worry, Higgins, I shan't steal this man's boat," says I, smiling. "Nothing of the kind."

I raise my voice to say to Mr. Fink, "I accept your terms. I shall give you half now and half on our safe arrival. Agreed?"

"Sure, girly-girl. Come on board and make yourselves comfortable. Ain't nobody in this world can't say that Mike Fink is a poor host, no sir!"

I take Mr. Fink's proffered hand and step aboard what I believe will be the new flagship of Faber Shipping, World-wide.

Chapter 14

Jaimy Fletcher
In the hayloft of a barn
In Pennsylvania, USA
In the company of Miss Clementine Jukes

"I love you, Jaimy," Clementine whispered into my ear. *I was lying on my back in the hay, and her right leg was thrown over me, with various parts of her female self pressed tightly to my side. My right hand was on her shoulder and her hair was in my face. It smelled good. I liked it, the way it felt. I looked up into the darkness.*

"And I, Clementine—"

That's as far as I got.

There was a squeak as the barn door was dragged open and the light of a lantern entered the barn. Both Clementine and I went rigid. *It's Pap.* There was a grating and creaking from the ladder, then his face, illuminated by the lantern swaying next to it, appeared over the edge of the loft.

"Hey, pretty boy, how yew doin'?" His words were slurred and his eyes rolled about, not quite able to focus on us in the dark. "Yew ready for some fun? Some manly fun, boy? Some…"

That's when the fact of two pairs of white eyes peering at him from the loft instead of just one suddenly registered in his sodden brain.

"What the hell? Clemmie? What yew doin' here?" He lowered the lantern and started back down the ladder. "That's it. Gonna kill the both of yew right now."

My mind, which had plainly been At Ease for the past hour or so, snapped back to Attention. *He's got the gun down below and he's going to use it. On us.*

I jumped out of the straw. "Get over there, up against the back wall!" I hissed at Clementine, and lunged over to where I had seen a heavy block and tackle hanging from its lines. It was probably used to haul heavy loads up to the loft. Its bottom hook was fastened to a metal hoop, but I was able to free it, so that the heavy block swung freely in my hand. I waited but I did not have to wait long. Pappy Jukes's head reappeared at the top of the ladder, and this time he had his rifle in his right hand, and, *damn!* a pistol in his left!

I swung the block toward his head, and as I did so, he fired the pistol. I jerked back as the ball flew by my face, nicking my right earlobe but doing no other damage. My aim with the block and tackle, however, was true, and it caught him in the middle of his forehead and toppled him backward off the ladder. I heard the thud as he hit the floor below, and I followed him down, leaping off the edge of the loft, hoping to catch him before he could aim the rifle.

I caught him all right. I landed with both of my heels on his chest, knocking the wind completely out of him. His rifle was lying off to the side, so I leaped over and picked it up.

I needn't have hurried. Jukes lay at my feet, his face contorted in agony. His left leg was twisted up under him at an odd, but to me rather pleasing, angle. I pointed the rifle at his head.

"My leg's busted, Clemmie, oh God, help me, Clemmie, my leg's busted." He moaned. "Fetch me that rake, girl, so's I kin stand up and git in the house. Oh Clemmie, fetch it fer me like a good girl."

Clementine appeared at the side of the loft, again clad in her flimsy yellow dress, took one look at him sprawled helpless on the floor, and climbed down the ladder. She gazed at her father in the circle of light cast by the lantern, careful, I noticed, to keep out of reach of his hands.

"Ain't fetchin' nothin' fer you, ever ag'in, you mean ol' man. You kilt Ma with yer meanness. You kilt any pet I ever had—my bunnies, my kitten, my ducklings—you kilt 'em ever' time you found out I was lovin' 'em, and you laughed when you did it. But you ain't gonna kill me, no, you ain't. I got half a mind to jest tip over that lantern and burn up this barn with you in it, I do, but I ain't like you, Pap, so I ain't gonna do it. But I ain't fetchin' nothin' fer you, neither. I'm leavin' here, I'm leavin' with Jaimy, and I ain't never been happier in my life."

Jukes looked at her, and then at me, with a cold, level glare of pure rage. "I'll git yew two, I will. Jest you wait."

"Clementine," I said, "get the horse out and tie it to the porch rail."

She went to do it, picking up bridle and reins on her way. The horse whickered quietly as she entered the stall. "There, there, Daisy, it's all right. We're leavin' here, and you'll never be whipped by that mean ol' man ag'in."

"You," I said to Jukes, "you move and I'll put a bullet in your head. I have been an officer in His Majesty's Royal Navy. I have been in battle, and I know how to kill a man, believe me. When she gets the horse out, I will bar the door from the outside, just like you did for me. If you connive a way to get out, I'll kill you out there. Is that clear?"

I was rewarded with an even more withering glare of hatred from the helpless Mr. Jukes.

Clementine backed the mare Daisy from the stall and led her out of the barn. I bent down and retrieved the empty pistol and, with the same hand, picked up the lantern. I went out the door, and from the now pitch-black interior I heard, "Yew come here. Yew steal my girl and then yew go and steal my horse. I place my curse upon yew. May yew rot in Hell."

Fine, old man, I thought as I closed the door and slammed down the latch, *curse away.*

Attending to the business at hand, I saw that Clementine had, indeed, tied the mare to the rail and had gone into the house. I followed with the lantern and found her stuffing some things in a sack.

"Blankets," she said, "pots, some flour, cornmeal, and we'll need a water jug…"

"How about gunpowder, balls…"

"That chest over there."

I went to the chest and found a powder horn, flints, and bags of balls, for both pistol and rifle, all of which I stuffed into an empty powder sack also kept therein.

"Money?" I asked, the last shreds of civilized behavior having been drained from me in this violent land.

"Oh, he's got some, but he never tol' me where he hid it. You could put hot coals to his feet and he'd not tell you where it was, I know that. Here, these're his Sunday-go-to-meetin' overalls. They're clean. I just warshed 'em. Only shirt he's got is the one he's got on."

I caught the overalls and put them on. It struck me that I had been essentially naked for the past twenty or so hours and was becoming quite used to it. I was becoming a savage in a savage land.

The rough garment was quite huge on me and hung loose on my frame. Only the shoulder straps kept it up. Upon seeing me in it, Clementine giggled, then said, "Oh, yes, and needle and thread, too. And here's some cloth to make you up a shirt." These items she also threw into her sack.

"What else?" I asked.

"Ain't nothin' else here," she said. "Not for me, anyways. Let's go."

I blew out the lantern and we went back outside. The first threads of the light of dawn were beginning to appear in the eastern sky. I made slings of our bundles and we slung them about our waists, there being no saddle to affix them to. I climbed up on Daisy's very broad back and reached down for Clementine. She took my hand and vaulted up and settled in behind me, and we rode slowly off.

I took one last look back at the silent barn, but she did not.

As we rode along at a slow walk, which is all I suspected that the massive Daisy could ever do in the way of speed, Clementine Jukes wrapped her arms about my waist and put her face against my bare back. I felt her slim body pressed against me. I felt her lips kiss me between my shoulder blades. I felt her long flaxen hair blow about my shoulders, and sometimes in my face, in the soft morning breeze.

"Mrs. Clementine Fletcher, *mmmm.* I really do like the sound of that, Jaimy, I do," I heard her purr.

Oh, Lord...

Chapter 15

We did, as Mr. Fink commanded, cast off immedi-ately, or almost immediately, for Higgins had to go sell the horses to Mr. Tweedie first. While he was gone, the rest of us stowed our gear below and then came back up on deck to await departure. When Higgins returned, he was not at all pleased, I discovered, as he stepped back on board.

"Damned thief! He knew we were at a disadvantage, so I could barely get more than the cost of our drinks from the blackguard!"

I put a restraining hand on Higgins's sleeve. "Dear Higgins, set your mind at rest. Right now the locals are having their way with us, but I promise you that it will not always be so. Let's live in the moment. All our gear is stowed and we should be at ease. After all, Higgins, the horses are sold, which means you do not have to ride one of them."

He agreed that this was a very fine thing, indeed, as he scurried about to see what cooking gear might be contained on this bark.

"Cast off!" roared Fink, standing aft at his steering sweep as soon as Higgins was aboard. "You, boy! Take off the stern line! Coil it down! Move yer ass, or I'll kick it all the way to Pittsburgh!"

Jim looked to me, angry. I gave a quick nod and mouthed *do it* and gave him a wink to let him know I understood the blow to his pride.

"Aye, aye, *Sir*," said Jim. He took off the line and coiled it expertly down on the deck, ready for its next use.

Our first day out on Mike Fink's flatboat is most pleasant. It's a fine, warm day and Fink, with what seems to be very little effort, keeps the boat on a leisurely course close to the eastern shore. I, naturally, waste no time in casing out the boat, which turns out to be a very well-made craft, well-found in her knees and planking. Quite new, too. As soon as I can, I go below, to thrust my shiv into various parts of the frame, but I can find no softness, no damp rot of any kind. A remarkable piece of work, I conclude.

The belowdecks area is fitted out with twenty bunks on each side, with curtains that can be drawn over each for privacy. In the center is an open hold for cargo, with a ladder going down into the bilges.

Jim Tanner is with me as we examine the inner hull of the flatboat. "Jim," I say, "I want you to watch this Mike Fink in every way, especially in how he handles this boat. Learn how to operate that sweep. Pretend to admire him and draw him out as to how this boat is run with a full crew on board. Appeal to his considerable vanity. I shall ask Higgins to do the same. All right?"

Jim nods, mollified now that he has a mission. I believe he is as happy as I am to be back on water, no matter fresh or salt and in spite of the boisterous Fink. There's not enough of a roll on this flat river to quicken the heart of any true sailor, but it's something.

Katy Deere, too, seems content to be here. With her skirt pulled up almost to her waist, she sits on the prow, her long legs dangling over each side. Her bow in hand, strung, nocked with a fishing arrow, and with its length of light line coiled beside her, she looks down into the dark water for whatever it might offer up.

Much later, when back on deck, I commend Mr. Fink on the quality of his craft and his skill in guiding it, and he guffaws in what I have already learned is his usual manner of speech...or rather, his usual mode of shout, "Oh, yes, and she's a fine one! Fitted out for passengers, as you've probably already noticed. Yeah, I seen you crawlin' and nosin' around down there. Jus' took thirty holy pilgrims up to a tent revival up in Jacob's Holler! Two whole dollars each!"

"As big and strong and manly as you so plainly are, surely you could not have gotten this heavy craft with thirty stout pilgrims aboard up this swiftly flowing river?" I ask, doing the arithmetic in my head: Thirty souls upriver at two dollars each equals sixty dollars, while we four poor souls were charged one hundred dollars for going *downstream*. Ah, Mr. Fink, I do think you've got it coming to you.

"Nah! I had a crew of ten and I dumped 'em off up there. Mike Fink don't need no crew to navigate downstream, no, he don't!"

He looks slightly offended, as if anyone could think otherwise.

"I see," I reply, and settle myself down on the edge of the low cabin. The cabin, itself, takes up most of the deck room, leaving only a narrow path for what I now know would be the boots of the crew as they poled this boat upriver, or guided it on its way down.

As I sit watching the trees on the banks go slowly by, Higgins comes up bearing a tin tray with a cup and steaming teapot upon it. Somehow he has managed to find a clean white tea towel, which he drapes over his arm before he pours the tea from the battered pot we had gotten at Katy's place into the cup he had picked up from God-knows-where.

"Thank you, Higgins," I say, lifting the cup to my lips. "*Ummm* . . . Wherever did you get the sugar?"

"It happened, Miss, that I—"

"Who the hell is she? Some kind o' princess or somethin'?" asks the mystified Fink upon seeing this performance, for performance it truly is. "And who the hell are you to be waitin' on her like that?" He squats on the stern next to his sweep and peers suspiciously at us.

"In a way, she is, Sir," explains Higgins, imperturbable as always. "She is the chief executive officer and major stockholder of Faber Shipping, Worldwide. I am an employee of the same corporation and, as such, am performing my duties in that regard."

"Well, ain't that somethin'," replies Fink, considering this concept in the dark recesses of his mind. "*Hmmmm* . . ."

"May I pour you a cup, Mr. Fink?" asks Higgins.

"Might's well. Ain't got no whiskey, and damned if I was gonna buy any off that damned Tweedie, neither, thirsty as I am, which is *very* thirsty. Thirsty enough to drain a middlin'-sized lake, if'n I drank water, which I don't. Ain't drunk nothin' but good corn likker since the day they pulled me offa my mama's teat, I ain't. Hell, ol' Mama, Torty Fink, which was her given name, liked her corn, too, so I figure the mother's milk I was gettin' outta her was a good fifty proof. It was a good way fer me t' get weaned, as I see it."

At this, Fink throws back his head and bellows out a song at the top of his plainly very huge lungs:

> *OH, IF THE RIVER WAS WHISKEY,*
> *AND I WAS A DUCK,*
> *I'D DIVE TO THE BOTTOM,*
> *AND NEVER COME UP!*
>
> *OH, "CORN WHISKEY, CORN WHISKEY,*
> *CORN WHISKEY," I CRY,*
> *IF'N I DON'T GET CORN WHISKEY,*
> *I SURELY WILL DIE!*

He goes into a high keen on the word *cry*, drawing it out to something like "CA-RYE-EEEEEEEEEEEEEE!" before finishing off the verse.

"Tha's a good song, don't tell me it ain't," says Fink, well satisfied with his performance.

"An excellent song, indeed, Mr. Fink, and so well done, too," I say, applauding. Actually it sounded like gravel rolling off a tin roof, but the song itself has possibilities. I shall have to get the rest of the verses. But not just now.

"Thank you, girly-girl," says Fink. "I sung that song in memory of my dear mama."

"Mother Fink has gone on to her reward?" I ask. "I'm so sorry."

Fink gives a mighty pull on his sweep to get us closer to the shore. As the boat swings over, he again takes up his eulogy. "Yep, 'bout ten years ago, Mama'd been held in the Pigtown jailhouse for three whole days without a single drink, and you *know* that didn't sit right with Mama. Her mouth got so dry that a brace o' desert rattlesnakes set up housekeepin' in her throat, yeah, and her mouth got so dry that ever' time she spit, she spit out pure dusty sand. They set up a cement mixin' operation next to her cell window, to take advantage of the sand. Warn't able to get her plug o' tobaccy to soften up enough so she could even taste it, and we all know that ain't right. Well, she decided she warn't gonna take it no more, so she raised up a mighty roar and rattled the bars so hard that the very foundations of the jail shook. Then the plaster rained down from the ceiling and the windows all broke, so's they had to let her out, else the place'd fall about their ears."

"Your mother sounds like a formidable lady," ventures I.

"Yep, Mama was a big woman," continues Fink, in all seriousness. "Them Frenchy trappers tell me they named the Grand Teton Mountains way out West after Mama, and I believe 'em, cause if'n there's one thing them Frenchies know, it's grand teats, and Mama had 'em fer sure. One time, when she was off on a tear, she swung around a bit too fast and took out half the town of Natchez. It still ain't been totally rebuilt since that calamity, no sir."

Fink shook his head in wonder at the magnificence of his mother's physical qualities and then went sadly on to recount her unfortunate end.

"Well, then Mama tramples three of them jailers to death on her way out of that slammer, and she hit the town runnin'. The first tavern she got to was the Dirty Dozens and she drunk it dry in under twenty minutes—that's beer, wine, them fancy lee-koors, and that fine, fine corn whiskey. She flung the last bottle aside and went into Horsehead Sally's and bellowed out for more. She drunk that place dry, too, of all their likkers and whatnot, even drank the birdbath dry, 'cause it was green and had feathers in it and stunk bad enough to be good. She kicked down the north wall of Sally's place and lurched over to Gypsy Judy's and done the same to that place, but, sad to say, the fact was that she was losin' her final battle. It looked like she was gonna be all right when she broke into Barkley's warehouse and found three fifty-gallon barrels of the best one-hundred-proof Kentucky likker. She clamped her teeth around the bung of the first one, pulled it out, lifted the barrel over her open mouth, and drank it dry. She paused to wipe her mouth—"

"As she was a lady, after all," I murmur.

"…and then she did the second. The townspeople gathered 'round in awesome wonder. Then she yanked the cork out of the third and drank it straight down, too…"

Fink pauses here, as if overcome with emotion, and then he soldiers on:

"Then she stood up, dropped the empty barrel, gave a mighty belch, which rolled over the countryside and blew out the windows of houses two hundred miles away, and then she just keeled over and died."

"Ah, so it was the drink that brought her down," I note. "Such a pity."

"*Nahhh,* that's what the townsfolk thought, and they sent for the doctor to come look at her mortal remains, which were considerable, believe me, and the doctor come and looked her over and shook his head. 'No,' he said, 'this poor woman did not die of the drink. She died of thirst.'"

"Of thirst?" I ask, mock incredulous. I do know how to play my part.

"Yep, it was thirst." Fink sighed, all grim. "There just warn't enough whiskey in that town to slake her thirst, poor woman. My mama died o' thirst." He sniffs back a tear.

I do not mention to Mr. Fink that I know of an Irish song that has the same punch line, because by now I've grasped the gist of this game and I enter into the spirit of the thing.

"My own dear mother also has passed from this world." I sniff, then work on coaxing out a tear of my own. "And she was of such purity of heart and soul that a band of a thousand angels came down from Heaven to take her up to her celestial reward. The archangel Gabriel himself played the Death March on his trumpet, and Saint Michael did beat his sword against his mighty shield to mark time for the holy procession. There were legions and legions of the saints and the sanctified on that Glory Road to Heaven, but none were deemed worthy to touch the hem of her snow-white garment. She sits now in glory at the left hand of God Him-self."

"Zat so? *Hmmm*," says Fink, considering this. "Well, no offense, girly-girl, but it sounds to me like your mama went up to Heaven with a stick up her ass, as I sees it." He clears his throat and goes on. "On my own mama's passin', now, fifty demons from down below come up and prodded her dear and gentle soul down to the lowest depths of Hell with their pitchforks, her hollerin' and squallin' all the way."

"So sad, Mr. Fink," I say. "May I offer up a prayer for her deliverance?" I press my palms together.

"Nah, don't bother," says Fink. "Soon's she got there, she

throwed Satan hisself out, sayin' she's gonna rule Hell all by herself, and she done it ever since." Fink takes a deep breath and nods at the truth of what he's telling. "Yeah, ol' Satan ain't been the same since, poor devil. Saw him a few days ago, upriver, beatin' his breast and mopin' about on the riverbank. Ain't hardly worth kickin' his tail no more, as he's lost all heart and there ain't no fun in it."

Mr. Fink heaves a great sigh over the problems of the underworld and goes on, relentless. "As for my mama's corpore-ree-al remains, well, there warn't an open space in Pigtown wide enough to dig a hole big enough to put her in, nor men enough to dig it, so they just got two hundred mules and hitched 'em up to her carcass and hauled her down to the river and floated her off. She floated all the way down past Natchez, past Memphis, past Vicksburg, past all them dirty little jerkwater towns, and finally ended up in the Gulf o' Mexico, where at last she come aground. Some birds landed on her and made their nests there, and turtles climbed aboard, too, and eventually she become the Island of Dry Tortugas, named that way 'cause of the horrible way Torty Fink died. Of an awful thirst. Amen."

"Amen," I reply. If it's one thing Jacky Faber knows, it's when she's beat. "But now, Mr. Fink, what will be for dinner?"

"Dinner? Ain't nothin' for dinner," answers our host. "Mike Fink don't eat nothin' 'cept raw, red meat, no, I don't. When I'm hungry, I grabs me the meanest old bear I can find and I eat him from the head on down, bones and all, and then pick my teeth with his foot claws when I gets down to them. Nope, nothin' for dinner. You didn't pay me enough for that."

Deeper and deeper into the slough of ruin do you place your foot, Mike Fink, I think. *And less and less sympathy I have for thee.*

Thinking unkind thoughts of Mr. Fink's hospitality and listening to my belly grumble, I notice Katy stiffen as we come around a bend in the river into some quiet water.

She lifts her bow and looses an arrow, then another. There are quacks, then squawks, then only the sound of the prey being hauled aboard.

"Ducks," says Katy Deere. "Ducks is what we're havin' for dinner."

Chapter 16

It's another fine day on the Allegheny River. The weather is good, the wind is calm, and the river churns along placidly between its banks.

Last evening, Katy bagged several more unlucky ducks. Higgins went below to get the biggest pot he could to fill with river water and set it on the fire to boil. When it got to a good rolling boil, we dunked Katy's catch one by one to loosen up the feathers, then plucked 'em. Higgins expertly roasted the ducks while Katy, who was more adept at primitive cookery than Higgins, made up some pretty good biscuits. There was some lard and butter that was not too rancid in Mike Fink's kitchen, and that made the preparation of the food easier.

I could have just sat idly by, but no, I rolled up my sleeves and helped pluck the birds. I mean, who am I to shirk work? I may be the owner of Faber Shipping, Worldwide, but at present its holdings are limited to my little *Morning Star*, which is now hanging in Dovecote's boathouse. Sure wish I had her here, but, hey, I'll work with what I got. Or what I am going to get. It's not just me I'm thinking about. I've got three employees with me who are not getting paid anything for their services.

Mr. Fink brought the boat into a cove next to the shore and dropped the stern anchor. When it caught the bottom to his satisfaction, he tied off the rope, and after we were moored for the night, we finished preparations for dinner and sleep. Flatboats do not sail at night, I was informed. Hidden snags and sandbars and that sort of thing, you know.

In spite of his declaration that he eats nothing but the raw meat of various creatures that live in this land—*bull buffalo's good if'n you let the carcass sit out in the sun for a coupla weeks afore you eat it*—he managed to eat more than his share of our ducks, which he pronounced to be good enough, for a light snack.

After dinner we gazed up at the stars for a while, Mr. Fink telling us many fanciful tales concerning their origins and how he placed them just so in the heavens and all, and then we turned in to our bunks, exhausted from both the journey that brought us to this place in the world and the day's travel 'neath the relentless tutelage of our Mr. Fink and his tall tales.

The bunks are wide, so after I claimed one, I pulled the reluctant Katy in with me, telling her it is part of her job on this trip to keep me from my nightmares by lending me her presence in my bed, since I do not like to sleep alone.

That settled, I curled up next to her and sleep came easy and I knew nothing till the dawn of this new morning.

Breakfast is tea and biscuits. Mr. Fink informs us that we will be stopping at the town of Kennerdell, about thirty miles up ahead, and we can buy things to eat there if we want but he is going to supply us with nothing.

That news gives me cheer, as I have much on my mind in the way of present gratification and future plans.

There are no chairs or benches on the flatboat, but the low cabin makes a fine seat anywhere you might want to place your bottom. I sit on the starboard-side middle, so I can see both Katy up at her post on the bow and Mr. Fink aft at the tiller. Jim sits by my side, watching Fink closely, while Higgins busies himself below. He reports to me that the kitchen is quite well fitted out and everything is remarkably clean. Higgins opines that Mr. Fink has not owned this vessel for very long, considering the rather dubious state of Mr. Fink's personal hygiene.

The cabin's top is a very good vantage point for observing life on the river this fine day. We pass some other boats toiling upriver and Fink flings a few good-natured curses in their direction. I study their method of poling their craft against the current and am glad that I will be going only downstream on this voyage. I see that two teams of men, one on each side, form lines facing astern, and as they dig their long poles into the shallow water, they propel the boat as they walk along the planking specially added along each side of the boat's deck. When each man reaches the stern, he turns around, walks back up to the bow, goes to the head of the line, puts his pole back in, and, poling all the while, trudges to the back, over and over again. Effective, if backbreaking and monotonous. Give me a sail and wind to fill it, any day, I say.

The men on the boats seem to dress in a very uniform fashion—boots, dark trousers, and loose white shirts with puffy sleeves and lacings at the open neck. A distinctive round black hat with a wide flat brim tops off their outfit. I reflect that I shall have to get us similarly outfitted, so as to blend in. I have taken out my light summer bonnet to keep the sun off my face, but I feel somewhat foolish in it.

There is something dreamlike in watching the shore slip away beside us—it goes from solid green bank of trees, to quiet cove, to small cluster of simple houses, to stretch of sandy beach, and then back again to a wall of trees crowding the bank. It is not at all like a voyage on the ocean, with wave upon wave upon countless wave numbing the senses and making time stand still and making one retreat into one's own little sphere of existence. No, it's like watching a long, long story that has no plot, and no end, unfold before your eyes.

I shake my head to rid it of these bootless thoughts and I pull out my pennywhistle, put it to my lips, and play a simple tune.

"Can you dance as well as you can sing, Mr. Fink?" I ask, after tonguing the last cascade of notes in the "The Dawning of the Day." I also stand up and do a few steps, Irish-style.

"Huh! You call that dancin'? Play somethin' better'n that and I'll show you, I will. Huh! Call that dancin'? In a pig's eye, that's dancin'. What's this world comin' to, to call that dancin'!"

"Higgins, if you would," I call out, standing flat-footed, fuming, and glaring daggers at our host. "Please bring up the Lady Gay." I know it is small of me, but I don't take criticism very well, whatever the source, be it from various captains, from teachers, from my mates, or from foolishly boisterous boatmen. *Just you wait...*

Higgins obligingly brings up my fiddle and bow from my seabag and hands it to me. I hop up on the low cabin top and lay the bow on the fiddle, give Mike Fink a ladylike sneer, and start out with "Tim Finnegan's Reel." When I finish, I rip off a few fancy steps and put up my bow and challenge him with my defiant gaze.

"Now that's music, by God!" shouts Mike Fink. "Here, boy, take the tiller," he says, and Jim takes it while Fink bounds to the top of the cabin to tower over me. I reflect just how much like a stage this cabin is. *Hmmm.* Food for thought.

Instead of going into a dance right off, he throws back his head and, for the benefit of anyone within five miles, bellows, "OOOOWEEEEEEEE! I'M A RING-TAILED WALLOPER WHAT HAS DANCED WITH THE DEVIL HIMSELF AND BEAT HIM TO A DRAW! HE PUT HIS FORKY TAIL 'TWEEN HIS GOATY LEGS AND BEGGED ME FOR MERCY! LOOK AT ME! LOOK AT ME! LOOK AT ME GO! HOLD ME BACK! HOLD ME BACK! I'M GONNA DANCE! I'M GONNA DANCE! WHOOOOOEEEEEEEE!"

I certainly had not intended to send him off into another fit of braggadocio, but I guess I did.

"All right, girly-girl, play that again, only faster! And I'll show you how to *really* dance!"

I put the bow to the Lady and tear it out. Fink puts one hand over his head and one behind his back and proceeds to stomp about mightily, more or less in time to the tune. The entire boat shakes. *Be careful of this deck, you great oaf! You'll splinter the damned thing!* I'm thinking, as he thunders about on the cabin top. I have begun to take a proprietary interest in this craft.

I look over at Jim and see him experimenting with the feel of the steering oar as Fink puts on his show. *Good boy.*

To prevent any further damage, I bring the song to an end, and Fink, with a final crash of his heavy boots, ends his dance as well.

"Now that's good dancin'! You can't say it ain't!" he crows in triumph.

"No, I cannot, Mr. Fink. You are as light and graceful on your feet as any ballerina," say I.

"Screw bally-rinas," says Fink. "Now play 'The Boatman's Dance.'"

"I'm afraid I don't know it, Mr. Fink, but if you'll hum a few bars of it..."

"You got to know it if you're on the river. Goes like this." He again throws back his head and roars out:

DANCE, THE BOATMAN'S DANCE, OH, DANCE THE
   BOATMAN'S DANCE,
DANCE ALL NIGHT TILL THE BROAD DAYLIGHT
AND GO HOME WITH THE GIRLS IN THE MORNIN'!

HI, HO, THE BOATMEN ROW, FLOATIN' DOWN THE RIVER
   ON THE OHIO!
HI, HO, THE BOATMEN ROW, UP AND DOWN THE OHIO!

It is a simple tune and I pick it right up and join in with my fiddle as he goes to the next verse.

WHEN YOU GO TO THE BOATMEN'S BALL
DANCE WITH MY WIFE OR DON'T DANCE AT ALL.
SKY-BLUE JACKET AND TARPAULIN HAT,
LOOK OUT, MY BOYS, FOR THE NINE-TAILED CAT!

Hmm. So the Cat rules on these waters, too. I think of the small raised scar I still wear on my back from my encounter with the nine-tailed lash, lovingly laid there by the late Captain Blodgett. Fink bellows out the chorus again and then sings on.

> THE BOATMAN HE'S A THRIFTY MAN,
> THERE'S NONE CAN DO AS THE BOATMAN CAN.
> I NEVER SEE A PRETTY GIRL IN THIS LIFE
> THAT SHE AIN'T SOME BOATMAN'S WIFE!

Another shouted chorus and he wraps it up.

"Beautifully done, Mr. Fink. Thank you. I shall add that fine song to my repertoire."

"Well you may. 'Course you won't be able to do it as good as me, but then, none can."

We share a few more tunes to pass the time of day, but eventually Mike Fink grows hoarse with bellowing and returns to his tiller.

I get with Jim up forward, out of earshot of our Captain.

"It ain't like a regular rudder, Missy," he tells me, "'cause it ain't got water streamin' past it. Y'see, the current's movin' at the same speed as the boat, so it's like you're dead in the water, no steerageway, like. So you've got to move the oar back and forth like a fish tail to get the boat to do anything. But I'm getting the hang of it."

"That's very good, Jim," I say, putting my hand upon the strong right arm of my stout coxswain, "because that skill is going to come in real handy, very soon."

He blushes and nods.

Katy doesn't have much luck bagging ducks this day—"Plenty o' bullfrogs sittin' on the banks, though. Too bad Lissette ain't here"—so she rigs up some fish lines, baited with balls of dough made up with lard and flour, and drops them over the side to see what that effort might bring.

Her mentioning my French classmate brings home to me just how recently the three of us, the serving girl Katy Deere, the aristocrat Mademoiselle Lissette de Lise, and I, sat knee to knee in a circle on the lowest deck, deep in the dark hold of the filthy slaver *Bloodhound*, munching on roasted rats, or "millers," as we called 'em, and glad for the meal. What a difference a month can make.

I go below to see Higgins and find that the dear man has made up a bath for me. It is only a large washtub full of clean, steaming water, but I shall be able to fit in it quite nicely. I notice that Higgins's hair is wet and he smells of fresh cologne, so it is plain that he is already washed.

"The hair first, Miss," he says, "if you would."

I doff my serving dress, beg Higgins not to drip water on my undergarments, and kneel next to the tub, my head over the edge. I close my eyes. After Higgins takes the pins from my hair and pours a pot of water over my head, I feel his strong fingers working in the soap.

"*Mmmm*, Higgins, that feels so good. Nobody can take care of me like you can."

"Well, you do require a bit of upkeep, Miss. The word *tomboy* continues to come to mind when thinking of you."

"Surely I have come some distance in the way of refinement, Higgins."

"Some, but may I remind you that you have spent the last hour or so stomping on the deck overhead with that rough buffoon of a boatman. I notice the back of your shirt is quite damp with perspiration. I shall have to wash it. Refinement, indeed."

"Ladies don't sweat, Higgins?"

"Not so it can be noticed, they don't. Rinsing now." I squeeze my eyes tighter shut and feel the rinse water wash over my head. Higgins takes my hair and wrings it out and piles it on my head. "All right. I'm going to put another pot of water on the fire. You finish undressing and hop in, now."

Gratefully, I do it. I have to sit cross-legged to fit, but fit I do. Then I wash the rest of myself.

"Higgins," I say, putting the soap to my feet, "when we get to this Kennerdell town, you will, of course, go off to buy some provisions. I also want you to buy some decent whiskey. One bottle, if you would, and, oh yes, see if you can pick up two glasses, too."

I can't see his eyebrows, but I know they go up in surprise.

"Why, Miss, your vow never to let spirits pass your lips, I—"

"Don't worry, Higgins, it's not for me. You'll see."

After I am dried and dressed in the fresh clothes that Higgins has brought me, I remark, "Ah, Higgins, how you do spoil me. What would I do without you?"

I go over to my bunk, on which rests my seabag, and I get paper and quill and ink, as there is something I wish to accomplish today. "I'll send Jim to come wash up in this water, then if you could make up a fresh tub for Katy, that would be good. When it's time, I'll wash her hair as I think she might be shy around you. Thanks, Higgins."

———

It is late afternoon when I sit myself down on the cabin top near where Mr. Fink stands steering the boat onward to Kennerdell. Higgins stands near me, gazing out across the water. We are ready to do our little act.

"Oh, Mr. Fink, is it not the most lovely day? Why, I fully expect to see nymphs and naiads frolicking about on yon sylvan shore. 'Oh, what is so rare as a day in June,' Mr. Fink?" I warble. I have spread out paper and have pen in hand. "I feel some wonderful poesy coming over me and just must get it down for the ages."

"What's she on about now, Higgins?" growls our Mr. Fink.

"Ah, Sir, 'tis the curse of the modern age," says Higgins, ruefully shaking his head. "It is the overeducated female in full feather."

"Huh! That's what I thought." Fink snorts. "Me, I likes 'em barefoot and preg-grunt. Them girls what signs their names with an *X* is good enough for me."

I see the opportunity and I seize it. "Can you sign your name, Mr. Fink, in addition to all your other accomplishments?"

"Sign my name? Sign my name? Hell, yes, I kin sign my name."

"Would you do it for me, then, Mr. Fink? In my travels I have taken up the hobby of collecting the autographs of the famous people I meet, and I would dearly love to add your name to that list of the renowned." I simper, holding up the quill. "I'd be ever so grateful."

Fink sticks out his lower lip and considers this challenge. He's trapped and he knows it. "All right, I'll do it. Boy, take the oar."

Jim, standing by as instructed, takes over the tiller, as Fink marches toward me. Not very happily, I notice.

He takes the quill and leans over the piece of folded paper.

"Right there, Mr. Fink. I will display your signature right next to Dr. Franklin's, I will. Oh, this is so exciting!"

He writes his name, very slowly and carefully. The letters are askew, not straight, and wander all over the page, but they do spell, to anyone's eye, Mike Fink.

"Hey, I've got one," calls Katy from the bow. There is the sound of a large fish thrashing about in the water. As Fink and Higgins hurry forward to see, I blot the paper, refold it, and place it in my vest. I give it a satisfied pat and smile as I, too, rush forward to see what Katy has caught.

That night, as I lie next to Katy, her freshly clean hair in my face, I think on the events of the day—the singing, the dancing, the stop at tiny Kennerdell, and the wonderful dinner of baked bass with all the trimmings that Kennerdell could provide. Then I let my thoughts go to Jaimy.

Poor Jaimy, you who are out there on that vast ocean, far from me, far from any of your friends...Here I lie snug and comfortable and safe in the company of loved ones while you lie in peril. It's not fair that you should be treated so cruelly, it's not. Oh, how I pray that they will be kind to you on that ship, and I hope you will be treated well when you reach England. Higgins assures me that it will be so, but I worry, especially in the dark of night when fears feel so much like reality. Know, Jaimy, that as I fall asleep, my last thoughts are thoughts of you. I pray that you are safe.

Chapter 17

Jaimy Fletcher
Somewhere in America
On the road to the Allegheny

Jacky,

We sleep wrapped up together in our blanket, as it is the only one we have. Most nights our bed is the hard ground beneath the stars, but that has been not that unpleasant, since the weather has been mostly kind. As we travel ever westward, several times we have been given a pallet in the house of some poor but kind and generous farm family, and to them I will be eternally grateful. But mainly we have been sleeping under the open sky, with Daisy grazing contentedly nearby, and the sound of a nearby babbling brook, the songs of the wild birds, and the nearness of each other our only comforts.

Clementine has proved most knowledgeable in what wild plants and mushrooms we can eat and those we cannot. With the rifle, I have brought down game, which is plentiful here. We cook over open fires and bathe in the many streams we cross. Clementine had the foresight to bring soap along with us on our headlong flight, and she washes our clothes in those streams and hangs them on branches at night, and they are dry by morning when we rise to continue our journey.

When we left the Jukes place, all those days ago, we rode farther and farther into the wilderness astride the very broad back of the good plow horse Daisy. When, on that first day, we had got about ten miles from Clementine's father's place, we came upon a well-kept farm and stopped to water Daisy. The farmer and his wife and all the many children came out to greet us.

"Good day to you, Clementine. It's good to see you."

"Good day, Mr. Parrish, good to see you, too. Is ever'body well?"

"Yes, God be praised."

"This here is Jaimy Fletcher. I'm goin' off with him."

"Cain't say's I blame you, Clementine. Your life's been hard, I know, since your mama died."

"Uh-huh. Anyway, Pap's lying back there in his barn with a broke leg."

"Uh-huh. Well, we'll be seein' to him. You best be gettin' on."

"Uh-huh. Thanks, Mr. Parrish. You always been kind to me. Missus Parrish, too. We'll be gettin' on."

I have told Clementine about my life in the Navy and the places I have seen, and she is a most rapt audience, her most common expression being "Oh, Jaimy, that must have been so wonderful. I ain't never seen nothin' like that." I tell her of the lofty ships, of the terrible battles, and of our friends, but I do not tell her of you. Right now she knows that I must find and follow a "Jacky Faber," whom I know she thinks to be a boy or a man. She does not ask what I want with you—she is happy enough just to be with me. I know that by the way she looks at me with those incredible blue eyes. Jaimy Fletcher, Heaven-sent to her. What a mess.

But sometimes as I lie upon my back and point out the constellations to her, her head resting on my chest, and listen to her murmured replies, I do not think it a mess. She usually falls asleep with a long, contented sigh. I listen to the gentle sound of her breathing. I wrap my hand in the softness of her hair. I'm sorry.

You ask how I could have gone off with this girl, and I ask you, what else could I have done? Leave her with her beast of a father? Abandon her in the next town? Leave her on the road? No, I could do none of those things. The poor girl has nothing in the world, nothing save an essential goodness that shines in her pretty face. She saved my life. It is the least I can do to offer her my protection. And my friendship. I am not sorry. And I ask you, Jacky, how often have you gone off from me?

I vow that when I do part with her, her life will be much improved, considering what it was like when I happened upon her... or she happened upon me. I will decide what to do later about this. Things will resolve themselves.

I writhe in mental anguish, but for now, my main thought is to get to the river, which, I am told, is three days up ahead.

I don't know what else to say....

Chapter 18

The next day dawns bright and full of expectation. I pop out of bed ready to get on with it. I nudge the still-sleeping Katy. Off with nightshirt, on with regular gear, tell Jim to get his lazy butt up and commence ship's work. *Things're gettin' right lax around here, by God, and I won't have it.* Higgins, of course, is already up and hot tea is ready at hand.

We are moored alongside the only dock in the town of Kennerdell.

"Thanks, Higgins. Any sign of our stalwart Captain?"

"I believe he came in about two in the morning at the behest of the townspeople who prodded him back aboard by many a pitchfork aimed at his backside. It is possible that he has worn out his welcome in this burg."

"He was not brought back unconscious?"

"No, he was his usual charming self."

"*Hmmmm.* Where did he sleep?"

"On the deck, next to his tiller. I believe he's still stretched out back there."

"At least we can be thankful for that, that he didn't come roaring into the sleeping quarters, disturbing our slumbers."

"That is true."

I have a suspicion that Higgins had stayed up the entire night, seated at the entrance to our sleeping quarters, his two pistols at the ready in case Fink returned with evil on his mind. More than a suspicion. Rather, more of a certainty. Good Higgins, are there any better than you in this world?

As we gather on deck to find out our sailing plans for the day, the recumbent Mr. Fink stirs, groans, and sits up. It is a very bleary but not totally subdued Mr. Fink who rises to face the day.

He stumbles to the side, leans over, and thrusts his head into the water, keeping it under there an impossibly long time. Long after we think him quite drowned, he jerks his head back out and shakes it as a dog shakes himself when he comes out of the water.

"Ah, that's better. Boy, cast off."

Jim takes in the lines and then pushes our boat out into the stream with one of the long poles. I reflect that I chose well in taking on Jim Tanner as my coxswain. He is really getting the feel of this kind of navigation.

"Are we suffering the effects of our carousing last night, Mr. Fink?" I ask, as prudish as I can make it.

He glares balefully up at me through red-rimmed eyes, but he is not to be subdued. "What? Hell, no! I ain't never had a hangover in my whole life, and that includes the night I drunk George Washington, Ben Franklin, Dirty Mary, and Man Mountain Murphy all under the table at the Dew Drop Inn down in Roarin' Springs." Mr. Fink pauses here to expel a huge rolling belch, and I believe he feels some benefit from it, as he resumes his tale with increased vigor.

"Ol' George was out West surveyin' somethin' 'fore he got

to be President, and he fancied that he could drink with the likes of us. Can you believe it? *Pshaw!* Thought he could dance, too. *Pshaw!* That East Virginny pantywaist was the first to fall, and us only four bottles into it. I drug him out and throwed his powdered butt in the horse trough. Went back in and found Dirty Mary a-sittin' and a-squirmin' on ol' Ben's lap and him a-laughin' away, but game as he was, and mighty good company, too, Ol' Lightnin' Rod didn't last too long after that. Hell, another bottle and he giggled and keeled over, his bald head thrown back, a smile on his face.

"Dirty Mary lasted a few more rounds, but finally she stumbled over and laid her head on Ben's slumberin' chest and passed clean out herself. I gotta say, for a woman she could sure hold her likker. Didn't look half bad, neither, if'n it was dark and you'd already had a few.

"Man Mountain Murphy, though, he took some doin', him bein' three hundred and fifty-five pounds o' pure dirt-dog meanness. Me and him was eye to eye over our cups till way in the mornin', but then he finally stood up and said, 'Lord, I'm a-goin' home,' and he keeled right on over." Fink rubs his chin as if he's recalling all this. "Yep. He fell straight down like a tree dropped with a sharp ax. 'Course it didn't hurt him none, him being so hairy from his beard to belly, to his bare and hairy toes, it was like him fallin' into a soft mattress, it was. Some fellas are lucky that way, I suppose."

"That must have been quite an ordeal, Mr. Fink," I comment, reminding myself to double his dose when the time comes.

"Ah no, girly-girl, far from it." Fink chuckles. "After I'd disposed of Man Mountain Murphy and the rest, I went 'round and drank what was left in their cups, then went outside and greeted the dawn. I butchered a hog, made up a four-foot stack o' pancakes, ate it all down, the hog included, from snout to trotters, and finished it off with a gallon o' coffee so strong you could melt nails in it. Then I took two promenades around the town square, got a shave and a haircut, shot a man for lookin' at me funny, and then went back to my boat, scrubbed her down from stem to stern, and cast off and went on my way. The town o' Roarin' Springs voted itself dry the very next day. Still cain't get a proper drink within fifty miles of the place, no sir, and it's a shame. I don't go there no more. Damn tight-ass teetotalers. Gimme that tiller, boy, and somebody get me somethin' to eat."

The morning passed uneventfully, with all of us doing our usual things: Katy the Huntress, with her bow and arrows, looking for food; Jim next to Fink, feigning admiration and pumping him for river lore; and Higgins and me casing things out down below for the final time.

"There are many tools, Miss, and they seem in excellent order," says Higgins.

"And that is good, Higgins, as we will need them. Oh, and rope, too. Let's put that coil next to the hatchway, shall we? Good."

We examine the hold till we feel we have exhausted all its possibilities, and then I say, "The whiskey, Higgins, if you would," and he produces the bottle.

I go over to my bunk and open my seabag and stick my hand in and rummage around till I feel what I am looking for—it is a small bottle, corked tightly with a coat of protective wax on the neck. I break through the wax and hand the bottle to Higgins. "If you would uncork it, please."

Higgins always keeps certain implements close at hand, one of which is a corkscrew. He produces it and quickly uncorks the little bottle and hands it back to me.

"Now the whiskey bottle, if you please."

He applies his corkscrew to that bottle and expertly draws the cork from it. He gives the cork a quick sniff and says, "Excellent."

"Good. Pour a bit out of it. Have a drink yourself, if you'd like."

"A bit early, Miss. However, I will save it for later." He surmises what I am up to and pours out into a cup an amount equal to what is in my little bottle and places the cup on a shelf, then hands me back the whiskey bottle.

I pour the contents of my bottle into the bigger bottle and hand it back to Higgins, who puts the cork back in and gives it a bit of a shake.

Ah, Mother's Little Helper, we meet again, I think. *Whatever would I have done without you, throughout this life of mine? You helped me find a home for my baby Jesse, you eased my pain when I was beaten, you helped my men when they were grievously wounded, and now you shall help me do this.*

That done, I go back up into the light and compose myself for the coming little drama.

Mr. Fink, now fully recovered from the revels of the night before, regales me with at least ten more tall tales as the day wears on. I contentedly sit and watch the panorama of the riverbanks slipping by in all its infinite variety—here a cove, there a beach, here a shady grove of trees hanging over the bank, there a quiet pool that makes me long for a lazy swim. Perhaps with a certain James Emerson Fletcher, *sans culotte,* hmmm…

"And then ol' George, he…"

"Excuse me, Mr. Fink, but might you get in trouble for blaspheming the name of General Washington?" I ask. "Back East he is hailed as the Father of His Country, you know." Several of Mr. Fink's stories have figured the late President in them.

"Not out here, girly-girl. He tried to slap a whiskey tax on us when he was Prez-ee-dent, and you know *that* bird didn't fly, father or not," replies Fink, with firmness. "We rose us up a rebellion and ol' George sent out the federals to put us down, but we whupped the hell out of 'em. I did most of the whuppin', of course. Was gonna make us a new country, but me and a feller named Shay couldn't come to terms on what to name it, so the rebellion fizzled." Fink shakes his head sadly over the vagaries of politics. "They took back the tax, though."

I reflect that, in most places in the world, the affairs of men are driven by love of country, by war, or by religion. Here, however, they seem to be driven by whiskey.

"What a shame," says I. "To think we could be traveling through the country of Finklandia right now."

He looks at me sharply. "You know, girly-girl, I git the feelin' sometimes that you're laughin' at me." He growls, not at all friendly. "You know, for all your ladylike airs, you got a mouth on you, and I mean to remind you just who's

Captain of this ark and if'n I take a notion to pitch you over the side, I'll do it. See if'n I don't!"

It is the opening I've been looking for.

I gasp and put the back of my hand to my forehead and go into a swoon, as if I am struck to my very core to be addressed so harshly. Me, who's been called every dirty name in the book, and generally deserving of it.

"Oh, Mr. Fink, how could you think that of me?" I cry, squeezing out a tear. "Why, I-I feel faint. I..."

Higgins is instantly at my side to lend comfort. He casts an accusing eye on the now slightly alarmed Fink. "Sir, please! She is of such a delicate nature! I fear you've brought on an attack of the female vapors." To me he asks, "Are you all right, Miss?" as he puts his hand to my back to steady me.

"Oh, Higgins, oh, please don't let him hit me! I fear I shall die!" I wail, as I bury my face in my hands.

"Ah, now, I warn't gonna hit her, you know I warn't. Oh, damn, please, girly-girl, stop crying now," pleads Fink, completely flummoxed.

"Shall I make up your bed, Miss, that you might lie down?" asks Higgins.

"No...no, it's too stuffy down there," whines I. "Perhaps if you helped me down the deck a bit, and then if you could bring up my medicinal spirits, I think I would be myself soon."

Higgins helps me limp about ten feet down the deck. While I sit back down, Higgins hurries below. He quickly returns, bearing a tray with the bottle and a glass upon it. He sets it down on the cabin top and pours an ounce or two into my glass.

I hold it up to the sunlight so Mr. Fink can truly appreciate the warm, deep amber color, a color with which I know he is very familiar.

I lift it to my lips and pretend to sip.

"Ah, that's much better," I sigh. "I'm sure my spirits will soon be restored."

Mr. Fink responds with a profound snort. "Here, boy, take the tiller." Then I hear his boots tromping toward me. He lifts the bottle and sniffs it. "Why, that's straight corn likker with some sugar in it! What doctor give you that?"

"Oh, no, Sir. This is a very special tonic. It has the most potent medicines from the mysterious Orient in it, and I fear for your health —"

"Aw, come on..."

"Nay, Sir, as weak and frail as I am, my constitution is used to the power of this restorative, and I fear that yours is not."

That does it, as it is a direct challenge to his manhood.

"I will have a drink of that bottle, as is my right as Captain of this here boat," he says, firmly.

"Very well," I sigh. "If you insist, but I shall bear no responsibility for what results. Is that understood, Mr. Fink?"

He nods and licks his thick lips, *not* a pretty sight. The little sniff of whiskey he has had so far has merely whetted his appetite, as I knew it would.

"Very well. Higgins, will you bring up another glass?"

Higgins goes below and comes back with the glass, places it on the tray, pours in the liquid, and hands the glass to Fink, who promptly upends it.

"Ah," he says with great satisfaction, "give me another."

"Sip, Mr. Fink. You must sip it like you would sip the

finest of liqueurs," say I, in warning. At my nod, Higgins refills his glass.

"Sip, hell," says Fink. "This is how a man sips the finest lee-koors." And again he drops the opium-laced whiskey down his throat. "Candy," he says. "It tastes like candy. Give me another."

"Others have said that, Mr. Fink," I say, noticing that Fink is starting to sway a bit on his feet. "But I fear for the consequences, I do." I nod again at Higgins and the glass is refilled, and again downed in one swallow.

Mike Fink places the glass back on the tray with what seems like extreme concentration. He then turns and gazes out over the water. He lifts his arm and points at something I know only he can see.

"Swans," he says. "White swans. Look at that...I ain't never seen swans on the river before...and there's women ridin' 'em like they was horses, with their legs wrapped 'round them birds' necks...nekkid women..."

Then Mr. Fink sinks down to the deck and keels over, a smile of wonder on his sleeping face.

"Quick!" I say, jumping up. "We've got to move fast. Jim! Steer over to the bank!"

Everybody leaps into action. Jim puts the tiller over and we turn toward the shore. Higgins dives below and brings up the coil of rope. Katy runs over and crouches next to the aft anchor. I watch for the proper place to do what we're going to do, and as I watch, I take off my shoes, dress, vest, and stockings. Higgins slips the rope under Fink's arms and ties it at his back and then stands ready at the side, holding the end of the line.

"There!" I shout, pointing at a stretch of open beach

where a tree with overhanging branches is growing. "Jim! Take 'er in! Katy! Drop the anchor!"

It is done. The anchor catches and holds, and the boat swings in to the shore.

I leap over the side into the shallow water, which is a mite colder than I thought it would be. I fall over but my feet find the bottom and I can stand. I reach up and hold out my hand as Higgins tosses me the end of the rope to which Mr. Fink is tethered, and I half walk, half swim to the shore. When I am there, I take the rope up to that overhanging tree and wrap it around the trunk, taking up the slack so it is taut.

"All right, Katy!" I shout, and I see her let slide the anchor rope around the butt to which it is wound.

The boat, pulled by the current, moves forward, and though I can't see him, I know that Fink's bulk is being pulled back toward the stern. In a moment I see his head appear over the edge, then his shoulders, the rope under his armpits, and then the rest of him plunges into the water.

Please don't wake up, Mike! I'm thinking as I pull him to shore, fearful that the shock of the water might restore him to consciousness. This was the only way we could do this, him being so huge and heavy and all.

"Hold the anchor!" I cry, and Katy ties it off and the boat stops moving. There is another splash as a shirtless Jim Tanner jumps into the water, as planned, to come help me drag my burden to the shore.

My fears are groundless—Fink doesn't wake up, but snores peacefully on as he is hauled to shore.

"Damn, he weighs a ton." I grunt as we pull him out of the water so that only his feet remain submerged. "But that's good enough. Let's go." Jim unties the rope from both tree and Fink and we start off.

Fink stirs and we freeze, but he only smiles and says, "Swans…"

Jim and I swim back to the boat and are pulled aboard. Jim goes to the steering oar and the anchor is hauled and taken aboard and we are under way again.

"I wish you the joy of your new command, Miss," says Higgins, smiling. "I shall lay out some dry clothes."

Still dripping, I jump up onto the cabin top and plant a wet foot on each side of the centerline, the better to feel the action of my boat.

Oh, how good it feels!

Chapter 19

We arise this morning at dawn as masters of our own fate—or masters of our own boat, anyway. We breakfast on biscuits, maple syrup, and bacon, and then head back out into the current to continue our journey.

Yesterday, after we had parted company with the redoubtable Mr. Fink, we continued on our way with much singing and revelry and bragging about what clever scammers we were, but it turned out to be not quite as easy as we had supposed—the current had picked up some, likely the result of a heavy rain upriver, and we were pitched about in a most unseaman-like way. I know that Jim was mortified at not being able to keep the boat's head up when we got spun around several times. We brought up two of the long oars—*sweeps*, as Mr. Fink had called them—and fixed them in their oarlocks and went to work, with Katy and me on one and Higgins on the other, and we were able to keep her bow to the west till evening, when, exhausted, we pulled in to the shore as night was falling.

Higgins whipped us up a good dinner from the provisions he had bought back in Kennerdell—some bacon, salt pork, a kind of dried beef called jerky, and even a good smoked ham. And a halfway decent bottle of wine made, it was said, from the fruit of the wild grapevines we had seen growing along the shore. "Fox grapes," Katy announced. "Ain't good fer nuthin' 'less you add pounds and pounds o' sugar to 'em." So we were rewarded for our labors and our good cheer was restored.

As we sat watching the evening sun go down in a glorious sunset, I got up and poured a libation of fox-grape wine over the bow, then said, "I christen thee the *Belle of the Golden West*! Long may you sail! Or float...or drift...or whatever..."

"Hear, hear," cheered my crew, raising their glasses.

Today, however, the water flows smoothly and the winds stay calm, and we are able to ship the sweeps and rely only on the steering oar. I set up a watch rotation such that every one of us four would become skilled at the handling of it. Under Jim's now-expert tutelage, we all do attain a measure of proficiency, but I certainly wouldn't want to do it for a living, as it takes a certain amount of brute strength to move the thing. There were several times when my feet were lifted from the deck in my efforts to make the damned oar behave.

It is plain that we shall have to hire more crew when we get to the mighty Ohio. How we will pay them, I don't know, but I'll worry about that later. Maybe we'll pick up some paying passengers in Pittsburgh. Going to have to get some good maps there, too, so's I can gauge distances and figure out what to charge my customers. By the mile, I think, and the money up front.

———

In the afternoon, as things are going smoothly, I sit with Higgins and we discuss the events of the past day.

"You do not think he will cry bloody murder when he gets up and finds his bearings but not his boat?" asks Higgins. "While it has been my pleasure to serve you these past years, still I would prefer not to be hanged by some unwashed, illiterate American mob for flatboat theft in this benighted wilderness. I had fancied a rather more elegant end to my days—something more in the line of a peaceful death after an honored life, followed by a stately but tasteful funeral featuring endless ranks of weeping but well-dressed mourners covering the casket containing my mortal remains with mounds of perfect yellow roses."

"Very poetic, Higgins," I say, "and I hope all that comes to pass for you, but not all too quickly, for I need you here by my side and not reclining elegantly dead in some vault in Westminster Abbey."

"Westminster Abbey," muses Higgins. "I do like the sound of that."

"Anyway," I say, breaking into his self-elegy, "when Mr. Fink wakes up, he will think that he fell overboard during a drunken stupor and he'll consider himself lucky to be alive. I'm sure he is right now making up a tall tale to fit the occasion. Shall I give it a shot? Very well: *Thar I was, throwed overboard by the biggest wave ever seen east of the monster waves of Bor-nee-oh, tossed down to the bottom o' the river whar I sucked up enough mud to chink all the log houses from Ohio to Saint Louis. I come back up to the surface and spit up all the dirt inta one big pile and that pile become Mount—*"

Higgins laughs, then says, "All right, Miss, very well composed. I think Mr. Fink himself would be pleased."

"Besides, Higgins, do I not have in my possession a Bill of Sale for this boat, signed by Mr. Fink, himself? Any court in the land would surely honor it." I had taken the piece of paper upon which Mike Fink had so laboriously penned his signature and I had written the Bill of Sale for the boat above it, all legal-like. The price was fifty dollars, the amount I had already paid him, which I think was fair. Serves him right, too, 'cause he shouldn't have been so greedy. Mr. Fink has found to his sorrow that it's not a good idea to try to cheat an old Cheapside hand.

"Yes, you have shown me the paper. I think Ezra Pickering, while aghast at the speciousness of the whole thing, would nevertheless be proud."

"So you see, Higgins," say I, "there is absolutely nothing to worry about. And, furthermore, if you think I feel guilty because of this, think again. Think how he cheated us on the fare he was charging us to Pittsburgh. And if you really think that Mike Fink came by this boat in any way honestly, well, I've got some stock in an under the English Channel tunnel company I'd like to sell you."

"Very well, Miss," replies a jocular Higgins, "I shall pass on the stock, put legal concerns out of my mind, and concentrate my thoughts on dinner. If you'll excuse me."

I go up to sit for a while with Katy and watch the shore slip by, all deep and dense and green. The cleared farms are growing fewer and farther between, as are the tiny towns. I wonder if there are any Indians lurking just beyond the edge of the forest?

Katy and I are both delighted to shed our dresses now that Mr. Fink has left our company—it's back to undershirt and drawers without stockings, just as we were dressed in the hold of the *Bloodhound*. Higgins expresses some concern that our attire might keep poor Jim in a state of constant excitement, but I reply that he'll have to get used to it, as the rivers are long and the work will be hard and dresses get in the way. I promise, however, to sew us up some heavier canvas trousers as soon as we can get the cloth. Meanwhile, randy Jim should keep his mind on his nautical studies and not on us. *Boys, I swear...*

We neither see nor catch anything edible, and so I go back to the spot on the cabin top right up in front of Jim, at his steering oar, and flop down on my back. Lolling about in the sun, I decide to call this spot the quarterdeck. I think on that: the quarterdeck of the *Belle of the Golden West*, Lieutenant J. M. Faber, Commanding.

Yes, I do like the sound of that, I do. And so, my bully crew, on to this Pittsburgh, where we shall see what we shall see.

Chapter 20

Jaimy Fletcher
Kittanning, Pennsylvania
USA

Jacky,

We reached the Allegheny four days ago at the town of Kittanning. It was a wretched little town with very little to offer, but it did have a dock from which I hoped to gain us passage downriver.

It was noon, with the sun high overhead, so we had time to take care of some things before finding a place to sleep for the night. I went to question the people at the dock as to our chances of finding a boat going downriver, while Clementine had the sad duty of taking Daisy off to sell her, the forests around the river getting so thick that we could not think of taking her farther.

I was informed that without money "y'ain't got the chance of a snowball in Hell of gettin' on a boat, but mebbe if one comes down needin' a hand, well, mebbe... You'll just have to wait and see what comes by."

Clementine came back, disconsolate, with a sack that contained two smoked hams and a jug of whiskey.

"It was the best I could do, Jaimy, I'm sorry, but at least the people seemed like they'd be kind to her." She turned away as her fingers brushed at her eyes. I knew, from the way Clementine would lay her face against the mare's neck on our journey here, that Daisy was the only thing in her former life that she could love and be loved by in return, if only in the simplest of ways: a neigh, a welcoming whicker, a happy toss of the head when the girl would come into the old plow horse's sight.

I assured Clementine that she had done well by both Daisy and me, and I put my arm around her and drew her to my side to lend her comfort. Then we trudged off to see what we could do in this town till opportunity presented itself. At least, finally, I had made it to the river.

There was a livery stable, owned by a Mr. Owens, and he offered me the job of shoveling manure and sawing and chopping wood in exchange for breakfast, dinner, and supper for Clementine and me. We could sleep in their barn if she would help Mrs. Owens with the house and laundry chores. We gratefully took the offer.

So, for the next four days, I endured some of the most grueling work I have ever done. I shoveled manure into barrows and then took those barrows out to fields and spread that same manure around, countless trips back and forth, back and forth.

Once, when I wheeled the barrow nearby the Owens's house, I heard Clementine inside singing as she went about her tasks.

Come all ye fair and tender ladies,
Take warning how you court young men,
They're like a star of a summer's mornin',
First they'll appear and then they're gone.

They'll tell to you some loving story,
They'll tell to you some far-flung lie,
And then they'll go and court another
And, for that other one, pass you by.

If I'd a-knowed before I'd courted
That love it was such a killin' crime,
I'd a-locked my heart in a box of golden
And tied it up with a silver line.

I stood there and listened, and it humbled me that while she sang happily in her present state, I grumbled and cursed. I picked up my barrow and moved on.

When I was not moving manure about, I chopped, sawed, and split wood for the coming winter's fires. I thought often, Jacky, whilst trying to neatly split a log with one blow of my ax, how you have often observed that no skill is worthless and that something can be learned from the meanest of jobs. And, while I cannot claim to like it, I have grown quite lean and sinewy in dealing with this harsh American life. I am probably in as good a physical condition as when we belonged to the Dread Brotherhood of the *Dolphin* and swung through the rigging like crazed little apes.

Not having the luxury of a razor, my beard has grown out, too. I have never been unshaven before, and I find my whiskers grow out black and fine. Clementine says she likes it, saying that while my chin formerly rasped her cheek, now it is all soft and silky. On our journey here, she was fond of smoothing it out with her fingers as we lay abed for the night. Yes, and she'd stroke it sometimes in the daytime, too, when we would lie on a verdant creek bank, taking the sun and...well, resting.

I caught my reflection in a horse trough one day and was quite shocked. With my long dark hair and pointy beard, I looked every inch the bloody pirate, except, that is, for my clothes. No piratical elegance there. My only two garments were Pap Jukes's overalls and the shirt that Clementine had sewn for me. The shirt, actually, was quite fine, but the rough overalls and bare feet made me appear to be the simplest of country bumpkins.

The nature of my situation is not lost on me: I cross the American wilderness in pursuit of one girl, while yet another girl stands by my side. If those two brigands had not waylaid me, none of this would have happened. I know that I would have caught up with you and things would be vastly different right now. But then Clementine, too, would have been stuck back at that awful place with no joy, no hope, no future, only vain wishes and prayers uttered by mountain streams, heard by nobody.

I do not know what to think and so I shall think about nothing. After our day's labor, we return exhausted to our nest in the hay and burrow in. She lies down next to me and we sleep deeper than I have ever slept before. I shall take it day by day.

I know I can only take one day at a time, but I also know I grow more and more fond of her every day.

It was on the morning of the fifth day in Kittanning, while I was filling yet another barrow with ordure, that I heard a commotion down by the river. It sounded like a boat coming in to the dock! And here I had been despairing of spending the rest of my life as a manure-hauler! With hope surging, I ran down to see. On my way, I saw Clementine up in the kitchen window of the Owens place and called out to her to come running and she did, catching up to me at the foot of the dock.

"I'm a-gonna kill 'er, that's for sure!" came the call across the water. "I'm a-gonna kill 'er! *Oooooweeeeee!* I'm a ring-tailed roarer who has been brought down sad, but I'm a-gonna kill her, I'm a-gonna flay her, I'm a-gonna skin her, I'm a-gonna tan her hide, and then I'm a-gonna wear her skin for my hat, and then ever'thin' will be all right! *Ooooooooweeeee!* Ain't nobody in this whirly world kin steal Mike Fink's boat and live, so I got to kill 'er and I will! I'll do it, you'll see! *Oooooooweeeee!* I'm a hidebound walloper born in a canebrake and ready to roar! *Ooooooooweeeee!"*

I hurried to the end of the dock to see what this hulla-baloo might be. The other people on the dock, formerly concerned with their daily occupations, suddenly got up and ran the other way, crying, "Christ, it's Fink!" which should have been a warning to me, but I was anxious to be on my way, so I stood my ground at the end of the dock. Clementine grabbed my hand as we watched this apparition approach.

He was in an open rowboat of about fifteen feet in length. There was little else in the boat except him, but of him there was a lot. Dressed in dark trousers, white shirt, boots, and wide-brimmed hat, he seemed a good four hundred pounds. He was also clothed in a good deal of hair—his great beard billowed from his chin almost to his eyebrows, which were equally bushy. Beneath those brows gleamed two beady and angry eyes.

"If you please, Sir," I ventured. "Mr. Fink, is it? We are desirous of a passage downstream, and—"

"What the hell you talkin' about?" demanded this Fink, while he brought the boat alongside the dock. I grabbed the lines and tied them securely to the posts.

"Please, Mister," pleaded Clementine. "We needs t'get downriver and we was hopin' you might help us."

"Wal, little girl, tha's more like it. How come he cain't talk straight like you?" Fink crawled out onto the dock and stretched his considerable bulk.

"He's from away and don't know how to talk right sometimes," explained Clementine. "But he's my man and I love him."

"Wal, there's some straight talk, I'll own," said Fink. "Now what about goin' downriver?"

"Well, Mr. Fink," I began earnestly, "while we have no money—"

"If'n you ain't got money, you ain't gettin' on my boat," said Fink, firmly.

"Yessir," piped up Clementine, blinking her eyes and wringing her hands. "But we got two good hams and a jug o' whiskey, and Jaimy could help you row the boat, and I could wash up things and—"

"Well, hell, whyn't you say so?" said Fink. "Get in the goddamn boat."

———

We made our good-byes to Mr. and Mrs. Owens, who, by and large, had been very good to us, Mrs. Owens even packing a bag of food for Clementine, and Mr. Owens clapping me on the back and saying that if I ever wanted a job as manure-hauler again, well, it was here waiting for me. I thanked him for his kindness, and Clementine and I went back to the boat.

I handed the jug of whiskey down to Mr. Fink, and then I got in and reached up my hand for Clementine and she hopped in and sat down on the bow seat. I picked up the oars and dug them deep in the water. This was how it was done in the Royal Navy, Mr. Fink, in case you didn't know.

I pulled us out into the stream and we were bound for the town of Pittsburgh, wherever the hell that is....

PART III

Chapter 21

"Hooray!" I exult as we finally bring the *Belle of the Golden West* to Pittsburgh. "It's a town, a real town! Look! Factories! Smoke! Dirt! Stink! I love it! Hooray!"

I am a city girl at heart.

The trip down was calm and leisurely, made more enjoyable because I was on a watercraft under my own command again. If I felt like it, I could order us anchored and we could go ashore to enjoy the charms of the land. We picnicked on grassy banks, swam in glassy pools, and explored the many small streams that emptied into the river. Jim would go off with his rifle into the woods in search of game, but it was mostly fish that we ate. While onshore we dug worms and with them baited our hooks, and we were most successful. We cut poles to tie our fishing line to, and it was most pleasing to sit on the cabin top with the baited line in the water, waiting for that thrilling jerk. That is, when we did not have to row, or take our turn at the tiller. Yes, and we practiced shooting, too, gaining proficiency with both pistol and rifle and alarming the bird population no small degree with our noise.

Along the way, we provisioned at various tiny towns

along the river's banks, and while there, we let it be known that we would carry passengers to Pittsburgh. But, alas, we got no takers, even though we promised them nightly musical entertainment. So we stuck to eating fish, buying only flour and lard and such to conserve our money, which was getting very low.

All in all, it was a most enjoyable cruise. But still, I was glad to see smoky, gritty Pittsburgh. It smelled, but to me it smelled like money.

"Jim! See the docks down there at the end!" I shout, pointing. "Steer for them. Man the sweeps!"

"Aye, aye, Missy," says Jim.

"The sweeps shall be manned, Captain," says Higgins. "But first you and Katy must dress, else I fear arrest."

"Oh, right," I say. I had forgotten.

Katy and I get into our Lawson Peabody serving-girl gear as fast as we can and then run back up on deck. We are much closer now, and I pick out a likely looking open space on a large dock as our destination.

"I'll take the helm, Jim," I say, placing my hand on the steering oar. "Take the starboard sweep with Katy." He does not protest.

With Higgins on the port oar and the others on the starboard, we start up the rhythm of the row.

"All pull," I say, and they do. These sweeps are curved in such a way that the rower can stand on the low cabin roof and put his full weight behind the pull or push. Very ingenious, I have thought, and even quite elegant, or as elegant as a boat can be that is not under sail. "All pull."

I see with mounting excitement that there are many taverns on the street running along the docks. *I can't wait!*

"Port, pull; starboard, hold," I call, judging the distance and the drift of the boat. Higgins pulls back on his oar, while Katy and Jim hold their oar out of the water. I swing the tiller bar to the right. "Port, pull; starboard, back." Higgins puts his oar in the water and pulls, while Katy and Jim dig theirs in and push. I put my rudder amidships.

We are swinging in. "Port, pull; starboard, ship your oar." Jim pulls in their oar, lays it on deck, and goes to tend the lines. I throw the tiller to the right and we slip alongside the dock, pretty as you please. Jim jumps over and ties her up. The *Belle of the Golden West* is moored.

The dock turns out to be a public pier, so the dockage fee is quite reasonable. Higgins goes to see the dockmaster and signs us up for a week, as there is much we have to do here. While he is gone, I go below to get myself into my remaining riding habit, the one I had bought in London. Tight dark green jacket with black velvet lapels and gold epaulets sitting up all jaunty on my shoulders and much creamy lace spilling out at my throat. On with the long black pleated skirt and my jockey boots. I figure why put on stockings when none can see them, as only the toes of my riding boots peek out 'neath the bottom hem of the skirt. Higgins comes back in time to fluff me up and brush me off. I top off my outfit with my rakish Scots bonnet, which, thankfully, Clarissa Howe did not grab when she raided my seabag to outfit herself on the *Juno*.

There. *That oughta show these bumpkins what a true*

international entertainer looks like. A puff of powder on the cheeks and we are ready to be off on the town.

"All right, let's go. Katy, you can pretend to be my maid…" I get a snort for that, but a nod as well. "Higgins, be your usual self, and Jim, stay here and watch the *Belle.*" I know he is disappointed, but his time will come. He nods and picks up a fishing rod, baits the line, and drops it over as he sits down to wait.

We stride out into the town.

The streets are muddy and pigs roam freely about and evidence of the passage of many horses is everywhere underfoot. The smell of coal fires and furnaces fills the air, but through it all, we can see the signs of many taverns—the Black Bear, the Harp and Crown, the White Horse, and there, the Sign of the General Butler.

I spy a passerby who looks like he might be of the sporting type, and I beg him to stop to tell me about the taverns that exist in this town and what sorts of entertainment they provide.

"Well, little lady," he replies, looking me up and down and grinning, "maybe you'd rather be checkin' in at one of the fancy houses uptown, like maybe Gypsy Sally's or—"

Higgins opens his jacket to expose the butts of the two pistols holstered there.

"Or then again, maybe not." The chastened sport gulps.

"A straight answer, if you please, Sir," I demand, my eyes demurely cast down. "And then we will be on our way, grateful for what information you may provide."

"Ahem. Well, Bob Erwin runs the White Horse, and he's a decent sort, and John Irwin, he does the Black Bear, and Molly Murphy owns the General Butler, and—"

"Thank you, Sir, you have been most helpful," says I, having heard enough. "A very good day to you, then." I dip down in a half curtsy as we leave him astounded in the dusty street.

"We will go to the General Butler," I pronounce, seeing the sign for the establishment swinging up ahead, "to see what we will see."

The interior of the General Butler is dark, smoky, and gloomy, but that is how it is supposed to look, and so I advance to the bar. I have found that I like working with landladies more than landlords, as the lords often tend to want a somewhat different kind of performance out of me than I'm willing to give.

"I wish to speak to Miss Molly Murphy," says I to the person behind the bar, who I suspect is Murphy herself.

I find I am not wrong.

"So, that's me," she says, without affectation. "So, what is it you want, dear?"

I like her already.

I puff up and say, "I am a musical and theatrical performer. I sing, I dance, I tell stories, I recite poems, I play the pennywhistle, fiddle, and concertina. If allowed to set up in your fine establishment, I will double your customers, guaranteed," I say.

"And how old are you, dearie," asks Molly, eyeing me not unkindly, "to be promisin' me all this?"

"Old enough, Missus," I answer, slipping into the Irish way of speaking. "Will you listen to this, then?"

Higgins hands me the Lady Gay, and instead of the raucous tunes I usually rip out at a time like this, I play a medley of the sad songs "Mountains of Mourn" and "Broom o' the Cowdennelles" and "Londonderry Air." It's the last one that nails her, which is good—if ever I can't make an Irishman cry with my fiddle, then I should hang it up and sit quietly by the fire forevermore.

The deal is struck. We get room and board for the four of us, and I will do two sets, one early evening and one that night. Katy will help out with serving the increased crowds, and Higgins'll provide security, with Jim to help out where he can.

We scope out where the stage is to be and then go back to the *Belle* to get ready for the night's revels.

Oh, I will be so glad to be back where I belong!

Chapter 22

Jaimy Fletcher
In the company of Mike Fink
On the Allegheny River
Pennsylvania, USA

Jacky,

It soon became apparent that Mike Fink intended for me to do all the rowing, as he plunked himself down in the stern, with his hand on the extra oar that he was using as a rudder, and guided us along while I provided the sole power. When I am done with this American odyssey, I shall be able to hire out as a circus strongman.

Clementine perched behind me in the bow seat and kneaded my shoulders to lend them relief. I had taken off my shirt in the heat and her hands felt good on my aching muscles.

Fink slumped in the back, mumbling curses over some recent bad luck he had recently experienced.

"Goddamn...goddamn...best boat I ever had, it was, too, and she stole it. Goddamn her to Hell and back. Fooled poor Mike Fink, who was good enough to give her a ride on his boat, then she stole it from him, bighearted, stupid Mike Fink. Damn! But I'm a-gonna catch her and I'm a-gonna kill her..."

I was sure this was just another interesting tale of mischief on the river, no doubt perpetrated on the wounded Mike Fink by some river slattern of low moral character, but I didn't ask for details. I knew it would come out, Fink being the braggart he most plainly was. It occurred to me that he was bragging even about being bested by this woman who had robbed him.

He left off his rant for a moment to peer closely at me and ask, "How come you're tryin' to get to Pittsburgh? Looking for work, I reckon."

"Yes," I said, mindful of Clementine listening behind me. "I am also trying to locate a friend, and furthermore, I would not mind catching up with the two men who robbed me on the road, taking all I had." I then recounted to him, between strokes of the oars, the story of my downfall and my rescue by Clementine.

"*Hmmm,*" he mused, stroking the massive mat of his beard, "so you mean to kill them fellers, I suspect."

"The thought had crossed my mind," I wheezed, pulling at the oars, "being that they clubbed me and stripped me and shot me and left me for dead."

"All right," said Fink, "we'll get down there and you kill them fellers and I'll kill that thievin' little bitch. Here's how I'm a-gonna do it: I'm a-gonna wrap my two hands around her skinny little neck till her face turns blue and them big brown eyes pop right outta her skull!"

Right about then a cold suspicion began to dawn on me.

It was the "little bitch" that first alerted me to an awful possibility. No, it could not be...

It was.

"She was there with those three others, her big fancy man and the boy and the other girl," Fink went on. "But you could see plain that she was the boss of all of 'em. 'Oh, thank you, Higgins,' she'd say for any little thing he done for Her Royal Majesty. And, oh, she'd prance around like the most frail and delicate thing, ready to swoon and faint away at the sound of any decent cussword. 'Oh, Mr. Fink, you are so very big and strong, you must be the very finest man I have ever met! Oh, please, tell me another story of your adventures!' she'd plead, and flutter those big brown eyes at me, and me, the fool, just lapped it up, when all along she was plannin' to steal my boat. It ain't right, t'ain't right, and I got to kill her."

I continued pulling away at the oars, hoping he would not pronounce your name. It was, of course, a vain hope.

"Yep, it won't be long now, as she's only got about three days' head start on me. Yep, Miss Jacky Faber has got about four days left on this earth," said Fink, with great satisfaction.

Oh, Lord...

Clementine's hands tightened on my shoulders, and then I felt them drop. Her freckled face appeared next to my left cheek, her blue eyes drilling into mine.

"I thought you said Jacky Faber was a boy," hissed Clementine into my ear, but loud enough for Fink to hear. "Why're you chasing her, Jaimy? You tell me. You tell me now."

I didn't have to respond, for Mike Fink exploded in rage. He pointed his finger at my nose and shouted, "You know her! Goddammit! You're part o' her filthy gang o' thieves! It comes to me now—you talk funny, jest like that Jacky Faber and her fancy man. Well, by God, yer gonna get it!"

With that, he threw over his improvised rudder, and we hit the shallows next to the bank. He jumped out of the boat, remarkably light on his feet for such a huge man. He paused to throw back his head and cry out with a mighty roar, then he lunged at me.

I rolled over to the opposite side of the boat to evade his grasp, but he managed to grab the suspenders of my overalls and hurl me onto the muddy bank on which we had just landed. I tried to gain my feet, but could not. Fink whipped me around like a toy and slammed me down face-first in the muck, his foot planted on the back of my neck. All my circus strongman illusions were gone, for I realized that the man was incredibly strong.

But he was also immensely vain. While he took a moment to rear back to beat his chest and loudly bray out his superiority to a pansy weakling such as the likes of me, I managed to scramble out from under his foot and jump to my feet.

I steadied myself enough to face him. I was breathing hard and thinking that I had endured just about enough of America and its brigands and river louts. Propelled by all my pent-up anger, I pulled back my right fist and punched him in the face where I thought his chin might be under all that matted hair. I hit with all the force and anger within me. Pain radiated up my arm—I feared that my knuckles were shattered and my wrist was broken.

Fink stepped back, surprised. He put his hand to his whiskered jaw and looked off, thoughtful. "Wal, now," he asked, working his jaw like a ruminating steer, "was that a

fly, a mosquito? Nah, must have been a gnat. A baby gnat...
Must've been. C'mere, boy, I'm about to show you what real
river fightin's like."

With that he snaked out a hand to catch me behind the
head and pulled me to him and smothered me in a great
bear hug, my arms pinned to my side, a hold I could not
break from.

"Y'see, boy," he whispered into my ear, "on the river we
don't box like little dancin' fairies. Nope, on the river we
rassles!"

Back we went, down into the mud again. On the way
down, he shoved a knee into the small of my back and
wrenched up my right arm behind me.

"See, boy, tha's how we do it," he snarled as he yanked
my arm further up my back. I shrieked with the pain of it.
"Steal my boat, will you?" he growled, grabbing a handful of
my hair in his other fist and pushing my head down into the
mud. When I cried out in pain, the muck oozed into my
mouth, my nose, and my eyes.

I was convinced that I would end my days here in this
stinking swamp, killed by a maniac. It was then that I heard
a steady *Thump! Thump! Thump!*

In my distress I thought it was a troop of marines,
marching to my rescue, but no. My vision cleared enough
for me to see that Clementine, wielding a four-foot-long
driftwood log, was standing over Fink and repeatedly
swinging it and bringing it to bear on the back of his head.

His eyes crossed on the first several blows, but he shook
them off. She, however, was relentless and kept on pounding
him. Eventually, his grip on my arm weakened, then let go.
Mike Fink rolled off me and slumped back in the mud.

"All right, girl, you kin stop now. Mike Fink's done." He groaned, his chest heaving. "And I don't blame you now for standin' up for your man. You're a good girl, I kin see. Just don't hit me no more. Ol' Fink's done." He shook his head to clear it. "We'll all go down this river. This boy'll kill them two fellers and then I'll kill this Jacky Faber and get my boat back and ever'body'll be happy. He kin bed her 'fore I kills her if'n he wants to, but that'll be the end of that. Jest put that log down now, y'hear?"

Clementine flung the log aside and stalked off to sit alone in the woods as Fink and I picked ourselves up.

Afterward, Fink and I stripped off our muddy clothes and Clementine washed them in the clear river and hung them on branches to dry, then we turned in for the night, Fink wrapped in a blanket in his rowboat, and me and Clementine under a bush on the shore.

Me, anyway. Clementine kept a good distance away from me. I could hear her crying in the darkness. Sobbing, Jacky, like I have heard you sob in the past, crying like your whole body was going to come apart. I lay back and waited. It didn't take long.

"I thought I was your girl."

"You are the best of girls, Clementine."

"Tell me this Jacky Faber and you is jes' friends," she demanded.

"We are friends. We were children together on that British ship I told you about."

"Tell me you ain't been with her like you've been with me."

Well, that's true, anyway.

"No, Clementine, I have not."

She sniffed in the darkness.

"What you gonna do, just leave me in the woods some-place when you find her?"

"I will tell you this, Clementine. Whatever happens, I will never leave you in a sorry condition. I will always do my best to take care of you as you have taken care of me. Do you believe me?"

She believed me enough to come to my side. She started out the night with her back toward me, which she had never done before, but in the morning we were again entwined as one....

Chapter 23

Jacky Faber
The Sign of the General Butler Inn
Pittsburgh, Pennsylvania, USA
At the headwaters of the Ohio River
July something, I've lost track
1806

Lieutenant James Fletcher
Somewhere in England, probably

Dear Jaimy,

I am writing to you in the same spirit that you once wrote to me—such that we might someday look back on these letters and have a good laugh at their contents. I cannot actually send it, of course, for it might be intercepted and read by those who pursue me. I will write to Ezra, however, and actually dispatch it, for I think that will be safe enough. I will tell him my news, and if you are in contact with him, well then, you, too, shall hear it.

Pittsburgh is a booming town, throbbing with commerce

and industry. There is the sound of hammers everywhere, and buildings and factories are going up all around. It is music to my mercantile ears. I almost wish I could stay to join in the progress that is going to be made here, but, alas, I cannot. I must journey down these rivers so as to get back to you, which, of course, is what I really want to do. I do miss you so.

I have a boat again, Jaimy, can you even believe it? I have named her the *Belle of the Golden West*. She is a river flatboat. Well, technically, she is a keelboat, because she has a hull that is built on ribs, not like the regular flatboats that are just floating boxes. She is pretty flat, though, because of the shallow water she has to navigate as we travel downriver, but she does have pointy ends, not like those other scows. She is quite elegant, in her way, in spite of the fact that she lacks sails. For now, anyway. I do have plans in that regard.

I am back to singing and dancing in the taverns. I know you don't want to hear that, as you always seem to want to have me tucked down in some safe, domestic place, but we must have money. Plus, I enjoy it hugely, and if you don't want the children to hear that their mother was a saloon singer in her youth, well, just don't read them this part.

The first night in Pittsburgh, I played at the Sign of the General Butler and was most pleased with both my performance, rusty as I was, and the warm reception I received. How I do love applause! We had sent Jim Tanner out into the town as a crier, telling the populace that Jacky Faber, the Toast of Two Continents, would be in solo performance at the General Butler, singing songs both happy and sad, fast and slow, telling funny stories, etc. You know, Jaimy, my usual patter.

Anyway, we had a good house that first night, and the

owner, Molly Murphy, a dear soul, pronounced herself most satisfied, so I was invited to stay as long as I liked. The second and third nights were even better, the crowd larger on each succeeding night. I think you would enjoy, Jaimy, the spectacle of a ninety-pound female sawing away on her fiddle while being guarded by a very large English gentleman's gentleman in full rig—a rig that includes the butts of two pistols peeking discreetly from beneath his jacket. Katy, too, proved valuable, helping out a grateful Molly with serving the drinks to the crowd. She was capable and efficient and earned herself some nice tips, too.

We have been hired to play at a wedding on Saturday and a barn dance on Sunday afternoon—no blue laws here, so it's my kind of town.

It is good we are making some money—for one thing, I get to pay Katy and Jim something for their labors to date. Upon receiving their coins, they hied off together into the town. Jim came back proudly wearing a black boatman's hat adorned with a red grosgrain band, and Katy returned with some new stockings and cloth for making a new shirt. I believe it was her first shopping trip ever, and it warmed my heart to see her quiet self pleased about something. I also have bought a boatman's hat for myself and one for Higgins, too. After all, I must keep my fair complexion away from this fierce American sun while we are on the water, and also I need to blend in with the river folk. Higgins, too, wears his, though it offends his sense of style, but he does realize the importance of blending in when we are under way. On shore, of course, he remains his well-dressed self.

The food is good at Molly's, and believe me, it sure was fine shoving my face into a big bowl of thick beef stew after all that fish. Good wines hereabout, too. I shall certainly stock the *Belle*'s wine cellar before we leave. For the passengers, of course—I do intend to offer a quality cruise.

Speaking of the wine cellar, we have hired a carpenter—labor and lumber are plentiful and cheap around here—to help us make some changes to the boat. We have built a partition across the back of the hold such that it makes a stateroom for me and my mates—two bunks, one over the other, on each side, and a curtain between. So Katy and I will be on one side and Higgins and Jim on the other. There is a door at the back so we have a private entrance, right back by the steering oar. A command post, as it were.

In the passenger section, Katy has sewn muslin curtains for each bunk, and Jim, under Higgins's supervision, has installed locks on the cargo section where the wine and spirits and kitchen supplies will be stowed. There is a bunk in the kitchen area for the cook we will have to hire. Higgins will cook for me, but not for ten or twenty.

I have also bought this journal in which I'm writing this down. I shall start keeping a ship's log like I did on the *Star* and the *Emerald*. I must now, however, put up my quill and get ready for this evening's performance.

It is my most fervent hope that you are safe and well. Higgins tells me not to worry about any trouble you might be in because of me, so I shan't.

Know that I think of you all the time, Jaimy, and that I remain,

Your girl always,

Jacky

Chapter 24

Jaimy Fletcher
On the Allegheny River
Pennsylvania, USA
Sometime in the summer of 1806
As I have lost track of the actual day

Jacky,

Fink has been pushing me to the limit, such was his deter-mination to attend to your quick execution and to reclaim his boat. I pull on the oars and hope for the best, having one angry but somewhat mollified female seated behind me and one female up ahead of me who will be very angry, too, should she meet either Mike Fink or Clementine Jukes. One day at a time, *I continually tell myself.* Just pull at your oars, Mr. Fletcher.

Mike—for I have been allowed to call him that, since we are now partners in pursuit of you—is dead set on your grisly demise. I have tried appealing to his better nature, hoping that one exists there in that mountain of hair and muscle and bone, but he persists in calling for your end. He has gone through many versions of what he hopes will be your last moments on this earth, some of which are quite colorful. The one concerning cramming a charge of powder up a certain posterior part of your anatomy and lighting the fuse with his cigar being one of them. I myself, in the past, have thought of paddling that same part of you into some sort of submission for your depredations against both society and my own well-being, so I had some perverse sympathy with his scenario, but still I pled your case.

"She really is a good girl at heart, Mike," I said. "And, yes, while it is true that on occasion she is given to larceny—it is, admittedly, one of her less admirable qualities—still I wish you would give her the chance to explain her actions. She does sometimes have a good, reasonable motive for the things she does."

"You sure do talk funny, boy," said Mike, ruminating on what I had just said. Upon some serious consideration, he went on. "Nope. Gotta kill her. Y'see, my reputation on the river depends on it. Why, if it got out that I was bested by that little twig of a girl, I'd be a goner. Ever'body'd be laughin' at me, and I couldn't have that. I've come to like you, boy, even if you do talk like a Baton Rouge girly-man, but no, my mama'd roll over in her watery grave and swamp two, three dozen boats in the process, and we can't have that, surely. Nope, Jacky Faber's got to go down." He clamped his jaw shut, and the case was closed.

I decided to keep silent on the subject and just row—for one thing, talking about you upsets Clementine. Sometimes she continued to knead my shoulders as before, sometimes not. Sometimes I felt her teeth gently nibbling on my neck, sometimes not... not gently, I mean. What I really plan on doing when we catch up to you is to get between the warring parties and appeal to sweet reason in both of you and arrange for you to give him his boat back with your apologies.

"But, Mike, they will hang you if you kill her," I said.

"Nah. They tried to hang me once for horse thievin' down in East Lick but it didn't take. Nope. I 'member it clear as day. The judge, he got up on his hind legs and hammered down with his little wood hammer and said, 'Mike Fink, you stand accused of stealing this man's horse and fer that I find you guilty! Guilty as hell, you thievin' rascal, since we found you a-ridin' on that very same horse and braggin' about it to boot!'

"Well, I couldn't deny that, so I tol' them to get on with it as I was a busy man. Then the little judge got up again and must've been consumed with his own eloquence, 'cause he said, 'Mike, there's gonna be a big card game tomorrow and all the local sports'll be there, a-sittin' at a big ol' table 'neath the big oak in the town square, and thar'll be piles o' money on the table and around that table will be the best gamblin' men in the country. But you ain't gonna be there, Mike Fink, 'cause tomorrow morning we're gonna take you out and hang yer sorry ass for the stealin' of this man's horse, and we're gonna hang it from that very same oak tree hangin' over that big card game. No, Mike, the cards'll be slappin' down but you'll never hear 'em 'cause yer dead butt'll be hanging over the game as a lesson to all those miscreants and yer soul'll be twangin' its harp up in Heaven or else be roasted by all the demons down in Hell, which we all find much more likely!'

"So they brung me out the next mornin' and done it,

sheriff and preacher and all, and they put me on a box, put the rope around my neck, and swung me off into eternity."

Mike paused to shake his head in wonder at the perfidy of the human race and then went on.

"Or so they thought. Y'see, the problem was that my neck muscles was too thick and strong, so I wouldn't choke t'death like they wanted. Oh, I gasped a bit and all, but nothin' serious, nothin' worse than a little ol' sore throat, the kind you get if'n you been drinkin' bad whiskey for a week or so. Anyways, after about ten minutes o' swingin' there, when ever'body was startin' to go home, tired of it all, I looked down and saw that the card table with all the sharpers was at my danglin' boot tips, and, damn, I couldn't let that go, so I begged for someone to come and take my boots and socks off, and who should come up but my good ol' girlfriend Sugartail Sophie, and it was she who pulled off my boots and socks, and bein' familiar with me and all, she didn't faint away when they come off, jest staggered a bit, is all. Good girl, she was."

Fink again stopped his narrative to make sure I'm rowing hard enough. Satisfied with our progress, he went on.

"So I played in that game with my toes four inches off the table. Had Sophie pull out the three quarters I had in my pocket so as to get in the game. Won the first hand o' Five Card Stud with two queens up and one in the hole and then won ever' hand—or, in my case, every foot—after that. Seven Card Stud, Low Ball, Texas Sweat, Razzle Dazzle Pass the Trash, didn't matter which game, ol' Mike Fink's luck was with him. I had Sugartail pull in the winnin's, but I handled the cards with me toes. Got so's I could deal pretty neat with them toes, too. Shuffle, even."

He took another deep breath and then concluded.

"Eventually I won all the money and most o' the real estate in that town. Told 'em I'd give 'em all their money back if'n they let me go and rename the town after me. And if'n they didn't, I was gonna give it all to Sugartail Sophie to set up the biggest whorehouse in the territory. Damned if they didn't agree. They cut me down and tol' me to get out of town and to never come back, which was all right with me 'cause I was sick and tired of their hard hospitality, anyways. I thanked Sophie for her help and lit out of Finktown fer good. Never been back there since, nope."

Mike Fink relaxed against the transom and said, "Tomorrow, we'll be there. Time to get some killin' done."

With that he closed his eyes and drifted off to sleep, leaving Clementine and me to navigate that last stretch on the Allegheny River.

What will tomorrow bring? I cannot help but shudder at the possibilities....

Chapter 25

This town calls itself the Gateway to the West, so I guess we ain't seen nothing yet in the way of real wilderness, though it sure seemed wild on the way down here. I have heard tales of the West and I worried some about that. River pirates and wild red Indians and all. I had also learned that much of Pittsburgh was made of the bricks from an old fort upriver that was torn down after it fell into disuse. It was named Fort Pitt and was used in what the locals call the French and Indian War, and so I resolved, first chance I get, to go exploring the warehouses and supply houses of this town to see what I might find in the way of discarded firepower.

My performances, both in the General Butler and elsewhere, have been going very well—I don't know whether it's the quality of the music and the entertainment, or the fact that there's so little of it out here that anything in that regard is welcome. I don't know, but I'll take it, either way. The tips have been most generous.

The barn dances that we've entertained at have been the most riotous affairs, fueled with high spirits and, of course, with the ever-present whiskey. The couples arrange themselves in squares, and "callers," men who call out instructions to the dancers in time to the music, sing out: "Swing your partner, bow to your corner, do-si-do, and promenade!" It is all good fun, and sometimes I wish someone else was playing the fiddle so I could join in the dance. There is much sparking going on among the young people, that's plain, and there's more than one good-looking lad.

On this particular morning, however, I put my mind back on the business of self-protection, and Higgins and I suit up and go off to scour the warehouses and supply houses that abound. That is the purpose, but it's also an excuse to sashay around in all my finery, nodding to them on the streets who recognize me, and, I must say, there are many. I can scarcely walk down the street without being recognized by my public. *I love it.*

Sure enough, we soon find a nice little three-inch swivel gun. That's a cannon mounted on a swivel so that it can be easily aimed. The three inches is the measurement across the barrel's mouth. We also buy a deadly looking four-inch cannon. These guns are small enough that they won't tear the deck of the *Belle* apart when they are fired, but they are large enough to be effective. We haggle over price and pick them up for a song, since to these people who are no longer at war, the cannons are only worth the brass that is in them. I order them brought to the *Belle*. They will shine up beautifully. I look forward to drilling my crew in gunnery.

I also buy powder and shot, a dozen cannonballs for each gun, and some bags of rock salt—I've no wish to kill anybody, and a tail full of rock salt can discourage even the most persistent of pests.

The hot work of munitions shopping done, we roll back up the street and into the General Butler and stick our noses in a couple of pints and pack in some lunch while I get a report from Molly. I had posted some hand-lettered notices about the docks, advertising the fact we were taking on passengers for a trip downriver and anyone interested could sign up at the General Butler.

"You got five passengers to Cincinnati. One man alone, a man and wife with two kids. All paid up. There's some more say they're goin' but need some time to scrape up the dollars."

"That's good, Molly, thanks."

"Oh, and a man named Cantrell wants to talk to you. Tol' him you'd be playin' tonight and he could talk to you then."

"All right."

"Looked like a real slick fella to me." Molly sniffs, with a bit of warning in her eye.

"Well, he'd best not try to flimflam an old Cheapside scammer like me." I laugh.

"And he's got a young black girl with him."

"What? Well, I won't have that," I say, firmly. "There is to be no slavery on my ship."

"Look, dearie, you can fluff up your feathers all you want, but if you're goin' all the way down to New Orleans, you're gonna have slave states on your left side all the way down, so you'd best get used to it."

"Well, I'll talk to him, anyway," I say and turn my full attention to the food in front of me, it being chops and gravy. "This is really good, Molly. You are some great cook."

Molly smiles, pleased, and wipes down the bar at which we are seated.

"Speakin' of that, Jacky, I recall you sayin' that you were lookin' for a cook for your ark?"

I nod. "Still am," I say around a mouthful of chop.

"Well, Crow Jane's in town and she's lookin' for work. She's good—can cook for five, can cook for fifty. Injun woman. Knows how to run a kitchen. Started off workin' for French trappers goin' up the Missouri, then she got onto the riverboats."

An Indian! I had seen some people that I thought might be Indians on my way here, but none definite, and none I could see up close.

"A very colorful name," I say, careful of my words, my mind conjuring up visions of painted faces and tomahawks.

"If you want, I'll send a boy to find her and tell her you want to talk. You gonna be back on your boat this afternoon?"

"Yes," I say. "And, yes, do send her by." I look at Higgins and shrug, and he shrugs back.

Quelling my usual urge to wipe my mouth on the back of my sleeve, I pull my handkerchief out of that selfsame sleeve and pat my lips.

"Come, Higgins, we must return to the *Belle*," I say, rising. "The guns will be delivered soon and I want to see them put in place. Cheers, Molly."

We are off.

The *Belle of the Golden West* is a hive of activity this afternoon.

The guns are brought aboard at one o'clock and we haul the four-inch cannon up forward and secure its carriage tightly down there, with the barrel sticking out over the bow. Katy will now have to straddle the gun if she wants to sit in her usual spot, but she says she doesn't mind, it's all the same to her.

We mount the swivel gun on the cabin roof, right in front of the quarterdeck. We make sure the apparatus holding the swiveling post that allows the gun to be aimed is anchored in good solid wood. Even though this is only a gun with a three-inch mouth, still, the recoil would be quite powerful.

When we get them in place, with the help of our carpenter, Mr. MacCauley, I stand back and admire them.

"Once again, Miss," says Higgins, with a certain dryness in his voice, "you stand in command of a warship. My congratulations, Captain."

"Thank you, Higgins," I say. "I know you are saying that with just a touch of sarcasm, but still, I like to hear it."

I set Jim to polishing the cannons and Katy to sewing up canvas covers for the armament—it's best that one's capabilities in that regard be kept from those who might be watching. Higgins takes off into the town to buy plates and other gear we will need for the feeding of passengers. The sign painter I had hired has arrived to paint *Belle of the Golden West* on either side of the cabin walls in big fancy gold and black letters. He sets up his buckets and brushes and gets right to work.

Having gotten some good maps and a set of dividers on one of my forays into the town, I spread out the maps on the quarterdeck cabin top and start figuring out distances so as to be able to charge the proper fares. The day is calm with no wind, so the maps do not blow around, and the sun is warm on my back. *All is good*, I reflect, taking a satisfied breath and then bending to my task.

"Miss Faber, I presume," I hear from the dock, and look up to see a very well-dressed man taking off his hat and bowing to me. Instinctively, now, I drop into a bit of a curtsy, then rise to look at him. He is dressed in black from bottom to top. Black trousers, black coat pulled back to reveal a black vest. His hair, which he wears cut short and not tied back, is wavy and black, except for gray at his temples. His hat, which he now puts back on his head, is curled in the brim, high in the crown, and black. The only spot of color is his red cravat, which is worn instead of lace, at his neck. I put his age at about forty-five, fifty, or so. I also put on the Lawson Peabody Look—back straight, chin up, lips together, teeth apart, and eyes hooded.

"Yes?"

"My name is Mr. Yancy Beauregard Cantrell, and I am bound for New Orleans." He smiles, and I see that, unlike many around here, his teeth are white and even. Except for a neatly trimmed mustache, he is clean shaven, which is also a rarity around here. All in all, he is a very handsome man.

"That is good, Mr. Cantrell, as I plan to journey there myself, on my boat."

"Alas, Miss Faber, I have only enough fare to travel halfway to Cincinnati, but I assure you, in all confidence, that I will gain the rest of the fare as we travel on. If I do not, then you shall be free to put us off wherever you choose. Agreed?"

I do not yet agree. I see some telltale bulges under his jacket and comment upon it.

"All guns are checked at the gangway, Mr. Cantrell, and believe me, you will be checked," I say, in warning.

"That is a very wise rule, Miss Faber," he replies, bowing again, apparently to my wisdom. He broadens the smile.

"What do you mean by 'us'?" I ask, suspicious. I have seen the Colored girl hanging back behind him.

"I have my girl, Chloe, here with me. She will be no trouble."

"I'll have no slaves on my ship, Mr. Cantrell."

"She is not my slave. She is my servant, and she is free to go at any time." He reaches back and brings the girl forward. She is clad in a dingy white shift, her slightly maturing figure evident through the thin cloth. From the bottom of her shapeless dress extend possibly the longest legs I have ever seen on any human around the age of sixteen, which age I suspect she is. Her hair is tied up in small braids, and on her face she wears an expression of the purest indifference.

"You agree with what was just said, girl?" I demand.

The girl nods, not looking me in the eye.

"She is mute, Miss Faber. That is all the answer you shall get from her, I'm afraid."

I think on all this, and I decide.

"Give me your hand on it, Mr. Cantrell," I say, as I walk to the gangway and extend mine. I feel the touch of his palm and know that his hand has never felt labor of any kind. He squeezes my hand and then raises it to his lips.

"Thank you, Miss Faber. I do not think you will regret your decision."

"I hope I shall not, Mr. Cantrell," I reply, withdrawing my hand and looking at him with my level gaze.

"And now, Miss Faber, I would like to move aboard, as I would rather give what money I have to you, rather than to some inn. Is that agreeable?"

We are more than a few days from departure, but what could it hurt?

"That will be acceptable, Sir. However, you shall have to take your dinners onshore, as we have not yet set up our kitchen," I explain.

"That will be just fine, Miss Faber," answers Mr. Cantrell. "I will take my leave now to go collect our luggage." With that, he bows again and turns to leave, walking back up the dock, the long-legged black girl loping in his wake.

Well, I think, and turn back to my task. According to my calculations with my dividers, Cincinnati is about four hundred and seventy-five miles downstream, so at twelve cents a mile, that works out to fifty-seven dollars, more or less, which seems fair, considering the fact that we are providing both food and entertainment. So that means that passage to Cairo in Illinois Territory will cost—

"Faber?"

Hearing this, I lift my head and look to the dock. Standing there is a woman, about five feet tall and three feet wide, a solid woman built like a door. She is dressed in a skirt of what I take to be leather, a fringed shirt of the same, and a red headband around her brow. Her hair is black, with streaks of white, and it is braided into two pigtails that are bound with bright ribbons. In her hands she holds the hilts of at least three knives and several pans.

"You must be Crow Jane," I say, somewhat taken aback at her appearance.

"Yep. Cook. Lookin' fer work. You the boss?"

"Yes, I suppose I am."

"Whatcha got?"

"Well..."

"Lemme look at yer fire," she says, and with that she steps aboard, her saucepans clanking about her. She heads for the hatchway down into the hold. I meekly follow her.

She rattles around the stove, opening doors and lifting lids. She checks out the wood stacked next to it, picking up a piece and holding it to her cheek. She nods in apparent approval and then examines the sleeping quarters.

"All right. What pay?"

"Uh...," I stammer, "...a dollar a day, room and board. A cut of any prizes." That last part sort of slipped out.

She turns to look at me, with black eyes 'neath lowered black brows. "Prizes? I ain't heard of *prizes* before."

"Prizes are anything we can take...steal, like," I say, lamely.

She gives a grunt of a laugh. "All right, then." She puts her pans on the stove and throws a sack I had not noticed before on the bunk that was to be hers. Her knives go into a slot on the side of the stove. Then she looks at me, sizing me up, I suspect. "Whatcha got fer crew?"

"Well, we have two girls, me being one of them, one young lad, and one big man," I say.

"You'll need more. At least two strong men. You got the Rapids of the Ohio to get through. Cave-in-Rock, too. More stuff after that. Where's yer supplies—flour and lard and such?"

"Down here below," I say, showing her the entrance to the lower hold. "Do you know of any that might serve?"

"Might. The Hawkes boys are both in the jailhouse. Due to get out tomorrow. Nathaniel and Matthew Hawkes.

They're good boys if you can keep 'em away from strong likker and wild women. Good boatmen, too. Grew up on the river. If you want 'em, best pick 'em up right from the jailhouse and bring 'em here. Don't give 'em no money or they'll just get in trouble ag'in. I'll go with you when you pick 'em up. They'll mind me."

What could I say to that? I now have a cook and some additional crew. I hope I have done right.

But now I must put all that out of my mind. I must finish up my distance figuring, compose an advertising poster for the *Belle*, and then take it up to the printer on Market Street. When I return, I need to get ready for tonight's show.

That night, during the second show, all was going really well, when, in the midst of me doing "Billy Broke Locks," there was the sound of a tremendous fight going on down the street. There were shouts and gunfire going off, and in the midst of it all, there was an oddly familiar roar that I could not quite place. Higgins went to the door to see what was up. He was gone for a short while, and when he returned, he reported, "It was a big riot going on down at the White Horse. The sheriff and his crew arrived and are beating men to the ground with truncheons. It seems to be ending. Even as we speak, men are being dragged off to jail."

"None of our concern, mates!" I crow. "Stay here and be gay, for there's nothing but trouble down there, and nothing but good fun here!"

And so they stayed and so we played, far, far into the night.

Chapter 26

Jaimy Fletcher
At Pittsburgh, Pennsylvania, USA

Jacky,

We got into Pittsburgh in the early evening and I suggested to Mike that we might put up for the night along the wooded shore and resume our search in the full light of day, the better to give me some time to work things out between you two, but he would have none of it.

"No, b'God! Mike Fink don't wait when there's killin' to be done! Nope, he gets right down to it and sends them souls directly to Heaven or Hell, dependin' on their inclinations, and I suspects that Jacky Goddamn Faber is goin' to the lower regions 'cause God don't put up with people who steal other people's boats. No, he don't," said Fink with great resolution and firmness of purpose in his voice. "Hey!" He sat up straight and pointed off to port. "That looks like my boat! Pull over there!"

With Clementine steaming behind me, I rowed in that direction.

Clementine has been steaming a lot, ever since she found out that not only are you not a boy, but, worse yet, my betrothed.

"That mean you gonna marry her, Jaimy?" she asked last night when we finally camped onshore, her hot eyes brimming with tears.

"I don't know what anything means anymore, Clementine," I answered wearily, "but I meant what I said: I won't leave you."

"What you gonna do, keep me in a shed out back of yer place when you marries her? Is that what you mean to do, Jaimy?"

"No, I don't. Now come over here and give me a kiss, and hush, now. Hush."

"Do you love me, Jaimy?"

I took a breath, held it, and then exhaled.

"Yes, I do, Clementine."

She waited a moment and then came over and lay next to me and put her hot, tearful face next to mine.

"I was so happy then, Jaimy, before...when it was just you and me on the road." She snuffled. "So happy..."

"Now, now. You'll be happy again, Clementine," I said. "I promise."

"It shore looks like my boat, but what are them lumpy things on deck? And what does that say on the side?" asked Fink, squinting in the gloom.

"It says 'Belle of the Golden West,' and I don't know what those things are," I said, trying to figure a way to divert his attention. It was his boat, all right, and I knew damned well what those canvas-covered things were: They were guns. I reflected that it did not take long for *La Belle Jeune Fille sans Merci* to commandeer a ship and rearm herself. "Let's put in there and then go check out the taverns. That's where she's most likely to be, night falling as it is."

"All right," growled Fink. "I could use a drink, anyhow. Do it."

I steered toward a landing, breathing a small sigh of relief as we hit the shore. If he had gone directly to the boat, all hell would have broken loose. I had recognized Jim Tanner standing guard on the deck of that boat. There's no mistake. *You are somewhere in this town, Jacky.*

Mike jumped out of the boat and headed toward the lights of the town, which were just now being lit.

I jumped out after him and said to Clementine, "You stay here and watch our stuff. Give me the pistol."

She handed it to me and said, "Oh, Jaimy, stay here with me! She ain't worth it, please, Jaimy..."

"Now, Clementine, I will be careful. You'll see."

And with that I scrambled after Fink, who was heading full tilt for the nearest tavern.

"Mike, wait!" I panted as I caught up with him. For a huge man, he can certainly move fast. I looked up and found we were at the entrance of the White Horse Tavern. From up the street, at another tavern, I heard applause and then a female voice say, "Thank you, thank you, you are all too kind. I would like to sing you now a song from the days of your glorious revolution, 'Billy Broke Locks.'" I knew in an instant it was you, and it was all I could do to keep myself from bolting up the street. But what I thought was good sense prevailed: I couldn't let Mike Fink at you just yet.

"Let's ask in here," I said to Mike, and shoved him in the door of the White Horse Tavern.

It was dark and smoky and smelled strongly of every bit of spilled beer or whiskey that ever soaked into the floor, but not smoky enough to keep us hidden from view. As soon as we stepped in, someone said, "Christ, it's Fink!"

"Goddamn right, it's Fink," roared Mike. "Now give him a drink a-fore he kicks some serious ass!"

"You got any money, Mike?" asked the landlord, fixing a suspicious eye on my companion.

"Hell, yes, I got money," said Mike, sticking out his lower lip. "So set 'em up!"

"Wal, then, Mike," said the landlord, "mebbe you kin pay me back for the damage you done last time you was in my place, drunker'n a skunk!"

Mike was outraged.

"HOLD ME BACK! HOLD ME BACK! I'M A RING-TAILED ROARER AND ABOUT TO DO SOME DAMAGE! OOOOOWEEEEE! I'M A-GONNA CUT EVER'ONE IN THIS PLACE A NEW—"

"You ain't gonna cut nothin', Mike," said a voice from the shadows. Into the light steps the hugest man I have ever seen. "'Cause I'm a-gonna toss yer dried-up carcass outta here, right now."

Mike Fink reared back and fixed his eye on this newcomer to the discussion.

"Wal, wal," he said, nodding his head in appreciation of the new situation here. "If it ain't Man Mountain Murphy, the biggest, stupidest, and ugliest man on the frontier. Heard you had a new job, Murphy—"

"Wha's that?" rumbled this mountain of a man.

"Standin' out in front of a doctor's office, makin' people

sick." Mike chortled. "Ha! I heard that ugly sits on you like stink on—"

"And I heard," said Man Mountain Murphy in a curiously high, piping voice, "that some little slip of a girl done stole Mikey Fink's boat. Tha's what I heard."

That did it.

Mike brought back his right fist and slammed it straight into Murphy's jaw. Murphy rocked back on his heels, but recovered quickly and grabbed Mike in a great bear hug, and together they staggered to the door and out into the street, the riotous crowd within following the fracas and egging on the participants.

I, too, went back out into the street, but not to enjoy the spectacle, oh, no—I was thinking this was an excellent time to race up the street, whilst Mike was otherwise engaged, burst into the tavern in which you were playing, be joyously reunited, tell you of Mike Fink's murderous intentions, and then light the hell out.

Such was not to be. As the main combatants fell to wrestling on the ground, other members of the audience chose sides and tempers flared. It seemed that Mike was not without friends in this port, and other fights erupted. I heard whistles blown and curses shouted and knew it would not be long before the police arrived. As I slunk away from the action, a hand fell on my shoulder and I was turned around.

"Friend of that Fink, ain't-cha, farm boy," said a grizzled old cove, and a fist exploded on the side of my jaw. I was dazed and confused. I tried to lift my fists to strike back, but I found I could not. "You like that, boy? Well, here's some more."

I was slammed on the other side of my jaw and I went to my knees, in shock. Then the man who was beating me was hauled back, and I dimly perceived a policeman telling me to get down on the ground, and then when I did not understand what he was saying, he brought his club around and struck me on the back of my head.

My last conscious memory that night was of Clementine shouting, "No! No! Git off him! Leave him alone! Git off my man!"

Chapter 27

Notice

All Persons Desirous of Waterborne Transport to
Louisville, Cincinnati, St. Louis, and Beyond
A Voyage to those Places will be Undertaken by

Belle of the Golden West

A Finely Fitted-out River Cruiser
which will be Departing Shortly
Possessing all of the Amenities including
Fine Wines, Spirits, and Tobacco.
Breakfast, Dinner, and Supper will be
Available for your Pleasure.

Entertainment Nightly

The Fare Being 12 cents a Mile Traveled:
Louisville $38
Cincinnati $57
St. Louis $93
New Orleans $234

The Belle of the Golden West can be viewed at the Publick Dock, and Reservations can be made at the Sign of the General Butler. Measures have been taken to ensure Passenger Safety when under way.

"Now, ain't that fine, Higgins?" I say, holding up one of my new posters. It's morning and they have just been delivered. I am again dressed in my finest clothes, since I will be going to the jail to bail out two miscreants. I want to look my best, responsible citizen and all, so it's the riding habit again. If fortune smiles on me in the future, I mean to get some new clothes. Maybe in New Orleans, as they are sure to have the latest fashions.

"Yes, Miss," says Higgins, pouring the morning tea. "And in the best of taste, too, echoing the refinement of the name of this vessel, painted on its sides. I am especially fond of the curlicues on each of the letters. Serifs, I believe they are called."

I almost snort some tea through my nose. "Now, Higgins, this is not London and we must do as the Romans do. We must not be shy, if we mean to make money." I settle back in my chair. We have got a small table and four chairs, and they are set up on the cabin top when the weather is good, which it is today. "You've met Crow Jane?"

"Yes, actually. We went over our stores yesterday and she was quite useful in pointing out what we lacked. Strange things, like buckwheat, and sourdough starter, beef jerky, and sorghum molasses. She seems to know what she is doing. I gave her some money to go off to buy what we needed."

"I have told her that you are second-in-command of this

ship, and that she is to take an order from you the same as if it came from me." I put a slice of buttered toast to the teeth.

"Ah, yes. First Mate on a riverboat on a river in the trackless American wilderness, hip to hip with a red Indian sous-chef. Surely every British butler's dream," replies Higgins, absolutely deadpan.

"Higgins, you kill me," I chortle. "You really do."

"And now you've gone and made a bit of a mess. Here, let me tidy you up."

Higgins applies the napkin to the jelly smears on my face, and then I return to my breakfast.

"*Mmm.* Good toast. And what is this?"

"Elderberry jelly, locally made. You will find it quite good, I think. And yes, the bread was made by Crow Jane. She was up early and had the stove going nicely."

A head appears at the passenger hatchway up forward. I see who it is and say to myself, *Why not?*

"Mr. Cantrell. Will you come share tea and toast with me?"

He looks over at me, at my table, removes the hat he had just put on, and says, "That is very kind of you. I will be happy to join you."

He comes up on the cabin top, and Higgins pulls out a chair for him, and he sits down, brushing back the tails of his coat.

"Lovely day, Miss," he says.

Higgins brings another place setting and I pointedly glance down at the Colored girl, who has also come up on deck to sit next to the railing and look out over the water. Higgins nods and goes below.

Higgins reappears, with another cup for Mr. Cantrell, which he fills from the teapot that sits on the table. He has also brought up two baskets of buttered toast, one of which he places on my table and the other of which he places in front of the girl. She looks up, suspicious, but she puts her hand in anyway and takes a slice and eats it.

"Yes, Mr. Cantrell, it is a most lovely day."

We spend breakfast in learning about each other's origins, him being from New York City and me being from Boston, which is as far as I am willing to go in revealing my past. It is most enjoyable, as he is a very amusing and well-spoken guest. Eventually, though, Crow Jane comes up with a stick in her hand and announces that it is time to go get the Hawkes boys out of jail, and I rise and bid him adieu.

As we approach the jail, or calaboose, as Crow Jane would have it, I ask her why people call her Crow Jane.

"Well, y'see, Boss, there's a tribe o' Indians out West called Crows, and a lot of folks think I'm Crow. But I ain't. I'm Shoshone, from up in the high parts of the Snake River. Early on, got me a taste for French trappers, whiskey, and tobaccy, so here I be. Got two sons, François and Jacques, trappin' up on the Missouri, and a daughter married to a trapper named Baptiste who runs the trading post on the Platte. Got some grandbabies by them, too."

We walk on a bit, and then she says, "Could be 'cause I had a tame crow onc't. Named Henri. Had his tongue split so he could say some words. Nobody could understand him but me, but they was words, I know. Died last year. Miss him. Jail's right here, Boss."

Boss Faber looks up at the edifice. It's made of brick and stone, and I'd hate to have to break out of this one, accomplished jailbreaker though I might be.

"The way in is on the other side," says Crow Jane, starting in that direction. I go to follow when I hear a familiar bellow.

"*Goddamn! It's her! Right there! The one what stole my boat!*"

I freeze for a second—*Good God, it's Fink!*—then I whip out my shiv and get into a crouch, expecting attack from any side.

But it does not come. Carefully I look around, and then I look up. There I see a very small, barred window about six feet up the side of the wall, and filling the entire window is the enraged face of Mike Fink.

When I see that Mr. Fink is safely confined, I replace my knife in my arm sheath and turn to talk to him.

"Good day to you, Mr. Fink!" I chirp, and drop down into a full curtsy. "How good to see your cheerful countenance again."

He manages to get an arm through the bars and seems to be reaching for my throat. I step forward and keep that throat about two inches beyond his grasp.

What he says is not coherent, but it seems to dwell mainly on a fervent wish for my imminent death by strangling.

"I am so glad you survived your fall into the river, Mr. Fink. We looked for you, you know, but as we were inexperienced, we were swept down the river. I ask you, what could we do?"

Fink gains his voice.

"What can ye do? You can bail us out of here and give me back my boat!"

"Ah, Mr. Fink, I have here next to my heart a Bill of Sale for that boat, signed by you," I reply. "Do you see your signature there? Do you deny that it is yours?"

"I'll kill you! I'll kill you! I'll kill you! Kill you, kill you, kill, kill, kill—"

"And just how long is your sentence, Mr. Fink? Twenty days? Ah, that is a very convenient time, Mr. Fink. I'm afraid I have no connection to the local law, and I and the *Belle of the Golden West* will be long gone before you get out. But don't despair. You may reclaim your boat in New Orleans, as I shall be done with it then. I shall leave it in good condition, better condition than when I found it. I am not greedy. I will name you a fair price for it."

I know it is evil to taunt him, but it is so much fun. Fink rages and tries to rip out the bars, but it is all to no avail. I think I hear someone else within the jail calling out, too. I think I heard my name shouted, but that's probably 'cause I'm getting so well-known around here.

"Well, Mr. Fink, this has been a most enjoyable conversation, but I must take my leave now, as business calls. My ship needs further outfitting before we embark for points south. Adieu, Mr. Fink. I do hope you'll enjoy your stay as a guest of this fair city," I say as I give him a slight curtsy while turning to leave.

"Wait a minute," Fink says in a more or less normal voice. I stop and wait. "There's a little girl, prolly sittin' by the front door of this here jail. She's got no one to watch out fer her, 'cause her man's in here with me. He's only got ten days while I got twenty. If you could do sumthin' fer her, I'd take it kindly. He would, too."

"Why, Mr. Fink," I exclaim, pleased. "That's the most decent thing I have ever heard you say. I shall see what I can do. Good-bye, Mr. Fink." I give him a little finger wave and my brightest smile.

"I'll be seein' you again, girly-girl, when you least expect it, but you'll know it's me who's killin' you, I'll make sure o' that," replies Fink, back to his old mean self. "And you know somethin' else? I know a secret thing that you don't know and I ain't gonna tell you what it is."

"To make rabbit stew, you must first catch the rabbit, Mr. Fink," I answer, all smug. "And I don't think I need to know your secret. Cheerio, Mr. Fink. I don't think we'll be meeting again."

I leave Mike Fink banging his head against the bars and go around the corner with Crow Jane to claim the Hawkes boys. I wonder, but not too much, about what secret he had to tell. I was glad to learn of Fink's being in jail, though— I was kinda worried he might catch up to us and cause trouble. And now he can't, for twenty days gives us too big a lead for him to catch up with us. Yes, this works out just fine.

Crow Jane chuckles. "Ol' Mike Fink, brought down by a girl. Wait'll the river hears about this. *Yiyiyiyi, wah-toh-pah!*"

I don't know what it means, but I can guess.

At the entrance to the jail is a bench and on the bench sits a girl. She is a little rag of a thing, with lank, strawlike hair, crudely cut across at the eyes, which are a washed-out blue. She is freckled all over her face and shoulders and even on her bare arms. A rag, too, is the old faded yellow dress she wears, its torn hem barely reaching to her bony knees. I suspect she has owned that dress a very long time, probably from when the hem came down to her ankles. She wears a white apron over the dress. Her nose is red, from crying probably, hands red from work are twisting in her lap, and her feet look like they probably never saw shoes. A fuzz of fine white hair grows on her lower legs. She's pretty clean, though, considering. At least there's no caked dirt between her toes.

"My name is Jacky Faber," I begin. "What is your name and how old are you?"

At the mention of my name, the girl jerks as if she has been touched with a hot poker. She glances up at me with a look of pure hatred, locking eyes with me.

"M-m-my name is Missus Clementine Fletcher. I am fourteen, if that is any bidness o' yours, which it ain't."

Well. This is a tough one.

"That's young to be married," I say.

"It's old enuff." She lowers her eyes and looks to the side.

"Boss, I'm goin' in t' get the Hawkes boys," says Crow Jane. "They'll need someone to vouch for 'em, say they got a job and all, or the sheriff'll jus' arrest 'em again for bein' vay-grunts."

"Good. Thanks, Jane," I say, and turn my attention again to Mrs. Fletcher. "I, too, have a boy named Fletcher, Jaimy Fletcher, and I hope to be his wife someday, but he lies far over the sea. Count yourself lucky to have your man out in twenty days. I would gladly trade places with you."

"Jes' bet you would."

"What does that mean?" *This is one strange girl,* I'm thinking.

"Nothin'. Go away."

Hmmmm.

"I told Mike Fink I'd see what I could do for you, but I'll be damned if I'll pay for your lodging, or put up with your lip. Get up. You can stay on my boat and work for your keep till we leave, or you can go to Hell, for all I care."

"All right. I'll go to Hell. Now just go away and leave me alone."

"What are you going to do for all that time? Just sit there?"

"Yup. If'n I have to."

I have to admire her loyalty, if not her intelligence. Why does she hate me so? Could it be my fine clothes while she sits in rags? Could it be that she's heard of my singing and dancing and doesn't approve 'cause that sort of thing's against her religion? I've found that there's lots of crazy cults that call themselves Christian in this country, that's for sure.

"Come along with me or you'll be arrested for vagrancy," I snarl. I am growing irritated. I am not used to having my charity spurned.

Just then Crow Jane comes out the jailhouse door behind two long and lanky young men who are protesting violently the fact that she's switching them unmercifully from behind.

"Crow Jane, now, you stop that! Yow!" begs the blonder of the two brothers. Both are clad in boatman's gear of canvas pants held up by a rope, loose white shirt, boots, and the boatman's black hat. Their unruly hair hangs loose and unbound to their shoulders. Each could use a shave and, from the smell of 'em drifting over to my nose, a bath.

"I'll stop, Matthew Hawkes, when you two polecats stop actin' like fools, drinkin' rotten whiskey, and chasin' *squa* ever' chancst y'git when y'got some jingle in yer pants," says Crow Jane, driving them relentlessly on till they stand in front of me. "This here's yer new boss lady. Take off yer hats. Ain't-cha got no manners?"

"A girl is our new boss, Crow Jane? Now that cain't be right," says the darker of the two. His hair grows back from a high forehead and he affects a pointy little chin beard. For his impertinence he receives another switch from Jane's rod. "All right, all right!" he cries. "She's our new boss!"

"Damn right, 'Thaniel Hawkes," says Jane.

The Hawkes boys take off their hats and hold them to their chests. "Pleased to meet-cha, Ma'am," they say in unison, exposing their teeth in what I'm sure they take to be winning smiles.

"Mutual, Messrs. Hawkes," says I. "I hope you will turn out to be good men. Now let us return to the ship and acquaint you with your duties. Clementine, come along."

The girl does not move.

"You want this *ikouessens* on the boat?" asks Crow Jane. "Then, here." And with that she reaches down and grabs Missus Clementine Fletcher's left ear and hauls her to her feet, howling in pain.

"Wait, wait!" cries the girl. "I'll go with you!"

"Thought you might," says Crow Jane, releasing her ear, which now glows a bright red from the pinch.

"Got our rowboat over there. Got our stuff in it," she says, rubbing her ear.

"Matty," says Crow Jane, and nods in that direction, "we're on the next dock over. The boat with all the fancy stuff on the sides."

Matty Hawkes, glad to get out of range of Jane's switch, lopes over to the rowboat.

It's plain who is the Captain of the *Belle,* and also who is First Mate. It's now also plain who is the Bo'sun.

"I'm glad you decided to do the smart thing, girl," I say to the sullen Clementine.

In all her sullenness I think I see a new look of cunning come over her face.

"I will come along with you, Miss Jacky Faber, oh, yes, I will," she whispers low. "It is the right thing to do, I see that now."

Could it be that I see a warning of danger in her hot blue eyes?

Chapter 28

Jaimy Fletcher
In the Pittsburgh Jail
Pittsburgh, Pennsylvania
In the Goddamned United States of America

Jacky,

I have been chained ankle to ankle with Mike Fink and various other lowlifes in this stinking jail cell since our arrest last night outside the White Horse Tavern. I have been massaging my swollen jaw and amusing myself by thinking up variations on USA. How about Ubiquitous Swine devoted to Anarchy? No? Then how's this: Unwashed Savages of Abysmal ignorance? I find myself longing for a civilized drawing room in London. Perhaps a soiree or a grand banquet, or at the Captain's table on a first-rate ship of the Line of Battle just before some Glorious Action? I, who have sat at the same table as Lord Nelson, himself, now sit on a cold stone floor in a squalid prison, shackled to . . . no, wait . . . squalid's a good word . . . let's see . . . Unabashedly Squalid and Asinine. That's a good one.

Or, as my present companions would say, "Tha's a good 'un, har-har, lesh haf another."

Oh, Jacky, how I languish in this land that you seem to thrive in.

Mike was standing up at the window, yelling at someone outside a little while ago, and it took my battered mind a while to realize that it was you he was addressing, and by then it was too late. *Always too late,* I moaned to myself. You, right outside this wall…*Damn, my head hurts!* I vow vengeance on yet another bloody bastard who has brought pain and anguish to me. That grizzled cove who last night caught me unawares, he shall pay, too, count on it. I have been making plans for what I shall do upon my release.

Earlier in the day, we were taken to court, Justice of the Peace Judge Otto Stottlemeyer sitting in judgement. It was my considered opinion, upon viewing this court, that this judge was only half literate and, similarly, only half sober—there being a glass of whiskey, which was constantly replenished, at his elbow during the entire proceedings.

The first cases were disposed of quickly—drunkenness, ten days on the work gang; fighting, twenty days; petty theft, ninety days; horse stealing, remanded for trial; and so on. I would have found the proceedings intensely boring if not for the fact that I was to be very similarly judged. That, and the judgement of a prisoner who came up just before us.

"Amos Beatty, you are charged with possession of stolen property, that bein' this man's saddle and bags. How do you plead?"

"Not guilty!" shouted this Beatty.

"Wha've you got to say, Mr. McWhirtle?"

McWhirtle stood and said, "I saw him take 'em off me horse, plain as day. Woulda stole the horse, too, if'n I didn't come upon him."

"Guilty!" said the Judge. "Guilty as hell! Fifteen days on the road gang for you, and give the man back his goddamn saddle. Next case!" Down came the gavel, and Mr. Amos Beatty was led away to serve his time. I smiled to myself... Mr. Amos Beatty, one of the two highwaymen who laid me low and left me for dead on that fateful day. *Well, well,* I thought, with some satisfaction, *sometimes Fate is, indeed, kind.*

Mike and I were up next.

We were stood up in our shackles while the Judge read out the indictment, there being no Clerk of Courts as far as I could see. Or any other court official, aside from the sheriff and his very burly deputies.

"Mike Fink, who is well known to this court, and uh...a Mr. James Fletcher, are each accused of Being a Public Nuisance," pronounced Judge Stottlemeyer. "What do you have to say for yourself, Mike?"

"Jeez, Judge, we just went in to the White Horse to have a drink and that little weasel of a landlord sicced Man Mountain Murphy on me for no good reason. 'Course I had to break his jaw; wouldn't you do the same thing?" asked Mike, the voice of sweet reason.

I looked over to see the wounded Mr. Murphy in the witness area, a very large man, to be sure, taking up two seats and looking very mountainous, and very aggrieved, as well. His jaw is bandaged and, I am sure, missing more than a few teeth. He shaked his massive head in denial.

"Guilty!" said the Judge, slamming down his gavel. "If you ain't guilty of this, you polecat, yer guilty of somethin' else twice as bad. Twenty days on the road gang and not a minute less! Next!"

Mike took a great deep breath and opened his mouth and I knew that he was going to go into one of his fits of braggadocio, and he barely got out a *"whoooeee"* before I rammed my elbow into his gut, cutting off both his air supply and the coming rant. He doubled over and coughed but said nothing further.

"Now for you, James Fletcher, how do you plead?" said the Judge.

I like to think that my sense of self-preservation never leaves me, especially in times of great stress or pressing danger, but at this moment, I started, unaccountably, to laugh. And to laugh uncontrollably. Me, Lieutenant James Emerson Fletcher, of His Majesty's Royal Navy, Decorated Veteran of the Battle of Trafalgar, charged with Being a Public Nuisance by these barbarians in this barbaric land, and this barely literate so-called judge about to pass sentence upon me! A Public Nuisance! It and the events of the past few weeks were all too much. I laughed out loud and I could not stop.

"I plead insanity, Your Honor," I crowed out. "Absolute and complete insanity! Ha-ha!"

"See if you find this funny, boy!" spit out the Judge. "Five dollars or five days, hard labor!"

Mike stepped on my foot to stop me from laughing. "This boy didn't have nothin' to do with the fight, Judge," said Fink, rather gallantly I thought, and I fought to bring myself under control.

"Your Honor," I managed to say without much giggling, "I am Lieutenant James Fletcher, an officer in His Majesty's Royal Naval Service, and I…"

I noticed that the place suddenly went dead silent. The Judge leaned over his desk.

"You mean you're a British officer, like the ones who've been runnin' around here tryin' to get the Injuns riled up ag'inst our settlers?" he asked, his unforgiving eye on me.

"No, Sir, of course, I—"

"I am sorry, I misspoke, Lieutenant Fletcher," said he. "Make that *ten* dollars or *ten* days at hard labor! Court's adjourned! Get 'em outta here!"

We were taken out, stripped of our clothing, hosed down with cold water, treated with delousing solutions to our heads and nether parts, and then thrown into our cells. We were given crude trousers and shirts, all imprinted with broad black and white stripes, and were told we would be working to build up the seawall on the southward side of the Ohio River come dawn tomorrow.

At night, the one window of the jail becomes a place for those connected to the inmates to come to talk and to lend support to those within, and to tell of news of family and friends. There are wives and sisters and brothers and friends, and in some cases, there are sweethearts who profess profound feelings of longing and of love.

Clementine, however, does not appear when it is my turn at the window, and a worm of worry begins to work itself into the mind of one poor prisoner.…

Chapter 29

"You're gonna sweeten up, Clementine, if you're gonna stay with us for a week, and I mean that, girl," I snarl, pointing my finger between the girl's sullen eyes when we get back to the *Belle* on this, her first day aboard. "Your job will be Cook's Assistant. You will take orders from Crow Jane, Mr. Higgins, and me. You will wash dishes, scrub floors, do laundry, and anything else you are asked to do in return for your keep. You will also be paid some money so that you'll have a little when your husband gets out, and maybe it will help you on your way. Is that clear?"

The girl nods, without expression. She stands there with a sack that holds what little she owns. It sounds like it contains a few pots, muffled like maybe they are wrapped in a blanket. There was a long old-fashioned rifle in the rowboat, too, but that we put away, as per the ship's rule about checking firearms before boarding. "What you want me to do now?"

"Stow your stuff down in the after cabin," I say, jerking my thumb back in the direction of our sleeping quarters. "That's where you'll be sleeping. Then report to Crow Jane. She'll tell you what to do. If she ain't got nothin' for you, then report back to me. This deck back here needs scrubbin'."

She nods again, and then goes to do it.

"Sure wish I had some holystone, Higgins," I say, looking down at the deck, which could surely use that kind of scouring.

"I shall check for availability, Miss," says Higgins, who had observed this last exchange, "but I fear I shall not have much luck. Very few Royal Navy ships dock here in this place."

"There is one here now, Higgins," say I, proudly. "HMS *Belle of the Golden West,* manned and ready for sea. Or river. Or creek. Or puddle. Or whatever comes."

"The girl?" inquires Higgins with one of his raised-eyebrow questions.

"A country girl. Says she's married to one of the men inside the jail. Mike Fink asked me to look out for her till the man's release, which'll be a few days after we leave. I said I'd do it."

"How very commendable of you, Miss. I knew there was a tender heart beating 'neath that cold, hard captain's chest of yours."

I cast my stern eye on him. "You are, of course, referring to how I have been treating this girl, Higgins, and think less of me for it?"

"*Um.*"

"Well, Higgins, when dealing with those whom you will command, you may start off harsh, and then later go softer as everyone finds their place and knows how things go, but," I say with teacher's finger in the air, "you can't do it the other way around."

"I suppose that's wise, Miss," he says.

"You, however," I say, "may be nicer to her. After she is

208

done with her chores, draw her a bath, if you would be so good. Back in our quarters. She is likely to be shy with you, so ask Katy to scrub her head and check her for lice. Is there anything you can do with that straw thatch of hers?"

"Well, after Katy washes it up, we'll see what we can do."

"Good. For now we must deal with our two new recruits. Remember what I said about starting out hard? Well, I think it truly applies to these two louts."

We both look forward and see the Hawkes boys lounging about the bow, smoking vile-smelling pipes and talking, talk that is punctuated with snorts and guffaws. They are facing away and cannot hear us approach.

"Garsh, Matty! Three girls aboard and all of 'em purty. Four, you count Crow Jane! Hot damn! This is gonna be the best job ever!"

"Well, I ain't that hard up, to count that Crow Jane," says brother Matthew, "but I gotta agree. You see the ass on the boss lady? She be skinny and meaner'n a snake, but that tail's still nice and round and fine," says he, describing a shape with his hands.

"Wouldn't kick it outta my bed, me neither, no sir, hot damn! This is the best boat we ever been on, Brother," says 'Thaniel. *"Geeeeeeez, we done died and gone to Heaven!"*

"That Katy girl, now she some long and tall, but that don't mean she ain't pretty, oh, no. Lord."

"And that little Clementine, Matty," added 'Thaniel, "if'n she ain't cuter'n a speckled pup, I don't know what is."

"Seems like these men need some cooling down," say I, loud and clear, "before Katy Deere puts a couple of arrows deep into their ardor, or I have them thrown in the river with some heavy chain around their necks."

The boys' heads jerk around, startled to find me standing there in a state of high indignation.

"Sorry, Boss, we didn't know you was listening," says Matthew, trying to stop his giggling but failing in the attempt.

"You two were supposed to be rigging the new oarlocks. Why are you not doing that?" I ask, with my stony Look firmly in place. "And stand up when I'm talking to you."

"Now, Boss, we're jest waitin' for the parts. That boy Jim went to get 'em. Here he comes now," says Nathaniel, getting to his feet and beginning to look a little worried.

"Never thought I'd ever say this, Mr. Higgins, but this ship just might need a cat-o'-nine-tails."

"Indeed, Captain," says Higgins. "One can easily be made."

"We'll get right on it, Boss...er...Captain, right now," says Nathaniel, putting an elbow in his brother's ribs.

Jim Tanner comes aboard bearing the hardware needed to rig up the oarlocks for the two additional sweeps, just as the girl Clementine comes out of the hold hatchway with a basin of dirty dishwater to throw over the side. He looks at her, and she looks at him and then goes back down below.

Yes, I had told this Clementine Fletcher to sweeten up, and against all odds, she did.

Oh, it was a slow process, from the surliness she showed on the first day aboard to a gradual lightening of mood on the second day, as she grew to know us and become more comfortable. She still continues to study me, like she did on our first meeting, though, as if she's trying to make up her mind about something—about what, I don't know.

I decided to have her bunk in the after cabin with us, what with those randy Hawkes boys sleeping up front, and so she put her belongings on the bottom bunk, under Katy and me. We sleep on the top bed, because we've installed some portholes for light and ventilation, and that's where the porthole is. I like to be able to look out when we're all locked down, and I also like the air.

That first night, Clementine started quietly crying.

"She's just homesick," I whispered in Katy's ear.

"Don't think she's got a home, from what she's said to me," whispered Katy back.

I rolled over and reached out my hand in the darkness.

"Come on, Clementine," I whispered. "It'll be all right, you'll see. Here, take my hand."

"No. I'll be all right," came the choked voice from below. I withdrew my hand.

The sound of weeping subsided. I had the feeling that she had shoved a corner of her pillow into her mouth to stifle her sobs.

"Prolly just misses her man," whispered Katy.

"That's gotta be it," I agreed, but didn't quite believe it. *There's something else going on here,* I was thinking. Then I put it out of my mind and went to sleep.

The next night, after a long day of boat work and a full evening of performance, we once again turned in for the night, and once again the weeping started up.

This time I said to Katy, "We'll switch beds. Send her up here. She's disturbin' everybody's sleep."

"Huh, it'd be a pleasure," said Katy, slipping out of the bunk, "what with you twitchin' and hollerin' and talkin' in tongues in your sleep half the time, then goin' stiff as a board sometimes and sweatin' the bed wet. Hell, yes, I'll send her up and git me a full night's sleep for a change."

I know she doesn't mean it, her and me being like sisters, and all.

Clementine slipped in next to me, not protesting but still sniffling. I put my hand on her shoulder and drew her to me.

She stiffened.

"Now, Clementine, you don't have to like me, but you do have to be quiet. Jim and Mr. Higgins are on the other side of that curtain and you are disturbing their rest. You don't want that, do you?"

I could feel her head shake. "No," she whispered.

I had noticed that in the doings of this past day, when work was stopped and meals were served at a long table set up on the bottom hold hatch between the rows of passenger and crew bunks, it was Jim Tanner and Clementine Fletcher who most often sat together. I further noticed that, when the work was done and all took their ease, it was Jim and Clementine who sat together with fishing poles to idle away the time. I even heard her laugh one time at something he had said.

I noticed also that before she would eat, she would put her hands together, close her eyes, and mumble some words, when none of the rest of us did.

"Good. Now go to sleep. Tomorrow will be a brighter day, you'll see. Soon we'll take you to the General Butler with us so you can see the show. Would you like that?"

I felt her head bob up and down.

"Good. Now go to sleep."

She settled into my side and gradually grew quiet. After a while her breathing became slow and regular. And then, after a while, so did mine.

That night, as I lay tossing and turning as usual, I had the most unusual dream—I dreamed that Clementine had gotten out of bed and gone down, as I supposed, to use the pot. Some dream time went on and I dreamed that there was, of all things, a cold pistol put to my temple, and I heard the sound of a hammer being drawn back and cocked. *What a strange dream*, I remember thinking. *It's not one of the things that I regularly dream and scream about. Funny, ain't it?* Then I dreamed I heard the sound of a hammer being brought back safely down to half cock, and presently Clementine crawled back into bed and I stopped dreaming till I woke in the morning, her flaxen hair across my face.

Chapter 30

J. Fletcher, Convict
On a road gang
Somewhere in the God-awful USA

Miss Jacky Faber
Also somewhere in this God-awful USA
But no doubt in a state higher than my current one

Jacky,

We shuffle out of the Pittsburgh prison at dawn, clad in our prison stripes, left legs shackled by the ankles to a long chain, after having been fed a ration of oatmeal, molasses, and weak coffee, made from some plant that grows wild here and isn't even remotely related to a coffee tree. Sailors on the meanest ship would complain of this fare, but so be it. I shan't complain. It is my lot and I will accept it.

Then we are all loaded onto a rough cart and taken on a jolting trip to the outskirts of the town, to a place next to the Ohio River where some seawall work needs to be done, and we are, of course, the ones chosen to do it.

I am, as Fate and the ever-so-humorous gods would have it, fettered next to Mike Fink, my supposed partner in my crimes against the Commonwealth of Pennsylvania, and must listen to his rants both night and day. He says he has taken a shine to me. God help me.

On the first day, we were shown the work that had to be done. There was a quarry where tons of what appears to be a sandy stone were blasted out of the quarry wall and hauled on carts by some convicts up to the rest of us, who would then use our hammers to break the bigger pieces into littler pieces that would be tamped into the space behind the seawall. It was called, not very poetically, the Rockpile.

While I was slaving away at the Rockpile, I added meaning to this deadly drudgery by picturing the many heads that I would very much like to have seen split, from Midshipman Bliffil to the pirate LeFievre to Captain Scroggs to Captain Blodgett to Captain Rutherford to many others I have met in this life. In my fury I even conjured up some half-buried jealousies and pictured smashing the knees of Robin Raeburne and the same of Randall Trevelyne. I am sorry, Jacky, but I am beyond rational thought. I swing my hammer with great gusto: *Here's one for your toes, Randall! Smash! You like that, you arrogant son of a bitch? Try to get on my girl, will you? Well, here's another! Smash!*

I was in an absolute orgy of jealous destruction, but I was restrained in time by my mentor.

"No, no, boy, y'see, y'gotta just do the least bit they require," said Mike with all the reasonableness of a schoolmaster. "Otherwise, if you do too good a job, they'll just nail you again as soon as you step outside the calaboose, 'cause they'll want you back. Y'see?"

I did see, and I slowed down my hammering and let my simmering resentment burn off. But I did not stop thinking and nurturing my resentments: There was the man Beatty to consider. Since I had grown a beard and pulled the ribbon from my hair to let my hair hang loose about my face, and affected an idiot's slow drawl when in his hearing, I do not think he recognized me. In fact, I was able to hear him talk to one of his compatriots to the effect that he and his partner, McCoy, would be heading south to a place called Johnstown after he got out of this hole. It warmed my heart to know that.

But my heart was not warm for long, for once again, that night Clementine did not appear at the jailhouse window.

Mike was sympathetic, in his way. "Should've kep' that one and got rid o' the other one. She seems like a good girl."

A good girl, indeed, *I thought, as I grasped the cold bars and looked out onto the empty street....*

Chapter 31

Clementine continues to sweeten. She arose singing from our bunk this morning and went straight to her work, helping Crow Jane get the stove started up from last night's coals and the breakfast on the table.

I had thought to take my meals in my cabin, separate from the others, as befits my station, but I decided against it. For one thing, I didn't want Higgins to appear to be waiting on me hand and foot, which, of course, I certainly enjoy, but it would damage his image as First Mate. Second, I liked the conviviality of sitting at the head of the long table and eating and drinking with my mates. Oh, sometimes I will take my dinner solitaire, when the occasion demands, but not now. The passengers will also join us at this table. The Hawkes boys must be taught some manners before that, though. I invite Mr. Cantrell to join our table and he does. I insist that the girl he has with him join us also, but she shakes her head and takes her plate to a corner to eat.

After serving, Clementine sits down next to Jim, who seems to appreciate the company. After the breakfast cleanup and the day's laundry are done, I'm sure the two again will be sitting on the bow, fishing and talking, their heads together.

The Hawkes boys sit at the very foot of this table, but they are learning their manners, very slowly but surely. There is hope for them, I think, crude as they now are.

I decide to take Clementine to the performance tonight, as a reward for her new cheerfulness, and I think it would be good for her to broaden her horizons some—I have the feeling she has seen very little of the world. I'll take Jim, too, since we can leave the *Belle* in the very capable hands of Crow Jane.

After the day's labor is done, Higgins and I set to work on Clementine's appearance. The hair is freshly washed and Higgins steps back and considers it, scissors in hand.

"*Hmmm.* We'll snip a little bit off here"—he applies the scissors quickly and surely—"and here. And we'll curl this, then tie this up in a bow. I think that will do it."

The girl does not know quite what to think, but she goes along with it. Higgins heats up the curling iron and goes to work.

"There, what do you think of that?" I ask, holding the hand mirror up for her to gaze upon her newly coiffed self. Two curled ringlets hang by either side of her face, the rest of her hair being swept up top and tied with a blue ribbon.

She is amazed.

"And what do you think your young man will think?" tease I.

"Ooooh. I don't know what he'll think," she says. "I don't know what to think myself."

"What's his first name, anyway?" I ask, putting away combs and pins.

"Jai—" she begins, and then coughs. "Jake. His name's Jake, short for Jacob."

"Is he a good man?" I ask. "And how old is he?"

"Yes, he's a good boy. 'Bout eighteen, I figure."

"Did he put those there?" I ask, pointing to some old yellow bruises high up on her arms.

"No. Pap done that. That's why I run away."

"Ah. What's Jake in jail for, if you don't mind me askin'?"

"Got caught up in a fight that warn't none of his concern."

"Ah, well, that happens, doesn't it? When the boys want to fight, sometimes you just gotta let 'em."

"I reckon," she agrees, softly. "Still, it tore me up to see him hurt like that."

"Well, he'll be out soon," chirps I, "and you'll have a most joyful reunion."

Strangely, she does not smile at the prospect but only nods and looks down at her hands.

"But as for now," I say briskly, "let's get you out of that dress and into something more suited to the evening. I shall lend you my serving-girl gear, which is what I usually perform in, and I shall wear my blue dress instead... Now, Higgins, don't look at me that way. I know it's a bit scandalous, but is not 'scandal' my middle name? Come on, be a sport and stuff me in."

I had fashioned my blue dress after a dress I'd seen worn by a Mrs. Roundtree. I had sewn it while I was on the *Dolphin* and figuring I was about to get kicked off. In which thinking I was absolutely right, by the way. Mrs. Roundtree was a lady in Palma de Mallorca, who practiced what is sometimes called "the oldest profession," but who was very kind to me in explaining how things work. I, myself, do not think hers is the "oldest profession"...I think runnin' a scam is the oldest, but let that go. As everybody who knows me realizes, I am a somewhat eccentric Biblical scholar. However, it is possible I could have picked a more modest model for my first dress, I will allow that.

With a heavy sigh, Higgins hauls the dress out of my seabag and goes to set the iron on the stove, and I turn to strapping Clementine into my serving-girl rig.

We are about the same size, but I think that's because she maybe ain't stopped growing yet.

So anyway, on with the black stockings—she's got a tattered pair of drawers, so that's good 'cause I don't have to give her one of mine—then she dons the blousy white shirt, black skirt, and then the black vest to top it off. I stand back and survey my work.

"Good," I say. "You look the very picture of the hardworkin' barmaid. When we get there, I'll set it up with Molly so that you'll be helping Katy—pickin' up and washin' the empty mugs, wipin' off the tables, carryin' in the trays of food and drink. Don't worry, you'll get the hang of it right quick. When you learn to count change, you can wait on tables in your own right."

She nods, smoothing out the unfamiliar cloth under her hands.

"All right, we are off to the merry dance," I crow as we leave the *Belle*, me and Higgins and Katy and Clementine and, right next to her, Jim Tanner.

Jane lights up her pipe and sits by the gangway, Jim's rifle over her knees, as we depart. Behind her the Hawkes boys sit with their long legs dangling over the side, whining, "How come we'uns don't get to go, too?"

"'Cause yer a pair o' no-good drunken louts who'd drink up all the profits and then start fightin' with each other and then get thrown back in the calaboose ag'in," says Crow Jane, "after we'uns been trainin' y'uns all week and y'uns eatin' up all the food and bein' nothin' but trouble. Nope. We got a 'vestment in y'uns and yer gonna pay it off if'n I got anythin' to say about it."

Aw, Janey...

The Sign of the General Butler is very nearly full when we get there to prepare for the night's show. I wear my cloak about my shoulders as if for warmth, though the night is warm enough.

I set it up with Molly as to what Clementine's duties will be, then I step up on the small stage we have had built, with Higgins taking his usual station behind me. I pick up my concertina to accompany the first song. Jim, without being told, goes to help Clementine. *Hmmmm...* In the beginning, I had half hoped that some sparks might work up between Katy and Jim, but nothing happened. Oh, they are good friends and trade jokes and gibes and all, but it's a brother-sister thing. But with Clementine, now, I think I can feel the heat between them. *But Jim, she says she's a married woman...*

I put that out of my head and turn my mind to performance.

"Good evening, gentlemen, and yes, ladies, as I do see some of the fair sex in the audience. All are welcome to the

Sign of the General Butler, and none may fear coarse or vulgar language. I will begin tonight's show with 'Handsome Molly' in honor of our gracious hostess!"

A cheer goes up for Molly Murphy, who acknowledges with a tankard held high, and I go into the song.

> *I wish I was in London,*
> *Or some other seaport town,*
> *I'd set my foot on a sailing ship*
> *And sail the ocean round!*
> *While sailin' round the ocean,*
> *While sailin' on the sea,*
> *I'll dream of Handsome Molly,*
> *Wherever she might be!*

That gets a round of cheers for both Molly and me. I play the melody on my squeeze box and look about and see that Clementine has wiped down a table and is looking about for more to do. *Good girl.* I do the next verse and another chorus.

> *Don't you remember, Molly,*
> *You gave me your right hand?*
> *You said if you should marry,*
> *I would be the man.*

I see that Jim Tanner is hangin' right close to our Clementine, and I suppose that is good. We've got to watch out for each other, don't we? I do the last verse, wherein Handsome Molly begins to stray.

> *I went to church last Sunday,*
> *You passed me right by,*
> *I could tell your mind was changin'*
> *By the rovin' of your eye.*

Clementine brings a tray of tankards up to a table and sets it down. Katy is there and she deals the drinks out to the table and Clementine is about to take the tray back to the bar when one of the gents reaches out his hand and runs it right up the back of her skirt. *Uh-oh, forgot to warn her about that...*

She stands up straight, shocked, and not knowing what to do while this cove runs his hand over her rump. I'm about to stop the song and sic Higgins on him when Jim appears at her side and grabs the bloke's hand and throws it down and sticks his balled-up fist in his face. The man looks up into the enraged eyes of the boy and decides not to push it. Clementine looks into Jim's eyes and I can feel the heat from here. I sing while playing the last verse and chorus.

> *While sailin' round the ocean,*
> *While sailin' round the sea,*
> *I'll think of faithless Molly,*
> *Wherever she might be.*

As I round the song off, I notice Clementine heading back to the bar with her tray. Could that be Jim Tanner's hand on the small of her back, guiding her on her way?

Amid the applause, I whip off my cloak and reach back for the Lady Gay and put the fiddle to my chin and rip into

"Billy in the Low Ground," and the crowd roars its approval, whether it's more for the tune or the costume, I don't know, but I'll take it either way. I made this dress three years ago, and while it still fits me, the parts of me that might have grown a little bit since that time tend to be my upper works, parts that seem to be trying to work their way out of confinement as I saw away at my fiddle. Perhaps Higgins is right—it might be time to retire this garment. Or at least alter it. Ah, well, who cares, as I am not shy in that regard.

After three or four more tunes, I do a poem, "The Boy Stood on the Burning Deck," and manage to wrest a few tears out of many a manly eye, then lighten the set with a reel, a couple of jigs, a sailor song, and then I take a break.

"Thanks, Molly," I say, putting my nose in the foam on top of a tankard of ale and drinking down a long swallow. "Oh, and my throat was so dry, I tell you true."

"Ah, well, Jacky," says Molly, "you've been doin' just fine. Sad to think you'll be gone in a coupl'a days."

"There'll be someone else who'll come along soon to play the old tunes, Molly, you'll see. I ain't the only songbird in the bush," I say, somewhat regretfully. I have enjoyed playing here, but I know I got to push on.

On the other side of the bar, Clementine and Jim are head to head and elbow to elbow, washing mugs and glasses. I know this is a chore that Jim would rebel at in ordinary times, but these, apparently, are not ordinary times for young Jim.

I finish off the mug, push it away, and again mount the stage. There are whoops and hollers as I launch into another set of songs, instrumentals, and patter. There are times when I look up and notice that Clementine, when not involved in work, or engaged with Jim, continues to study me with those cold blue eyes.

I reflect also that it is a lot of work holding a crowd in the palm of your hand all by yourself, and it is often that I long for the company of my old partner Gully MacFarland, he of the magic fiddle and the knowledge of a thousand songs. True, he was a drunk and a no-account, but still he had his charms. I think of one of his old jokes, which he used to break up a set, and looking around at the females in the crowd and judging that they're a quite bawdy bunch of women, I decide to recount it. I put up my bow and begin telling the joke.

"There once was a Scotsman who was far from his native land, in Pennsylvania it was, and not far from here, in fact. He had drunk his fill in the local tavern and then stumbled out into a nearby field, to answer the call of nature..."

"Hear, hear, go on, go on!" says the crowd.

"...and he did relieve himself, but in trying to return to the revels in the tavern, he found that he had already drunk his fill and so keeled over on his back, fast asleep in the heather..."

"Sounds like a damned Scotsman," says some bloke, and another tells him to shut his gob. *Peace, all, please,* I think to myself.

"...and he lay there till mornin', peacefully slumberin' away, when who should come upon his sleepin' form but two young maidens out to take the cows to pasture. Seein' him there, one says to the other, 'I've heard that Scotsmen wear nothing under their kilts. What say we find out, Sister?'

"And so, being bold Pennsylvania girls, they go and lift up the front of his kilt and find..."

Guffaws and snickers all around.

"...and find that he indeed has nothing on 'neath his kilt. 'Lord,' says one of the maidens, 'look at that, will you!' and the other says, 'We must be going on, Sister, but how can we leave him a message that we have been here to observe him in all his manliness?'"

I give a bit of a pause to build it up a bit, then proceed.

"'We will do this, Sister,' and she pulls the blue ribbon from her hair and ties it...about...well, you know what she ties it about," say I, blushing mightily, my eyes cast down in fake modesty. "Then she pulls his kilt back down, smooths it out, and the two girls go off on their way."

I take a deep breath and look off into the rafters, as if the story is done. I give it a beat or two, and then I resume.

"Presently, our Scotsman wakes up, and again feels the call of nature and goes off to the nearest bush and raises his kilt." I look all wide-eyed and innocent about the place. "He looks down at his...uh...member, with the blue ribbon around it, and exclaims, 'I don't know where you've been, laddie, but wherever it was, it looks like you won first prize!'"

And with that, I slam down my bow and tear into "Scotland the Brave," and the place explodes in laughter. That's one thing I like about the frontier: You can tell the oldest joke and it'll be new here.

The rest of the night went well, and all left very satisfied. When I ended off with, as I always did, "The Parting Glass," me and Gully's closing song, I noticed that Jim and Clementine were off in a darkened corner, slowly dancing to the tune.

Chapter 32

This will be our last day in Pittsburgh and we are making the most of it, doing our last-minute outfitting, loading on supplies, and saying our good-byes.

I've arranged with Molly for Clementine's lodging till her man gets out. She'll do chores at the General Butler in return for her room and board. Today she's here doing our laundry, the tubs being set up outside on the deck to keep from steaming up the hold. I've given Jim an errand to run in town so maybe she can get some work done. He has been most attentive to her this past week, and I don't think she has minded the attention. He's getting all gloomy now that we'll be gone tomorrow and she'll still be here. Ah, the pangs of young love. Poor Jim.

We've got a total of nine passengers, most of them bound for ports this side of Cincinnati—'tis plain that the passenger trade ain't going to do it for us in the way of getting rich, that's for sure. Nope, performance has got to be the way. They've gotta be hungry for entertainment out in the wilderness, that's what I'm thinking. Higgins reserves judgement on this.

In that regard I've had Carpenter MacCauley make up some wide boards that hook together at their edges, which we can lay from the *Belle* to any dock we might be next to, making a sort of stage area, where we can put on shows for the people in these port towns and thereby not have to find an accommodating tavern in which to perform. Jane says taverns are going to get scarcer and scarcer as we move on, anyway, so I think it's good we're doing this. We have also built some light benches for future audiences, which we've stowed down in the still-empty cargo hold—wasn't able to find a cargo yet, 'cept for livestock, and I don't want to smell up my newly beautiful *Belle* with any of that.

I'm glad we are moving on. It's not good to grow stale by staying in one location too long—first whiff of that and you are toast, and old, cold toast at that. Nope, always leave 'em wantin' more, as Gully MacFarland used to say. Our good-byes were said last night at the Sign of the General Butler and all pronounced themselves sad to see us go, and that is as it should be.

Come time for lunch, I have my private table set up on the quarterdeck, as it is a lovely, mild day, and I invite Mr. Cantrell to join me, as he is amusing company even though I know he is a rounder of some sort—just what kind, I don't know yet, but if he stays with us long enough, I'm sure I will find out.

"Thank you for inviting me, Miss Faber," he says, pulling out my chair for me. *Ah, I do like gentlemanly manners.*

"My pleasure, Mr. Cantrell," I purr, and slide into the chair as Katy comes up with the tray. The tea is poured and the food is served and we fall into a wide-ranging conversation that winds up with me lamenting the lack of a cargo to take down the river.

"It's got to be clean and compact, and short of carrying a cargo of gold, I can't think what that could be." I sigh, resigned to having an empty hold.

"I have a suggestion, if you don't mind," he says, smiling. He smooths back his mustache with the top of his forefinger.

"Please. I'd like to hear it," I say. I've noticed that men with mustaches do that smoothing bit a lot.

"It seems to me that..."

From up forward I hear Clementine's voice, raised in song. *Hmmm.*

I stand up. "If you'll please excuse me for a moment, Mr. Cantrell? And please hold your thought on my cargo problem."

He stands up as I do and says, "Of course."

I recognize the song as "Fair and Tender Ladies." I know that song, 'cause Katy taught me the words. 'Course there's an old English version, but the American tune is much more sorrowful. Wonder why that is with the Americans—they're so wildly optimistic about their burgeoning country, yet their songs are so sad and lonesome?

> *Come all ye fair and tender ladies,*
> *Take warning how you court young men,*
> *They're like the stars of a summer's mornin',*
> *First they'll appear and then they're gone.*

I walk over the cabin top and look down upon her bent over the scrub board. She has a good voice and she sings with great feeling. She does the verse about love bein' a killin' thing, and she sounds like she really means it. I wonder where she's been, to have such intensity. Then she does the bit about wanting to be a tiny sparrow...*spay-row* is how she says the name of the little bird.

> *I wish I was some little sparrow*
> *And I had wings and I could fly,*
> *I'd fly away to my false true lover,*
> *And all he'd say, I would deny.*

As she starts the last verse, I join in. She starts at the sound of my voice joining hers, but she doesn't miss a beat, nor stumble on a word.

> *But I am not some little sparrow,*
> *I have no wings, and I can't fly,*
> *So I'll stay right here in my grief and sorrow*
> *And let my troubles pass me by.*

She turns to look up at me as we finish the duet.

"You have a very lovely voice, Clementine," I say. "And I think we sounded very good together, don't you?"

"Yes, Miss."

Well, I guess you have to answer that way, Clementine, whether you think it or not. I consider the girl, who returns to her scrubbing. "You say your husband is a good man, and I believe you. You have proved to be a good worker in your own right. That said, should you catch up with us in your rowboat, I will give you both employment. What do you think?"

She turns to look at me and a slight smile crosses her features.

"I'll ask him," she says. "Tonight. I'll be leavin' this evenin', since you're goin' in the mornin'."

From the corner of my eye, I notice that Jim Tanner has chosen this moment to return from his errand and has heard this exchange. I see his shoulders sag.

"All right," I say.

"And, Miss," Clementine goes on, "you said you might pay me somethin' for my work…"

"You shall have it, Clementine. It was good having you aboard," I say, and with that I return to my lunch with Mr. Cantrell.

"That was a lovely duet," says Mr. Cantrell, as we settle back in. "I must say that my first thought when you got up from the table was that you were going to chastise the girl for disturbing our luncheon."

"Voices raised in song *never* disturb me, Mr. Cantrell," I reply, a bit severely.

"Nor me, Miss Faber," says Yancy Cantrell, with a slight bow. "I, too, take delight in music, all music, however simple the source." The mustache is stroked yet again. "I must say that over the past week I have perceived depths in your character that I had not previously discerned. My compliments."

Oh, you are so smooth, Mr. Cantrell.

"I, too, am a very simple sort, Mr. Cantrell, having been raised as a homeless orphan on the cruel streets of London. But let that go," I say. "Now, what were you saying on the matter of cargo?"

"Simply, Miss, that instead of hauling gold, you might consider *amber*," says Mr. Cantrell.

"Which means?"

"Whiskey, Miss, is what I mean. The very finest of bourbon whiskey," he says, pulling out a long cheroot. "Do you mind if I smoke?"

"Not at all, as long as the smoke doesn't drift my way and you don't set my ship afire," I say. "Whiskey?"

He pulls out one of the newly invented matches and fires up the foul thing. "Yes, Miss. It is clean, compact, and, ounce for ounce, very valuable."

"Hauling whiskey to New Orleans sounds to me much like hauling coals to Newcastle," I answer, doubtfully. "I've been to New Orleans. It seemed it was fairly awash in spirits. Need they more?"

"What you tasted was rum, Miss, or at best rye whiskey, not fine bourbon whiskey. They don't have the ingredients down there, nor do they know the secrets of the sour-mash process." He leans across the table and points the cigar at me. "Now, as we journey down the Ohio, you will presently find Virginia on our left, and then, after a time, you will find the state of Kentucky, and there, Miss, is where the very finest of whiskeys are made. And, where you can pick it up for a good price." Satisfied he has made a good case, he settles back in his chair and watches me for my reaction.

"Well, as for tasting rum in New Orleans, that did not happen. I have taken a vow never to drink spirits, and I have not, except when certain men of low character have forced it between my lips…"

"Even more depths…," observes Mr. Cantrell under his breath, and his eyes narrow and look very sly.

"…but I will take your words under consideration," say

I, again rising. "But now I must get back to work. Thank you for your company, Mr. Cantrell, and for your advice."

That evening, at six o'clock, Mrs. Clementine Fletcher gathers up her belongings and goes off the *Belle of the Golden West*. She gives Jim a squeeze of the hand and a kiss on the cheek, which I think is proper under the circumstances, she being a married woman and all, in spite of her age. He looks very down in the mouth, but I figure he'll get over it, 'cause you generally do.

She throws the strap of the rifle over her thin shoulders and picks up the bag she arrived with all those days ago, and starts off, not looking back.

I stand with Jim and watch her go, her too-short yellow dress blowing about her knees as she trudges off into the night.

I put my hand on Jim's shoulder and give it a shake, but I don't know if it helps any.

It starts to rain.

Chapter 33

The Convict J. Fletcher
at Hard Labor
in a foul American jail

Jacky,

We got off the road gang later than usual this night, the rotten jailers getting an extra hour of work out of us, the sods. With aching muscles I sit down on the floor of the jail, my back to the wall, eating the bowl of gruel dished out to me. I don't even want to think on what's in it.

My boon companion, Mike Fink, slumps down at my side.

"Ha, boy, only twelve more days! Hell, I could do twelve days standin' on my head with my thumb up my ass! Ha!"

In former days, a statement like that could make me lose my appetite, but not now. I shovel in the landsmen's burgoo. Isn't the worst I've tasted, being Royal Navy and all. *Or, rather, used to be Royal Navy,* I think with some lingering regret. How proud I was to be…never mind.

"Now, you, boy, you got less'n a week or so to go," contin-

234

ues Fink. "Hell, that's so short a time that I don't think I can even start up a long conversation with you 'cause I wouldn't get to finish it. I mean, that's so short a time that—"

"Jaimy."

I freeze with the gruel still on my lips.

"Jaimy. It's me. Clementine."

I fling down the bowl, its contents spilling over the floor, and leap to the window.

Looking out, I see her small and forlorn figure standing there in the rain in the dwindling twilight. She has nothing with her, just herself—wearing her yellow dress and white apron. The dress is becoming soaked in the rain and is clinging to her. She stands with her arms held straight down at her sides.

"I'm here, Clementine," I say. "I was so worried about you. I—"

"Shouldn't have worried about me, Jaimy. I found me some people what took care of me, so I was all right."

I notice that her hair is fixed different, with ringlets on the side of her face, and a cold feeling comes over me.

"You...you didn't...sell...anything, did you?"

She raises her blue eyes to me. "I don't know what that means, Jaimy. No, all I sold was the labor of my hands, as that's all I'm good at. That what you mean?"

"Clementine, I—"

"No, hush now, Jaimy, and let me talk. I'll be gone off soon."

Chilled to my soul at that, I listen.

"I seen her, Jaimy, I did. I had to see what she was like to make you want her so. And I found out. I crept up outside the place where she was singin' and dancin' and tellin' stories and all. I seen her all right, and I seen that she can do all those things I cain't do. Dress up and act like a fine lady like she was born to it...sing, dance, play all them musical things. Ever'body in the town just loved her, I could see. Me, I cain't do nothin' 'cept wash dishes and clothes."

She pauses here to take a breath. I can see her thin chest rise and fall. Myself, I can hardly breathe.

"I'm cutting you free, Jaimy, 'cause I know it's her you want and not me. I ain't gonna make no sense now, 'cause I'm just gonna ramble on so maybe you'll know why I'm doin' this...

"Now, don't say nuthin' and don't you worry about me, Jaimy. I've seen me some shows and some city lights, and I've learned to dance slow. I've met a sweet young boy. I've drunk me some drinks and et some things I never seen before, and I seen some sights. You was right, Jaimy, my life has got a lot better since I found you. God sent you to me and I still believe that, but now I'm thinkin' He sent you to show me that I could go off and have a better life even without you, on my own, like, and I thank Him for it, and I thank you, too, Jaimy, for taking me away.

"I got me a good job, taking care of the kids in this family that's going upriver to a new homestead. They was nice to me and fixed up my hair like this, and, no, Jaimy, I ain't sold 'em nuthin' 'cept the labor of my hands."

I know that it is not raindrops that are streaming down her face, but I say nothing. I only look into those sad blue eyes.

"One night when she was playing in that tavern, I snuck aboard the boat she stole from Mike Fink, just to look around. You know she got a paintin' of you above her bed, dressed in your fine uniform? Yup. It looks just like you. Oh, Jaimy, it just about tore my heart out to see you there, looking like that—all fine, fine as she is and fine as I never can be. Oh, yes, you and her, you both talk funny, you do, so I guess you belong together."

The rain pours down now and the ringlets are gone from her hair.

"Clementine, you're going to catch your death—"

"Don't you worry about that none, neither." She gulps, sobbing now. "But listen to this: I've left the rifle and pistol and the other stuff at the General Butler tavern. Ask for Molly. She's been real good to me, too. I left the money I earned with her, too. The rowboat's down at the pier."

She stands there for a moment longer, then says, "I think that's all I got to say. Good-bye, Jaimy. I loved you so."

She turns and walks away. Just before she gets out of sight, she stops for a moment, and when I don't call her back, she goes on and disappears into the night.

I slump down, my back against the wall of the cell.

There, my rational mind thinks, *my problem is solved, just like that.*

So why do I feel so wretched and alone?

And why do I feel so damned rotten?

Chapter 34

"Jake said he wanted to go north with some trappers. Tol' me I could go with him if'n I wanted to," said Clementine when she appeared back at the boat that night, standing soaking wet in the rain, with no rifle, no bag, no nothing...nothing but her poor self, her arms wrapped around her shivering form.

"Tol' him I didn't want to. Tol' him I didn't want to go off with a bunch of dirty trappers. No tellin' what they'd do with me if'n his back was turned," she said, not moving from the place where she first appeared. The expression of total resignation that was writ on her face also did not change. "If'n the work of Cook's Helper is still offered to me, I'll take it and be grateful for your kindness. If'n not, I'll be on my way."

"Of course you can go with us, Clementine," I say, reaching my hand up to welcome her aboard, but my hand is beat to it by a joyous Jim Tanner, who bounds up to the dock.

"*My dear girl!*" he exclaims as his hand takes hers.

She looks up at him. "I warn't really married to him, not like in church and all. My real name is Clementine Amaryllis Jukes, named after my mother."

"Well, consider yourself the newest employee of Faber

Shipping, Worldwide, Clementine Amaryllis Jukes," I say, taking her by the arm. "And stand off, James Tanner, as we've got to get her below and get her dry."

Strange, but I thought I felt her stiffen a bit when I called Jim "James."

The morning dawned glorious, as it often does for me when I am off on a new venture. The sun shone, the sparkling wavelets were dancing merrily, and all was well in our watery world.

There was the hustle and bustle of getting the passengers aboard with their luggage, the last-minute payments of dock fees and such, which gives me time to sit down at my topside table and write my first entry into the log:

Belle of the Golden West log. Preparing to cast off from the port of Pittsburgh, Pennsylvania, USA, on the Ohio River, bound south for New Orleans and all points between. Passenger manifest as follows:

Mr. Yancy Beauregard Cantrell, with servant
Mr. Manning and daughter Elaine
Mr. and Mrs. Pankowski and family, homesteaders
Mr. McDaniel, lumber merchant
Mr. Brady
Miss Umholtz, schoolmistress, Cincinnati Normal
    School
Under way, 10 o'clock. Weather clear, all secure.

"Cast off!" I cry, exulting in two of the sweetest words in the sailor's language. The lines are taken in and we shove off the dock and pull out into the stream, finally, on the Ohio River.

"Man your sweeps!" I joyously sing out. Nathaniel is on port forward oar, his brother Matt on the starboard forward one. Behind Matt stands Jim Tanner on aft starboard, Higgins on port aft oar, and between them, on the cabin top, stands me on the tiller. Katy's on bow lookout, watching for snags and debris and other shipping that might impede our progress, while Clementine is below helping Crow Jane get the noon meal together.

When I see that all the oars are ready in the up position, I call out, "All...pull!"

The oars dip into the water, the stroke is pulled, and they return to the up position.

"All...pull!" and it is done again. And again.

When we're well clear of the dock area I say, "Port, hold! Starboard, pull!" I throw my tiller over to the right and the *Belle* turns neatly to the left, pointed downriver and parallel to the shore.

After several more pulls by all, I say, "Secure the after oars; forward oars pull together," and Higgins and Jim ship their oars and secure them. "Jim, take the tiller if you would. Keep her about fifty yards offshore and be alert if Katy spots a snag." We're going fast enough that we can get by with just the Hawkes boys on sweeps, and they know each other well enough that they don't need the strokes called out. We'll reserve that for tight situations, like coming in to dock and such.

Jim takes the tiller and I go forward to mix with the passengers for a bit. As I go, I step over the blue line I had the sign painter draw on the deck. It runs from the port gunwale over the deck, up the side of the cabin, across the top and down the other side, over the starboard deck to the gunwale on that side. That line separates the quarterdeck from the rest of the ship, and all passengers have been told that, for safety's sake, no one is allowed abaft that line 'cept crew—can't have some little brat hangin' off the tiller bar, now, can we? The real reason is that I like the separation. I've got three young females back here and I don't need any nonsense in that regard. Plus, we must separate the officers from the crew, the crew right now being the Hawkes boys, but I suspect it might grow. I offered a bunk back aft for Crow Jane, but she let it be known that she'd rather sleep next to her stove. For one thing, I know she didn't take kindly to my rule of no smoking at any time in Officers' Country, as it has become known. For another, I think she just liked it better there, next to her stove, with the Hawkeses for company. They've known each other a long time and are comfortable with that, and I can certainly understand.

About midway through our stay in Pittsburgh, I had promoted Jim from coxswain to Third Mate, with great ceremony and cheers from all about. With the title, he gets a slight increase in pay, which doesn't really matter much, for I can't afford to pay him anything at all now, but I know he appreciated the recognition. More than once when in the taverns, I saw him put his thumb to his chest and announce to others gathered about him that he was "Third Mate on the *Belle of the Golden West*, the best damned keelboat on any river in America!" It seems to me that the bragging and boasting tradition of the river has taken hold of our Jim Tanner.

All the passengers are out on deck, watching the riverbank slide by and remarking on the other shipping and the beauty of the river and of the day. I greet Mr. and Mrs. Pankowski and comment on the beauty of their children and am about to turn to engage others in small talk, when I look up and see a sight that sends me running back to the quarterdeck.

There on the bank, downriver, is a gang of convicts in black and white striped shirts and pants, toiling away at building a seawall. I can hear the sound of their hammers smashing rocks, to be pounded into the space behind the big rock wall that has already been put up. And there, as we draw closer, I see that at the top of the pile of rocks stands none other than Mike Fink, King of the River.

"Higgins!" I shriek. "Please, my fiddle!"

J. Fletcher, Convict
On the Rockpile on the bank of the Ohio
Pennsylvania, USA

To Jacky Faber or anyone else who might be the least bit interested in my wretched life:

I was in an extremely surly mood this morning, and in no temper at all to listen to any more of Mike Fink's drivel, or anything else for that matter. The other convicts have learned to stay clear of me, as I have been in several fistfights with a few of the more unruly ones and they have come out the worse for it. Harrumph—to think they would try to best an officer of the Royal Navy with any kind of weapon, including fists. Think of it—I, who have sat at the same table with the great Lord Nelson, now bruise my knuckles on the unshaven chins of ignorant American rabble in a squalid jail in the trackless wilderness.

Fink, of course, continues to think of me as his protégé in the life and the lore of the rivers, not getting it through his thick head that I could give less than a tinker's damn about all that.

Yes, it is true: Clementine's departure last night has wounded me to my core.

"Boy! Lookee there!" shouts Fink from the top of the pile. I am down at the bottom of the hole, tamping the broken bits of rock into the base of the seawall. I poke my head up over the top of the wall. "Out on the river! What's that say on the side of that boat?"

"It says, you illiterate brigand, 'Belle of the Golden West.' What of it?" Uh-oh, I say to myself—I believe I've seen that craft before.

"I'll be damned if that don't look like my boat, all gussied up like a fifty-cent whore!"

I look with a good deal more interest now. I can see people, a lot of them, on the deck and in the stern, and then what appears to be a girl with a fiddle jumps up on the cabin top.

Then, as the boat comes abreast of us, we can hear the strains of a fiddle and a voice raised in song.

> *Dance the boatman's dance,*
> *Oh, dance the boatman's dance,*
> *Dance all night till the broad daylight,*
> *And go home with the girls in the morning!*

I ripped out the melody of the "Boatman's Dance" and then put up my bow to sing the chorus, 'cause I knew Mike would enjoy it so, then I play and sing the verse that most pertains to the poor convicts' situation.

I went on board the other day,
To see what the boat girl had to say,
And there I let my passion loose,
And they crammed me down in the calaboose!

"Oh, look, Higgins, how he does rant and roar! Is this not just the finest thing!" I gloat.

"Have you never heard of the ancient Greek concept of hubris, Miss? If not, there are definitely some gaps in your education, to say nothing of your philosophy," says Higgins, observing the scene with a lot less relish than do I.

"Oh, bother all that," I say. "Here, I'll give him more of the tune and maybe a bit of a dance to cheer him and those poor convicts. How could that be bad of me?"

I don't wait for an answer but instead put bow to the Lady Gay and tear out the song, both with fiddle and feet. I'd like to take off my dress so that my legs could more freely move, but I've got passengers aboard and I cannot. However, in my skipping and jumping, I make sure my dress comes up well over my knees, because I am not shy in that way and I mean to bring only joy to those who watch.

J. Fletcher, astounded
Behind a stinking seawall in stinking Pennsylvania

Jacky,

I will address you directly, Jacky, since it is you that I see dancing on the deck of that boat out in the river. Not much sur-

prises me in this life anymore. The only thing surprising is that you still have any of your clothes on. My ankle shackles hold me down in this pit, such that I can only get my eyes up over the edge of the wall to watch you. Mike, however, is in full appreciation of your performance.

"Ah, is she shaking her tail for us poor convicts? To give us some cheer? Aw, that's right nice o' her, considerin' she knows I intends to kill her when I catches her. I know it's a shame, it is, but it's gotta be done. Law o' the River, and all. But till then, hey, lookit her shake those tail feathers! She's a game little hen, she is."

Ordinarily, I would rise in anger and demand satisfaction, but now, no. I merely watch and take joy in watching you cavort. What a thing you are, Jacky Faber.

"Mike Fink, King of the River, in the calaboose, and me, Jacky Faber, loose on that same river! Ain't life grand sometimes, Higgins?" say I, handing him back the Lady Gay. We have gone around the bend, out of sight of the poor prisoners. I do hope I brought them some joy.

"True, Miss, but sometimes it is not best to antagonize the natives in the land you travel through."

"Oh, he can't hurt us now. I bet he's got a good twenty more days on his sentence and we'll be long gone by then."

"Is this being said by the same Captain who maintained that nothing could ever catch the *Emerald*?" asks Higgins. He has put the Lady Gay back in her velvet-lined case.

"That was an unlucky shot, Higgins, and you know it. If that ball had not caught our mainmast—"

"*If* is the biggest little word in our language, Miss, but no matter. Will you dine with the passengers today?"

"I believe so. What's for dinner?"

"Crow Jane has made up a very acceptable *boeuf ragout.*"

"Ah. Beef stew. Sounds good. Crack out some burgundy to go with it, if you would."

"Certainly, Miss."

"Now, calm down, boy. Iffen you catch up with her 'fore I do, you'll marry her skinny tail and you'll have a mess of runny-nosed little brats, and she'll make yer life miserable, count on it. Plenty of time for stuff like that! Enjoy this!" says Fink.

"Enjoy what? Being a convict in a barbaric land?"

"Hey, this ain't so bad. Three hots and a cot, it could be worse. Say, jus' how close did you git to that little bundle, hmmm? Does she wiggle? Does she squeal and shout? Come on, warm a poor convict's heart, boy!"

"A gentleman doesn't speak of such things. Fink, I swear you are the most uncouth man I have ever met."

"Jest as I thought, boy. Oh, she prances, and she dances, and she says 'Oh, Mr. Man, you are just the very finest of men,' but when it comes down to tearin' up the sheets together, she's gone all prissy church lady and won't deliver the goods. 'Why, Suh, I hardly know you…' I can hear it now. Yup, she's the teasin' kind, I can tell."

"You do not know her, Mike."

"That's all right, boy. You think what you want. You go catch her and love her up good, till such time as I can get down-

river and kill her. And hell, boy, after we've done her good and proper, you stay out on the river with me. It's the only life for a man and you know it to be true."

Dance on, Jacky, dance on—

Jaimy

PART IV

Chapter 35

And so we traveled down the Oh-Hi-Oh, singing and dancing as we went. It's been a good week since we left Pittsburgh behind us, and we have long since left the Pennsylvania shores to find the state of Virginia on our east, and Ohio on our west. Virginia is a slave state and that makes me somewhat nervous, what with Mr. Cantrell's girl being on board and all. But I've got to get used to that, 'cause soon we'll have slave states and slave territories on both sides of us.

I lose some passengers as Mr. McDaniel gets off at the squalid little town of Wheeling, Virginia—no taverns to play in, pigs runnin' free in the streets, whole place stinkin' to high heaven—and Mr. Brady leaves at East Lick, but I pick up another one there, and at the very last minute, too. Just as we are about to pull out into the current again, I hear a cry of "Wait! Wait! Please wait!" and this man jumps out of the bushes and leaps onto the *Belle*. He is a tall man, thin, and dressed as a preacher, stiff collar and all, and what he has clasped in his hands seems to be a collection box. He looks over his shoulder as if he fears pursuit but calms down as soon as we get far enough midstream.

"I am the Very Reverend Jeremiah Clawson," he says, smoothing down his coat and smiling the smile of the blessed and holy.

"I am pleased to meet you, Reverend Clawson," I answer, dropping into a medium curtsy. "I am the Very Mercantile Jacky Faber and the fare is twelve cents a mile, prepaid, Reverend." He nods and harrumphs and roots about in the box to come up with the fare, an amount that'll get him at least as far as Cincinnati.

He is not the only new addition to the *Belle.* After leaving East Lick, while we were swinging around a bend in the river and coming close to the shore, two buckskin-clad forms, each carrying a long rifle, dropped silently from an overhanging tree onto our deck. Katy sees them drop, rolls over from her place on the bow, nocks an arrow, and has that same arrow drawn and pointed at the chest of the taller of the two.

"Katy, wait!" cries Crow Jane, who had just come on deck for a smoke. "It's Lightfoot and Chee-a-quat! They're all right! Don't shoot! Boss, come here!"

I jump down to the main deck. There stand two men. One is an Indian with both sides of his head plucked bare and feathers stuck into the remaining crest. He's bare-chested and is wearing a breechcloth and fringed leather leggings, with beaded moccasins on his feet. In addition to his rifle, there is a knife and a tomahawk in his belt. *Lord! My first real Indian!* Except for Crow Jane, of course. True, I had seen some small encampments of what I had been told were Indians on the shores that we had passed, but here, standing before me, was a true Indian brave, skin bronze and gleaming, nose hooked, and eyes black as coal.

"They'll pay their way when they're aboard, trust me on that," promises Crow Jane. "They'll hunt and get game. And when you get to Cave-in-Rock, you'll be glad to have 'em on your side!"

The other man is a white man—or maybe once was a white man. His skin is just as dark and tanned, and he is dressed much as the other, but his eyes are green and they bore into the eyes of Katy Deere, whose arrow point has not wavered one inch from a point dead center on his chest. Unlike his friend's, this one's chest is covered with an over-shirt of beaded, fringed buckskin. Not that it would in any way stop Katy's arrow on its way to his heart, should she choose to release it.

"Katy," I say. "Stand down."

She brings down the arrow, to point to the deck, but does not relax the bow.

"Your name is Lightfoot?" I ask of this frontiersman.

He nods but says nothing. He keeps his eyes on Katy and her still-nocked arrow.

"Where are you bound?"

There is a pause, then...

"Goin' to the Arkansas," he replies, slowly bringing his eyes over to bear on me. "Who the hell are you, girl?"

"Jacky Faber. Captain of this boat, that's who the hell I am. Why are you goin' to the Arkansas?"

"Huh!" he says, considering my captainhood. Then, "Man there. Needs killin'."

Hmmm...

"Well, Crow Jane vouches for you and that's good enough for me. So welcome aboard. Just follow the rules and we'll get along."

They don't say anything but instead seat themselves cross-legged on the foredeck, and there they sit in silence.

Later, when we anchor for the night, Lightfoot and Chee-a-quat slip off onto the shore to sleep in the forest, and I find that will be their usual way throughout this trip, and, right now, that's all right with me.

The second day they are with us, they come back aboard in the morning with a full-grown deer slung across Lightfoot's shoulder. When he steps aboard, he drops the carcass at my feet and turns away to resume his spot up near the bow, say-ing nothing.

Seeing this, Crow Jane comes up and grabs the dead beast by its hind legs and drags it off to butcher it. Thankfully, she does it out of my sight, but I must say the dinner that night was excellent, and a welcome change from the fish.

I expect my crew to do their jobs, but I ain't the type to just make work for people, so there's plenty of time for lounging about in the sun. I heard the Hawkes boys fooling around with a song and went forward to join them. They stand up as I approach. *Good boys, you are learning.*

"What's that you're singin'?" I ask.

"It's called 'Ground Hog,' Miss," says Matty. "We learned it as babies, didn't we, 'Thaniel?"

"Yup. It's about a critter what lives aroun' here. Some-times called a 'whistle pig' 'cause of the sound it makes when it's standin' next to his hole, 'bout to dive in. Learned to eat 'em and learned to sing their song, too."

"So sing it, then," say I, crossing my arms across my chest.

They ain't shy about doing it. They each have these little

metal things they call jaw harps, and they whip them out of their pockets and stand up next to each other. Then they cup them in their left hands and press them against their teeth, and with their forefinger, they strike the twangy part of the mouth harp to make the sound. By working their jaws up and down, and I suspect some tongue action inside, they make something that sounds almost like a melody. It certainly seems to fit the tune they start to sing. After the boys hammer away at the tune to set the mood, Matty stops playing his and howls out:

> *Grab yer gun and whistle up yer dawg,*
> *Grab yer gun and whistle up yer dawg,*
> *We're goin' to the wild woods to hunt ground hawg!*
> *Ooooooh, ground hawg!*

Matty slaps his jaw harp back up to his mouth and twangs away while 'Thaniel takes up the next two verses.

> *I dug down but I didn't dig deep,*
> *I dug down but I didn't dig deep,*
> *Found a little whistle pig fast asleep!*
> *Oooooh, ground hawg!*

> *Here come Sally with a ten-foot pole,*
> *Here come Sally with a ten-foot pole,*
> *Twist that whistle pig outta his hole!*
> *Oooooh, ground hawg!*

My sympathies fast attaching to the unfortunate rodent, I listen as Matty now steps to the fore to bellow out the last two verses.

Here come Susie with a snicker and a grin,
Here come Susie with a snicker and a grin,
Ground hawg gravy all over her chin.
Ooooh, ground hawg.

Little piece o' cornbread, sitting on a shelf,
Little piece o' cornbread, sitting on a shelf,
You want any more, you can sing it yourself.
Ooooh, ground hawg!

The Hawkes lads round off their number with both of them on jaw harp and their feet pounding the deck in a dance I take to be the "clog" that others have told me is common to this area.

When the last foot has stomped down, I give them a delighted round of applause, which is echoed by the passengers who have gathered about, and the boys blush and say, "*Pshaw!* Warn't nuthin'; anyone kin do thet…"

But I, for one, know that isn't true. I find out later that they also know how to call out the square dances, and I figure that could prove mighty useful. I resolve to have them teach the skill to me. In return, I might include them in my act—I can see us in a line, with me and my fiddle and maybe Clementine, too, all of us twanging and singing and clogging away. *Hmmm.* We shall have to work on it. First I've got to make the Lady Gay sing that high, lonesome sound, and neither she nor I have got it yet.

Jim Tanner, alas, has no music in him at all, and his voice is that of a tone-deaf frog. Oh, he likes the music, especially when Clementine is doing the singing—he just can't sing, is all.

I have started Clementine on her ABCs and simple numbers, and have required Jim to become more proficient at both those studies, and since he gets to sit next to Clementine, he does not protest too much. Actually, he does know how to read, basically, so he takes over most of the education of Clementine Jukes. When they don't think I am looking, they hold hands under the table. *Oh, Jim, I wonder just who's gonna be getting the education here?* She and I work on duets and are coming along quite nicely. If only we had some audiences. Crow Jane says there ain't gonna be much in the way of that till the town of Maysville, on the Kentucky shore. I think on it and come up with a plan—sending Jim ahead to scare up a crowd. Tell 'em showboat's a-comin'. But how to get him there? *Hmmmm.*

During this leg of our journey, I find myself more and more frequently inviting Mr. Cantrell back to my table to dine with me. As we travel farther south, the sun grows steadily more fierce, so I had the Hawkes boys install a sort of canvas canopy over my quarterdeck table to shield me and whomever I might invite to join me.

On this day, Yancy Cantrell fans a deck of cards out across the table. I look at them, and then up at him, with disdain.

"I do not believe in gambling, Mr. Cantrell," I say, severely.

He smiles and smooths back his mustache.

"Neither, Miss Faber, do I."

I consider this for a moment and then nod. He smiles and smoothly deals out the cards.

And so begins my education as a card sharp. First I learn the rules of the various games of faro, three-card monte, baccarat, and poker. Then, I am taught the odds of drawing certain cards in each of the games, the better able to gauge my chances of winning. After that I practice the art of the bluff. This is how to win when you have nothing in your hand and have only the steady eye and confident demeanor that convinces your opponent that he is the loser, and not you. And then, I learn the dark arts: how to deal smoothly from the bottom of the deck, how to deal seconds, how to palm a card, and how to use marked and shaved cards. I, of course, would never use such cheating skills in an actual game. I study them only for amusement, much as a magician learns sleight of hand. It helps pass the time as we float down the river, that's all. And Mr. Cantrell is an amusing companion.

We pass by Ohio on our starboard side and slide into Kentucky on our port side and glide into a place called Vanceburg, where we act upon Mr. Cantrell's advice and take on a cargo of Kentucky bourbon whiskey.

"The purest whiskey you will ever find," promises the distiller with a great amount of pride, counting out the money we put into his hand. His pride notwithstanding, Higgins taps each twenty-gallon barrel we put below, to make sure we are not being had. Everything seems to be in order. Mr. Cantrell assures us, with a wink, that our cargo will come in very handy, in spite of the draining of our very meager resources.

Until we can find a regular way to get Jim downstream to stir up a crowd for the showboat, I figure I'll send him ahead with Lightfoot and Chee-a-quat. I'm anxious to try a show out here on the frontier, and Crow Jane says that Maysville might have enough people around there to make up an audience. When I propose that they do this, Lightfoot looks at Chee-a-quat and says, *"Wah?"* and Chee-a-quat says in return, *"Wah!"* and Lightfoot and the Indian pick up their rifles and lope off into the woods at an easy gait, with Jim hurrying after them, plainly buoyed by the kiss that Clementine gave him as he set off on his mission.

Chapter 36

Jaimy Fletcher, ex-con
Pittsburgh, Pennsylvania
USA

Jacky,

I was released several days ago, bidding farewell to the Pittsburgh jail and to Mike Fink, who graciously wished me luck in my search for you, saying, "Love her up good, boy, 'fore I come down and mess her up for good and ever. After she's down at the bottom of the river with an anchor chain wrapped 'round her neck, maybe you and me'll bring my boat back upriver. Haul some cargo, buy us a coupl'a fancy ladies, have us a time. Wha'd'ya say, boy?"

After assuring Mike that I would take that under serious consideration and after enduring a manly hug from him that nearly broke several of my ribs, I walked out of the jail a free man and went directly to the General Butler tavern, hoping that Clementine might still be there. Alas, those hopes were dashed when I was informed by the landlady that she had indeed gone, and to where the landlady did not know. Or said she didn't. Molly Murphy handed over the items that Clementine had left for me—the pistol, rifle, bag of sundry items, and three dollars and seventy-five cents.

From her look, I could see that this Molly Murphy had very little use for me. "She also paid for two days' lodging for you," she said, as she slapped down the coins on the counter.

I looked down at the coins. *That dear, sweet girl…*

"How old are you, Fletcher?" she asked, her arms crossed on her chest and her gaze stern and disapproving.

The question took me aback. "Why, nineteen," I answered. "But why—"

"You nineteen, a grown man with a beard, and that poor girl just fourteen? You ought to be ashamed. Your room's at the top of the stairs," said she, biting the words off short. "You've got today and tomorrow and then I want you out of my place."

With that, she turned her back to me and stalked off.

Her words hit me like a punch in the stomach. *Fourteen! Oh, Lord, I now know that I am surely going to spend eternity in Hell.*

I did stay those two days at the General Butler in spite of the coldness against me, as I needed to rest and eat some decent food to get my strength up: Mr. Beatty will get out of jail in four days and I intend to be ready. I have kept my beard, for Beatty's partner, McCoy, has been hanging about town, waiting for his release, and I did not want to be recognized as their former prey. I followed him one day to another tavern and stood at the bar near him, having a drink on the generous Clementine, and listened to his conversation with another lowlife. I was gratified to hear that the two brigands still intend to go down to that place called Johnstown, and there's only one road there.

I did make one other purchase with Clementine's money: I found a rusty cavalry saber with scabbard at a secondhand store. It will look ridiculous hanging at the side of a barefoot man wearing overalls, but I don't care. I reflect that there's a lot I don't care about anymore.

I spend a good deal of time sanding the sword clean and sharpening it to a razor's edge. That, and plotting my revenge, for if I am going to be condemned to roast in Hell for my deeds, I intend to have company....

Chapter 37

As soon as we pull into the dock at Maysville, Jim is there to meet us, rocking on his legs, in a state of total exhaustion.

"Missy! They ran all the way! My lungs are about blown out! I'm a sailor, not a damned greyhound! We gotta do this a different way next time. Please, Missy!"

We bring him aboard, and soothing female hands are put to his fevered brow. It turns out that he and his fleet escort have been around to all the farms in the area and spread the word that there would be a show at Maysville landing tonight, one show only, starting at dusk. It also turns out that Lightfoot and Chee-a-quat are capable of running, flat out, for an entire day, and have, in fact, the ability to run down a deer if they have the running room. Poor Jim. We assure him that a different way will be found, and I leave him to the tender murmuring ministrations of Clementine Jukes and go out to supervise the preparations for the evening's show.

Matty and 'Thaniel bring up the boards that attach us to the dock, and after the boards are put down and fastened, the brothers bring up the benches and put them in a rough semicircle, facing the stage area of the *Belle of the Golden*

West. I go down to tune up the Lady Gay and to get into my finery and prepare for the performance.

"I think the blue dress would be just the thing tonight, don't you, Higgins?"

"Yes, Miss. But maybe with your black shawl around your shoulders, as we do not know the nature of the crowd."

The people come trickling in well before the fall of night and sit down quietly, their children on the ground before them. The young people, those in their teens, stand behind their elders, and I notice that many pair off, shyly. All are as silent as the grave. The older people are dressed simply, the men in overalls and the women in shapeless linsey-woolsey dresses. The children wear garments that appear to be made of flour sacks. They make not a sound.

This don't look good, I'm thinkin' as I get ready to go out. There are no signs of enthusiasm or excitement.

Yancy Cantrell strides to center stage. The lanterns have been lit all about him. He throws back his head and shouts out, "And now, ladies and gentlemen, I give you the Toast of Three Continents, Miss Jacky Faber, the Lily of the West!"

With that, I jump out onto center stage and rip out "Mrs. McCloud's Reel," the best I ever played it. From that I go to "Dicey Riley," and end that up with a couple of fancy dance steps. I hear some murmurs of appreciation from the passengers behind me, but from the audience in front of me...

Nothing.

I then pull out my concertina and do "Queer Bungo Rye," a merry little tune and story that never fails to bring the laughs.

Nothing.

I tell some jokes, then do some hornpipes with my pennywhistle, complete with dance steps. I do "The Galway Shawl" without accompaniment, and end that with an elegant curtsy.

Nothing.

Desperate, I try to appeal to the kids. I do "Froggy Went a-Courtin'" and "I'll Tell Me Ma," mugging all the way. The kids look at me wide-eyed, but...

Nothing.

Maybe poetry will help. I try "The Boy Stood on the Burning Deck," the poem about a boy of thirteen on a warship at the Battle of the Nile, who remained at his post even though all others had fled.

> *There came a burst of thunder sound—*
> *The boy, oh, where was he?*
> *Ask the winds that far around*
> *With fragments strewed the sea!*
>
> *With mast and helm and pennon fair*
> *That well had borne their part,*
> *But the noblest thing which perished there*
> *Was that young faithful heart.*

Now, I have brought pirates, murderers, corsairs, assassins, even, to their knees, blubbering in their beers in ports on three of the Seven Seas, with my rendition of that poem, but here...

Nothing.

I give up. I give the full performance, as I always do, but

expect nothing more from it. I round up with "The Parting Glass," and then I dive below, mortified.

I throw myself into a chair and sit there fuming over the worst performance of my life. "They hated it. They just hated it!"

Clementine puts her hand on my arm. "You're wrong, Miss. They loved it. They just don't know how to show it."

I am furious and beyond comforting. I take hold of her arm and snarl, "Don't you try to cozen me, girl! You weren't out there dyin'! You don't—"

Clementine grabs my hand and throws it off her arm and says evenly, "You go to Hell, girl! You think I owe you somethin', but I don't owe you nothin'! I give you some-thin' you ain't never even gonna know about! You can sleep with your own self tonight, you mean thing, you!"

She storms out of our cabin, and she does not come back in. *Let her go,* I say. I'm sick of this horseshit.

There is silence for a bit, and then Katy says, "She's right, you know. Just wait a bit and you'll see."

They are both right. A little later I am told by Crow Jane that people have been dropping by sacks of vegetables, corn, and other produce. She asks me to come up to see and I do. The townsfolk drop their offerings on the deck and I shame-facedly nod in thanks.

There, in the bucket set out for tips, is a sack, a sack that squirms about. I reach in and pull it out and open the draw-string at its top.

Out pokes a pink little face, the face of a perfect little piglet. It wiggles and squishes its nose against my hand. I am astounded.

"Well, there's tomorrow's dinner, anyway," says Crow Jane.

Chapter 38

James Emerson Fletcher, Highwayman
Pennsylvania, USA

Jacky,

"Stand!" I shouted as the two mounted men rounded the curve in the road. "Stand and deliver, you murdering swine!"

I had left Pittsburgh two days ago and walked down the Frankstown Road till I came to a likely spot—thick woods on each side and a little hillock where I could sit and see the traffic coming either way, and there I did sit for a full day and a half till I finally saw two men on horseback, riding hard, their long riding coats flapping out behind them. It was them.

I positioned myself in the middle of the road, pistol in my left hand and rifle in my right, both fully primed and cocked, so I was ready for them when they rounded the turn.

"Stand be damned!" shouted the man on the left, who I saw was Beatty. They both pulled back hard on the reins, and the horses squealed in fright and reared up above me. I could see both men pulling out weapons from beneath their long coats, and I aimed and fired my pistol. The bullet caught Beatty high on the chest and he spilled backward from the saddle. I sprang back just as McCoy's pistol was fired and I felt the bullet buzz past my cheek like an angry hornet. I lifted my right hand and fired my rifle, but in my haste I missed him as clean as he missed me.

His horse ran by me, but I reversed my rifle in my hand to swing the butt of it at his head with all the fury that was in me. I felt it connect and he tumbled out of the saddle, to thump heavily to the ground.

I drew my sword and stood over him, but even as far as I have fallen from civilized ways, I could not kill him in cold blood.

He rose slowly to his knees and then stood up, glaring at me balefully.

"You the boy from the prison?" he asked, as he drew the sword from his own side. I recognize it as being my old sword, the one they had stolen from me when I was ambushed and left for dead. It will be good to get it back.

"I am Lieutenant James Emerson Fletcher, late of His Majesty's Royal Navy," I said with a slight bow. "I am also the man you waylaid and left for dead up on the Allegheny. I have been schooled in swordmanship since I was fifteen. *En garde.*" I went down into the ready position.

I saw uncertainty in his face at that, but still he snarled, "You look like a goddamned hayseed t' me!" and he raised his sword to take a swing at my head. It was pathetic. I parried it easily and pinked him on his sword arm. When he went to put his hand over the wound, I lunged and put the point of my blade in his belly. When I felt it grate against his backbone, I pulled it back out. He looked shocked, dropped his sword, and then fell to his knees. He held that position for a moment, and then went over on his back.

"Lord, you have killed me," he bleated, as he looked down at the blood spreading over his shirt and trousers.

"It appears so," I said coldly.

"I ask for mercy."

"I will give to you the same mercy you gave me." I reached down inside of his coat to check for more weapons and I found another pistol. It was loaded. I noticed that it was of the new percussion-cap design and reflected that thieves like this would certainly have the latest of equipment as part of their evil trade.

"If you could turn me to my side a bit to ease my pain, I would thank you for it," said McCoy, looking over my shoulder.

It occurred to me that if McCoy had two pistols, then—

I heard the cock of the hammer and hit the ground in the same instant. The not-quite-dead Mr. Beatty pulled the trigger, the gun fired, and the bullet sailed across my breast to bury itself in McCoy's leg. I turned over, cocked the pistol that I held in my hand, and fired at Beatty. The ball went in his right eye socket and took off the back of his head.

I got to my knees and took a deep breath. I looked over and knew that we would hear no more from Mr. Beatty. I knew also that I had to clean up this mess, for if anyone came along, I could find myself with much explaining to do, and I had no wish to end my American adventure being hanged for murder.

I ran up to my little hillock and looked about and saw that no one was coming either way, so it looked like I had some time, at least for a while. I went back and gathered up the horses and led them into a small meadow I had previously noticed, hobbled them, and set them to graze. The beasts seemed content. Then I hurried back to the road.

Mr. McCoy was singing his death song.

"Lord, I've been to the river and I've been baptized and I have heard the Word of the Lord. I know that today will be my dyin' day, Jesus, and I beg You to take this poor sinner in Your lovin' arms and carry me away."

"Like He carried away the souls of all those poor travelers you murdered?"

McCoy turned his head to look at me as I took the feet of his former partner under either arm and dragged him into the bush. I have scouted out a deep ravine up near the hillock to hide the bodies until such time as the wolves find them. I got Beatty's body there and rolled it in and then went back to McCoy.

"I know I've been a sinner, but I know my sins will be washed away in the Blood o' the Lamb, yes, I know my redemption is at hand!"

"You've got a damned strange concept of religion in this land," I said as I gathered the fallen weapons from the ground. I broke off a pine bough and swept the ground of any signs of the mortal struggle that took place there. Time then for Mr. McCoy.

I put my hands under his armpits and dragged his groaning body through the woods to the edge of the ravine that was to be his grave.

He started singing, or rasping, really.

> *I am a pilgrim, and a stranger,*
> *Travelin' through this wearisome land,*
> *I've got a home in that yonder city, good Lord,*
> *And it's not—*

Someone's coming. I ran to the hillock to see a buckboard coming down the road from Johnstown. Man, wife, two children. *Damn! They'll hear him rant!*

McCoy heard the rattle of the buckboard, too, and grinned up at me.

"All I got to do is shout, boy, and they'll be up on you faster than hounds on a possum. And you'll be taken off and tried and hanged for the murderer you are. Ain't that some fine? I may not be here to watch it, but trust me, I'll know, wherever I might be."

I watched the approach of the buckboard. The family in it was singing gaily, looking forward to a holiday in the big town. I had to agree with the wisdom of what he had said.

I took my sword out of my scabbard.

"You ain't got what it takes, boy," giggled McCoy. "You was just Fink's fancy boy back in the lockup. That's all you was. You ain't got the balls."

It turned out I did. I glided the edge of my saber across his throat, pulling back hard. His eyes opened wide, but he never again said another word. Not in this world, anyway. I wiped my blade on his coat and pitched him over into the ravine and looked upon him no more.

The merry family passed by, completely unaware of what had just happened here.

I continued on the road down to Johnstown, figuring that I'd better go in that direction rather than returning to Pittsburgh, because the people back there might remark on the once penniless, funny-talking, ex-convict hayseed, who suddenly came back to town with two saddled horses and money in his overalls.

So I continued on down the road to Johnstown, to fit myself out for further travels.

In going through the bandits' effects, I found myself richer by seventy-five dollars. Johnstown turned out to be another godforsaken frontier town completely lacking in any grace or style, and was actually little more than an overlarge Indian village. I managed at least to sell the extra horse and saddle, no questions asked, as well as the old flintlock pistol and rifle that belonged to Clementine's father. I kept the four percussion-cap pistols that formerly belonged to Beatty and McCoy, and purchased what was represented to me as a "Kentucky squirrel gun, the most accurate rifle available today, yessir." It does have the new-fashioned grooved barrel that's supposed to spiral the bullets more accurately at the target, and I am anxious to try it out.

I did not strip the bodies back at that ravine, for I have never had a desire to wear dead men's clothes. However, in Johnstown, I found that there was no place to buy civilized clothing of any kind, so I bought the buckskin breeches and fringed leather shirt of the frontiersman off an Indian woman who was selling them by the roadside. She tried to sell me a hat that had the head of some unfortunate animal on the front of it, but I demurred. I kept the shirt that Clementine made for me, but threw away the overalls, hoping never to see the like again.

Apart from my sword, which hangs again at my side, there was one other object that McCoy had of mine in his saddlebag—it was the miniature portrait of you, Jacky, that you had painted with your own hand those years ago when you were at school, or when I thought you were at school. It fairly tore my heart out to see it, and it renewed in me the desire to track you down and bring you to bay, for that is the way I see it now.

I stayed overnight in a meager inn, had something to eat, and set out the next morning overland to get back to the river.

I won't be writing again for a while....

Chapter 39

"Mr. Cantrell," I say, putting on my stern Look. "It appears that your fare is only paid up to this point. You had said you would make good your fare as we went along. What do you mean to do?"

I am half joking, of course. I am perfectly willing to wait for my money till he finds more fertile grounds on which to practice his profession.

"Ah, yes, Miss." He sighs. He finishes his morning coffee and rises. "I had hoped that I might find some gentlemen of the sporting class on this cruise, but, alas, I found none. A more square-headed, Bible-toting bunch I have yet to see. But no matter." He looks off to the left. "I see that we are coming up on a small town on the Kentucky side...Augusta, is it? Yes. A fancy name for a squalid little town, but it will do quite nicely. If you could pull in there, Miss Faber, I'll go ashore and get your money."

Mystified, I give Jim, who's on the helm, the order to pull in to the rickety dock, and he throws over the steering oar and we drift in and tie up.

As soon as we are secure, Yancy Cantrell puts on his black hat, smooths down his lapels, and steps onshore. He gives a quick whistle and his black girl jumps to her feet and follows him off.

What is going on? I wonder.

But I do not have the time to muse on this because I hear a strong *ahem!* from Jim and see Reverend Clawson off to starboard on the main deck, his hat in his hands.

"Passenger Clawson," he says, a hopeful look on his face, "requests permission to cross the blue line, Miss. I would like to speak with you on matters that might be mutually beneficial."

"Come ahead, Reverend Clawson, and seat yourself," I say, graciously waving him to the seat recently occupied by Yancy Cantrell. "Clementine. A cup of tea for the Reverend, if you would."

Clementine appears shortly, bearing the cup, saucer, and spoon, and she pours from the teapot that already sits on my quarterdeck table. The girl has been coming along quite nicely. Later in the evening of what I thought was my disastrous performance back in Maysville, I sought the girl out and found her huddled up in one of the unused passenger bunks. I put my hand on her shoulder and said I was sorry for what I had said to her in anger and asked her to forgive me my rash words. She did, and all was well between us again. Later still, when we were in bed for the night, I asked her what she meant by having given me something that I never would know about, and she just said, "Don't mind me, Jacky, sometimes I just talk out of my head. It ain't nothin'."
Still, this girl is a mystery.

"It's this way, Miss," begins the Preacher, "I've been workin' this river...er, preachin' the Word of the Lord, up and down here for a while and I learned some things, chief of which is this: You've got to know the kind of people you're gonna be comin' up on, you got to know what the crowd'll be like. I think you found that out back in Maysville. I coulda told you what was gonna happen there, but I thought it best you find out for yourself," he says. He puts four rounded teaspoons of sugar into his cup, stirs it, and pauses in his speech to give it a slurp. "You being a high-spirited girl and not liable to take any old advice."

I nod at the wisdom of this.

"So what do you propose?"

He leans forward. "You sent young Tanner downriver before to scare up a crowd, and he did. What you should have done was to have him make two trips, the first being to have him case out the town, then report back to us on what sort of town it is. If it is a sanctified town, with hard-rock churchgoin' folks, then we'd put on a revival; if it is of a more open nature, you would put on your regular show; and if it is truly a wide-open town, then who knows what sort of show we could put on?" He winks broadly at me. "Do you get my drift?"

I begin to realize that this Reverend Clawson is a man of many parts.

"I do indeed, Reverend Clawson. And in the revivals, what part would I play?"

"Oh, Miss, the spiritual music is not far off from what you already play. I know you could do it up proud," he replies, smiling. "Yep, I just know you could get 'em rockin' and a-rollin' in the aisles, comin' up to testify and a-praisin' the Lord to the very high heavens themselves! You've got the gift. I know you do."

He chuckles and leans back to let me soak it all in, and I do.

While I am taking in all of this, he continues. "And there's another kind of show you ain't considered, and it's perfect for podunk places like Maysville."

Here he gets all conspiratorial and leans in close.

"You've got a whole lot of good whiskey down below. We could pick up a bunch of empty medicine bottles in Cincinnati, pour in some colored water, maybe add a few herbs, cut it half and half with some of your good ninety proof, paste on some fancy labels, and put on a medicine show. Same sort of thing you did at Maysville, but a lot shorter. I make the speech, you play a few tunes in your skimpiest outfit, we give out a few tiny samples, and we rake in what they got, be it coin, paper money, or barter. Then we pull up the stage and are back in the stream inside of two hours. Believe me, we will get no complaints on the quality of the medicine, because we *know* it will make everyone feel much, much better."

Now *this* is a man of the cloth I can relate to.

"So," I say at last, "if we could pick up a small sailboat, one that could be handled with oars if the wind was contrary...," I say, musing.

"I'm sure the proper boat could be found in Cincinnati. Y'see, I know the Ohio, down to Cincinnati, but I don't know the river the rest of the way, nor do I know the Mississippi." He looks off, all dreamy-eyed. "The Big River, the Father of Waters, oh, I'm so anxious to go, Miss. Can you imagine the multitude of souls who need saving all along the Big Muddy, all the way down to the evil dens of New Orleans?"

I look over at Reverend Clawson and realize that he would not be found terribly out of place in those evil dens.

"This has been a most interesting conversation, Reverend Clawson," I purr, "and I believe you may be safe in now calling yourself part of the crew of the *Belle of the Golden West*."

He gets up and bows. "And it is a singular honor to be named as such, Miss Faber. I look forward to a long and profitable relationship." Then he takes his leave of the quarterdeck.

I sit back in my chair and look out over the broad Ohio River and I think on what he has said. After a while I get up and go down to my bunk to rummage through my seabag and get out my carving tool, it being a V-shaped sort of blade that I've used before in woodcuts and in scrimshaw. I go down into the lower hold and find a nice smooth piece of hardwood.

Returning to my quarterdeck table, I set to work. Taking my pencil, I sketch out the words, backward of course, since this will be a print.

Captain Jack's Elixir
The finest of Tonics for the Cure of Catarrh, Ague, Liver Dyspepsia, Choleric Humor, Contrary Children, and Female Vapors, Nerves, & Hysteria

If I can find a printer in this upcoming Cincinnati, I will add more to the label. If not, this will have to do. I set to work on the wood square and let the chips fly.

———

I am finishing up the third line when Yancy Cantrell comes back aboard.

"Thank you for waiting, Miss Faber," he says, coming up to me and putting the fare money into my hand. I notice he has some more money, which he puts back into his pocket. "If you would shove off now, I think it would be good."

"Jim. 'Thaniel. Matty," I call, getting up and dusting the chips from my lap. "Let's be on our way. Cast off."

"Thank you, Mr. Cantrell," I say, bending back to my work, "but really, I would have trusted you for the money."

"I knew that, Miss Faber, but I felt it best that we keep accounts square," says Mr. Cantrell. Then, unaccountably, he says, "If it is not too much trouble, if we could keep close to the left bank, I would appreciate it."

This sounds a bit strange to me and I lift my head from my work. It is then that I notice that Cantrell's black girl is not with him. Grave suspicion grows in my mind.

"Where is your girl?" I demand, rising from my table.

"I sold her," says Yancy Cantrell, calmly, "for my fare, and for my stake in the next high-stakes card game. If you'll excuse me, Miss Faber, I believe I'll wash up for dinner."

"Higgins!" I shout. "My pistols! Now!"

Bearing the two firearms, Higgins bursts out of our quarters, a look of alarm on his usually placid face. I grab the pistols from him and train them both on Mr. Yancy Cantrell's forehead. He falls to his knees.

"You low-down, no-good son of a bitch! You sold that girl into slavery! Get off this boat! Get in the water now, before I blow your brains out! Now get out! Over the side! Now, you slimy bastard!"

Cantrell, seeing the fury in my eyes, puts his hands up in

front of his face and pleads, "No, please, Miss. Don't shoot. Just wait a few minutes, please. You'll see. Just wait. Stay close to the shore. Please."

The *Belle of the Golden West* slips by the southern bank, and as it does, I hear a splash, then the sound of someone swimming, and someone swimming quite well. I look over the port side and see Cantrell's girl stroking along, tawny arm over arm, and coming briskly alongside. Katy Deere reaches over the side and hauls her aboard.

"Now, if you could get to the middle of the stream, that would be good," says Mr. Cantrell, still looking fearfully down the barrels of my cocked pistols.

When I see the girl safely aboard, I put the pistols at half cock and lower them.

"So what's the scam, then?" I demand, not in the least mollified.

"We have done it many times before, Miss Faber," says Cantrell. "When we are in need of money, I take her inland, sell her, and return to the river. She makes her escape, and believe me she is expert in that, and she rejoins me downriver and we go on our merry way."

I am incredulous. "What happens if they lock her up?"

The girl looks at me with her dark eyes, water dripping from her hair. She pulls out a necklace, and from it dangles what I see is a set of lock picks. She shakes it and it tinkles like little bells.

"She knows how to get out."

"What if she can't?"

"I return and buy her back. Say I've had a change of heart. It's only happened once or twice."

I hand the guns back to Higgins. "All right, Mr. Cantrell. It is a good scam. But I will tell you this: I know I am barely sixteen years old, but this is *my* boat and I will say what scams get run from it, and you will never again do that particular one. If that ain't clear, you can get off now. What do you say to that?"

Yancy Cantrell bows his head and says, "Agreed." He turns to the black girl and says, "All right, Chloe. Go down and get dressed."

She gets up and says the first words I have yet heard her say.

"Yes, Father."

And she goes below.

Chapter 40

Mr. Cantrell is being chastised for running that risky scam, and while I know I will forgive him eventually, for now he is banned from my table. I do, however, ask that he invite his daughter for dinner with me that afternoon as we approach the town of Cincinnati.

She emerges from the lower decks, the ribbons and braids gone from her hair, hair that now falls in glossy black ringlets to her shoulders. She wears a gray dress of a quite nice cut, with a white shawl about those same shoulders. White stockings and neat shoes on her small feet complete the outfit. All gaze upon her in astonishment.

When she comes back on deck, she takes Cantrell's arm and he brings her up to me.

"Miss Faber, may I introduce my daughter, Chloe Abyssinia Cantrell?" says Mr. Cantrell. The girl lowers her eyes and dips down into a very acceptable curtsy.

I return the same.

"Her mother, my late and very much missed wife, was a teacher of the Coloreds in New York City," said Cantrell, by way of explanation for the girl's appearance here on the *Belle of the Golden West*.

"I am pleased to make your acquaintance, Miss Faber," murmurs this Chloe creature.

"Mutual, I am sure," I say. "And now will you join me for dinner so that we might become better acquainted?"

"I would be delighted, Miss Faber."

Will wonders never cease?

The dinner is laid out by Higgins, himself, this time. I think it's mainly because he wants to listen in to the conversation that will surely ensue, being as curious as to the nature of this girl as I am.

We go to my table. The canopy is up, this time because it looks like it might rain. She sits, tucking the dress under her bottom as she settles in. Napkin in lap, face composed. *Hmmmmm...*

"How came you to be here, Chloe, if I may call you that? Thank you, Higgins."

Higgins pours the tea and steps back. He gestures and Clementine brings up the platter of meat and potatoes. Chloe picks up the tongs and expertly nails a piece of venison. The platter comes to me and I do the same. This girl knows her way around a table, that's for sure.

"My mother was a teacher at the Abyssinian Academy in New York. She was educated by her parents, her father being a well-known Abolitionist preacher, who often addressed the students and teachers at King's College on the 'Peculiar Institution' of slavery. Her mother was a former slave, who had been indulged and set free by her owners. After I was born, Mother set herself to educating me to the highest level possible, believing that education was the way to advancement for any of the Colored race." She says this last with a wry smile.

"You don't agree with that?" I ask.

She cocks an eyebrow at me. "With my education, I could have become a tutor, maybe a governess."

"And that was not enough?"

"Enough for a black girl, you mean?"

I catch the edge in that. "There were times in my life, Miss, that I would have rejoiced to be either one of those. I have a book for you to read sometime. It was written by a friend of mine. It concerns my early life as a beggar on the streets of London."

"I would be glad to read it," she says, attending to her dinner. "This is very good. Thank you for inviting me."

"Yes, Janey's a very good cook," I say, applying myself to my own dinner. "I am sorry about your mother. Has she been gone long?"

She nods and, I think, loses some of her icy composure. "It's been two years. The yellow fever. I was devastated. Father returned home several days before she died, and was with her at the end," she says, "as was I."

"Mr. Cantrell was away at the onset of her illness?" I prompt, gently as I can.

"Father was away much of the time, pursuing his many...enterprises. We never knew what they were, but he generally returned with enough money to sustain us in the style to which we were accustomed," she says, a smile returning to her lips. "Grandfather Burgess never quite approved of Mother's choice of Father, but then one must follow one's heart, mustn't one?"

I take another sip of the tea and ask the question I have been dying to ask. "Your father...and mother...from such different...backgrounds, as it were. Was there not much talk?"

"Him being white and she being black, you mean?"

"*Umm.*"

"Well, they did not go out together in public much, not that Father gave a damn what anyone thought." Done with her dinner, she pats her lips with her napkin and places it on the table. "Besides, Mother was very beautiful, and Father was not untouched by the tar brush, as they say."

"Which means?"

"Father is from New Orleans. He is what is called an octoroon."

"Which means?"

"Which means a great-grandparent of his was a black man. Or woman, which is more likely the case."

"And so...?"

"In New York, people left us alone, and after Mother died, Father told me of his life and offered me the choice: Stay comfortable and bored in New York, or go off with him. I opted for the risky game."

I smile at that. "We are going to the South, you know, into the slave territories."

"I can play the po' little ol' black girl, as you know."

I think on that. "You know, you just might prove valuable on this journey, Miss Cantrell. Are you musical?"

"I can play the harpsichord, Miss Faber."

I have to laugh at that. "We are hardly likely to find such an instrument in Cincinnati, but who knows? As for now, let us talk of the 'risky game,' as you put it. Higgins, will you uncork us a bottle of the burgundy?"

————

After that very pleasant meal is done and cleared away and I'm at work at my table, I hear the call from 'Thaniel Hawkes: "Captain! We're comin' up on Cincinnati!"

I reach down to scratch the ears of my little pig, who lies asleep at my feet, and say, "Bring her in, Master Tanner, and let us see what this town has to offer the *Belle of the Golden West* and her weary travelers."

Belle **Log. Arrived Cincinnati, Ohio. Moored starboard side. Set out and secured performance boards. Disembarked passengers.**

What Cincinnati has to offer is about fifteen hundred human souls of many backgrounds, and about fifteen thousand souls of the swine variety, many running freely in the streets. We are told early on that this town is nicknamed "Porkopolis," and one's nose certainly verifies that it is indeed aptly named. No matter, we shall be quickly gone from here.

Our passengers debark and all proclaim that they had a most enjoyable cruise and would recommend us highly to all their friends. We send out the Hawkes brothers to plaster the town with posters to gain us new passengers on our journey south, and Jim Tanner goes about announcing tonight's show.

While Higgins and Crow Jane go off to buy more provisions, I take Clementine to see if we can find her a more presentable dress than the yellow rag she wears. I plan to use her in the performance tonight—we shall sing several duets of lonesome mountain songs to see how that goes over.

Reverend Clawson will deliver a Dramatic Recitation as well, so the cast of the Great American River Musical Revue is growing. It will be good not to have to bear the whole burden myself.

We find a general store and are able to buy some light blue material to make Clementine a nice little frock that will look good in performance. With Katy and Clementine both doing the cutting and sewing, it should be ready by nightfall. When Clementine finally does put it on, she fairly glows with the pleasure of wearing it. Jim Tanner is equally appreciative.

Miracle of miracles, while Higgins and Crow Jane were out and about, they found a harpsichord in a secondhand store and somehow managed to drag it back to the *Belle*. Evidently some poor family thought they could bring it west with them, but, alas, it was too heavy for their small flatboat. Fortunately our *Belle* is much bigger, and now Chloe can add to our musical efforts.

When we start to sign on passengers, we are perplexed by the number of people who want to go only to Shawneetown, a very small village on the Illinois side of the river. Upon some investigation, we find the reason. It is because of the fearsome outlaws who lurk at the place called Cave-in-Rock.

"Y'see, Miss, what they do is this. They send someone aboard to guide you down through the Rapids, but if the guide sees that you've got a lot of good cargo, what he'll do is run you aground near the cave and the other bad men will swarm all over you. They kill the people and slit open their bodies. Afterwards they stuff them with rocks to sink them in the river, and then they steal their boats. No, it's true, Miss, ask anybody. But, if you make it to Elizabethtown, which is right downriver from that place, well, we'll sure ride with you all the way to Cairo, yes, Ma'am."

Hmmmm. Fearsome, eh? Well, we'll show 'em fearsome...

It is now evening and the Very Reverend Jeremiah Clawson spreads his arms wide as he addresses our pretty good-sized audience.

"Good evening, ladies and gentlemen, and welcome to our show, a night of music, song, and story, starring our very own Miss Jacky Faber, the Lily of the West!"

Chapter 41

It has been a good week since we left Cincinnati, the river town that proved to be such a handy place. There I found a glass factory and arranged for one hundred half-pint bottles to be blown and ready for us two days hence, complete with corks, all at a very reasonable cost. From a local apothecary I purchased some herbs and spices—cloves, mallow root, and the like—ingredients that I knew would not be harmful to my customers, even if they proved to be of no actual help, medically speaking. And glory of glories, I was able to buy two whole gallons of tincture of opium, and if a bit of that in our elixir doesn't help soothe the mind, relax the body, and regulate the bowels, I don't know what will. I was glad to find sassafras root, too, which I had first tasted back at Dovecote and which was sure to give my concoction a medicinal taste. I would add no sugar—best make it strong tasting so they are convinced of its curative power. A crude print shop was found to print up the labels and we spent some time gluing them to the bottles.

After hearing of what could await us at Cave-in-Rock and the Rapids of the Ohio, Higgins and I purchased enough guns to fit out our regular crew of the *Belle:* a rifle and a pistol each for Crow Jane, the Hawkes brothers, Clementine, Katy, the Reverend Clawson, Chloe, and Yancy Cantrell. That supplemented the firearms Higgins and I, and some of the crew, already possessed. Lightfoot and Chee-a-quat were already as armed as they needed to be. Jim requested a tomahawk and was given one. Powder and ball for all was purchased, and the new armament was put under the care of our new Master-at-Arms, Mr. Higgins, who locked everything away in a sturdy cabinet. Can't be too careful, I figure. We had bought much more powder than we originally planned, because we had been practicing with the two cannons ever since we got them aboard—trying ever harder for greater accuracy and speed in reloading. I finally pronounced us as ready as we could be for any emergency.

I also bought a ship's bell. No, it didn't come from any ship way out here, 'cause there ain't any, but it was a bell nonetheless—all bright and shiny brass—and I had it mounted by the helm. No, we shan't ring out the hours, 'cause we ain't got an accurate enough clock for that, but still, if we need to ring an alarm, we'll be ready.

Oh, yes, and now we tow a jaunty little sailboat behind us that we picked up for a song. It's only about twelve feet long, gaff rigged, and equipped with oars to use when there is no wind or when the river gets too narrow. It's a sweet little sailer and big enough for the Reverend Clawson and Jim to sail down ahead of us, moor at a likely town, figure out what show would go best in that particular place, then spread the word to the populace in the village and to farms thereabouts.

But before Jim is ready to take her on short jaunts downriver, he practices sailing her and delights no end in taking Clementine about and showing off his skill. I can hear her squeals of excitement as the boat heels over in a stiff breeze and rips along on a splendid beam reach.

They both beg me to let Clementine accompany Jim on his excursions downriver, but I cannot allow it. For one thing, it's too dangerous. I worry enough about having Jim off alone on these short trips—even if Reverend Clawson, who knows nothing of sailing, is along. And two, how do I know that Clementine and Jim won't crawl off in the bushes somewhere for a bit of a romp? Besides, the small sailer is really too small to carry three people. I hate acting like Mistress Pimm back at the Lawson Peabody School, 'cause it's certainly not in my nature, but sometimes I have to.

I do, however, let Jim have the honor of naming the little boat, but tell him he cannot name it after anyone aboard. After some serious consideration, he decides on the *Evening Star,* which I find rather poetic of my Jim Tanner.

We cruise placidly down the river and very soon find the territory of Indiana on our starboard side. The days are pleasant, as is the weather, by and large, and we settle into a comfortable routine aboard the *Belle.* As for the education of my young crew, I now have Chloe Cantrell to help in the education of Clementine, Katy, and Jim, too, for he doesn't know as much as he thinks he does. As for my own further education, I find that Crow Jane knows the sign language that the various tribes in this area use to communicate with each other and I demand that she teach me. Katy, too, seems anxious to learn. The signs are graceful, eloquent, and it is fun to learn them.

It is also fun to play with my little piglet, whom I have named Pretty Saro after the song that tells of a poor immigrant who comes to this country and, I reckon, that speaks to my case.

> When first to this country a stranger I came,
> I placed my affections on a handsome young dame,
> She was lissome and lovely and light in her frame,
> And Saro, Pretty Saro, was her given name.

I generally keep her tied to a leg of my table when she's not sitting in my lap revelling in having me scratch her ears. She does enjoy that and gives out little grunts of pleasure when it is done. She sleeps back by the tillerman, where her little messes are easily washed over the side with a bucket of water.

Crow Jane repeatedly gazes upon her, running her knife over her whetstone, sharpening it to a razor's edge. I shiver and look away. I have said that we would not do that till Pretty Saro is older. Would it not be better to have a whole pig, rather than just a little piglet? Jane grunts and walks away, sheathing her knives, for the moment.

Trouble is, Pretty Saro grows bigger every day.

The territory called Indiana is well named. More and more do we see Indian camps along the shore. Naked children are laughing and splashing in the shallows. Laughing, that is, till they see us coming round the bend, then they scurry off and are silent. I envy them—I'd like a swim, too, and although my crew already knows me for one who sometimes flouts convention, what with the passengers aboard, I really can't do it. So for now I have to be content with baths in the washtub down in our quarters. I have noticed, however, that Chee-a-quat bathes often. I have many mornings seen him in the water next to the bank on which he and Lightfoot had camped the night before. By the movement of his arms and how he holds his face up to the sky, the bath seems to be not only for cleanliness but also a ritual.

Chee-a-quat will not speak directly to me in English, although Lightfoot says that his friend does understand it—it's just that he refuses to speak it, calling it a "lying tongue." He will, however, answer in like manner if I sign to him… after waiting a moment or two to remind me of my place. Like the time we went close to the bank several days into the journey from Cincinnati and came upon an encampment of Indians, mostly men, and, as far as I could tell, mostly drunk. There was much shouting and wailing and waving of weapons at us as soon as we were spotted. Chee-a-quat, who was standing near me on the quarterdeck, his arms crossed on his chest, barked out a string of what I suspected was insults and then spit in the direction of the shore group. There was one Indian over there who I suspected was the leader. He had his hair plucked out on either side of his head, leaving a scruffy crest on top, and half his face was painted red. He did not look friendly.

I turned to Chee-a-quat and made the sign *What?* by holding my right hand open, palm toward him with fingers spread and then turning my hand at the wrist several times.

He brought his dark eyes to bear upon me and lifted his clenched right hand to the left side of his bare chest, which he then lowered to his side, opening the fingers, one by one. *Bad,* it meant. Then he made the sign for *shame.*

The figures on the shore increased their wild howling upon seeing Chee-a-quat, and they started toward the canoes pulled up on the riverbank. I was about to run over to ring the bell in alarm, but Chee-a-quat calmly lifted his rifle, aimed, and shot. There was a yelp from the shore and one of the Indians fell over into the mud.

I was shocked by this casual murder, but Chee-a-quat seemed unconcerned. He lowered his rifle and pointed to the throng on the shore, which was now clawing their way back into the cover of the woods, and he made the sign for *cowards*.

Crow Jane, hearing the shot, came up on deck and looked over the scene, as did Lightfoot.

"*Squee-eh-squash!*" she said contemptuously, adding a stream of spit of her own to those ashore. To me she said, "Renegades. Outcasts. Murderers who kill their own people. Drunkards who sell their own women. Thieves who steal from anybody. They come from all of the Five Nations. You Whites have your bad ones. We have ours."

I nodded and looked at Chee-a-quat and said, "*Wah!*"

I swear he almost smiled as he turned and walked away.

We practice with the weaponry, as well, on the way south, to the great amusement of the passengers, especially the children. When we fire the cannons, the kids cover their ears and fairly scream with delight.

All the males in my crew are well enough versed in firearms, including the Preacher. Yancy Cantrell is expert. We drill Clementine and Chloe and Katy in how to load the rifles and pistols: First, the proper measure of powder is poured from the horn into the barrel and tamped down with the ramrod. Second, the bullet is dropped, and after that, the wad is pushed down, tamping the whole thing solid. Then the percussion cap is put on the nipple, the hammer cocked, the gun aimed, the trigger pulled, the gun fired, and the bullet goes on its murderous way.

Katy finds the loading process too slow compared to how fast she could loose arrows from her bow, but she learns all the same.

It's not all armament and murder. We put on shows at Louisville, Kentucky, a bustling little town, where our performance goes over very well, as it does farther downriver at Evansville, on the Indiana side. In between, though, we try a revival at the little town of Owensboro, Jim having gone down and found it a place more suitable for our sanctified show, and so he talked it up some. The word spreads and we draw a good crowd. The Reverend Clawson takes center stage with his Bible-thumpin', Hell-raisin', Judgement's-a-comin, brimstone-breathin', fire-eatin' sermon, while Clementine, 'Thaniel, Chloe, Matty, and me with my voice and fiddle do our best from the sidelines, belting out the holy songs and all of us together getting them rockin' and rollin' and writhin' in the aisles. The Preacher saves at least thirty souls that day, and lays hands on more than a few and cures 'em of what ails 'em. A couple of bottles of Captain Jack's Elixir passed around just before the service doesn't hurt none, neither. It gets 'em in the mood, like.

At the end the Reverend calls upon the faithful to give what they can for our ministry. "Which is bringin' the word of God to the poor miserable heathen Red Savages what don't know no better 'cause they don't know the love of God yet, but would surely shine in the glory of the Lord and be no longer a pestilence to us white folk. Give! Give what you are able to give to this noble cause! The Lord Jesus will take you to His side for your kindness to these poor wretches! Ride on, King Jesus, ride on and conquer all evil, ride on!"

The Preacher is really getting worked up at this point, but he pulls himself together enough to lay his hand upon his chest and intone, "And now, the angel Evangeline will take up your offerings. Bless you, oh, bless you...," and Jim kills the footlight lanterns and fires up the light behind me where I'm now standing on the cabin top. I'm wearing a long white gown, which Katy and I have sewn, that flows from my throat to my ankles, and we have made up a crown of gold leaf that now rests on my head, glinting in the light. It is not a halo, but it is close. There is a quiet gasp from the congregation as they behold me there. I hold the pose for a moment and then descend and go into the crowd, holding my basket before me. *Bless you, oh, bless you.* I hear the coins tinkle into the basket and smile my beatific smile. *Oh, bless you and bless your children.* And I mean it, too, as I weave through all these happy, smiling faces, knowing that we have put on the best show we could—and I do love putting on a good performance, whether sacred or profane.

Log of the *Belle of the Golden West*. 14:30, arrive Shawnee-town, Illinois. Debark passengers. Prepare for battle.

The passengers get off in Shawneetown, Illinois, a small place that seems to make its living chiefly by providing for the needs of travelers who prefer to portage rather than face the dangers of Cave-in-Rock. It ain't big enough to be worth our show, so we push the *Belle* off and head downstream and get ready for the fight.

When we moor for the night, fifteen miles above Cave-in-Rock, I invite my entire crew in for a grand dinner on the passenger deck, and so we sit and eat and drink together, British and American, Indian, Negro, and somewhat White. For some of us, who knows, it might well be our last.

Dear Jaimy,

As I lie here in my bunk next to a girl named, of all things, Clementine Amaryllis Jukes (can you imagine such a name?), I think fondly of you back in Jolly Old England doing I don't know what. What I do hope is that you are safe and well and that maybe we might meet up again soon. It'll take me a while to get to New Orleans, and if I can take passage there for Britain, then that'll be another three weeks, at least.

Ugh! Clementine has just turned over in her sleep and I have to push her back a bit or else I'll be pushed over the side. I know she is a bit nervous about what will happen tomorrow, but she is a tough, brave little thing and I know she'll be all right. What? Wait…she is talking in her sleep, saying something like Ja-Ja-Jaimy? No, that can't be right. There she goes again…J-J-Jim…Ah, that's who she meant. While I can't blame her, I'll be keeping an eye on those two, that's for sure, otherwise there'll be a swellin' of a certain belly soon, and I don't need that, and neither does she.

I don't really want to be doing this thing that I will be doing tomorrow, Jaimy, for you know that I am really, at heart, a peaceable coward and would like nothing better than to lie back on my quarterdeck and soak up the sun as I float gently down to New Orleans, maybe bringing some people a bit of cheer as I go.

Ah, but that is not to be. As so often happens in this world, there are evil people who stand in the way of such a peaceful idyll because they seize boats carrying goods of any value and commit rape and murder for personal lust, and so I must do what I must do. What else is there? Abandon my ship and creep around the bandits at Cave-in-Rock and take off again with nothing and nothing with which to pay off my loyal crew? Nay, we must push through, for the tales of the foul deeds that those fiends have committed sicken me even to think of them, and they must be stopped.

Pray for me, Jaimy, as I pray for you.

Chapter 42

We round a bend in the river, all of us at our usual stations: Katy at the bow on lookout, the Hawkes brothers on the forward sweeps, Jim on steering oar, and me at my quarterdeck table, with First Mate Higgins at my side. I have on my black cloak and am covered by it from neck to boot top. Clementine and Chloe sit on the cabin top, in plain sight of anyone with a long glass, sewing away at a quilt and chatting sociably. All others are below, the better to make us look like helpless and easy prey.

"A fine morning, Miss," observes Higgins. He is wearing a long riding duster over his usual clothes, the better to conceal the two pistols he wears tucked in his vest.

"Indeed it is, Mr. Higgins," I reply. I put down my teacup and look out over the river, which does seem to be working itself up into a faster flowing stream. On the shore, I see bigger and bigger boulders sticking out of the water. I suspect the Rapids of the Ohio are not far downstream. In front of me is a map, which shows what we know of Cave-in-Rock, which is not much. It is apparently a fifty-foot cliff on the Illinois side of the river giving anyone standing on top a clear view of the river traffic coming down. In the cliff itself there is a large cave twenty feet high and thirty feet across its mouth and a hundred and fifty feet deep, wherein the outlaws and their hangers-on live.

"What do you think, Miss?" asks Higgins, refilling my cup from the pot that sits on the table.

I consider this and say, "There are evil men there, Higgins, men who think they are powerful and cunning, and we shall be meeting them soon, I think, but I try to hold down my fear." I add, "For are we not, you and I, Royal Navy?"

"Yes, Miss, we are."

"Then, they don't stand a chance, do they?"

"No, Miss, they do not."

"I thought not, Higgins," I answer. "However, if they do manage to prevail against us, I want you to know that I consider you the best friend I have ever had in this world and I will die happy knowing that I had your friendship to the end."

"The feeling is mutual, Miss, but you should not let—"

"Man in boat to starboard!" shouts Katy. "Callin' out to us!" Higgins rises from the table and goes to the side.

Ah, that would be our guide through the treacherous Rapids of the Ohio . . . or to be delivered to what other treachery might lurk there.

I look out and see a man standing in a rowboat, waving his hat to us.

"Pull over by him," I say to Jim, and the *Belle* glides over to the small boat.

"What do you want?" calls out Higgins to the man.

"Sir," announces this person, "I am Mr. Fortescue, Frederick Fortescue, as it were, and I am a most experienced pilot. I would be glad to guide your boat through these wicked waters for a *most* modest sum. What do you say?"

"Bring him aboard," calls out Higgins, who will be acting as Captain for a short time. The man scampers up our side, leaving his rowboat to fend for itself. He shakes Higgins's hand and strides back to the quarterdeck and stations himself in front of Jim at his steering oar.

Hmmm. Not a good sign in a waterman, I'm thinkin', *leavin' his boat adrift like that.*

"Off to the left there, boy. Now rudder amidships! Steady as she goes!"

"You are experienced in these waters?" asks Higgins, affecting a pose of hopeful indecision.

"None better!" crows this creature. "Why, I know ever' rock in this river better'n I know the hairs on the back of my hand!"

Well, we shall see about that. I sense him for a fraud right off, but I have been told that there are honest guides on this river, as well as the rogues, so I hold my tongue, at least for the time being. We head down the river and the stream gets faster and faster and the rocks appear more and more frequently at our sides.

While this man is guiding us along, I rise from my table and approach this Mr. Fortescue, with my eyes cast down, and ask in a tremulous voice, "Please, Sir, I beseech you for myself and on behalf of the other helpless females aboard this craft that you will do your best to see us through to safety."

He looks at me, and then at Katy and Chloe and Clementine sitting up forward, and then smiles a smile that I recognize as being full of absolute joyful anticipation. Of course, I know he would not be high on the pecking order, but I also realize that *he* knows he'd have a run at us after the big tough men were done.

"Don't you worry, Miss," says he. "This is all gonna work out jes fine. Jest you settle back, now."

Finally, after the river rounds another bend, Cave-in-Rock comes into view. It is much as it had been described: a high cliff with a cave in its face. It has low-growing bushes about the mouth to the cave, and some more growing across the top. Bigger trees are at the bottom.

Mr. Fortescue guides us toward the middle of the river.... Should he bring us in the slightest way to the right, then we will know for sure that he is a bad one, and we will go from there.

"Steady as she goes, boy," he says to Jim, and Jim nods.

The cliff is now about a half mile downriver. I can see figures moving at the top of the bluff, and I see a boat putting off from the shore that lies beneath the looming cliff.

"Take her off to the right, boy," says Mr. Fortescue, sealing his fate.

"Belay that, Master Tanner," I order, standing and flinging off my cloak, revealing that I am dressed in full military array—my beautiful blue lieutenant's jacket with all its gold trim, black boots, white britches, and leather straps across my chest holding my two fine pistols. I withdraw one of the pistols and point it at Mr. Fortescue's forehead and say, "On your knees, scum."

He gapes and does not move.

"On your knees, *now!*" I warn. "Or I'll scatter your brains all over the river." I click back the hammer. *"Now!"*

He drops to his knees, too shocked to say anything.

"Higgins! Pull him over to the other side of the cabin! Put him down and bind him!" Higgins grabs him by the scruff of his neck and drags him over to the side. Higgins had laid out two short lengths of rope for just this purpose, and now he uses them to truss up the hands and feet of the false pilot. Higgins uses his booted foot to force him face-down onto the deck, out of sight of anybody watching us with a long glass from the cliff.

"Help me, boys! Help me!" bellows our prisoner.

"Best gag him, Mr. Higgins, before he alerts his friends."

Higgins takes a handkerchief from his pocket and crams it into the captive's mouth. Aside from muffled curses, we hear no more from him.

The boat I had spotted before is now about a hundred yards ahead, and I can plainly see that it is full of men, probably a good ten or twenty of them, with no guns in sight.

Good. That means they didn't leave many behind to guard their fortress.

"Ready, everybody," I call, trying to keep my voice from trembling. *Legs, stop shakin'!* Katy and Chloe get up and go into the foreward hatch, while Clementine comes around the starboard side and goes down into the rear hatch. All in the crew had been given permission to get off with the passengers and meet us downstream, no hard feelings, but none took me up on it, not even the Preacher.

The boat is now fifty yards directly ahead. The men in it wave and *halloo* and yell out things like "Come visit our tavern!" and "Good entertainment up at the Cave!"

Twenty-five more yards and the charade is over. We see the men in the boat raise their rifles and point them at us, calling out, "Pull up, pull up there or forfeit your lives!"

I hear a *pop* and see a puff of smoke rise from the boat. The bullet hits the top of the cabin down and to the right of me.

Wait one more second, till they are in point-blank range...
Now!

I throw over my table and whip the canvas cover off the swivel gun that lies beneath it, calling out, "Rudder hard right! Matty, pull! 'Thaniel, back!" and Jim throws the rudder over and the *Belle* swerves to the left, swinging her stern to face the oncoming boat.

I throw the levers that allow the gun to swivel on its base and to be raised or lowered. Then I point the barrel down to aim it directly at the enemy boat, lock down the levers, yell *fire!* and pull the matchlock.

There is a roar as five pounds of sharp nails spray our would-be murderers. Then there are screams as many claw at their bloody faces while others curse, but some don't say anything at all.

"Reload! Jim, keep bringin' her around! Matty, pull! 'Thaniel, back! Bring her around!"

At the sound of the blast, Clementine, stripped to undershirt and drawers for ease of movement, bursts out of the crew's quarters, carrying a charge of powder. Higgins is already swabbing the barrel. Clementine slides the bag down the barrel and steps out of the way as Higgins rams in a wad. She picks up another cloth bag, this one containing more nails, and puts that in. Another wad, another ram, and ready again.

I swivel, aim, and *fire!*

More screams, more shouts, but the boat with its cargo of killers is not yet done. There are several of the bandits who remain untouched and are shaking their fists and demanding revenge.

At the sound of the first shot, as planned, Lightfoot, Chee-a-quat, Cantrell, and Katy hurry back up on deck, their rifles at the ready. Katy, like Clementine, has stripped down to her old fighting gear—drawers rolled to her knees, white band around her head. She also has her strung bow across her chest and a quiver full of arrows hanging down her back. The three of them take up positions on the cabin top and begin shooting with great effect into the other boat. Katy and Lightfoot say nothing as they set about their grim work, but Chee-a-quat stands straight and tall and sings what I suspect is a death song.

The *Belle* has now swung completely around such that her bow again points directly at the brigands' boat. I bound across the cabin top and yank off the canvas from the forward fixed cannon. There is, I know, a four-inch round ball deep in the cannon's throat, resting on a full charge of powder.

The Preacher has come up on deck with swab in hand, to help me with the gun. Feeling that it would not be right for a man of the cloth to be actively killing people, howsoever vile they might be, he has elected to be gun loader on the forward cannon. It is still a dangerous job, as bullets continue to buzz about us. One bullet takes off his hat and sends it skidding across the deck.

I take the ratchet bar and crank down the barrel, then call out to the Hawkeses. "Matty, back! 'Thaniel, pull! Keep doing it till you hear this gun fire!"

They do it and the barrel of the gun swings into range of the attacking boat. I have only to wait till it comes to bear. *A little bit more, a little bit more…* The gun points at the water, then the gun points at their hull…now…*Fire!*

The recoil from this much more powerful gun shoves the *Belle* ten feet back in the water and knocks both the Preacher and me from our feet. It may do some damage to us, but it is nothing compared to what it does to the other boat. The ball slams into their starboard side, opening a huge hole, and the boat goes straight down. Or down as far as it can, which is about two feet, before it hits bottom. Those in the boat who are still able climb out and head for the bank. Lightfoot and Chee-a-quat take down a few before they reach the safety of the shore. Several even try to climb aboard the *Belle*, but showing no mercy, we club them down with the butts of our rifles. They sink and try us no more.

I keep telling myself, *These are murderers, girl… They have killed helpless men, women, and, yes, even children… You should not care what you do to them…* I tell myself that… but still…

Cradling in her arms a bag of powder, Chloe, in the same state of undress as Katy and Clementine, emerges from the hold to reload the fore cannon.

At the sight of her doing her job, I shake myself out of these bootless thoughts and look over the battlefield and, satisfied with what I see, call out, "Plan B!"

At that, Katy returns to her lookout position and I go back on the quarterdeck. I remove my long glass from its rack to scan the cliff. *Hmmm.* No sign of much activity, yet. Then I lower the glass and scan the bank on the right.

"Anything, Katy?" I ask.

"Nothin' yet…wait! Got bottom…'bout six feet down… sandy…some rocks…now about four feet."

I had spied before a large tree trunk that had fallen from the bank into the water, its roots still anchored to the shore.

"Jim! Steer for that tree! 'Thaniel, pull! Matty, hold! Now pull together! Katy?"

"'Bout the same...no...bottom comin' up. Two feet now, still sand and a few rocks, now..."

There's a grating sound as the *Belle*'s keel slips up on the shoal, but we are close enough such that her bow noses up to the fallen trunk.

"All right! Go!"

And Lightfoot and Chee-a-quat and Katy leap up on the trunk and disappear into the woods. Their mission: to keep the robbers from taking their booty out of the cave. I don't want Katy to go, but she insists, saying that she can cover them with her arrows whilst they reload their rifles, and so I let her go. She'd have gone, anyway; my authority only goes so far on this bark.

"'Thaniel and Matty! Push us off, boys!"

The Hawkes brothers take their sweeps from the oarlocks and stick them into the sandy bottom and push with all their might. It is not enough, though, so Higgins and Reverend Clawson come up to add their backs to the push. Reluctantly, the *Belle* slides back into the stream.

"Get your oars reset and pull us out!" *Out, so I can have some firing room.* "Stroke! Stroke!"

I look up at the cliff and as soon as I can see the cave opening, I say, "Drop the anchor, Jim!" and he does it. We can feel the hook take hold by the dragging of the deck below our feet, and I go to the forward cannon.

I crank up the elevation as high as it will go. I will aim it side to side with the help of the Hawkeses.

"'Thaniel, back. Matty, pull. Keep doing it till I say 'hold.'" They do it, and the barrel of the cannon slowly swings over toward the mouth of the cave.

"Hold," I say. Then, as the momentum takes us a few more degrees to port, I say, *"Fire!"* and pull the lanyard of the matchlock.

The cannon barks out its ball and we stand and wait for the results. It hits above and to the right of the cave mouth. I think I can hear cries of alarm from up there. It is good that the shot was high, for I can get no more elevation out of this gun. I take the ratchet bar and crank down two. The Preacher and Chloe have already reloaded, and I have only to yell *fire!* and pull the lanyard.

This time the ball hits the right side of the cave wall and careens into the interior. There are more screams and people spill out. I note with dismay that some are women.

But I harden my heart, and when the gun is reloaded, I fire it again. This time the ball goes straight into the mouth. I think I hear glass shattering.

"Let's have a hot one this time," I say, as Chloe and the Preacher reload. "Jane! Bring up a hot ball!" and Crow Jane struggles out of the hold, grasping in big tongs a red-hot cannonball, which had nestled in the coals of the stove for many hours. She drops it in the barrel and I waste no time in firing it, for the heat of the ball could set off the gun all by itself.

It, too, goes right into the cave mouth, followed by more shrieks and howls. Smoke begins to pour out of the opening. I lift my glass and watch. And then I hear the popping of rifle fire. That would be Lightfoot and Chee-a-quat firing at the retreating robbers. Their orders are to prevent the outlaws from hauling off any booty with them, but I fear they might be doing much more than that.

"Hold fire," I order, as I notice a woman come out of the cave, holding a baby. A few minutes later I see a figure on top of the cliff waving a red piece of cloth. It is Katy, and it is the signal that the place is taken.

"Secure the cannon. Lift anchor. Bring us back to the shore. Well done, all."

The *Belle* swings back into the shore and again runs gently aground. I hop out into the shallows and call out for Higgins, the Hawkes boys, and Cantrell to come with me, leaving the ship in the capable care of Jim, Clementine, Chloe, and the Preacher. I lead my party into the woods.

We find a well-worn trail that we know will lead up to Cave-in-Rock, and we work our way along it, pistols at the ready should we meet any disgruntled former inhabitants of the place. We meet none.

Eventually we reach the top to find Lightfoot and Chee-a-quat leaning on their rifles. From Lightfoot's belt hangs a bloody swatch of what looks like human hair.

"Where's Katy?" I ask, and he nods his head in the direction of the cave mouth. "And what's that—on your belt?"

Lightfoot considers this, then says, "'Member when I said I was goin' downriver 'cause there was a man down there who needed killin'?"

"Yes...?"

"He don't need killin' no more."

Ah.

Higgins and I go off to find Katy, while the Hawkes brothers strip the bodies on the ground of any valuables they might have. I notice that two of the dead men have arrows sticking out of them. Another looks like he was done in with Chee-a-quat's tomahawk. I look away from that.

I find her coming out of the mouth of the cave, dragging the smouldering bedding that had been set on fire by the hot cannonball. The cave entrance was clearing of smoke.

"What have we got, Kate?"

"Some food. Powder. Bullets. Guns. Piles of stuff. The place looks like pigs've been living in it," she says. "I think Lightfoot dropped the one that was trying to get away with the money box. But then again, I think the real prize is down there..." She points down toward the water, and there, nestled amongst the greenery of the shore, float two boats, one a flatboat, the other a keelboat like the *Belle*. It's plain that they are boats stolen from innocent, luckless, and now-dead travelers. There is a path that leads down to the boats.

"I think you're right, Katy," I say, already making plans in my head.

"There's a child in there, too," adds Katy, nodding toward the cave. "Boy child. Sick. Maybe dead."

I look at Higgins and we go into the cave. It's plain that there's another entrance to this place, for a breeze blows through and the smoke is all but gone. The place is indeed a sty, but what would you expect from an outlaw den?

There is a natural stone aisle that leads right into the cave—it is almost as if stonemasons had carved it, it is so straight and regular. On either side of this passageway are relatively flat rock ledges, shoulder high, that extend to the cave edges and have plainly served as sleeping areas—some seem almost to look like family hearths, with bunks and beds laid in a circle. I decide not to think on that.

Following the aisle to its end, we come to a large, domed room, which has a small hole at the top, through which sunlight twinkles. There are remains of a large fire in the center of this room, and a trickle of smoke trails up to the vent hole at the top. *What a perfect fortress,* says the pirate in me.

There are piles of clothing and barrels of whiskey and tons of other booty the river pirates have taken and that now belong to us. Back along the right side of the cave is one of the living areas, and in one of the beds there, I see the recumbent form of a child, lying faceup.

I go over, with Higgins beside me, and look down. "What do you think?"

Higgins puts his hand on the boy's forehead. "He is about eight years old and still alive, at least, but very feverish." He opens the boy's shirt and looks at his chest. "No measles, no chicken pox, no smallpox...I think it's influenza. He is barely conscious." The boy moans and twists in the bed. He is covered in sweat.

"All right," I say. "If he's still alive when we're ready to quit this place, we shall take him with us. Now let's get loading."

I leave Higgins to supervise the loading of the goods and go back out to the Hawkes brothers, who are now through with their grisly work.

"Matty. 'Thaniel. I'm going back to move the *Belle* over next to those boats you see down there. We'll load whatever we can take from here into them."

They both answer, "Yes, Skipper," as they get down to the business of stacking up the booty.

"And, lads, you could not have been more brave today when those bullets were whizzing around and yet you stood at your posts, manning your sweeps. We could not have done this without you, and I want you to know that."

"Ah, *pshaw*," the boys reply together, blushing, but I know that they are pleased.

I make sure that Lightfoot and Chee-a-quat are continuing to guard against the return of the remnants of the outlaws, and then head back to the *Belle* at a dead run.

"We're gonna move her about fifty yards downriver to load cargo. Everybody on the poles to pull her off!"

The *Belle* comes off the shoal fairly easily and we slip back into the stream.

"Mind the rocks now, Jim…There! You see those two boats tied up there? Head in!"

We slip in beside the other boats and tie up.

"I'm going back up," I say, leaping onto the deck of the flatboat and then onto the other keelboat. "Clementine, you, too." With a delighted yelp, she follows me off.

She falls a bit behind me 'cause it's always been my pride that no one beats Jacky Faber in climbing the rigging, and nobody beats her on a steep trail, either.

There is a rustle in the bushes next to me, and startled, I turn to face a very large, extremely wet man with rivulets of blood coursing down his face. Apparently he is one of the men from the robbers' attack boat, obviously his rifle is wet and useful now only as club, and plainly he wishes to kill me. He swings the rifle butt at my head as I manage to raise my shoulder in time to deflect the blow, but still it knocks me facedown in the dirt, stunned.

Looking up, I see with horror that there is a bayonet at

the other end of the gun. He reverses the gun in his hand and lifts it over his head and prepares to use all his force to drive the point through my back and pin me to the ground.

I can't reach my pistols, I can't... Oh, God, I'm gonna...

I hear two shots, one right after the other, and two blossoms of red appear on the man's chest. He drops the weapon and falls back, still as a stone.

I roll over to see Clementine standing over me, her two smoking pistols held out at shoulder level.

"Thank you, Sister," I say, my voice quavering as I get to my knees and then shakily stand. "He'd have skewered me for sure."

She nods, looking dumbly at the smoking pistols in her hands. *I know how that feels, Clementine, when you kill someone, no matter how vile they might be, but we'll deal with this later.*

"Reload, Clementine. There might be more." Given this simple task to do, she does it, and we continue on to the cave, with me being much more watchful this time. *Stupid thing, you! Keep watch!*

We gain the cave mouth and the Hawkes boys begin taking the plunder down to the boats. I go around to the side, where Lightfoot and Chee-a-quat and Katy are standing guard against a possible return of the thieves, and I call Katy to me. As she comes toward me, I notice Lightfoot watching her as she goes. *Hmmm.*

"Katy," I say. "Stand guard on Matty and 'Thaniel as they take the goods down. I was almost killed by one of the survivors of the bandits' boat on my way up here. If not for Clementine, I'd be dead right now."

"*Um,*" she says, nods, and lopes off after the boys.

Clementine and I go into the cave to find Higgins separating what we can use or sell from that for which we'd have no possible use.

"So, Mr. Higgins, just what do we have here?"

"Well, Miss, we have this," he says, handing me a sort of flat wooden box. "A man attempted to escape with it, but he did not make it past your dragoons. Katy brought it down."

I lift the lid. Inside is an assortment of watches, gold and silver coins, brass buttons, gold buttons, brooches, hairpins, necklaces, pearls...*How sad,* I think to myself when I pick up an exquisite cameo to examine. *This was probably some poor girl's most prized possession. It is all just so sad...the evil that exists in men, I cannot understand it.*

"Good," I say out loud, snapping the lid closed and handing it back to Higgins. "There will be a payday in Cairo when we get there, and I'm sure, since no one has gotten any pay yet, all will welcome that. What else did you find here?"

"Powder—whiskey, mostly. Several dozen chickens. Clothing we will be able to use or else sell. And one item in particular that might interest you, Miss," says Higgins. "But first I must show you this."

With that he strides over to the pallet that holds the sick boy. The boy's eyes are still half shut and he is shivering. Higgins reaches down to lift the bottom edge of the blanket. Around the boy's thin, grimy ankle is a shackle to which is attached a short length of chain and attached to that is an iron ball of about twenty pounds.

I draw in my breath. "A captive, then," I say. "And not one of the scum. We must take him with us."

I turn to Clementine. "Run back down to the boat and

get Chloe. Tell her to bring her lock-picking tools. Both pistols in your hands, now, and keep a sharp watch."

She looks at me with those cornflower blue eyes and nods, a slight smile on her lips. She pulls the pistols from her belt and heads out and down.

That look she gives me sometimes...it's like an I-know-somethin'-you-don't-know look...Nah, it's just my imagination.

I turn back to Higgins. "When we get it all loaded, leave a big bag of powder in here. We'll run a line of gunpowder from it and out the front, and when we're done, we'll light it off to burn anything in here that the robbers might find useful should they return. I want to hear their rotten teeth gnash from wherever I am when they discover that they don't even have their foul beds to sleep on."

"Aye, aye, Lieutenant," says Higgins, knowing how much I like the title. "And here is the item you might find interesting." He holds up a wooden thing that must be a musical instrument, for it has a hollow body, a fret board, and six strings.

I take it in my hands and strum the strings. It gives off a deep, mellow discord. "What is it?" I ask.

"I believe it is called a *guitarra*, Miss. It's a Spanish instrument," answers Higgins.

Yes, of course. I saw a woman in Kingston playing one the time I was there with the *Dolphin*. And, yes, of course, this is definitely *mine*.

In time, Clementine and Chloe come panting into the cave. Shown the shackle lock, Chloe has it off in under a minute. *I, myself, am going to have to take some instruction from this remarkable schoolmistress of ours.*

———

We finish loading up by early afternoon. The last load is carried down, and the charge set. Higgins has taken the child down to the *Belle* and put him in a clean bunk in the passenger area, where cool compresses are put to his fevered brow. We don't hold out much hope for the kid, but we'll do what we can for him.

I call Lightfoot, Katy, and Chee-a-quat back down from the top of the cliff, and I apply my flint striker to the trail of gunpowder leading up to the bag deep in the cave. It catches and the flame sizzles its way up and into the mouth of Cave-in-Rock. We wait and are soon rewarded with a *whoosh!* and a tongue of flame that roars out the cave's mouth. It looks like the mouth of Satan, himself, clearing his fiery throat.

"*Wah!*" exclaims Lightfoot, in appreciation.

"*Wah!*" echoes Chee-a-quat.

And Katy, surprisingly, also says, but much more quietly, "*Wah.*"

Hmmm.

"Well, that purifies the place, at least till the vermin come creepin' back," say I, satisfied with both the spectacle and the outcome of the day. "Let's get back down to the *Belle.*"

I realize that everyone is weary, I know I certainly am, but I feel we've got to push on. I don't want to stay moored here tonight when any survivors of our attack might have leisure to take potshots at us.

I see that Jim has already put the towlines on the other two boats and we are ready to take off. I jump up on my quarterdeck.

"Stations, everyone!" I call out, and the oarsmen leap to their sweeps.

"Push us off!" and off we go into the stream to face the Rapids of the Ohio. A little white blur skitters around my feet—it is Pretty Saro squealing in delight at seeing me and at being back up on deck again, she having been sequestered below for the duration of the fight. I give her a quick scratch and say, "Later, baby. Work to do now," and I attend to business.

"Bring him up here," I order, and Higgins pulls the miserable Mr. Fortescue to his feet. "Cut off his leg bindings." It is done. I withdraw one of my pistols and hold it to his head. "Stand here. Do you have a good view of the river, Mr. Fortescue?"

"Y-Y-yes, I do, but..."

"Good. Then you may prolong the length of your miserable, rotten life a bit longer. We are now going to go down through the Rapids of the Ohio and you will guide us. If we so much as touch bottom or hit one rock, I shall blow your head off. Do you understand that, Mr. Fortescue?"

"Y-yes...but what kind of fiend are you, that you would do this to me?"

"Ah, Mr. Fortescue, I am not half the fiend that you or any of your former friends are. I am, however, in many parts of the world known as Jacky Faber, Pyrate, and even as *La Belle Jeune Fille sans Merci,* 'the beautiful young girl without mercy.' You may discount the 'beautiful,' but I advise you not to discount the 'without mercy.' It would be at your peril, Mr. Fortescue."

I pause here and call forward, "Crow Jane."

"What, Boss?" Her head pops up above the front hatchway. I suspect she has been slaughtering chickens for tonight's victory feast.

"Bring up our worst tablecloth and spread it over here on Mr. Fortescue's left side. Should it happen that I must shoot him, I will do it from the right side, as I don't want to spill his brains all over my clean quarterdeck."

"Yes, Boss," she says, as she goes below to get the cloth.

I look over at our sorry river pilot and ask, "Any orders to the helm, Mr. Fortescue?"

His face fades to an even whiter shade of gray and he says, "Right rudder. Get to the center. Might hit that rock on the right. Hard right, now..."

Six wild hours later and we are through the Rapids without a scratch, on any of the three boats. We drift into the now quiet center of the river and heave great sighs of relief. Then we reflect on what to do with Mr. Fortescue. I have my table set up again and convene the trial. Good smells are drifting up from Crow Jane's kitchen. I rap my knuckles on the tabletop.

"The good people of the Ohio River Valley versus the False Guide and Deceiver Mr. Frederick Fortescue. How do you plead, Sir?"

"Not guilty," he answers. "I'm but an honest river pilot trying to ply my trade."

"Right, Mr. Fortescue," say I. "Will anyone else speak in his defense?"

Not a word is spoken. The defendant squirms in his bonds.

"Is there anyone who wishes to speak against him?"

"He did order us over to the right, in order to ground us and to put us at the mercy of the river pirates," testifies Jim Tanner.

"I was there and heard that order myself," I concur. "I call for a verdict. So say you one, so say you all…"

"Guilty!" comes the call from all those aboard. Mr. Fortescue looks noticeably uncomfortable.

"Let us proceed now to the penalty phase. All in favor of hanging him, say *aye.*"

There is a goodly chorus of *aye*s.

"*Hmmm,*" I say. "Will anyone speak for the condemned?"

"Your Honor, if I may," says Preacher Clawson, rising with hands outstretched. "Whatever his past crimes, I beseech you to extend mercy, for is he not still one of God's creatures, even though he has gone wrong?"

"*Hmmm.* Very well, Reverend, we will take your recommendation under consideration."

I sit back and pretend to deliberate. Then I say, "Mr. Tanner, prepare the gangplank."

Mr. Fortescue looks aghast.

"Yes, Mr. Fortescue, for your crimes against the good people of this country, you shall, indeed, walk the plank. You and your cohorts thought they were true pirates, but, Sir, you do not know *real* pirates." I clap my hands together. "Let's get this unpleasant work done. Strip him down to his underclothes and put him on the plank. Prepare some heavy chain to wrap around him so that his body does not float up."

The Hawkes boys grab the quivering Mr. Fortescue and relieve him of his outer garments. Clanking chain is brought up and placed near him. His eyes begin to go out of focus. The brothers put him on the gangplank that extends over the port side of the *Belle.* I go up behind him, cocking my pistol. He stands, his hands bound behind him, his knees shaking.

"Mr. Fortescue," I say, "you are, indeed, fortunate to have fallen into our hands, for unlike you and your sort, we are not murderers of the innocent, nor even of the guilty." With that, I take out my shiv to cut the bonds from his hands.

"We have shown you mercy, Mr. Fortescue, kindness that you and your type have shown no others. It is to be hoped that you remember this, whether you sink now, or are able to swim to safety. I do not care which."

I put my foot in the small of his back and push him over. There is a splash and I do not turn around to see whether or not his head bobs up.

We have a great, triumphant feast that night, all three boats nested up and anchored in a quiet cove. Bottles of our best wine are opened and Crow Jane's fried chicken is received with great acclaim. Even Lightfoot and Chee-a-quat join us in this celebration. Tales of individual bravery are told and retold. Praise is heaped upon every brow. Songs are sung and more stories are told and eventually we go off to bed. It has been a very long day.

Clementine and I tumble into our bunk and begin to settle ourselves for the night. When we are set and quiet, but before we blow out the candle, I say, "Thank you, Clementine. You saved my life today, you did, and don't deny it."

She sniffs and maybe nods but says nothing else.

"I mean it," I go on. "And if there's anything I can do for you, please tell me."

At that, she gets up on one elbow and faces me. "All right. You see that?"

She points to my miniature painting of Jaimy, which I keep above my bed.

"Yes," I say. "That is a picture of my intended husband, Jaimy Fletcher, he's—"

"Uh-huh," she says. Then, "You done that picture?"

"Yes, though he's much better looking than—"

"Uh-huh," she says and settles back down into the pillow. "Then, if you'd make one of Jimmy, uh, Jim Tanner, for me, I'd be grateful...and then...we'll be even."

"Of course, I will, Clementine. I'll start on it tomorrow," I answer, preparing myself for the sleep that may not come, not for either of us. For I know I will have a new nightmare, that of a man standing over me with a bayonet, ready to gut me like a pig, while she'll be dealing with the fact that she killed a man.

Dona Nobis Pacem, Pacem, I sing over and over to myself as Clementine and I lie wrapped in each other's arms against the terrors of the night. *Dona Nobis Pacem...*

Give us peace.

Chapter 43

Belle log, midsummer. 12:35. Arrive town of Cairo. Debark passengers. Look out over Mississippi River. Personal observation: I had thought that we had been on mighty rivers these past few weeks, but I have never seen anything like this. Good Lord.

We had picked up our former passengers at Elizabethtown the day following the Battle of Cave-in-Rock. They expressed both delight and surprise that we were still alive, and climbed eagerly back aboard. All of them would get off at Cairo, most of them going upriver to St. Louis, which seems to be the only big town around here, and that mainly a trading post. Before leaving Elizabethtown, we informed the town fathers that we had cleaned out the nest of outlaws up at Cave-in-Rock and it would be well if they could send some good men up there, well armed, to keep the bandits from creeping back in and setting up their vile business again, which would surely help the future hopes of their little town. Whether or not they did so, I don't know. Prolly not.

Higgins had taken to calling me Commodore Faber on the way down to Cairo, but alas, that title was not to stick.

We had such a torturous time keeping the three boats in a line that we decided to sell the latter two at Cairo, it being the meeting place of the Ohio and the Mississippi, where boats like these would be in great demand. When I finally did get a good look at the mighty, turbulent flood that was the Big River, all doubts were dispelled: No way was I going to take three boats tied together on the crest of *that*. Hell, there were *houses* floating by, for God's sake, to say nothing of massive uprooted trees, and other nasty snags what could gut the *Belle* and put all of us under in a minute. One thing you never know about a river: On one day it can be calm, then within minutes all that can change into a roiling mess that doesn't begin to calm down for several days.

We call a general meeting up on the cabin top soon after we dock and all the passengers have left.

Mr. Cantrell thought that it might be nice to keep one of the boats as a sort of floating tavern and gaming place, but I countered that by pointing out if we stopped carrying passengers, we could do the same thing with the *Belle*. And so it was decided and all agreed: No more passengers unless they could contribute to our general enterprise. They were mostly a bother, anyway. You had to feed them and all. Plus we would have had to hire on more crew, and I want no more of that. I know Crow Jane was relieved—she was cooking for enough people right now. No, it would be the *Belle of the Golden West* and our performances—Sanctified, Minstrel, or Medicine—that would see us downriver, and if they don't pay, well, we will just eat catfish and bullfrogs till they come out of our ears.

We all stand on board this ship as brothers and sisters! So say you one, so say you all! Good. It is agreed.

We set about in a great bustle of activity, selling some things we took from the Cave, stowing others. Higgins sets off into the town to sell the two captured boats, while Yancy and I set about making changes to the *Belle*. We hire carpenters and have half the passenger berths taken out on the starboard side, to be replaced by a good, sturdy bar with shelves and racks behind to hold the bottles of spirits. Our long mess table will serve as tavern seating. Lanterns and lamps are set about to provide the warm and welcoming lighting. Cantrell wants a small, round table set to the side, seating maybe six, for serious players. I admonish him that I will brook no cheating nor skinning of helpless country boys, and he assures me that only serious members of the sporting class will be allowed to take their place at that table. On the floor to one side of that table, we install a trapdoor, with a secret pull-lever handy to the head chair, to take care of any unruly patrons. There is much hammering and sawing going on as I take my leave of the place, to go out into the town, satisfied that all is going well.

The boy? Oh, yes, that boy. He does recover, against all odds. On the second day, his eyes pop open to stare about him in wonder, seeing three young females about him, mopping his brow with cold compresses and murmuring soothing words. It has to be quite a change from his former company.

When he is able to speak, he tells us that his name is Daniel Prescott and tearfully relates that he was captured by the river pirates last year, along with his father and uncle, neither of whom survived the attack. When I tell him of our successful attack on those same vermin, he expresses great joy to hear it.

"I hope you killed them all. Warn't a good one in the bunch. I hate them."

"And I hope that you do not let that hatred fester in your heart, young Daniel, for it will mean that they managed to hurt you for the whole of your life," I say, placing my hand upon his arm. "Never fear, many of them are dead, Daniel, and you are alive, here, and safe."

In his delight at being aboard the *Belle,* he is soon up and about and getting into everything. When we get him clean and presentable, I stand him up in front of me and inform him that his billet is to be ship's boy, and in that capacity he is subject to the orders of every single person aboard. In addition to any chores the others assign him, he has the job of looking after Pretty Saro, scrubbing her down and keeping her in the pink, and she seems to thrive under his care. Crow Jane, with plenty of new slabs of bacon and butts of ham now in her food locker, has given up gazing pointedly at a contentedly sleeping Saro whilst running her thumb along the edge of her knife to test its sharpness. My piglet is safe, for the time being, at least. But every day she *is* growing larger, and very soon we will no longer be able to call her a piglet.

Crow Jane has an unlooked-for delight in this port when she meets up with someone from her own Shoshone village high up on the Missouri and Snake rivers. There are exclamations of happiness at the meeting, expressed by a sort of shuffle dance done with thumb in mouth, then great hugs and squeals of joy. The girl, who turns out to be Crow Jane's niece, has with her a little boy of about two, Jean Baptiste. She was captured, as a child, by the Hidatsa Indian tribe and then later sold to a French trapper, who made her his wife when she was old enough to be a wife and to be gotten with child. I think to myself, *Huh! A lot of say she had in the matter,* but the travails of her life don't seem to bother her overmuch. She eats and laughs with great gusto and charm as she recounts her travels, in both French and English. I find that she has been on that Lewis and Clark Expedition across the new Louisiana Territory that Amy Trevelyne was going on about back in Boston. That expedition is now breaking up, the leaders heading back to Washington to report to President Jefferson. 'Tis no wonder the men on the expedition took her along, as I am sure she brought them much cheer in their darkest hours. Now she's been hired as cook on a boat going downriver. Of course, she'll take her son along, too. Her name in English is Bird Girl, and we invite her to dinner and avidly listen to her tales of the wild wonders she has seen, especially me, and, curiously, Katy, too, who seldom expresses enthusiasm for anything. And this Indian girl has even seen the Pacific Ocean on the other side of this massive country. Jeez... Even I ain't never yet seen the Pacific. We sit there far into the night, listening with chins in hands, rapt, until she finally rises, picks up her child, thanks us for dinner, and leaves to continue her journey downriver.

"Wouldn't that have been somethin' to have been along on that trip?" I sigh, after all have left and we undress for bed.

"Yes," says Katy Deere, simply, but I catch an edge of real longing in her voice.

Higgins has managed to sell off some of the goods, and so, on our third day here, we have a payday. We break it down this way: Faber Shipping gets ten shares—after all, we have to pay for resupplying, repairs, and renovations, as well as to pay Higgins and Tanner. All others receive one share, except for Daniel, who gets a quarter share. It works out to fifteen dollars a share, and all pronounce themselves satisfied. Matthew and Nathaniel Hawkes head for the nearest taverns, with orders to be good. If they land in jail, they will be left here, and they know that. I don't know where Lightfoot and Chee-a-quat go, but then, I seldom do.

Mr. Cantrell pockets his pay and goes off looking for a game. Chloe, dressed in her best, goes off with him. As elegant as they both are, I cannot help but think of the circling sharks I have seen in various waters.

Jim and Clementine run off, hand in hand, laughing, to taste the charms of the town, and, I am sure, the charms of each other. *Oh, well...*

That night, the *Belle* is left in the capable guard of Crow Jane, the Preacher, Katy, and Daniel, who was allowed enough time to go buy himself a folding knife, of which he is most proud.

Higgins and Lady Gay and I go in search of a tavern, where music might be wanted and where the company should prove kind.

On the day before our departure, the Hawkes boys return. We have not seen hide nor hair of them since they went hooting off with some jingle in their pockets, and I despaired of their return, thinking them surely in jail, or drunk in some ditch—but no, here they are, and instead of looking sodden, seedy, and dirty, they are quite spruced up. They had plainly found a barber, for they are freshly shaven and their hair is neatly cut. They each have a new jacket and hat, and I would be amazed at this change in their appearance had not the reasons for it been simpering by their sides: There stand two girls, dressed identically in frilly pink dresses with matching pink hats. Hats, that is, not the usual bonnets of the frontier, and the girls are, in fact, twins. They look as out of place on this rough dock as the girls of the Lawson Peabody looked two months ago when confined in the belly of that vile slaver *Bloodhound*.

Nathaniel Hawkes takes his girl by the hand and leads her up the gangway, to face me where I stand on the deck of the *Belle*. Yancy Cantrell stands by my side, as we have been discussing the final outfitting of the bar.

"Pardon, Boss," says 'Thaniel, taking off his new hat, "but this here's Tupelo Honey. Tupelo, honey, this here is the skipper of the *Belle of the Golden West*."

The girl dips down in something like a curtsy. "Charmed," I say, not meaning it much.

"And this here's Honeysuckle Rose," says Matthew, proudly handing his girl up from the dock. "We'd be much obliged if you'd allow these girls to ride down to New Orleans with us, yes, we would."

I cross my arms on my chest. "Now, Matty, you know we decided not to take on any more passengers, lads, so I'm afraid we—"

Honeysuckle decides it's time to speak up. "Oh, Miss, please hear us out! We're stranded here, my poor sister and me, and we just want to get back home to dear ol' New Orleans."

Both the girls have blond hair that they perhaps were not born with, that hair having something of a brassy sheen. They are quite ample of chest and tail, with nipped-in waists, which I suspect are kept so by strong whalebone corsets. Their dresses end at mid calf, and frilly white pantaloons show below. They each hold a pink parasol.

"And just how did you ladies come to be stranded here?" I ask.

"Why, Miss, cruel, cruel fate had dealt us a very bad hand. A gentleman down in New Orleans said he had work for us upriver, at St. Louis—we are artistic dancers, you know—and so we agreed to go with him. But when we got up there, he turned out to be not a gentleman at all, no." She pulls a handkerchief out of her sleeve and dabs at her eyes, in which I can't really make out any tears. "He wanted me and my poor innocent sister to do awful things with men. Oh! I can't bear to think of it! I can't!" More dabs at eyes. Tupelo, taking the cue from her sister, whips out a hanky of her own and picks up the story, her sister being overcome with emotion.

"So Honeysuckle and me, we cut and run and made it down to Cairo, where we fell ever so gratefully under the kind and lovin' protection of these fine gentlemen." She bats her eyes up at Nathaniel.

I take this all in with more than one grain of salt. "I have friends in New Orleans. Have you ladies ever heard of a Mrs. Bodeen?" I ask.

They exchange a quick look.

Aha.

"Why, no, ah don't believe we are acquainted with that person, no," says Honeysuckle.

Uh-huh.

"And you know, Miss," chimes in Tupelo, hastily, "we'll work to pay our way."

Right, and I can imagine exactly what sort of work you have in mind.

"*Hmmm,*" says Yancy, looking the amply endowed sisters up and down. "They could tend the bar, while you and Clementine and Chloe provide the entertainment. We do have the cabin room."

"What is your last name, girls?"

"Why, it's Sweet, Miss…"

Of course.

"We are the Sweet sisters. Or were." Tupelo giggles, looking up at Nathaniel. "Now our last name is Hawkes."

What?

I cut my eyes over to the Brothers Hawkes. Nathaniel blushes mightily, the red of his cheeks matching those of his brother's. "We all got married up yesterday."

Oh, lads, what have you gone and done?

I heave a large sigh. "Well, I guess that settles it, then. You will have to work to pay your way, but I think you will find me fair. You will tend bar, wait on tables, wash glasses and dishes, help with the laundry—and ladies"—here I pause and give each of them a serious, level look—"above all, you will behave yourselves. Is that clear? Good. Welcome aboard my ship. You may call me Miss Faber."

"Oh, bless your little ol' heart, Miss Faber!" gushes Honeysuckle. "Thank you so very, *very* much!" She rushes forward to envelop me in a big ol' hug. I endure it stiffly, enveloped as well in a cloud of rose-scented perfume. "And ain't you got just the cutest little ol' accent, you!"

Lord.

So, changes are made in the living quarters. Higgins will get a cabin of his own, as will Yancy Cantrell, and so, too, the Reverend. Jim and Daniel share a cabin that has upper and lower berths. Matthew and Nathaniel each have a cabin and a Honey. All pronounce themselves well satisfied.

The former officers' quarters now become a girls' dormitory. We take down the canvas curtain that divided the male space from the female. Clementine, Katy, and I retain our old beds, and Chloe takes Jim's former bunk. *A much better arrangement,* I'm thinking. This will make bathing and other personal matters much easier. Plus, I'm glad to get Jim out of the same room with Clementine. I knew that some night soon I would wake to find Clementine not in my bed, but in Jim's, and this ship don't need any more marriages, no it don't.

Everybody's back. We push off in the morning on the biggest river of them all.

PART V

Chapter 44

We are some days out of Cairo and things are going very well. Now we have Tennessee to our east and Missouri to our west. We have made stops at Dorena and Tiptonville and Point Pleasant and Caruthersville and other places whose names I forget almost as soon as we leave them, but we do leave them happier than they were before our arrival.

When we approach a likely town and the weather is fair, we put Chloe's instrument up on the cabin top, and with her pounding away on the harpsichord and me sawing on the fiddle for all I'm worth, well, they gotta know something special's coming. And something special it is, with the *Belle of the Golden West* all bright in her new paint, and all of us girls up on deck dressed in our best, waving and singing. Kids, told of our coming by Jim Tanner, watch out for us, and when we come around the bend and into their town, they scamper off to spread the word. *The showboat's here!*

In some of the places, we've been able to put on all three of our shows. We arrive, set up the performance boards and curtain frame on whatever dock the town has to offer, and send Jim and Daniel around to announce the times of the show. We run the Sanctified Show, the Very Reverend Jeremiah Clawson, Harvard Divinity Class of '82, presiding, with the Calico Angels (singers Clementine and me, and Chloe at the harpsichord) at noon or thereabouts. Then we do the Medicine Show at three in the afternoon, and the Tavern Show at night, inside the *Belle*. We charge no admission; we merely pass the collection plate after the church service, sell bottles of Captain Jack's Elixir in the afternoon, and sell drinks and food at night. So far, we prosper.

The Captain Jack's Tonic Hour of High Hilarity, our medicine show, not only has the sales pitch with Reverend Clawson holding up a bottle and pointing to the label while reciting the list of complaints and ailments the elixir would cure, the bottles for sale lined up on a table before him, but the show is also filled with comical songs and skits. In one of them, I play a bit of a tune on the fiddle, and every now and then I stop and Matty and Nathaniel, acting out the parts of a farmer and a lost traveler, have a little exchange of words. It goes like this:

MATTHEW: Say, Farmer, does this road go to Sharpsville?
NATHANIEL: Wal, Stranger, I've lived here all my life and it ain't gone nowhere yet. It just sorta lies there.

Then I come back with the tune again, and then in a bit, I stop.

MATTHEW: Say, Farmer, you ain't very smart, are ye?
NATHANIEL: Mebbe not, Stranger, but I ain't lost, neither.

Once more I play the tune, then again pause.

MATTHEW: Say, Farmer, just how do I get to
                    Sharpsville, then?
NATHANIEL: Sorry, Stranger, you jest cain't get there
                    from here.

Back again with the fiddle, the Hawkes boys join in with
their jaw harps and some fancy clogging, and we finish it
off with a flourish. Corny, yes, but it works. We get laughs
every time.

Then there's the testimonial. While the Reverend's making another pitch, I nip into the cabin, put on a white apron
and a child's bonnet, and pop back to give a testimonial:
"Oh, good people, onc't I was a very bad little girl—wouldn't
mind my elders, took fits, sayin' swears, but ever since my
mama started givin' me a teaspoonful a day of Captain
Jack's All Season Tonic and Elixir, why, I've been good as any
angel!" Here I rub my belly and put on my idiot's grin and
say, "And it tastes good, too! *Mmm, mmm!*"

Sales of the tonic are brisk.

We end the Medicine Show with a playlet I have written,
called *The Villain Pursues Constant Maiden, or Fair Virtue in
Peril.*

The Cast of Players

Miss Jacky Faber as Miss Prudence Goodlove, maiden
Master Daniel Prescott as Timothy, her sickly little brother
Rev. Jeremiah Clawson as her father, Col. Goodlove,
away at war

Mr. James Tanner as her betrothed, Captain Noble
Strongheart, away at war

Mr. Yancy Cantrell as the evil Banker Morgan

The Scene: Inside the Goodlove home on Babbling
Brook Farm

We open with Chloe playing some happy, down-home
music, and when she lets it trail off, Higgins steps up and intones in his best British accent, "The Scene is in the parlor of
the Goodlove home. Miss Prudence Goodlove has just received some disturbing news," and then he steps off. The
Hawkes boys open the curtains, revealing Daniel and me. I
am dressed in my special white dress, one that I purchased
in Cairo and had altered to suit this play. Daniel is neatly
dressed, his hair combed and parted down the middle.

TIMOTHY: Sister, Sister, whatever is the matter? What
distresses you so? (*Daniel rips out a few
convincing coughs.*)

PRUDENCE: Oh, Brother Timothy! The worst of news!
The foreman has just informed me that the
locusts have come and eaten our crop!
(*I put the back of my hand to my forehead
to show great distress.*) We shall have to
mortgage the farm. Oh, that dear Papa
were here. Oh, that the cruel war were
over!

TIMOTHY: Surely, Sister—(*cough! cough!*)—surely
there is another way!

PRUDENCE: No, dear Brother, there is not. We must pay
the help. We must have money for food.

We must do it. (*I wipe away tears.*) I will
send the foreman for Banker Morgan right
now.

CURTAIN

The curtain closes as Chloe plays a very sad and mournful
adagio and then Higgins again steps forward to gravely announce, "The very next day." Behind him, the curtain opens.

TIMOTHY (*cupping ear*): Hark! I hear hoofbeats outside.
It must be Banker Morgan! Oh, Sister, I
hope you do not rue this day! I do not like
Banker Morgan!

PRUDENCE: Now, Timothy, we must have hope. There
is still time to get in another crop before
the fall. We must have faith and trust in
God.

(*There is the sound of knocking.*)

PRUDENCE: Come in. (*Yancy Cantrell enters wearing a
black hat and cloak, looking evil, shifty-eyed,
and sinister. Chloe does a two-handed,
anxious-sounding tremolo.*) Mr. Morgan,
how good of you to come so quickly to our
aid. Thank you so much.

MORGAN: You are welcome, my dear. (*He pulls a
sheaf of papers from his cloak.*) I have
the papers right here. If you will just
sign them, your troubles will be over.
Heh, heh.

I lean over the table we have set up, take up a pen, and sign the notes. Yancy, behind my back, runs his eyes up and down my form, leers whilst twirling his mustache, and winks broadly at the audience, which is beginning to work up a few hisses for the villain.

PRUDENCE: There. It is done.

MORGAN: Not quite, my dear. You must first give me the deed to your farm to hold until the note is paid in full.

PRUDENCE (*opening a drawer in the table and pulling out a paper*): Here. (*I hand the paper to Yancy, but instead of taking it, he grabs me by the wrist and pulls me to him, encircling my waist with his arm.*)

MORGAN: Come with me, my honey, my sweet, and you'll never worry about money again, I promise you. (*He rains kisses on my face and neck.*)

PRUDENCE: Please, Sir! Let me go! (*I struggle in his grasp.*)

TIMOTHY: Unhand her, you cad! (*Daniel rushes at Yancy, his puny fists flailing at the man. Yancy kicks him away. The boy falls to the floor, coughing. The crowd's hissing redoubles.*)

MORGAN: Out of the way, brat! This is man's business!

PRUDENCE: I shall never go with you and lead a shameful life! Let me go! (*I struggle out of his grasp.*) I am promised to Captain Noble Strongheart. Oh, would that he were here

now, he would give you such a thrashing!
Give me my money and leave my house,
Sir! (*I point offstage, my face full of righteous
indignation.*)

MORGAN: Very well, my reluctant beauty. (*He scoops
up the fallen deed and flings a bag of coins
at my feet.*) Just remember, my winsome
lass, that the note is due on the first of
October. The payment must be in full,
or you shall be put out of this place! We
shall see what happens then, and in what
form payment will be made! (*Banker
Morgan pulls his cloak over his face so that
only his evil eyes show. He exits to loud hisses
and boos.*)

PRUDENCE: Oh, poor, poor brave Brother! (*I kneel
down next to the fallen Timothy and lift his
head. The audience gasps to see a thin trickle
of blood at the corner of his mouth. I turn
my tearful face to the audience.*) Oh, was
pure Virtue and Brotherly Valor ever, *ever,*
more sorely tried!

CURTAIN

Higgins advances to center stage, his steps in time to the
gloomy dirge Chloe is playing. "The first day of October,"
he intones, dolefully, shaking his head sadly as he walks off.
The curtain opens, showing Prudence Goodlove seated at
the table, crying. Her brother is lying in a bed, covered with
a sheet, coughing.

TIMOTHY: Sister, dear Sister, why do you weep so?

PRUDENCE: Oh, Timothy, I am so sorry to have awakened you from slumber! It's just that the crop is not yet ripe and we cannot harvest and today is the day the mortgage is due! I fear that Banker Morgan, that detestable man, will come and demand his money, which I do not have! I fear—

(*There is a loud knocking heard.*)

PRUDENCE: My worst fears realized! Oh, Lord, save our humble home!

(*Enter Banker Morgan to loud boos. He casts a snarling look at the hissing audience and advances on Prudence. She falls back, swooning.*)

MORGAN: Miss Goodlove, I will have my money now, or I will have this farm!

PRUDENCE: Please, Sir! Our crop is almost in! Please won't you grant us a few more weeks? Oh, please! Heaven will bless you for it!

MORGAN (*laughing evilly*): Ha-ha! Never shall that happen! Pay up or I shall put you and your brother off this land right now.

PRUDENCE: But he has the consumption, as you can plainly see! It would kill him to be cast out in the cruel elements! Oh, have you no mercy, Sir?

MORGAN: Mercy? Ha! I have none, but you, my dear... (*He crosses the stage and throws his arms about Prudence*)...you have a choice:

Surrender up your virtue to me, consent
to be my mistress, and I will tear up the
mortgage. Refuse, and you will lose the
farm and your brother will die!

TIMOTHY: Do not do it, Sister, dear! Do not…(*He
passes out.*)

PRUDENCE: Woe is me! What am I to do? Keep my
sacred honor and watch my brother die, or
give in to the fiend's foul demands? Oh,
what shall I do?

MORGAN: You shall make up your mind, girl, as my
patience grows short!

With that, Yancy reaches up, grabs my dress at the neckline,
and rips it down, the specially weakened side seams giving
away, revealing me standing openmouthed in naught but
my chemise and drawers. The gasps from the audiences on
that little move can usually be heard three counties over.
That, and the scream I deliver.

PRUDENCE (*arms crossed on chest*): Oh, I am undone!

MORGAN: Not yet you aren't, but you surely shall be
soon! Come here, my lovely!

(*Loud hissing and shouts of* shame! shame! *as he chases
me around the table two or three times.*)

PRUDENCE: Shall no one save me? Must I yield to
dishonor?

(*Enter, offstage right, Captain Noble Strongheart—Jim
Tanner, dressed in my midshipman's jacket, pistol by his*

side, with drawn-on charcoal mustache to give him some years.)

STRONGHEART (*offstage*): Prudence, darling! I have returned from the war! How I have longed for this moment! (*He strides into view and is visibly shocked by the scene before him.*) But what madness is this? Prudence? Banker Morgan?

PRUDENCE: Oh, dear Captain Strongheart, you have come to save the day! Oh, thank the merciful heavens! Banker Morgan has been pressing his unwanted attentions on me most vigorously.

STRONGHEART: You, Sir, are a bounder and a cad. Stand away from her at once!

(*Strongheart takes Morgan by the shoulder and throws him down to the floor and goes to put his arm around Prudence. Morgan rises and pulls a small pistol from under his cloak and fires it at Strongheart.*)

MORGAN: Curses! Missed! But no matter, I have another! Die, Strongheart! You may have survived the war, but you will not survive this! (*He pulls out another pistol.*)

STRONGHEART: It is you who will die, villain, for your dastardly assault upon the honor of this frail flower! (*He fires before Morgan can get off his shot, and Morgan is struck in the chest.*)

MORGAN (*staggering with his hand to his chest*): You have killed me! I am done for! It's the fires of

Hell for me! (*Loud cheers from audience as he falls to floor and lies still.*)

PRUDENCE: My hero! (*Embraces Strongheart.*)

(*Enter Rev. Clawson as Col. Goodlove, stage left.*)

COL. GOODLOVE: Daughter, Son, I have returned! (*Surveys scene.*) But what has happened here?

PRUDENCE: Oh, Father, dear, you could not be more welcome. I had to mortgage the farm and the note was due today and Banker Morgan was forcing himself upon me, but brave Captain Strongheart came and saved me from a fate worse than death!

COL. GOODLOVE: Worry yourself no more, my dearest daughter! I return with much money, money enough to pay the mortgage, money enough to get poor Timothy to a hospital back East where he shall surely be cured, money enough to give you a generous dowry so that you and this fine man might be married!

PRUDENCE: Oh, happy day! Oh, happy, *happy* day!

CURTAIN

I said it was a play, I did not say it was a good play. Higgins is of the considered opinion that my talents, when it comes to the theater, might be best confined to acting out words written by others, but I will have none of it.

"Give 'em a villain to hiss, a little action, a little leg, and

345

they go away pleased with their theatrical experience is what I say, Higgins," says I, not in the least wounded by his wry review of my playwriting skill.

The part with the dress we added after the first few performances—without it the play fell a bit flat. So now, when we stay over in a town for two nights and we perform it twice, we sell out on the second day, every time. The word gets around about my little playlet, and gets around fast. One time the audience got so worked up that we were afraid someone was going to take a shot at Yancy in his role as villain, so we had to stop the play for a bit to calm things down and to remind them it was, indeed, only a play.

We end our days at these ports of call in our Golden West Tavern, in the belly of the *Belle*. We serve food and drinks and have entertainment just like any land-bound tavern, except that we float.

I do my usual tavern show, helped by Chloe and Clementine. I have dropped some of the British and Irish ballads from the sets and adopted many of the high-country, lonesome hill songs that I have learned from Clementine. It's a good mix, and we are always warmly received.

I was wrong in being suspicious about the Honeys—Honeysuckle Rose and Tupelo Honey have worked out very well. They are cheerful in their daily duties and truly shine at night. Honeysuckle tends the bar, and Tupelo serves the tables. They have that talent that all good barmaids have—the ability to be friendly to the customers without letting it get too far. Their husbands, the Hawkes boys, still bask in their new state of wedded bliss. At night Matthew is stationed at the hatchway to control the entrance and to screen the crowd for any troublemakers, and Nathaniel is posted inside. It is plain that each is well armed.

Mr. Yancy Beauregard Cantrell sits at the gaming table should any of the local sports want to try their luck. He keeps his winnings modest, within reason. He makes sure that at least one of the men seated at his table leaves as a winner, so he gets the reputation of running an honest game. He always plays with his sleeves rolled up.

When I am not singing, playing the fiddle, or dancing, I am the hostess. I welcome customers and direct them to tables or to the bar. I keep an eye on things. Once, when in a lumber-cutting town—Pikesville, I think it was named— there was a lad, probably not yet sixteen, who had a bit too much to drink at the bar, and when I noticed, I gave Honeysuckle the finger-across-the-throat sign that meant *Cut that boy off,* and she nodded, and in few minutes the boy got up and walked unsteadily over to the gaming table where sat Yancy, alone. The boy sat down, pulled out his money, probably all the money he had earned in three or four months of backbreaking work cutting timber. It was money which, when he was sober, I'm sure he fully intended to get back to his poor ol' mama back on that poor ol' homestead.

I shook my head at Yancy and he nodded.

Yancy took the deck that lay in front of him, shuffled it, then offered it to the boy to cut. He did. Yancy then dealt two hands of five cards each, face up, one to him and one to the boy. He dealt himself a royal flush—ace, king, queen, jack, ten, all in spades, the highest hand in straight poker— and to the lad, he dealt deuce, trey, four, five, seven, all in various suits, the lowest hand in straight poker. He scooped up the cards again, shuffled, had the boy cut again, and this time

347

dealt himself a full house—three aces over two kings—and to the boy he dealt another full house, this one three queens and two kings, which though a powerful hand, would lose, and lose big to the former. The lad looked on in amazement.

"Boy," said Cantrell, "if you've a thin dime, put it on the table now, next to mine." Yancy reaches into his vest pocket and pulls out a coin and snaps it down.

The youth, dazed, fished in his own pocket and pulled out a ten-cent piece and put it on the table.

Yancy shuffled the deck and put it on the table and said, "Cut for high card."

The boy reached over and cut a three. Yancy cut and showed—a deuce.

"Take them up, lad, and go, secure in the knowledge that you will be able to say to your friends as you go through this life, 'I sat down at a table to play at cards with Yancy Beauregard Cantrell and stood up a winner, as very few have ever done.'"

The boy lurched to his feet, picked up the two dimes, and went out the hatchway.

I beamed my best smile at Yancy Cantrell.

Another time—in Gold Dust, I think it was—we had a much rougher customer.

We had a good crowd, but I noticed him right off—he was probably half tanked before he even arrived, loud, obnoxious, and meaner than a snake. We were between sets when he came up to me, reeking of a liquor not as fine as the bourbon we sell. I saw that Nathaniel had noticed as well, and had loosened his pistol in his holster.

"Hey. You the madam?"

"No, Sir, I am the hostess. And the entertainment."

"Well, entertain this, girly. That nigra gal up there playin' that fuss box? How much for a little time with her in one of these here cabins?" He pulled out a roll of bills.

"I'm afraid none of the young ladies here present are for sale, Sir," I said, my voice low and even.

"What about you, then, sweetie?" he asked, showing yellow teeth with more than a few gaps. "You talk funny, but you damned cute, too."

"This is not a brothel. Now, if you want to enjoy the food, the drink, or the—"

"Huh! I get it...You girls must take care o' business amongst yerselfs, ain't-cha? Eh? I heard o' thet. Makes me sick, but I heard of it."

He spit on the floor and turned from me. Nathaniel looked at me with eyebrows raised in question. *Should I throw his ass out?*

I shook my head, for I saw the man heading for Yancy's table. He sat down and pulled out his money. There were several other players there, but upon seeing him join the table, they picked up their money and went back to the bar.

Yancy looked up at me. I put two fingers to my right eyebrow, our signal for *Take him for everything he's got!*

Yancy smiled and nodded, and I turned back to my hostess duties.

It was not long before the whole company heard a row.

"You cheated! You double-dealing bastard! You took all my money!"

"Cheated?" said Yancy, calmly reshuffling the deck. "Please, don't think I didn't notice your clumsy attempt at second dealing on the last hand."

There was an ashtray on a stand next to Yancy, in which burned the butt of a cigar. But it was not only an ashtray, oh, no, it was also the lever to release the trapdoor artfully concealed under a small rug upon which sat our loud customer.

The man jumped to his feet, brushed back his coat, and grabbed the butt of a small, well-concealed pistol, but he never drew it, not on this deck level, anyway, for the floor fell away beneath him and he tumbled down, to hit hard on the bilge boards six feet below.

"Please, everybody!" I sang out. "It is but a momentary disturbance caused by one intemperate in his habits. Just stand away from the hole and none shall be hurt!"

I carefully went over to the edge of the trap. "Sir, if you will be so good as to throw up your weapon, we may resolve this matter."

"You go straight to hell, bitch!" came the response from our unrepentant guest.

"Ah, well," I said. "Katy? The snakes, please, if you will."

"Snakes? What snakes?" came the cry from below.

"Oh, just your common cottonmouth, rattler, and water moccasin, Sir."

Katy Deere, in her food-foraging expeditions along the shore, had, on my request, captured a number of harmless though fierce-looking snakes, snakes that we keep in a burlap sack for just this purpose. She untied the bag and tipped the squirming, twisting contents into the hole.

The gun came flying out of the hole. "Get me out of here!"

"Take off your clothes, please," I said. "You may keep

your drawers. Then we will lower the ladder and you may go away. And thank you ever so much for your patronage."

And so we roll on down the Big River, under the sun that burns down upon us during the day, under the stars that wheel about us in their great soaring courses at night. We roll on and we sing, we dance, we play, we prosper.

Chapter 45

"You must hold still, Jim. I'm almost done."

Jim Tanner, dressed in my midshipman's jacket with some foamy lace spilling out at the neck, sits rigidly in a chair set up across from me. His hair is neatly combed and tied back with a black ribbon. I am at my table, with my colors arrayed about, concentrating on the small ivory oval in front of me. I am painting him in profile.

We have erected a canopy over the quarterdeck area to keep off the sun, which grows hotter by the day. We are all, with the exception of Jim, in our lighter clothes, and I, for one, look forward to a swim in a quiet cove when we anchor for the night. There will be no port visit today, as we are passing through some sparsely populated country, with Tennessee on our left and Arkansas now on our right.

Clementine sits next to me, resewing the weak seams in my Prudence dress to get it ready for the next performance. Where each inch of a seam usually has about fifteen stitches in it, these seams have only two per inch, and Clementine sews with the weakest thread we have.

I glance over at her hands as they sew, the fingernails bitten to the quick. Several days ago she was nearly out of her mind with worry when Jim failed to return from a scouting trip downriver. For two whole days we all waited anxiously, but none more anxiously than she. Each night, before going to bed, she knelt by the bunk in prayer for a long time, and in the daytime she seldom left the bow, her eyes constantly scanning the river south of us. It was her exclamation of joy that alerted the rest of us to the *Evening Star*'s sail and Jim Tanner's safe return. It seems he ran into that pack of outlaw Indians, the ones we had fought off back up on the Ohio, and he had to flee south, for the wind was against him, and as it was, he just barely managed to outdistance the renegades as they pursued him in their swift canoes. He knew it was the same band of Indians, for their leader was the man with his face painted half red. Jim explained all this while standing on the deck of the *Belle*, with Clementine wrapped around him, her face pressed to his chest, sobbing with relief.

Daniel, back on the stern, scoops up buckets of water and pours them over Pretty Saro, who grunts contentedly and goes back to sleep. Nathaniel is on tiller. From up forward, the Honeys laugh and chatter as they hang laundry along the rail. Crow Jane is below, cooking up lunch, while at the long table, Higgins, Yancy, Chloe, and the Reverend Clawson play at whist. Lightfoot and Chee-a-quat sit crossed-legged on the deck, cleaning and oiling their rifles. Matthew Hawkes tends some fishing lines and Katy is on forward watch. Life on the *Belle of the Golden West* drifts contentedly along.

Some more highlights in the hair... There, yes... and there and... Done!

"What do you think, Clementine?" I ask, holding up the miniature portrait for her opinion. "I know I didn't make him handsome enough."

"Oh, yes, you did," she says, a smile lighting up her features as she looks upon the painting. "You did just fine."

"Good," I say, basking as ever in any praise that might come my way. "Now let's start one of you, for darling Jim to clasp next to his heart. You can get up now, Jim."

Jim Tanner gets up and stretches, grateful to be able to move again. He takes off the jacket, comes over and looks at the picture of him, blushes becomingly, and voices both his approval of it and his ardent desire for one of Clementine. I put the painting aside to dry—later it will be put under glass and framed—and choose another ivory oval as Clementine moves over to the now vacant chair. I think I will try her in three-quarter view rather than the profile and I—

"Somethin' in the water up ahead," comes the call from Katy up on the bow.

I rise and look forward, shading my eyes with my hand. "Is it a snag?"

"Nope. Seems to be somethin' swimmin'."

I pick up the long glass from its rack and go forward to stand next to Katy. She points off to starboard and I bring the telescope up to my eye, and I spot it.

"It's a man," I say to the others who have gathered around. "He's swimming. But what in the world is he doing in the middle of the Mississippi River?"

I lower the glass. "Jim, take over the helm from 'Thaniel. Matty, get on the sweeps with your brother and steer for that man. He must be in need of help." The crew hops to it and the *Belle of the Golden West* points her bow at the swimming man. "Daniel, put this back." He takes the long glass from my hand to return it to its rack. No need for it now, as the man is clearly in sight, and in a few minutes we are upon him.

"It's a burrhead!" reports Matty on port sweep. He, being higher up, can see the man better.

"What?" says I.

"It's a nigra man," says Matty. "What do you wanna do, Skipper?"

"Bring up alongside of him. We'll see what he's about."

We get close and the man spots us and tries to frantically swim away, but it is plain that he is tiring.

"Ahoy, there!" I call. "Slack off! We won't hurt you! We are not slavers! We are a showboat! From the North!"

The man stops swimming to tread water and look at us. His eyes take in the *Belle* and her gaudy paint.

"Here! Grab the sweep and rest!" I nod at Matty and he extends his oar toward the man. The man grabs on, panting hard. Matty pulls in the sweep and the man is brought to the side of the boat.

"Who are you and what are you doing out here?"

"My name is Solomon. I was runnin' away," he wheezes, "from Marse Wilcox. He's a bad man, him. Couldn't take no more, no."

"I am sorry to tell you this, Mr. Solomon," says I, "but you are swimming from the slave territory of Arkansas to the slave state of Tennessee. What could you hope to gain?"

"I didn't have no choice, Miss," says this Solomon. "Listen up careful and you'll hear."

I lift my head and cock an ear. From the Arkansas shore I hear the not-so-far-away sounds of a pack of baying hounds. *Ah.*

I think on this for a moment, and then I say, "You do have a choice now, Mr. Solomon. You can continue to swim across and gain the other shore, work your way north through Tennessee, through Kentucky, and so into Illinois, a trek of a mere two hundred or so miles of territory very unfriendly to free-roaming persons of your color..."

The man leans his head against the oar.

"...or, you can ride with us down to New Orleans, working with us on board to pay your way. When we get there, and you have worked hard, we will pay your passage on board a ship bound for a port where you can be free. What do you say?"

"What if you take me there and then sell me?"

"You shall have to trust me on that," I say. "Chloe, will you give me a testimonial?"

Chloe Cantrell comes to the side and looks down at the man in the water, and he looks up at her. "You can trust her," she says simply and turns away.

"All right. I will trust you. And I'll go with you."

"Very well. There is a short ladder at the back of the boat. You may come aboard. Stay out of sight by the side of the cabin till we clear this area, in case someone is watching from the other shore. Welcome aboard, Mr. Solomon."

And so we add yet another member to our motley crew of Brits, Americans, Africans, American Indians, plus one fine pig. For now, we are all getting along.

Chapter 46

Yesterday, when Solomon was brought aboard, we discovered that he was shirtless and wore only a ragged pair of pants that ended just below his knees. Well, we can't have any member of Faber Shipping, Worldwide looking like that, so I asked Higgins if he could round up something in the way of shirt and trousers, and he said he was sure he could find something presentable in the stash of clothing we had taken from the outlaws' cave and stored below.

While Higgins was searching, I sent Daniel down for my medical kit, then said to Solomon, who was seated on the deck, his back to the cabin and out of sight of the Arkansas bank, "You can get up now, Mr. Solomon. Please sit in that chair. Straddle it, facing the back, if you would. Oh, thank you, Daniel, put it down there."

Solomon sits down, his forearms on the back of the chair. His eyes are guarded, fearful, as if expecting a blow.

I root about in my kit and pull out my can of healing salve, open it, and begin to apply it to his back, which I can plainly see has been recently whipped. He flinches when I touch him, and somehow I don't think it's from the pain. I think it's just from my touch.

"Why did they whip you, Mr. Solomon?" Many of the crisscrossed welts have begun to heal, but not all.

"Talkin' fresh. Talkin' back. Speakin' up when things ain't right. Sometimes I just cain't help myself."

"Well, this will make it feel better. I know, 'cause once I had that done to me."

He turns his head to look at me. "You, Miss, you were whipped?"

"Aye. I was captive on a slave ship." I lift up the back hem of my shirt to show him my welt, my souvenir of Captain Blodgett's *Bloodhound* and his cat-o'-nine-tails.

"What did you do?"

"Same sort of thing you did, Mr. Solomon. Bein' a smart mouth, leadin' a riot."

"Solomon ain't my last name, Miss. It's my only name. So you shouldn't be callin' me a mister. Git us both in trouble."

"Very well, Solomon, I believe I'm done here, and I hope your back feels better. Ah, here's Mr. Higgins with some clothing for you. Go below and Crow Jane will direct you to an unused cabin. Go in, change into those clothes, and then look up Mr. Tanner. He'll put you to some useful work. Tell him I want you to learn the ropes around here, man the sweeps and all. Settle in, Solomon. You'll find there's plenty to do."

"There's one thing I already know how to do," he says, taking the folded clothes from Higgins.

"And what might that be, Solomon?"

He points to my guitar, leaning against my table. I had been messing with it this morning, with very poor results, I must say, just before the painting session.

"Teach you how to play that thing *right*, is what."

Hmmm. He *does* have a smart mouth. *How do you know how I play, Mr. Solomon?*

Higgins and I watch him walk forward.

"He is a fine figure of a man, is he not, Higgins?" I say. Solomon is about six feet tall, has wide shoulders and narrow hips. He is strong looking, but not overwhelmingly so. He has a fine head of closely curled hair, the good, strong features of a pure African, and skin the color of burnished ebony.

"Oh, yes, Miss, he is most certainly that!" says Higgins with very obvious appreciation.

And for that, Higgins gets my elbow in his side.

Later that day, Lightfoot comes up to me on the quarterdeck and says, "Ain't no towns of any size for three, four days of travel, so you won't be doin' any shows or runnin' any tavern. Me and Chee-a-quat is gonna take off and go visit our people. There's a big camp nearby. Chee-a-quat's wife and kids are there. He wants to see 'em. Figure we can meet up with you three days downriver."

"That's fine, Lightfoot, but I want to go with you."

"How's that?"

"When I was a child I wanted certain things. I wanted a Cathay Cat and a Bombay Rat and I wanted to see the Kangaroo. Seein' a real Indian village is part of that. I know you don't understand, but still, I want to go with you. To see."

Chee-a-quat was standing nearby and Lightfoot looked at him and they said, "*Wah?*" with shrugged shoulders, which I believe translates to "Might as well humor the stupid girl," and I was in.

"Tomorrow Lightfoot and Chee-a-quat are going to a big Indian village near here and I'm going with them. Isn't that grand?" I say to Crow Jane a little while later. "Could you pack us some provisions?"

"Huh," says she. "Why they goin'?"

"Chee-a-quat wants to see his squaw."

Crow Jane straightens up and turns from her stove, bringing her black eyes to bear on me. "Don't use that word, Boss."

"What word?" I ask, all innocent.

"*Squaw*," she says, her voice harsh.

"Why not?"

"'Cause *squaw* means that part of you that you got between your legs, girl. How'd you like to be called by that, instead of by your name, huh?"

I stand openmouthed. *What? Of all things...*

"It's a northern Injun word. From back East. White men picked it up and spread it around. Injuns don't like it." She points her finger at my forehead. "The Shawnee word for woman is *kweewa*. Use *that* when you talk of someone's wife or daughter. And you listen to what them two got to say when you're back in Injun country. Injun girls don't act the way you do." She snorts and turns back to her stove. "Huh! Ain't no girls act like you do, far as I can see."

"I know, Janey," says I, putting on my contrite look. "It's 'cause I wasn't raised up proper. But I will take your advice to heart. And I have been called by that name several times by angry men, but it was with the white man's word for it. And no, I didn't like it one bit."

Tomorrow, Jaimy, I shall go to a real red-Indian village! Can you imagine? Oh, I know that you—sitting back there in London, probably at your club—would feel that it is a dangerous thing, but it is not, as I am to be a guest of Chee-a-quat and the mountain man Lightfoot, who is given great respect by the Indian tribes hereabouts. I hear rumors that the great chief Tecumseh might be in the neighborhood, seeking to forge an alliance twixt the Five Nations, which are the Choctaw, the Shawnee, the Chickasaw, the Creek, and the Cherokee. If he manages to do it, it will be a formidable force...and on whose side will they be? On the side of the British, or on our side... wait...what am I saying here?

Good night, Jaimy. I'll think more on this later.

Be safe.

Chapter 47

Jaimy Fletcher, Frontiersman
At the confluence of the Ohio and Mississippi Rivers
In the American Wilderness

Miss Jacky Faber
On the Mississippi River
On board her ship, the Belle of the Golden West

Dear Jacky,

I have collected my thoughts, my raging temper, and myself,
after the events of the past few weeks, enough to continue these
letters to you, letters that I compose in my head, having no
paper or pen with which to write them down.

After my settling with those two bandits on the Frankstown road in Pennsylvania, I made my way to the Ohio
River, and there I managed to purchase, with the money I
emptied from the pockets of the recently deceased McCoy
and Beatty, a canoe called a bull boat. It has a light wooden
frame over which has been stretched a buffalo hide, taut as

a drum. It is quite fast and very maneuverable and I like it quite a lot.

I have become a very good marksman with my rifle, so I do not go hungry. I hunt, I fish, and I buy what flour and lard and such that I need from the small towns I pass. I camp on the shore and when the weather is wet, I sleep underneath my overturned canoe. What I catch or shoot I cook in the pots and pans that Clementine had left me, and I must confess I feel a pang of regret every time I use them, thinking of the sweet, simple girl who is forever lost in the northern forests of this wild land.

Yes, I have heard many tales of you and your boat as you make your way down these rivers and I paddle my way down after you. I have heard of the shows you have performed and guessed at some of the deeds you have done—the blackened hole that was once the outlaw stronghold Cave-in-Rock has your mark upon it, for sure.

I figure I am maybe a week behind you now, since your boat must be largely drifting on the current of the river, while I can paddle and gain a few knots per mile. While I have had to avoid several bands of hostiles—one in particular led by a rascal who paints his face half red—I feel that I am gaining on you.

My hopes are of seeing you soon, Jacky, hopes that I know in the past have been cruelly dashed at the very moment of fulfillment, but still, still, I hope for the best....

Chapter 48

We have been going along this trail for several hours now, at a half-walk, half-lope pace. They are certainly not making any allowances for me, that's for sure. I've got on my serving-girl gear, the skirt knotted at the side for ease of movement, and I'm able to keep up, but just barely, so I'm both startled and grateful when an Indian warrior appears on the trail in front of us. It seems that he is a sentry, guarding this particular path into his village, and it also appears that Chee-a-quat and Lightfoot and he know one another very well, as there is much talk and laughter among the three of them.

I hardly get a glance, let alone an introduction, but I do get to put down the sack of trade goods I've brought along and to catch my breath. Crow Jane had lent me an Indian shawl to put over my head so I wouldn't be quite so noticeable with my light hair when we got to the encampment, and I put it on now, as we are surely getting close.

Presently we all four start up again, and within several hundred yards, we can see the village, or town really—there are about fifty tepees grouped together on the banks of a small river. There seems to be great excitement among the people of the town.

"What's going on?" I ask quietly of Lightfoot, who has fallen back next to me as we enter the village.

"Chiefs of the Five Nations gatherin' to talk. The Creek and Cherokee here now. The rest soon. Tecumseh comes tomorrow."

Hmmm...Big doings. Best keep alert. If these Indians do decide to get together and go on the warpath, it could bode ill for the Belle.

"Me and Chee-a-quat gonna go see our father now. I'll put you with the girls. You behave now, y'hear?" he warns.

I nod. *Of course I'll behave myself. Don't I always?*

"Your father?" I ask, as we get deeper and deeper into the town. All along there are calls of welcome and greeting. Lots of folks think Indians are always solemn and reserved, but that's only when they're in the company of strangers. When they're with their own, they laugh and cavort as much as any people, which is what they're doing now. I am starting to draw some attention from the younger members of the tribe, I notice.

"When I was a young'un, I ran away from home, and my father Tak-a-lay-to took me in and made me his son. Chee-a-quat is my brother. I am Shawnee," he says, with a good deal of pride.

Ah. Well, that explains a lot, I'm thinking. We come up on a group of girls, mostly my age as far as I can tell. They are dressed in very handsome buckskin shirts and skirts that come to their knees, and they are wearing moccasin leggings that come up to mid calf. Their clothes are decorated with much beading and quillwork and are very handsome—it must be their good clothes that they have on for the occasion of this grand powwow. Lightfoot speaks to them in Shawnee, and one of them, a girl only slightly taller than I and totally without expression, comes forward and takes my hand to lead me off, to what, I don't know. The other girls follow silently.

I am led around the back of a group of tepees, down a path, and to a small meadow next to the river. They stand in a group apart and regard me, saying nothing.

Well, we can't keep this up forever, can we? And I've found that nothing breaks the ice like a good tune, so I whip my pennywhistle from my sleeve to play "Poll Ha'penny," and accompany it with my dancing feet. As I do it, my shawl slips from my head, revealing my hair, which Higgins just this morning had put up in a French style with a blue ribbon holding it all together.

Now, I ain't a true blond, not like Clarissa Howe, I'm more of a sandy-haired type, but compared to these girls with their raven locks, I am surely a *jolie blonde,* no doubt about it. They stand astounded at both my appearance and my music.

I slip the whistle back up my sleeve and regard my audience. I put my tightly closed right fist in front of my face, my fingers toward me, my knuckles facing toward the girl who escorted me here. Then I point with my index finger to the girl, my hand moving away from my face as I do so. It is the sign for "What's your name?"

"Tepeki-kweewa-nepi," she answers, and makes the same sign back at me.

"Jacky Faber," I reply.

"Yaw-kee-a-berra," she tries, and at this, all the others are consumed with fits of laughter. "Yaw-kee-a-*berra!* Yaw-kee-a-*berra!*" they chant over and over. With my keen sense of when I'm being mocked, I assume that my name, when mispronounced by them, means something crude or silly in their language.

Then Tepeki-kweewa-nepi gets control of herself and admonishes the rest of them to knock it off and they do, which is good, for I didn't come here to be laughed at. She makes the sign for *sorry* and then pantomimes me playing the pennywhistle again, so I pull it out and start playing a simple dance tune.

Immediately the girls get into a circle around me and commence a shuffling kind of dance, punctuated with songs and high trills, and I can tell from the signs that they are making that it is a dance of welcome.

When they are done, I put my right hand at my shoulder level and bring it down sharply four inches or so. It is the sign for *sit down,* and they look at each other, but they do it. I open my bag of trade goods and pull out the string of sleigh bells I had gotten for a song back in Pittsburgh, and using my lacings from my vest, I tie up the bells in groups of three for each length of lacing. Then I kneel down and tie three bells to each girl's left ankle. I have just enough bells and just enough lace to do them all, with one bell left over, which I toss back into the bag. Never know when it might come in handy.

"All right, everybody up," I say, motioning with my hands. Some things don't have to be in sign language. "Now let's do it again." And I play the same simple tune again, and again they do their shuffle dance, but this time it's shuffle, shuffle, *ching!* shuffle, shuffle, *ching!* shuffle, shuffle, *ching!*

Their delight is plain on their faces. Tepeki, after singing an especially joyous song that the others respond to with *yip*s and *yi-yi-yi-yi*s and various other vocalizations that I do not understand but that do seem to fit, motions with her hand and the group shuffles and *ching!*s toward the center of the town. I'm beginning to suspect that this Tepeki is maybe a chief's daughter or something, 'cause she seems to have a good deal of cheek.

We take our dance through the town and are applauded with shouts and, of course, many *wah!*s and *yi-yi-yi-yi*s. I think we are a hit.

We stop, eventually, on the outskirts of the village, at the tepee of a very old man, who sits cross-legged outside his home. By his side is a collection of many flutelike things. Tepeki shushes the other girls and sends them away. I suspect they are going back to the meadow next to the river. Then we sit as she addresses the old man in a very respectful tone and then gestures for me to play on my whistle.

I do "Willow Garden," a slow and wistful piece, and when I am done, he nods and then picks up one of his own flutes and begins to play. He plays the thing by blowing across a hole rather than through a whistle, and the sound that comes out is breathy and woody and wondrously beautiful. He plays a sad song in a tuning I have never heard and will never be able to play, but it is plain why Tepeki brought me here—she brought me to sit at the feet of a master.

When he is done, I take my pennywhistle and extend it to him as a gift. He takes it and runs his hands over it and smiles. Then he reaches over and picks one of his flutes, one that is similar in size to my pennywhistle, and he hands it to me. Tepeki gives me a nudge and we leave to go join the others in the meadow.

No, it was not the same pennywhistle that Liam Delaney gave me back on the *Dolphin*—no, not that battered but holy old relic, which rests in honor in my sea chest, no—rather it's one of many that I have picked up in my travels. And now, in exchange for it, I have an American Indian version of the same.

When Tepeki and I get back to the meadow, I once again take up my bag of trade goods and begin passing out gifts. There are mirrors and combs, of course, always a big hit with girls, no matter who they are or from what country, and yards and yards of ribbon to tie back their hair. There are satisfying expressions of delight.

When all is passed out, Tepeki jabbers off some orders and two of the girls fly off to the town. Tepeki takes me by the arm and leads me down to the river, and there, they begin to undress me. And they begin to disrobe themselves.

I express alarm and make the sign for *Men?*

Tepeki shakes her head and signs, *No... Men. Girl. Swim. Place.*

Ah. So I let them take my clothes.

They exclaim at the fairness of my skin and the pinkness of various of my parts and the blondness of my hair in all the locations it chooses to grow, but really, skinwise, I'm not much lighter than they are, especially in those places where I am tanned. They are certainly not red.

My arm sheath raises some eyebrows, and my tattoo of course gets a lot of attention and comment. I cannot, however, come up with enough signs to explain that little item away.

We plunge into the water and have a great time of it, hooting and hollering and splashing one another, just like any girls in the world, but before we get out to let the sun dry us off, Tepeki takes me to the edge of the river and cups some water in her hands and pours it with great ceremony over my head, intoning, *"Wah-chinga-sote-caweena-que-tonk!"* This, I suspect, is my new name.

The two girls who had left come back, and we get out of the water and dry off with the blankets they have brought. They also bear gifts for me, and wondrous gifts they are.

I am dressed, again with great ceremony, in a soft buckskin shirt that is embellished with much fringe and beadwork, its lapels decorated with porcupine quills. Then I step into a fringed skirt made of the same fine, almost-white buckskin, and I marvel how they could have tanned these fine things, not having tanning chemicals and such. The skirt comes to my knees, and then moccasin leggings that go up to mid calf are pulled onto my feet, laced, then tied up, to complete my costume.

Tepeki signs to me, *You Shawnee now, Wah-chinga.*

I sign back, *Thanks, Sister.*

Tepeki signs to me that we should go get something to eat, and I'm all for that, so we walk back into the village together and—

"Gor, blimey, Sarge! There's a little blond Injun there!"

My jaw drops open as I see, lined up next to a tepee in the middle of the American wilderness, a squad of red-coated British Regulars, well armed and all spit and polish, and all of them staring right at me.

"Damn me if it ain't," replies the sergeant. "Hullo, darlin'," he says, looking down at me standing there all astonished. "And what might your name be?"

Damn! What the hell is this?

"She's a darlin', she is," says one of the privates. "Wonder what the chief o' these here Hottentots 'd take for her?"

"Trade him some bangles and stuff," says another. "I'm sure the wog'd go for it."

"Roight, Willie," says yet another. "We could save her from these savages and have a bit of fun with her 'fore we gets her back to civ-il-za-tion and sets her back on the true and righteous path."

"Sure, and she's got to have been around the block a few times, livin' here wi' these red fiends. Won't be no loss to her virtue, for certain," chimes in another. So far I've heard Welsh, Cockney, and Irish from this randy crew, and I'm about to flee when the sergeant says, "Tenn-HUT!" and this parcel of rogues snaps to attention as the tent flap on the tepee next to them opens and a Captain of Cavalry steps out...and a very splendid Captain he is, too. No crossed belts across the chest for him, no. He wears a coat of the deepest scarlet with the purest white turnouts, with a good froth of lace at his throat and wrists. White britches, black boots, and a fine sword swinging at his side. He is young, maybe twenty-two, his cheeks still downy. His hair, which is tied back with a scarlet ribbon, is not very much darker than mine. *Hmmm...*He is quite good-looking, I notice in all my confusion.

He doesn't see me right off, and I think about slinking away, but I don't...Those are *very* nicely tailored white britches, to be sure...

"At Ease, men," the officer says. "Sergeant Bailey, the Special Agents will stay in this tent. I want a round-the-clock two-man guard posted at the front. We will bivouac around back, where there is an open space. See to the pitching of the tents...What the hell is it, Sergeant?"

Sergeant Bailey peers around his superior officer and points at me. "Lookee there, Sir. It's a white girl."

The Captain turns about and gazes upon me. "Well, *ahem,*" he says, "and who might you be?"

I shake my head and make the signs for *no* and *speak,* and then, by drawing my right forefinger across my eyes from left to right, *paleface.*

"*Hmmm.* It's obvious she doesn't speak English. A captive, no doubt. Kidnapped as a baby, I suppose." He walks slowly about me as I stand straight and unmoving. "It's none of our concern, of course, but still it is a shock to see that blond mop in the midst of all this." He reaches into his vest pocket and pulls out a long cheroot. If I thought it was going to be a little present for a poor Indian girl, I was mistaken. It is a long black cigar that he takes out and places between his lips. "Set up the camp, Sergeant. Let's get to it."

He turns back to me. "Can't a man get a light around here?" he says, tilting the long thin cigar up by thrusting out his lower jaw.

I pretend not to know what he is talking about, but Tepeki-kweewa-nepi, practiced, I'm sure, in the ways of tobacco, nudges me toward a fire laid in front of a nearby tepee, and I go over and reach in to grab the cool end of a stick that is burning at its other end. I take it to the Captain and hold it up to him. He sticks his cigar into the flame and puffs deeply. Satisfied that he has a good light, he straightens up as he says, "Thank you, my dear. You are a neat little trick. We could have some real fun together. We surely could."

And with that, he turns to go join his men, leaving me still standing there in astonishment. After a moment I turn and go with Tepeki to have dinner with her and her mother, my thoughts still churning.

What the hell are these men here for?

The dinner is good, a kind of stew made with meat and rice, eaten with the fingers with great gusto amongst Tepeki's sisters and little brothers. Her mother is nice to me, and I think she is pleased when I sign *Food. Good. Thanks*. And I was right, Tepeki is the chief's daughter.

Later that evening, more chiefs from the Five Nations arrive and there is great ceremony of welcome and much joyous dancing. My group of jangle-ankled, buckskin-clad dancers shine, and we are much appreciated.

The celebration goes on far into the night, but eventually things calm down and I bid Tepeki good night and go into Lightfoot's tent to sleep. I don't know what he told them, whether I was his wife, or his daughter, or what, but here is where I end up this day.

I curl up on the ground, wrapped in a hide blanket that Tepeki has given me, and close my eyes.

I am awakened much later when Lightfoot comes in to sleep. After I hear him settle in, I ask in the darkness of the tepee, "Lightfoot, the girls gave me a Shawnee name today. What does *Wah-chinga-sote-caweena-que-tonk* mean?"

"She-Who-Dances-Like-Crazy-Rabbit."

Hmmm…I guess that's all right. I've been called worse.

After a bit, I again have a question. "Lightfoot, what do you think those English agents are up to?"

"Don't know. But I 'spect they're up to no good. Prolly stirrin' up trouble. 'Tween the settlers and the Injuns, is what I figure. Bad medicine."

I think on that for a while and am about to drop off to sleep again when Lightfoot says, quietly, "You know that Katy girl?"

"Yes?"

"Nex' time you talk to her…"

"Yes?"

"Tell her Lightfoot's willin'…"

"Just tell her that?"

"Yep. She'll know what I mean."

Silence falls on us again, and I close my eyes and slip back into sleep.

Good night, Jaimy. You wouldn't believe where I am right now, but be safe and soon…soon…

Chapter 49

I help make breakfast with Chee-a-quat's wife, Nee-ah-hanta, a proud, handsome woman, brisk in her preparations for the morning meal, and not at all awed by my presence. To her, a girl is a girl, dark- or light-skinned, and, as such, should help tend the fire and stir the pot. I do it, of course, grateful for the chance to help in return for her hospitality.

The breakfast is a porridge made mostly of rice and berries, as far as I can tell, and when it is hot enough, I take two bowls into the tepee and put them in front of Chee-a-quat and Lightfoot, and in return I get a couple of grunts that I take for thanks. Then I duck back out to get my own and to help Nee-ah-hanta feed her two kids, a boy of about two and a girl of about four. I plop the plump little fellow on my lap, sing him a song, and manage to spoon a good bit of the porridge into him. After I clean him up, I sign *thanks* to my hostess and go off to find Tepeki.

I find her in the middle of the village, where more chiefs are arriving with their bands of warriors. Tepeki's father, as chief of this village, welcomes them all, and there is much public exchanging of formal greetings and gifts, after which the chiefs duck into tepees to talk in private. The village continues to buzz with excitement, with much sparking going on twixt the boys and girls, same as it ever was, no matter what the country or who the people.

I haven't seen the British agents yet, but I am keeping my eyes peeled. When I got up this morning, I had put my hair in twin braids, so as to not stand out so much with my shaggy blond mop. I also keep Crow Jane's shawl over my shoulders to cover up if need be. No telling who those agents are or what they're up to.

Tepeki and I wander about, hand in hand, taking in the sights and getting caught up in all the excitement. Every party that enters the town is dressed in their finest, and some fine stuff there is. There are feathers and plumes and brightly colored cloth. The men of some tribes have full heads of hair while others have plucked theirs to form high crests down the centers of their heads. Some wear feathered headdresses, while some sport turbans. Tepeki points out who's Creek and who's Chickasaw and all that, and—

"Hey, girl."

I look up alarmed. The British Captain of Cavalry stands next to me. I put on my frightened-doe look, which ain't hard considerin' the fact that if I get recognized by these people it's the noose for me for sure.

"Yes, you. Come here."

I drop Tepeki's hand and whip Crow Jane's shawl up over my head and look about for an escape route but find none as he grabs my arm and drags me out of the village and into the woods. I try to tug away, but his hand is too strong. I hear Tepeki running off. I think about pulling out my shiv, but no, not yet.

"You come along, girl. Come on, I won't hurt you. We'll just have a little talk, is all."

We come to a small clearing and he makes me sit down on the grass that grows there. I gather my skirt under me as he sits down beside me. He reaches out and pulls my shawl back off my head.

"Now, my little light-haired woodland sprite, let's have that little talk." He points to his chest and says, "Me Richard Allen." Then he points at my chest and says, "What's *your* name?"

"Wa—wah-chinga-sote-caweena-que-tonk," says Dances-Like-Rabbit, feeling very much like a scared rabbit under the fierceness of his gaze. I notice he has a scar on his right cheek. Probably from a saber, I'm thinking.

"Why, that's quite a mouthful, ain't it, sweetheart," he says softly. "I think I'll just call you She-Is-Pretty-Thing-What-Showed-Up-in-the-Woods-Against-All-Odds-to-Cheer-Me-for-a-Little-While-in-This-Godforsaken-Hellhole-of-a-Country. She-Is-Pretty-Thing, for short. What do you think of that, Pretty-Thing?"

I decide a little smile on Pretty-Thing's part wouldn't hurt, as he is quite good-looking—slim, tall, with a rugged yet fine-boned face—the very picture of the dashing young officer, a type I have always found most attractive. Plus his words are sweet, and what could it hurt?

It could hurt a lot. He takes my smile for Full-Speed-Ahead-Not-a-Moment-to-Lose and slides his hand up the inside of my leg.

"Wha—" I gasp. In my shock I almost say *what,* but change it to a *wah!* of shock and surprise.

A smile spreads over his face. "I've often wondered what Indian girls wear under their skirts. Now, Pretty-Thing, I know. Sort of like what people wonder about Scotsmen, eh? But you don't understand a word I'm saying, do ye? Well, maybe you'll understand this." Without taking his hand off my inner thigh, he leans over, puts his other hand behind my head, pulls me forward, and puts his mouth on mine.

My eyes open even wider.

"How did you like that? Bet your Indian fellows don't do anything like that. How about if I was to buy you? Give old Sasquatch some firewater and haul you away with me? What do you think of that, girl? It'd be better than living here with these savages, wouldn't it, you Pretty-Thing, you?"

A long rifle barrel appears at the Captain's temple. He starts and then looks cautiously to the side and then up the barrel to the man standing there, his finger tight on the trigger. "She ain't fer sale, soldier boy," he says, with real threat in his voice. Lightfoot is well named—I did not hear him coming and neither did Richard Allen.

"You watch your mouth, man," says the Captain, his eyes gone as flinty as Lightfoot's. His hand goes to the sword that hangs by his side.

I quickly sign *This Man. I. No. Speak. Paleface.*

Lightfoot nods, understanding what I mean. "And you watch what you're doin' when you're here in this place, soldier boy," he says.

Captain Allen gets to his feet. Lightfoot moves the barrel of the gun to point between the officer's eyes. I get up and stand behind Lightfoot, my hands on his waist, my face all wide-eyed and wondering as I peer at the officer.

"And if I do not do that, renegade?" asks Allen, unabashed.

"I'll kill you and take yer scalp and put it on my belt here with the others. Tell ever'body it come all the way from London just to hang here," says Lightfoot. "And you watch yer own mouth when it comes to callin' a man sumthin', y'hear?"

Captain Allen's eyes go to the grisly bunches of hair and dried skin that hang at Lightfoot's middle and he says nothing. Lightfoot grins at the man's discomfort.

"Draw that pigsticker and you're one dead Englishman," he says. "Remember, soldier boy, you're on Shawnee land here, and I am Shawnee and you sure as hell ain't."

"She's a white girl. You have no right to keep her here," says the Captain. *He* is not smiling.

"She's Shawnee, too, and you got no right to take her away from here." I reflect on the truth of this statement, in that I *was* made a member of the tribe just yesterday. Then I hear sounds of drumming coming from the direction of the village. Lightfoot puts up his gun and says, "You best go tend to yer lobsterbacks, soldier boy. Sounds like the great man's comin' in."

With a final glare, Captain Allen turns and goes to form up his men for the arrival of Tecumseh.

"I thank you, Lightfoot," I say, putting my hand on his arm and looking up at him gratefully.

"*Wah,*" he says, striding off. "Go sit with the women, girl."

Meekly, I go do it. But before I do that, I go back to the tepee I share with Lightfoot and get the bundle of clothes that I wore here, pull out the drawers and, with my knife, cut them off just below the crotch. Then I put them on under my leather skirt. I reflect that I might have cut them a little bit farther down, but too late now.

I join up with Tepeki and the other girls, and we watch the coming of the great Chief Tecumseh and his band of about twenty warriors. He's a tall man, almost six foot, with a fine, proud bearing. He has a long, thin nose and olive skin and hazel eyes that flash with determination and a certain cheerfulness. On his head he wears a red turbanlike headdress from which hangs a single feather on a string of wampum, and on his body buckskin leggings and a jacket of the same, bound around by a red sash. All in all, a splendid-looking man. I wish I could have Lightfoot by my side to translate what's being said by him and others as the welcome is made, but I can't. For one thing, he can't be caught hanging around with a girl, and for another, I can't draw any more attention to myself than I already have. So I'll just have to guess at things. One thing I don't have to guess at is the amount of esteem in which everyone here holds this man.

After Tecumseh has settled into the largest tepee in the town, to hold court with all the other chiefs, and all the young warriors have been thoroughly checked out by us girls, we are of a mind to sneak off for another swim at the women's bathing place. There are some new girls with us, undoubtedly girls from other tribes. From their looks in my direction, I suspect my Shawnee friends wish to show me off, and that's all right. After all, I *am* a performer by trade.

But it is not to be. Not now, anyhow, for when the mob of us, chattering away, are no more than halfway to the bend in the river, an older woman bursts upon us, waving a long ladle and pointing downstream, reminding me of nothing so much as good old Peg, back at the Lawson Peabody, scattering us serving girls back to our chores when we would grow lazy of a summer's afternoon.

It becomes plain to me that we are to gather food, and we all change direction and head for a group of canoes tied up to the bank. The girls take this change of plans with good grace and run laughing and calling out *yiyiyiyiyiyi!* to the boats and clamber in. Tepeki chooses one and motions me to join her and I do, picking up a paddle and shoving us off into the water.

When we head downstream, I find that there is a paddling song in which all the girls join and to which I try to add my voice, mainly in wordless harmony, and then when we pull into the marshes where the food grows, they fall into what I know are call-and-response songs—songs wherein one voice calls out a verse, mainly concerning another member of the party, like, say, what particular boy one particular girl has her eye on, and there are hoots of laughter and that particular girl gets to pick another girl or boy or whatever to comment on, and so on and so on.

We come to a thicket of rushes, and Tepeki puts up her paddle and pulls the tall greenery over into the boat and begins shaking it, and wonder of wonders, black kernels of wild rice fall into the bottom of the canoe. It is early in the summer, so not all the rice is ripe, but some is and we gather what we can. We then move on to a growth of cattails, and the girls take both the brown-capped stalks and the roots of the plant.

Satisfied that we have done enough, we head back to the

village to prepare lunch. The rice is divided up by the women, the cattail roots are peeled and pounded to a pulp, and the cattails themselves are twisted from their stems to form a golden yellow powder that, when water is added, turns into another paste, which can be baked into a bread. *Crafty people, these Shawnees,* I reflect, biting into a hot cattail cake and again looking out on the festivities of the day.

It is then that I finally spy the two English Special Agents. They have come out of their tepee and stand blinking in the sunlight, with an Indian man dressed in white man's clothing by their side. The older one, a disagreeable toadish-looking man with thick lips and a half-bald head, is dressed all in black, while the other one, a large and very handsome fellow, is dressed in navy blue, suggesting a possible naval officer. The younger man looks damned familiar, but I can't quite place him, and I can't stand there staring at him, that's for sure. I duck back out of sight behind a tepee and tuck the shawl tight about my face and peek out.

The Indian man, whom I take to be their interpreter, says something to them and points down the row of tepees to one near where I am standing.

Tepeki, her own chores done, has come to seek me out, and when I see her come up to me, I sign to her *Quiet. I. Listen. Palefaces.* and nod at the men entering the tepee. She glances over, then nods, and we go around the back and lie down on the ground such that we can put our ears to the opening below the hide covering of the tepee. This Tepeki doesn't lack for cheek, that's for sure. I grin at her and put my finger to my lips in the universal *shush!* sign and she grins back. I cock my ear to the conversation inside.

"Please tell Blue Hand, Great Chief of the Cherokee, that

His Majesty King George of England sends his fondest greetings." This from the older cove, I'm thinking.

The translator speaks and Blue Hand says something in return.

"He says he is happy to receive greetings from his brother King George and welcomes you gentlemen to his tepee."

"Thank the Chief and tell him that King George sends his Cherokee brother this fine pistol as a token of his esteem. Lieutenant, if you would?"

Lieutenant...hmm...

There is the sound of a case being opened and then an appreciative *wah!* from Blue Hand. I hear the hammer being cocked. Then the Chief speaks again.

"He says many thanks for the pistol and asks what he can give his brother George in return."

I hear the agent take a deep breath before he begins on what I feel will be the heart of the matter.

"Chief Blue Hand, it has come to your brother King George's attention that the American settlers have been moving into the lands of the Cherokee, and this has filled his heart with sorrow..." Here he pauses to let the translator do his job. After the Chief hears it and gives an *ugh!* of agreement, the agent goes on.

"This taking of the sacred land of the Cherokee has saddened him so much that he wishes that he could rise up and smite these settlers and free his Cherokee brothers from their transgressions, but, alas, he cannot do that, for he is too far away, across the great ocean from here." Again a pause, and then again he goes on.

"But the great and noble Cherokee and their brothers the Shawnee, the Choctaw, the Creek, and the Chickasaw *are* here, and the King urges them to rise up and take the path of war against these invaders who, in their great numbers, will not stop coming on Indian land till the last red man and his woman and his child are thrown into the great waters to drown!"

There is more translation, and angry sounds now from Chief Blue Hand. On the agent presses.

"The King will help his Indian brothers in their rightful anger against these settlers," says the agent, "by putting in your hands five American dollars for every white man's scalp, three dollars for every woman's, and two for every child's."

I am barely able to suppress a gasp. *This can't be true! Englishmen can't be doing this!*

As this is spoken in Cherokee, Tepeki, too, understands and looks at me in sorrow. Our happiness with our little adventure in eavesdropping is now gone. *How can people be so cruel?*

Blue Hand responds that he will have to talk it over with his fellow chiefs, but he has taken the white man's words to heart and it has brought gladness to him.

Farewells are said and the Special Agents take their leave.

I stand up, fuming. Tepeki also gets up and signs *sorrow* to me, her eyes cast down. I take her to me and whisper, "Tepeki and Wah-chinga," and by putting both of my hands into fists and then crossing my arms on my chest, I make the sign *affection*. Then I take her by the shoulders and put a kiss on her forehead. She nods and I motion for her to follow me.

We stride along the backs of the tepees, me intent on following these bastards back to their lodging to see what else they've got to say when they think no one else is listening. A very subdued Tepeki comes along with me and again we lie down with our ears to the bottom of a tepee.

There is the sound of shuffling as the men make themselves comfortable. I hear a bottle being uncorked and the *tink* of a bottle laid against a glass and then the gurgle of liquid being poured, then...

"Ah, that's much better," one of them sighs, the older one, I believe. "So what do you think? Will they go for it?"

"I think it's all up to Tecumseh. If he goes for it, the rest of the bloody savages'll fall in line. At least we've gotten Half Red Face to sign on now—the rest of the malcontents from this bunch should fall into line with him even if Tecumseh refuses to sign on." This from the younger man, and it's plain their Indian translator is no longer with them, or else they don't care about insulting him. "When do we get to talk to the main man?"

"Tonight, after they've all had a chance to powwow with him. That Blue Hand seemed ready to go on the warpath, though. You could see the greed in his eyes."

"Maybe so, but I must tell you, Sir, that I don't like the sight of all those armed braves strutting around. And here we are, sitting on a box of money. They've all got guns, too. Hell, I thought they was all supposed to be carrying bows and arrows. Or spears. Damn! And where's that damned Allen, who's supposed to be providing for our safety? Off chasing some skirt, no doubt, the randy bastard!"

"Sergeant Bailey did say something about there being a white girl in this camp."

"Oh? And how old?"

"Midteens, Bailey thinks. Small, but full-grown. Quite pretty, too, I hear. Doesn't speak English. Probably captured as a baby after her family was slaughtered."

"Hmmm..."

"Put that out of your mind. We are well acquainted with your own reputation as regards the ladies, Flashby."

Flashby! That's why he looked so familiar! He's that cove what tried to drag my passed-out drunken body off to do me on that black day back at Dovecote! Of course he would end up in some dirty business like this!

"If you want to keep your hair, I suggest that you'd best wait till we get back to the fleshpots of New Orleans."

Now I'm really gonna have to stay out of sight! If he gets a glimpse of me...

There is a growl of assent from Flashby. "Aye, aye, Mr. Moseley, but I hope she gives the arrogant son of a bitch a good dose of the clap."

The older man laughs. "She might at that, we shall see. But right now I'm hungry. See if Private Quimby can whip us up some decent rations. I'll be damned if I'll eat that Indian slop—ain't hungry enough to eat stewed dog. Not yet, anyway."

I've heard enough. I tap Tepeki on the shoulder and we quietly get up and go back to join the other girls. I've got a lot to think about.

It turns out that the girls are now keen on having that swim that was denied us earlier, and so we all charge on down to the women's bathing place. After what I have just heard, I could use a good cleansing bath. Plus, the girls-only nature of the women's bathing spot makes it a good place for me to lay low and stay out of Flashby's sight.

We strip down on the bank and hang our clothes on nearby branches. I am truly fond of the buckskin outfit the girls have given me, and I fold it over carefully, as I intend this to be my costume for the rest of the journey down the river.

After getting some *ooohs* and *ahhs* over the nature of my skin, hair, and, of course, tattoo, I plunge into the water and join the frolic, putting the rest of the day out of my mind.

We have a merry time of it, hooting and splashing about, and after a bit, my feet find that there's a quite deep channel next to a high part of the bank. Taking a deep breath, I dive under for a look.

The water is quite clear, and I see no obstructions—roots, branches, or the like—in the deep under the bank. There are some holes in the underwater bank that are probably the entrances of some creature's den, but they ain't bothering me, so I shan't worry about them. I dive down further and see some clamlike things sticking upon the bottom. *Hmm...* I'll wager I ate some of those things in the last stew I had. I kick around the bottom a bit more, and when I've been down about a minute I shoot back up to the surface.

I'm astounded to see Tepeki's worried face in front of me, her black hair streaming about her face. Hey, I was only down for a minute or so. I look downstream and see that some are combing the shallows for my drowned body. Tepeki's expression changes to one of anger. I sign *sorry* and then *Sister*. She looks stern and then forgives me, throwing

387

her slippery arms about my neck in relief. I return the hug and then clamber out of the water and go up onto the high bank.

I decide to give them my backflip first. Feet together, arms held out forward, I bend my knees and spring backward, legs overhead, and then feetfirst into the water. *Not too bad*, I'm thinking. *Could use a little more height, though.* When I come back to the surface, I get hoots and a few *yiyiyiyiyi*s by way of applause. I climb back out, intending to treat them to my swan dive. This so reminds me of my time in my beautiful lagoon, back when I was marooned in South America.

Gaining the bank, I put my toes over the edge, heels together, and arch my back and extend my arms gracefully out to the side.

I see shocked looks from those below. What? This isn't that shocking? It's just a dive, and it's a lot easier one than the backflip...But then I realize that it ain't me they're lookin' at. I smell the unmistakable odor of tobacco wafting from behind me and I look over my shoulder. There stands, smoking his usual cheroot, Captain Richard Allen, a broad smile on his face.

"I think I was hasty before in naming you She-Is-Pretty-Thing. I now think that She-Has-Saucy-Tail would be much more appropriate. Or would Pretty-Bottom be more to your liking?"

I can't let him see my tattoo! is my only thought and concern as I hastily dive into the water, much less elegantly than I had planned. I hit the water and go down to the bottom to think for a second. *Did I stupidly speak in English when I was showing off before the girls? Had he been hiding in the bushes the whole time and spot my tattoo?* I don't know, I only know I've got to go up for air eventually, and so I kick off the bottom and resurface, showing only the bridge of my nose and my furious eyes, which I fix on the arrogant Captain Allen.

Matching me for fury is Tepeki who, with a fine string of what I assume are Shawnee curses, sends a little kid off to get someone to set this interloper straight, and then charges out of the water herself, picks up a handful of mud, and wings it at the officer, who steps aside to avoid the missile.

"Now, now, Pocahontas, settle down. I'll be gone long before that old squaw you sent the little brown dumpling off for comes down and chases me off...But you know, you're a right handsome one, too, Pocahontas...Ah, yes, a man could have a real good time here. 'Tis a pity I can't tarry." He takes the cigar out of his mouth and points the slippery wet end at me. "You, I'll see later," and he turns and walks unhurriedly off.

I rise up and watch him saunter away.

The insufferable cheek of that man!

Chapter 50

We are getting ready to leave. At breakfast, when I deliver their bowls to the men, Lightfoot looks up at me and says, "Stay."

I look at him and raise my eyebrows in question.

"That Katy girl," he begins, and I swear he looks embarrassed, shy, even. "I-I got her these." And he holds up a finely tooled and decorated leather quiver that is full of arrows. "Our best arrow-maker, old Sequi-tan, made these. Ain't none better. Think she'll like 'em?"

I smile at his discomfort—the strong and brave mountain man Lightfoot, who could kill ten men without blinking, all fumble-mouthed when talking to a girl about another girl.

"I think she'll like 'em just fine, Lightfoot," I answer. "But when it comes to girls…" I finger the collar of my fine buckskin shirt and the hem of my fine buckskin skirt.

"Ah," he says, taking my meaning.

"She's about the same size as Tako-hah-yoe," I say as I leave the tepee. He nods. She's a Shawnee girl I know from our swimming sessions whose name means Willow-tree, and she's probably the tallest girl in the camp.

———

Had it not been for the fact that Lightfoot had to go hunt up the outfit he wished to give to Katy, we would have left right after breakfast, but as it was, I had time to go look up Tepeki to say good-bye. I found her looking for me in the center of the village.

"*Wah-ho-tay*, Wah-chinga," she says by way of greeting, and I return the greeting, and we join hands, and I lead her toward the backs of the outlying tepees yet again. I intend to have one more listen to the agents to see if anything was decided last night in the big powwow. They were all at it far into the night, I know, but since Tecumseh's tepee was square in the center of the town, with people all about, I knew I couldn't just plop down and listen in as I did at Blue Hand's abode.

I lie down for a last listen. If I find that Tecumseh agrees with the agents' fiendish scheme, we'll have to spread the alarm to warn settlers as we take the *Belle* down the river. Tepeki lies down beside me.

"Dammit to hell, Flashby, why can't these damned savages ever make up their minds?"

"Probably figures he's got to go on a vigil first," says the other man, "have some sort of heathen vision to show him the way."

Good. It seems that Tecumseh hasn't yet agreed to do their murdering for them.

"Aye, and it's all up to him, too. If he goes along with it, the others will follow and—"

"What have we here, now?" says a voice above me. "Captain Allen, come look!"

Uh-oh...

I'm shocked to see a pair of shiny black boots next to my face. I try to get to my feet to make a run for it, but one of the boots is lifted and placed in the middle of my back, pinning me to the ground. I hear Tepeki getting up and running away.

"What's going on out there?" demands Moseley from inside the tent.

"Caught that little white girl sneakin' around back o' yer tent, Sir," says Sergeant Bailey, the owner of the heavy foot that holds me down. I'm having trouble breathing.

"Prolly lookin' to steal something. Like the rest of them thievin' savages," says Bailey.

Yes, yes! That's it! Please believe that and let me go!

More pairs of boots come into my vision.

"Why, I'll be damned, if it isn't Pretty-Tail," says a voice I recognize as Captain Allen's. He squats down next to me and peers into my face. "Were you looking to steal something, sweetheart? *Hmmm?* Or were you just looking for me?"

I turn my face the other way, but when I see Flashby and Moseley coming around the tepee, I turn back to Allen so they can't see my face.

"So what is this?" asks Moseley.

Captain Allen stands up. "The sergeant thinks he's caught himself a thief. Me, I think she was just curious about the white folk."

"She seemed to be listening under your tent, Sir," says the obstinate Sergeant Bailey.

"I thought she didn't understand English," says Flashby.

"Well, stand her up and let's have a look at her."

Sergeant Bailey takes his foot from my back and I roll to the side, leap up, and go to run, but his hand catches me by the neck and holds me fast. And I'm wishing that my hair were not in tight braids so it could hang about my face. My worst fears are realized.

"Oh, my God." This from Flashby, and I know I am lost.

Flashby comes grinning up to me and places his hand on my shoulder. "In my capacity as a lieutenant in the Royal Navy on detached duty with British Intelligence, I arrest you, Jacky Faber, in the name of His Majesty King George the Third of England."

"Whatever are you going on about, Flashby?" asks Moseley, irritably. While I am sweating buckets, to him this is just an annoyance.

"Well, Sir, this female is the wanted criminal, the notorious Jacky Faber, and I have just made myself a neat two hundred and fifty pounds sterling by her capture," crows Flashby with great satisfaction. "Surely, Sir, you remember the notice the Admiralty has been circulating? The wanted posters stating the reward? They have been most anxious to get their hands on this girl, and now they shall have her. As will I." He puts his finger on my nose. "You and I have some unfinished business to attend to as well, as I'm sure you recall."

"Come now, Flashby, what would a criminal wanted in England be doing deep in the wilds of America?" asks Captain Allen.

"Oh, probably she has gone over to the Americans in return for their protection, and they've sent her out here to thwart our dealings with the Indians. It doesn't matter," says Flashby. "Later, when we're far from here, she'll tell us everything she knows. Count on it." Again he points his finger at my nose.

"And just what proof do you have? Look at her, standing there trembling," says Captain Allen, whom I am liking more and more every minute. "She's just a captive, more Indian than white now, and should be pitied for it."

"Pity, my ass. Do you see this eyebrow where the hair has grown in white over the scar beneath? That's one of the items from the description." He points to my damning eyebrow. I have yet to say a word. "Plus, there's the fact that I was introduced to this girl at a dinner party in Massachusetts several years ago, and I remember her very, very well. I almost bagged her then, but I will most certainly bag her now."

"I still say this is preposterous. You're going to cause an incident with the Indians."

"That's true, Flashby," agrees Moseley. "You must be careful."

"*You* be careful, Bailey," Flashby warns the soldier holding me by the neck. "She's known as a wily one. She's escaped captivity twice and has killed more than a few men."

"This little thing, Sir? I can't believe that," says Sergeant Bailey, giving me a bit of a shake to prove my helplessness. I flop like a rag doll to lend credence to his words.

"There's one last and final proof," says Flashby with a leer. "She has a blue tattoo on her right hip. It is an anchor with the words HMS *Dolphin* above it. Will you believe me then, if it is there?"

"Lift her skirt," says Moseley, "and let's be done with this."

Sergeant Bailey reaches for the hem of my lower garment. *Time for the knife now, for sure.*

I run my right hand up my left sleeve and slide out my shiv and put the point of it to the throat of a very surprised Redcoat sergeant.

"Let me go or die," I say. "Your choice, Sergeant."

"Well, I'll be damned," says an equally surprised Captain Allen.

The sergeant lets go of my neck and I spin and turn and make for the woods.

If I can get there, I'm safe! Lightfoot and Chee-a-quat will track me and take me back to my ship and—

It is not to be.

Three of the privates are between me and the forest, and they are skilled enough in the art of knife fighting to crouch before me, hands out, and circling just out of the reach of my blade, one sayin', "Now, dearie, let's just drop the knife. We won't hurt you, come on now, dearie..."

I might have been able to fight my way through, but that doesn't matter, as all they have to do is delay me enough for Sergeant Bailey to come up behind me, encircle my waist with one arm while the hand of the other arm grasps me by the wrist of my knife hand. One of the privates comes up and puts his thumb in the soft underpart of my wrist and pushes *hard*.

My shiv falls out of my hand.

"Now we'll see about that tattoo," says Flashby.

I squeal and twist, but I am thrown to the ground once again, and hard hands hold me there, on my back, as my skirt is flung up and the waistband of my drawers drawn down.

"There it is," says Flashby. "Are you all satisfied now?"

There is murmur of assent, then I hear a new voice.

"What the hell you doin'?"

It is Lightfoot, his long rifle cradled in his arms, the barrel pointing at Flashby. I see Chee-a-quat and Tepeki standing next to him, all lookin' grim.

"Get yourself off, you goddamn renegade," orders Flashby. "This girl is a wanted fugitive."

Tepeki, her face a mask of fury, shoulders her way through and kneels next to me and pulls my skirt back down over my bare legs. I lie there with my chest heaving great racking sobs borne of frustration and shame. She stays beside me as her father, the chief of this village, comes up. It is plain that he is alarmed at this turn of events. The Indian interpreter is also present and begins translating, for there is much conversation going back and forth.

Finally the chief turns to Chee-a-quat and Lightfoot and speaks low and careful to them. They do not change expression, but I know what the chief is saying: *The powwow is too important to be disrupted by a mere girl. Let the palefaces take the paleface girl. It is no concern of ours.*

Chee-a-quat and Lightfoot say nothing, but they do put up their rifles. Lightfoot says, "She is nothing to me. Take her." With a final glare at the agents, he spins on his heel and leaves.

I am pulled once again to my feet. Tepeki, seeing that all is lost, reaches down and picks up my shiv and, holding it before her to part the ranks of Redcoats, runs off.

"Get her down to the boat," orders Moseley. "We're leaving now. We'll find out Tecumseh's answer soon enough."

"Break camp!" bellows Sergeant Bailey to his squad. "Brisk, now! Move it!"

I am tied fast to a tree for the time it takes them to make their preparations, and then my hands are tied behind me, a rope put around my neck, and with Redcoats all about me, I am pulled along a trail toward a boat, which I know must lie waiting on the Mississippi.

This is a different trail than the one we came in on three days ago. We have not gone a great distance along it when Moseley orders a halt.

"Be quiet, all of you," he orders, and for several moments we stand there and listen to the silence. "Sergeant, draw your pistol and point it at the girl's head."

My knees turn to jelly and I think I might fall. *Why is he—*

"You out there!" shouts Moseley. "You, the white renegade, and any Indian cohorts you might have with you! A gun is pointed at the back of the girl's head! If anyone fires even one shot on us, she will be instantly killed! Do you understand that? Instantly, and without mercy!"

Silence in the woods. "All right, Captain Allen, let us proceed," Moseley says more quietly, and we move forward once again on the Captain's command.

"If you would, Sir, could you please direct the sergeant to shoot her in the back should we be attacked, instead of in the head?" asks Flashby. "You see, a good part of the reward still stands if I bring back only her head, and it would be distasteful if her skull were all shattered by a bullet."

"Make it so, Bailey," growls Moseley, getting fed up with all this.

It is hard to walk with my hands tied behind me, and several times I stumble and eventually I trip and fall. I fall hard on my shoulder and my head hits the ground and it hurts. The soldier holding the rope about my neck didn't slack off quickly enough as I went down and so the rope burns into my neck and I feel so miserable that I just let go and cry, the tears pouring out of my eyes and into the dirt beside my face. I bring my knees to my chest to curl up as much as I can into a ball of pure misery.

"How can you be so m*eeeee*an to me…I didn't do anything to you-hoo-hoo." My face contorted, my eyes squeezed shut, I bawl out my total pain and despair.

"Christ. Get her up. We've got to keep moving!" Moseley orders.

I am pulled roughly to my feet.

"Stand up, you," growls the soldier who lifted me up.

"Here, here, none of that," I hear Captain Allen say. "No need to be rough. She'll come along nicely now, won't you, dear? Come on, now."

Encouraged by a half-kind word, I nod and walk along as they start out again. I notice that Captain Allen walks by my side now, I think to catch me should I fall again.

"No need to be rough? Ha!" Flashby laughs. "Wait till later when she'll find out what rough really means."

I sense that Captain Allen stiffens at that, as do I, but he says nothing and we trudge on.

I cannot rid myself of the notion that this time I am truly captured. I will be taken down to the boat that lies on the river and from there it will be down to the sea and thence across the ocean, and, ultimately, to my doom.

The Black Cloud rolls in and I am helpless before it.

Chapter 51

The British Special Agents and their escort have a keelboat much like mine, moored in a little estuary of the Mississippi. I notice that three men have been left behind to guard the boat in the others' absence, and they look at me with undisguised astonishment as I am brought aboard. I notice also that tents have been set up on the outer decks, the lower decks being reserved for the officers, I suppose.

My dishonor and degradation is complete when, as we sight the boat, I speak up and say that I have to attend to a need of a personal nature.

"What the hell do you mean by that?" asks Moseley.

"I think she means she has to relieve herself. It happens, you know. Even in the best of girls," says Captain Allen.

"Well, then squat down, girl, and do it," says Flashby.

I lift my face and begin to cry again, the tears of humiliation real.

"You know, Flashby, you really are something of a cur," says Captain Allen, his hand on the pommel of his sword.

Various black looks have been exchanged between Allen

and Flashby all along this journey, looks that have not gone unnoted by me.

"Here, I'll have none of that," says Agent Moseley. "You can go at each other when this mission is complete, but not now. She can go behind that tree there."

"Please, Sir, I must have my hands free...to manage my skirt, like."

"All right, untie her hands," says Moseley.

"Wait a minute," snarls Flashby. "Let me check that neck rope. She ain't getting away this time."

Lieutenant Flashby examines the knots and then leans into me and says, "There's a bowline and three half-hitches on this noose. You can't hope to get them off. Try to run and I'll snap your neck. Got it? Good. Now go do your business. *I'll* hold the rope."

My hands are untied, and I go behind the tree, lift my skirt, drop my drawers, and do what is necessary. Then my hands are retied, again in back of me. Flashby is taking no chances with his prize.

"Take her below and tie her to a chair," says Flashby when all are aboard. "And get us something to eat and drink. We've got some hot work ahead of us," he says, with a smirking look at me.

Two of them take me down into a sort of common area and a chair is found and I am tied to it. They simply lift up my arms and slide them over the back of the chair and then bind my feet, each to a leg of the chair. It is Privates Quimby and MacDuff, I believe, and since I don't think they're enjoying this job overmuch, I bring on the tears and the heaving chest again.

"Damn me, I hate to see a girl cry," says MacDuff.

Hearing that, I redouble the volume of my cries.

"Steady on, Archy," says Quimby. "There ain't nothin' you can do about it."

"They're gonna torture me, lads," I wail. "They're gonna hurt me, I just know it, and I ain't got nothin' to tell 'em!"

"Now, Miss, they ain't gonna do nothin' o' the kind," says Archy. "After all, they's proper English gentlemen."

The proper English gentlemen come down into the hold.

Seeing that the binding job is done, Moseley orders the soldiers out, saying, "I told you that you are never to talk to this creature, and here I hear you babbling away with her. I catch you again, it's ten with the Cat, understood? Good." The soldiers leave in a hurry.

Moseley and Flashby stand regarding me.

"You, too, Allen," says Moseley. "Out."

"What?" asks Captain Allen, incredulous.

"What will go on here is an Intelligence matter and of no concern to the Regular Army."

"What are you going to do to her?"

"We will conduct an interrogation. There is reason to believe this girl has turned traitor and gone over to the American side…"

Here I shake my head vigorously back and forth. "No, it's not true!"

"…and we mean to find out the truth of the matter."

"I remind you, Allen, that this girl is *my* capture and I'll do what I want with her," says Flashby. "She is nothing more than gallows bait, after all, and as such, she has absolutely no rights."

"And I remind you, *Lieutenant* Flashby, that I outrank

you and, as such, am the Officer in Charge of military operations on this expedition!"

"We are merely going to ask her some questions, Captain Allen, that is all. Now if you would kindly step outside, we will get on with it."

Allen, furious, says, "Very well, Mr. Moseley. You have one hour. My men must be fed and put to their rest without disruption. One hour, no more."

And with great emphasis on his last utterance, he leaves the hold, and with him goes any hope I might have had of some protection.

Flashby grins at me and pulls a cigar out of his pocket. He licks the end of it and then steps over to the stove behind me. There is a rattling of metal and when he comes back into my sight, the cigar is lit. He pulls up a chair next to me and puffs a great cloud of smoke in my face.

"Do you mind if I smoke?"

I don't answer. The acrid smoke gets in my eyes and makes them leak tears all the more.

Mr. Moseley shuffles through some papers till he finds the one he wants. "It says here that you are wanted for piracy. What do you say to that?"

"Not true. I was a privateer, in the service of King George. I had a Letter of Marque."

"One that was revoked."

"They didn't tell me, when they revoked it. How was I to know? I was at sea, doing what I thought was my duty," I say, my voice full of honest resentment.

"*Hmmm.* What about the charge of misappropriating one of His Majesty's ships?"

"It wasn't his; it was mine. It was my share of the prize

money from those ships I took as commander of the *Wolverine*."

"Well, I'll let you settle that with His Majesty. Now, this business of your involvement in a French spy ring…"

"I *uncovered* the spy ring; I wasn't *involved* in it. I know I saved many lives by my actions, and I take comfort in that," I say. "Not like you, who seek to pay the Indians to murder innocent men, women, and children. How could you be so vile?"

"Ah, so you know about that? You *are* good at sneaking about," says Flashby. He takes a few more hard puffs on his cigar and then knocks off the gray ash, exposing the end, glowing red-hot. He reaches over with his other hand and flips my skirt back from my knees, exposing my legs to mid thigh. Seemingly by accident, he brings the glowing ember close to one knee. I can feel the heat of it and terror grips me, as I know his intent.

"Very well," says Moseley. "That takes care of your past actions, actions for which you will surely swing, *after* Naval Intelligence gets done interrogating you concerning the spy ring. Now, as to the present. How came you to be here, and what are you up to?"

"I ain't up to nothin'. I was taken prisoner by Captain Rutherford of the *Juno*. I escaped, and having no place to hide, I ran for the interior and met up with Lightfoot. I had some money and I hired him to take me down to New Orleans, where I have friends. That's all there is to it."

"Ah. You'll have to do better than that," he says, reaching over to slap me hard across the face.

I cry out, shocked by the suddenness of the blow, and then I blubber out, "I can't tell you anything else! God help

403

me, I don't know anything else! Please believe me! *Oh, please don't hurt me!*"

"It's reported that, as *La Belle Jeune Fille sans Merci,* you tortured prisoners on board the *Wolverine,*" says Flashby, leering into my face. "How do you like it done to you, *hmmm?*" And he puts the hot tip of the cigar to my leg.

"*EEEEEE-eeee!*" I screech, and thrash about in my bonds. "*No, no! Please, no more, oh please, God, save me!*"

Flashby blows on the tip of his cigar and again brings it down on me.

"*EEEEE-eeeee oh God! No, please, not again! EEEEEE-eeeee!*"

Through my pain I hear the hatch door thrust open and the heavy boots of Captain Allen come into the room. Flashby hurriedly pulls my skirt down over my knees to hide the burn marks. I hang my head and sob.

Allen, furious, demands, "What the hell are you doing to her?"

"Now, now, Captain Allen, she is just overreacting to our simple questions," says Moseley. "She sees you are sympathetic and seeks to prey upon your emotions. Can't you see?"

"What I see is that the interrogation for today is over," states Allen, flatly, looking at Flashby with murder in his eye.

"Who are you to be telling us that, Captain?" says Moseley, his toad face turning bright red. "I remind you that I am the head of this expedition, Sir!"

Allen turns on him and says coldly, "Look outside this hold, *Sir*... You will find nine soldiers dressed in red uniforms, very much like mine. They owe their loyalty to me, *Sir;* they take their orders from me, *Sir;* and as hardened as they are, they are *very* distressed over the shrieks they hear coming from a young girl held down here by the likes of you. If you want us to abandon you and Flashbutt out here in the wilderness to fend for yourselves, just say the word, and we will be gone, *Sir*."

Flashby is on his feet, glaring at Allen.

"Anytime, Flashbutt, anytime," says Allen, holding his gaze.

"You just want that bit of quim for yourself, admit it," snarls Flashby.

"Anytime, any weapons, Flashboy. Right now is fine with me." His eyes have not wavered from Flashby's. I do my job by continuing to gasp and sob, which ain't hard, given that my face still smarts, my leg still burns, and I despair of my future.

Moseley pulls Flashby to the side and whispers something to him, and then says to Allen, "We were through for the day, anyway. Let's lock her up and see how she likes spending the night in the dark with no food or water. That should make her more cooperative tomorrow. Captain, call down three of your men."

Captain Allen, with a final black look at Flashby, goes to the hatchway and calls out, "Sergeant, come down here with Jackson and McMann."

In a moment the men are in the hold, awaiting orders.

"Empty that closet of its contents," says Moseley. "Here's the key."

Sergeant Bailey takes the key and walks behind me with the other two men. There is a click as the door is unlocked, and then there is the sound of goods being moved.

"Done, Sir," says Private McMann.

"Make sure there's absolutely nothing left in there," warns Flashby. "This female is extremely clever and has twice escaped custody, and I'll be damned if it's going to happen on my watch."

"Nothin' in there, Sir," says Bailey. "Kind o' small, though."

"We'll be the judge of that," Moseley snaps. "Untie her feet. Just her feet."

The one named Jackson squats down and does it.

"All right, now tie her ankles together. Good."

I have not stopped bawling this whole time, and I think it's getting to the soldiers.

"If...if you tie me too tightly, my hands and feet will go numb and then turn black and fall off and I'll d-d-die," I sob. *And I won't be worth so much then, you bastards.*

"Make sure the bonds are firm, but don't cut off her circulation."

Sergeant Bailey slides a finger between the ropes and my ankles, then my wrists. "Should be all right," he says.

"Then lift her up and put her in."

Strong hands take me up and turn me around, and I get to see what will be my prison while I am here: a box three feet wide and four feet long, not even big enough for me to stretch out in.

"Oh, how could you *beeeeee* so *cruuuuuel*?" I wail, shaking my head back and forth, making my pigtails flail about my face.

"I must protest this treatment of a prisoner," says Captain Allen. "You can be sure that both my superiors *and* yours will be informed of this when we get back."

"Captain Allen, you may report all you wish. I think *my* superiors would be most pleased with my actions in this matter," says Mr. Moseley, tersely. "The female will be uncomfortable, yes, but in pain, no. Now direct your men to put her in the closet."

A pause, then, "Do it."

I am lifted from the chair and carried to the box and put in.

"Please, please, don't, *pleeeeease...*," I scream as the door shuts and blackness surrounds me. The key turns and the lock is secured. I hear low voices from outside and then nothing.

I keep up my caterwauling for a while and then taper off into groans of despair, followed by mere sniveling and whining over where cruel fate has cast poor me. Then I take stock of my situation.

I'm lying on my side, facing away from the door. I twist around to reverse myself and... *good. There's a crack of light at the edge of the door.* I can see the lock's lug where it enters the jamb—I won't be able to jimmy it, having no tools, but at least I'll know when it is withdrawn.

First things first. With my fingers, I work the rope binding my wrists down as far as I can toward my hands. Then I slide my bound hands under my rump and down to behind my knees. Now for the hard part. I try to work my hands farther down, but I can only reach to my ankles. That's all right, 'cause now I can get my fingers on the clumsy granny knot that I saw the landlubber Private McMann tie previously. Thank God it wasn't tied by a sailor or I'd be havin' a lot harder time of it. No time to lose, though—I've got to have a look at the knot on my wrist binding before they turn out the light over there.

There! My feet are free. Now I can slide my wrist rope up to my right heel, over and into my arch, then over my toes.

That's one leg, now for the other. I make short work of that and... *at last!*... now my hands are in front of me and I can hold them up to the dim light of the crack to check out the knot. *Good!* A simple set of half-hitches.

I set to work with my teeth.

"Worst watch I ever stood in me life, Archy," I hear from outside my box two hours later. It seems the watch over me is to be changed. "She cried the whole time, poor thing. But, remember, you can't even talk to 'er or you'll get the whip. And you'll want to talk, believe me, but don't do it."

"Still don't believe she done all those things they say she's done," says Archy MacDuff, plainly plopping himself down in the spot just vacated by Private Quimby. "No way to treat a girl, no matter what she done."

I've got my nose planted right up against the crack so as to suck in what fresh air I can, and I let out a low moan, followed by a few gasps and sobs.

"There she goes again, Arch. I don't envy you your time here."

"*Ach,* 'twill be a hard night, Willie. Get you off. See you in the morning."

Inside the box, I listen. Quimby has left the hold. I've loosely retied the bonds on my feet again, and I am ready to throw my hands behind me should I be inspected during the night, but no such inspection comes. I softly cry some more and then...

"Archy MacDuff, I know you are of Scottish blood, and you know I am not, but I was born in the north of England and so that's close enough to Scotland, it is, so that we share some common blood, yes, we do, and oh, Archy, pity me in my state of total disgrace and humiliation, pity me with all your heart...My hands are tied behind me, my feet are bound. Oh Lord, how can I survive such torment, such pain? And I'm thirsty, so thirsty, my mouth is as dry as a desert and oh, oh, oh, I'm sorry, I just can't keep from crying, I can't, Archy. I know you can't speak to me, Archy, and I know it's hard on you 'cause you want to talk to me and try to ease my pain, but you can't, you can't, I know you can't. But when I was a wee bairny, my mother used to sing me a Scottish lullaby called 'Schmeag Schmore' that went sort of like 'Hush, little baby, ever'thin's gonna be all right, the sheep's in the meadow, and the cow's in the corn,' and I know you can't sing it to me, Archy, but if you were to hum it real low, it would give me great comfort in my time o' need, Archy, it would..."

Chapter 52

It was a long night, one of the longest I have ever spent, but finally light began to creep through the door crack, and though I am cramped and achy, I make myself ready and steel myself for the attempt, for I know that this will be my only chance at escape before I am once again trussed up, helpless and doomed.

Facing the door and never taking my eye off the now-visible lock bolt, I lie back with my shoulders pressed against the far end of the box for extra leverage. My legs drawn up, my knees to my nose, I grip in my hand the whip I made out of the binding ropes by doubling them and knotting the ends.

I note footsteps approaching, and then I hear a voice I recognize as Moseley's.

"Report, Private Merrick."

I had all six of the private soldiers on guard last night, and while they could not talk to me, I could talk to them, and by now they all know me very, very well.

"She's been cryin' all night, Sir. She's quieted down some now, though."

"Well, let's get her out and bound up," says Lieutenant Flashby. "Here's the key."

That's three of them in there. No more, please.

"Aye, Sir," says Merrick. There is a rattle, and the bolt slides back.

Now!

With all my might I drive my feet against the door. It flies open and Merrick, taken by surprise, falls over backward as I vault out of the box and make for the hatchway door which...*yes! It's open!*

"Damn!" shouts Moseley, and he makes a grab for me, but I swing my cat-o'-four-tails and catch him full across the face. He shrieks in agony and falls to his knees, and I charge on toward the light.

But Flashby gets between me and freedom. "Oh, no, you don't!" he snarls, reaching for my neck.

Again I swing the whip, aiming at his face, but he manages to get an arm up to take the blow harmlessly on his sleeve, and then with his other hand, he rips the flail from my grip. Both his hands for the moment occupied, I dart to the side, and bouncing from a box on the deck, get up behind him and loop my last remaining piece of rope around his neck. With either end of the garrote wrapped around each of my hands, I pull with all my might. He begins to choke. I wrap my legs around his waist so he can't shake me off.

"Back us out the door or you'll never take another breath again, you scurvy dog!" I shout into his ear. He lunges wildly across the room, trying desperately to dig his fingers under the rope, to take that awful pressure off his windpipe, but he cannot. He can do nothing but gag. I am little, but I am strong. "The door, dog, or die!"

Again Flashby careens across the hold, this time in the general direction of the door. Another door opens and from the corner of my eye, I see Richard Allen, shirtless, step into the room. He takes in the scene—Moseley still on the floor, moaning, and Flashby staggering above him with a luridly purple face, and the Captain bursts into great gales of laughter.

"Nothing like a brisk ride of a morning to get the blood pumping, is there, old boy?" crows the delighted Allen. "Of course, I myself prefer to do the riding, rather than being rid, but then there is no accounting for taste, and I hear you Navy chaps do like your fun a little, well, *irregular. Hmmm*...It looks like she's got the bridle a bit tight, doesn't it. *Tsk, tsk.*"

"Get her! Tie her down!" This from Moseley, who has recovered enough to stand. "If she gets out the door, she is gone!"

Flashby is starting to sink to his knees. 'Tis plain he ain't gonna carry me to the door. I let go and leap for the opening. *If I can get out and into the water, I might yet save myself!*

"Allen, I order you! I swear I'll have you court-martialed!"

Captain Allen stops laughing long enough to say, "Oh, very well. *Ahem!* Sergeant Bailey, please apprehend that demon who has brought at least five hundred pounds of His Majesty's finest Intelligence Agents to their knees. Careful, now."

I'm out the door and there is the shining Mississippi and never did it look better, but there also is Sergeant Enoch Bailey, looking very large and very determined and very much in my way.

"Aye, Sir," says Sergeant Bailey. He whips out a hand and gets me by the neck—for a big man, he is very fast.

But I am very fast, too, and I use every dirty trick I know to try to break away. First I box his ears—bringing my two cupped hands together hard on his ears—he winces, but does not let go. Then I bring my knee up quick into his crotch—he doubles over and gasps, but he does not let go. Finally, I sink my teeth into the soft part of his shoulder next to his neck and I bite down as hard as I can. He does not let go.

"Archy...Alfie...help me," he wheezes, and the two soldiers are by his side, and they pry my now-defeated form off of their sergeant and carry me back inside and plop me in the chair. Rope is found and I am securely bound once again.

"Remember, no food, no water," says Moseley to Allen, as he prepares to leave. "I don't care what else you do with her, but no food, no water. And she had better not escape," he adds with a threatening look at the languid Captain Allen, who leans back in a chair, his booted feet crossed. He has on a loose white shirt now, but no coat. It is summer and it is hot. He also has a pistol in a holster by his side, I guess in case Flashby takes him up on one of his many challenges to duel.

"Don't worry, Guv'nor, she's in competent hands now," says the insolent Captain Allen, blowing an excellently formed smoke ring in Moseley's direction. I gather that Moseley and Flashby must journey back to the Shawnee village to find out what will be Tecumseh's stand on selling settlers' scalps for money.

Flashby, for his parting word, leans close to me and whispers, "The time to settle our unfinished business will come. You can mark me on that. When we get to New Orleans, goddamn Captain bloody Lord Allen will be gone, but you will still be my captive. We will see just how frisky you are then." He puts his hand to his neck, which is red with vivid rope burns. "And you may mark me on this, too. After I deliver you to the Admiralty and they are done with you, I shall give up fifty pounds of the reward for the privilege of putting the rope around your neck and pulling the lever to drop the trap myself. I am glad to inform you that I am quite highly regarded as a man up-and-coming in the Intelligence Service, and I am sure they will accede to my wishes. I will make sure that the drop will be the short one, not the long, so I can watch you strangle." He runs his finger over my throat when he says that.

I have not had a drop to drink in over twenty-four hours, but I manage to work up a gob of spit, and I sling it in his eye. Enraging him doesn't matter anymore, he will do to me whatever he will do.

He starts back, wipes his eye, and brings the back of his hand across my face. I shudder and hang my head and wait for another blow.

It doesn't come. Moseley and Flashby leave the hold.

I continue to hang my head and sag in my bonds. I try an experimental whimper.

"Well, you did spit in his eye, dearie, you can't deny that. I'd have smacked you one, too, for that."

"Would you, to someone tied in a chair? I think not, Captain Allen."

"I don't know about that, as I've never tied anyone to a chair. It ain't my style." Allen rises and locks the hatchway door and puts the key in his pocket. After he glances up at the clock—you can always trust the military to be watching the clock—he goes to a cupboard and takes out a bottle of wine and one glass. He draws the cork with his teeth and fills the glass. Then he pulls up a chair next to me and sits down.

"Do you know what Moseley and Flashby are doing at the Indian camp?" I ask.

"Oh, stirring up trouble, I suppose. They haven't seen fit to let me in on it yet, and that's fine with me. My only job is to protect the politicos, and that's what I'm doing."

For some reason, it gladdens me to hear that.

"How long will they be gone?" I ask with a sniffle. "Till they come back to torture me some more?"

"Oh, four or five hours. And I won't let them torture you. Oh, you'll have to suffer a little, but I won't let it get too far."

"Too far? Will you lift the edge of my skirt over my left leg a few inches?"

He grins. "Why, I'd be delighted." He gets to his feet and comes over and flips up my skirt. The angry red burn marks are plain on my leg.

Captain Allen's face loses its smile.

"Flashby's cigar. Just before you came in, he held it close to my eye. I-I thought he was going to blind me. But then he decided to brand my leg instead."

"It won't happen again. I'll remain in the room when they question you further."

"I must name you my friend and protector, then, and give you my heartfelt thanks," I murmur.

"Nay, don't name me that. It doesn't suit me being considered honorable."

"I think you like to paint yourself as a rogue when, in fact, you are not," I say, watching him take a long, slow drink of his wine. "Though you are torturing me by drinking that in front of me." Time for big, sorrowful eyes now.

"*Hmmm.* Moseley said no food, no water, but he did not say anything about wine," says the Captain, musing. "Very well. Here." And he holds the blessed cup to my lips and tilts it such that the liquid pours into my mouth. *Oh, Lord, that's good. So good.*

"Thank you, Sir," I say, running my tongue over my lips. "Thank you so very much."

"You are quite welcome, my dear. Now tell me something of yourself."

"Is this a further interrogation? Will you beat me, too?"

"No, no," he says. "It is just to pass the time. The agents seem to think you've been up to some pretty adventurous antics. Hard to believe, though, to look at you." He has another sip of wine and then puts the glass to my lips. "Then again, that was a right impressive rain of curses you were calling down on my poor sergeant's head as he tried to subdue you, so…"

I consider, and then I begin telling him of my early life as a beggar in London, of my time on the *Dolphin,* of the Lawson Peabody School for Young Girls, and of Dovecote, of the *Wolverine* and my *Emerald* and the *Bloodhound.* I am helped along by many, many sips of the glorious wine. When I am done, we are on the second bottle. In my telling of my story, I did not mention the fact that I was not unfamiliar with wine, so that when I begin acting a mite bit tipsy, he is not surprised. He only smiles secretly to himself, or so he thinks, the rogue.

"...And so I was arrested by Captain Rutherford, escaped, hired the mountain man Lightfoot to guide me to New Orleans, and here I am, tied to a chair. End of story."

"A remarkable account," observes Captain Allen, nodding. "Remarkable, indeed." He rises to go to the stove to light up a cigar.

"And now let us hear of your life, Captain. Surely you have had some adventures, too," I simper. "I heard that Flashby call you *Lord* Allen. Could you actually be one?"

"Well, my father is, anyway, the cantankerous old fart, and I could have been one, too, if I had been good, which I wasn't...Here, another sip, my dear? There you are...No, I messed up in school, got into fights, got into the wrong politics, got several daughters of the local gentry in trouble. *Le droit de seigneur* should have applied in those cases, I thought, but others thought differently...Would you like a puff, dear?"

"The 'right of the lord' to mount any girl in his fiefdom on her wedding night? Certainly an out-of-date custom, my lord," says I, shaking my head to his offer of a puff on his cigar.

"One they should have kept. A country breeds a better sort of bastard that way," he says, blowing a perfect smoke ring. It rolls and curls in on itself and then settles about my head. He grins and then continues.

"So the old man bought me this commission in the dragoons, knowing I'd be shipped out of the country, *tout de suite,* and so I was. I survived several battles on the Continent, and here I am."

"Dragoons? You are a cavalryman then?" I ask, knowing full well that he is.

"Yes. And where's my horse, you might ask? He's back with the rest of my company, getting fat and lazy, the rascal. I got in a bit of a tiff with the Colonel and got put off on this wretched 'detached duty.' Something to do with his lovely wife, and trust me, she was *very* lovely."

Captain Allen gets up to stand next to me, the butt of his pistol very close to my face. "And speaking of lovely women," he says, "it's been a long time for me, stuffed out here in these woods." He runs his finger down my cheek.

"And so you would force me, a helpless captive? I should not think a man as handsome as yourself would need to do that." I drop my chin and look up at him through my eyelashes. "I am scarce sixteen, and yet a maiden, and you are what, twenty-two, three?"

"A maiden? You?" he snorts. "From your reputation, I should think the last time you suffered that state was when you were twelve or so."

"It is the truth, my lord, in spite of what you might think."

He stands looking at me, thinking. At last he says, "You said in your story that you count yourself a commissioned officer in the Royal Navy. Do you?"

"Yes, I do. I earned that commission."

"Um. Then do you understand the meaning of *parole*?"

"I do. It's when a captured officer gives his word of honor that he will not try to escape in return for a measure of freedom until such time as a prisoner exchange is arranged. It is a common thing, but I will not give you my parole. I cannot," I say, "for if I am delivered to London, it will not be for repatriation, it will be for death."

"All right, then, how about a conditional parole? One for, say, a half hour. You'd be able to stand and stretch your legs, or…whatever else might occur to us."

I pretend to consider this, then I say, "Very well, I give you my parole for half an hour, and thank you."

Allen puts his cigar out in the ashtray on the table and proceeds to untie me. While he is bending over, undoing my feet, I look over him at the clock. It is exactly six minutes to twelve noon. *So twelve twenty-four, then.*

When he is finished untying my hands, he rises and says, "There, you can stand up now. But remember, on your honor…"

I rub my wrists and then stand and stretch my arms above my head, my back arched. "Oooh, that feels so good…Oh!"

Pretending to lose my balance, I fall against him, giggling. "Oh, my lord, my head is spinning so!"

His arm comes around my shoulders. "Here, let me steady you, my dear. Come sit at the table. I'll get another glass for you." He seats me on the bench and goes to get it. I notice he picks up another bottle on his way.

"You are probably dizzy from the confinement. Here, a glass of wine with you, to clear your head," he says, pouring out a generous dollop.

I notice that he allows the pistol butt to be within grabbing distance, and I have the feeling he is testing me to see if my honor will hold. I am quite sure he would seize my hand in time should I try for the gun. *Not, yet, Captain Allen.* It is now twelve-oh-three.

I take a goodly slug of the wine, sigh a heartfelt sigh, sit back, and put my elbows behind me on the table. "Ah, that is much better, Richard. May I call you Richard, my lord?"

"Of course, you may, Jacky." He sits next to me so that our shoulders touch.

I lean into him. "Richard, my lord, my lord, Richard," I prattle. "Such a fine name, such a fine man." I put my hands to my face to stifle more giggles.

He puts his arm around me and squeezes. With his other hand, he puts two fingers to my forehead and says grandly, "And I name you my own Lady Jacky, Duchess Pretty-Bottom, my dear little woodland sprite."

The woodland sprite does not shake off his arm. Instead she puts two fingers of her own to his brow and says, "You are a very forward fellow, Lord Richard. That was very naughty of you that day, to come upon me when I was bathing. I fear you are a rake, Sir."

"It was the vision of your loveliness that drew me there, Jacky, and I was glad I did it." He slides his arm down to my waist.

"Have I a pretty bottom? I have no way of telling."

"Oh, yes, Jacky," he says, beginning to angle his face toward mine. "The very finest I have ever seen. I shall never be the same again."

"And a flatterer, as well, Lord Dick," says I, with a small, ladylike burp. I wriggle a little bit away from him to free up both my arms and then unloosen the rawhide ties on the front of my shirt, opening it to the middle of my chest.

"Woo, but it's warm in here. Are you warm, Richard? I certainly am." I take the front of my shirt and give it a few flaps to set up a bit of a breeze inside it. Captain Allen's face *is* getting a bit red. *Twelve-oh-seven.*

"I sure wish I could take my leather shirt off, but since I have nothing on underneath, alas, I cannot," I lament. "But, Richard, if you would be so good as to take off my moccasins, I would be most grateful. I fear if I were to bend down to do it, I might swoon." I bat the eyelashes becomingly.

"Of course, my lady," he says, smiling broadly. I put the knees together as he kneels before me and begins unlacing the legging of my right moccasin. In a moment I feel it slide off. In another moment the other one joins it.

"Oh, Richard, that feels *soooo* much better," I purr. Then I feel his hands caress my calves and feet. "Oooh, that feels good, too." I relax and let the knees come a bit apart. Then I feel his lips on my left knee and, while that feels good, too, I figure he's about to start workin' his way up.

I pop up off the bench and bounce around the room. *Twelve ten.*

I stop in front of the mirror, look at myself, and decide to take my braids apart. *That should buy me a few minutes.* I take out the ribbons and untwist the braids. There is a comb there in a cup, and I take it and comb out my hair, fluffing it up about my face. Then I turn to face him. *Twelve twelve.*

"What do you think, my lord? Do you like me better as Dances-Like-Crazy-Rabbit, Shawnee Maiden, or as Jacky Faber, Fine Lady?"

"I like 'em both, so bring 'em both back over here." He is again seated on the bench, and he is patting his knee. I see that my wineglass has been refilled.

I prance back across the room, lift my glass, take a slug, and plop myself down in his lap and put my left arm about his neck. I know that the pistol is right next to my left buttock, as I can feel it there. His hand goes on my hip.

"How came you by that, my lord?" I ask, as I trace with my finger the deep scar on his left cheek. "By duelling?"

"Nay, it was at the Battle of Assaye, in India. It is a saber cut. The fighting was hot, close, and dirty."

"My poor, poor Richard. Here's a kiss for your bravery." And I put my lips on his and close my eyes. When I open them again, I see *twelve twenty-two. Two more minutes!*

I snuggle into his side and move my bottom in his lap. "Again, Richard," and again I feel the rasp of his cheek as we bring our lips together once more. Our breath is getting rapid, and I, for one, ain't actin'. I am finding this not at all unpleasant duty.

His hand, which formerly rested on my hip, now slides up the inside of my right leg. My lips open and I can taste the tobacco, I can taste the wine, and I can taste *him*, and I moan, "Oh, Richard..." And when I open my eyes again, I see that it is *twelve twenty-six! Get hold of yourself and move, girl!*

Another moan, another squirm, and I have my hand on the pistol's butt. I jump back, jerking the gun out of the holster, and I train it on the chest of a very shocked Lord Richard Allen.

"It seems, Captain Lord Allen, that you have lost not only your senses, but all track of time, as well," I say, my chest heaving. "You will notice that my parole is up and so is our dalliance. You liked me in my other guises, so how do you like me as Lieutenant Jacky Faber, *hmmm*?"

He looks over at the clock. He is not smiling.

"Now take the key out of your pocket and open the door. Then you will stand back away from it. You will note the pistol is on full cock. I am an excellent marksman."

"I won't do it," he says, his expression not changing. His eyes, steely now, bore into mine.

"You must, or I will kill you. I know where the key is. If I have to take it from your dead body, I will. Do it now." I hold the pistol in both hands and point it now at his face.

"No. I cannot. I may not have much in the way of honor, but I have some. So shoot me. If you get back to England, I hope that you'll get word to my parents that I died honorably. They would like to hear that."

"Screw honor!" I shout. "Open that damned door!"

"No."

The barrel quivers as I keep it pointed at his face. *Damn it! Damn it all to Hell!*

I give it up. I lift the pistol's barrel, put the hammer back on half cock, and throw the gun onto the table. I cross the room, sit down in my usual chair, and put my hands behind my back, my face red with indignation and fury. *Goddamned male bloody goddamned honor! I am truly lost!*

Captain Allen calmly rises, picks up the pieces of rope from the deck, and reties me securely. He says nothing, his expression does not change. After I am trussed up to his satisfaction, he goes back to the table and retrieves his pistol, but he does not put it back into his holster, oh no, he does not.

Instead he checks the charge and comes back to stand in front of me, his mouth a hard, grim line. He lifts the pistol and points it at my face.

"You did not have the stomach to pull the trigger. You will now find that I, in fact, do." He pulls the hammer back to full cock.

Tears pour out of my eyes. "Please, Captain, not in my face, please..."

He pulls the trigger, there is the sound of the flint hitting the metal and making the spark that ignites the powder in the flashpan as...

...as nothing...The gun was not loaded.

Captain Allen grins. And then he roars with laughter. "Did you really suppose I would be so stupid that I would have a loaded pistol lying about after seeing you take down Moseley and Flashby and half my squad? Did you think I would leave a loaded pistol within reach of Bloody Jack, or fairly close to Lieutenant Jacky Faber, or even in the same room with *La Belle Jeune Fille sans Merci,* the Scourge of the French Coast, the Caribbean, and who knows where else? Ha!"

He comes to my side, as I lie limp and quivering in my bonds, and he rumples my hair as one would a playful puppy. "Oh, Jacky, you are *such* a pistol, you are! I might even be in love with you! Ha!"

There is a sound from outside, and Captain Allen says, "Uh-oh. I think the agents are back. And just in time, too. For lunch, that is, which I'm afraid they will not ask you to attend. Perhaps that will be your punishment for trying to mislead poor, gullible Dick Allen. *Hmmm?*"

I reward that speech with a glare. He takes out his key and opens the hatch door, and Moseley and Flashby enter.

"What is this?" demands Flashby, upon seeing me with my hair down and my leggings off. The three empty wine bottles on the table do not escape his notice, either.

"She got hot," says Captain Allen, with an ill-concealed leer, "*very* hot, indeed, if you take my meaning." He makes as if he is buttoning up his trousers.

"Look, you…"

"Is she bound up, just as you left her?" asks Allen, his eyes steely again.

"Yes, but…"

"Then shut the hell up, Flashby. It's time for lunch."

"Yes, it is," replies Moseley, with a satisfied look. It is apparent he has received some good news today. *Damn! Did Tecumseh agree to the plot?*

The three arrange themselves at the table and food is brought down and I have to watch them eat it. But that's all right, I have gone hungry before and I suspect I will again, if I survive this ordeal.

As they are finishing, Moseley says to Allen, "After we are through here, I need you to take some men and scout downriver. I have heard of some encampments of savages down there that it might profit us to talk to."

Captain Allen cuts his eyes to me, as does Lieutenant Flashby, who smiles into his cup of wine. *Uh-oh…*

My head sinks down. *How much more of this can I take?*

Suddenly, all four heads in the room start up at a strange sound from outside.

"It sounds like music," says Moseley in wonder.

Yes, it does, says I to myself, hope rising in my breast once again. It is indeed music, and it is Scarlatti's Sonata in G for Harpsichord and Violin, played now with only the harpsichord, but it is sweet, oh, such sweet music to my ears!

Chapter 53

"What the devil?" asks Moseley, cocking an ear at the sound of the harpsichord.

Don't change expression, girl! Don't say a word! They'll get suspicious!

I keep my face calm, I let my head hang and my body sag as if I'm still without hope, but I am not, oh no, I am not. It is all I can do not to sing and shout for joy.

In a moment, there's a knock and Sergeant Bailey's florid face appears in the open hatchway. "Your pardons, Sirs, but there's a big keelboat anchored next to us. There's girls all over the boat, too." He glances off to his left for another look. "Pretty girls."

"We'll see about this," answers Moseley. He rises from the table and goes to the hatchway. "Come along, Flashby. Captain Allen, you stay here and watch things while we investigate."

"Girls, eh? We'll certainly have to investigate," says a grinning Flashby.

He and Flashby exit the cabin and I hear Reverend Clawson boom out a welcome to them.

"Gentlemen, may I introduce myself? I am Mr. Jeremiah

Ezekiel Clawson and this is my *Belle of the Golden West*, the finest showboat and tavern on the Mississippi River! We have superb food and fine wines and the best Kentucky bourbon made! We have music and entertainment and the most beautiful and cultured young ladies to keep you company!"

I hear some *yoo-hoo*s and feminine laughter, and I suspect that Honeysuckle and Tupelo and Clementine and Chloe are standing on the cabin top, smiling and waving and flirting shamelessly with the soldiers out on deck, who must be in a state of total amazement.

"It's been a long time since I've had a decent drink," says Flashby. "Or an indecent girl. I say we see what they got, Sir."

I can't hear Moseley's reply.

"Shall I send our boat over for anyone who would like to sample our offerings, gentlemen?"

"Very well, Mr. Clawson. Send the boat," says Moseley. He comes back and pokes his head into the hatchway, then says, "Allen. Lock the door from the inside. Keep an eye on her. You'll get your turn later."

He disappears and Captain Allen closes the hatch. "Imagine that, a floating whorehouse out in the middle of absolute nowhere. Will wonders never cease?"

He fishes the key out of his pocket, puts the key in the lock, and turns it. "There," he says, "I believe we shall have some privacy now." He goes to the table, picks up a piece of ham, and comes over to stand in front of me. "Open," he says, and I open my mouth, and he tosses in the chunk of meat. I chew and swallow. It is wondrous good.

He gives me a few more pieces and then holds his wine cup to my lips.

"Thank you, Richard. That was very good of you. To disobey Moseley's orders and all," I say, giving him the full big-eyed waif look.

"Well, my dear, he didn't order me not to feed you this time, did he?"

"If he had ordered you to go off on that scouting trip, would you have done it?"

"To leave you here alone with the gallant Flashby? I'm afraid I would have had to obey that direct order or face a court-martial and a possible firing squad, either of which I would have found most unpleasant. I love you, Jacky, but not quite enough for that. Here, have another sip."

After giving me another taste of the wine, he crosses to the stove and lights another thin cigar.

"Pity we can't have you give your parole again and pick up where we left off, but those two could come back at any moment, and since we can't have them finding you sitting in my lap, whispering sweet words in my ear, we'll have to pass the time in genteel conversation." He pulls up a chair next to me and puffs away contentedly.

It is the last bit of contentment he will enjoy for a good long while.

There is a sudden *crrrack!* of cannon fire followed by shrieks of pain from the soldiers outside. I also hear a blood-curdling Indian battle cry as well as a few *yee-haw!*s from, I suspect, the Hawkes boys.

"Damn!" says Captain Allen, jumping to his feet and fumbling for his key.

There is another *crrrrack!* and more agonized cries, and I hear Higgins call out, "Those guns were loaded with salt!

Now we're reloading with grapeshot! Throw down your guns and surrender!"

"I'll be damned if we will!" shouts Allen. He gets out the key, unlocks the door, yanks out his pistol, and runs up the stairs....Then he walks slowly backward *down* the stairs, with Lightfoot's long black rifle barrel pointed, once again, between his eyes.

"You been havin' fun with her, soldier boy?" I see Lightfoot's finger begin to tighten on the trigger. He comes fully into the cabin, with Katy Deere right behind him, an arrow nocked in her bow, her eyes searching the corners for any threat.

"Lightfoot!" I shout. "Don't kill him! Please! He helped me, he did! As best he could!" I feel a bump, which I know must be the *Belle* being grappled alongside.

"Then put the pistol down, boy, and stand back against that wall. Lift the gun and you're a dead man."

Captain Allen puts his pistol on the table and steps back, furious. "Friends of yours, no doubt," he says to me.

"The very best of friends, yes," I sob, overcome with relief.

"We got 'em all rounded up, Mr. Higgins," I hear Matthew Hawkes say.

"Good," replies Higgins. "Get their guns and take all their weaponry to the *Belle*. Be careful, Matthew. Remember, those men are trained soldiers."

"They don't look much like that now, no sir! Look like a bunch of crybabies to me." I can hear the sounds of sobbing from outside. Salt under the skin *does* hurt.

Higgins comes into the cabin, takes one look at me, and says, "Very becoming outfit, Miss. The Noble Savage, as it were. Quite handsome, and rather appropriate, too, considering your nature."

"Spare me your wit just now, Higgins. If you could see fit to untie me, I would appreciate it."

Higgins has me loose in a few moments. I stand, rub my wrists, and address Captain Richard Allen. "Captain Allen, do you surrender yourself and your men to me?"

"To you?" He looks at me with very little love in his eyes. "Why to you?"

"Because I am the Captain of the *Belle of the Golden West*, the ship alongside of us at the moment, which, I must point out, has just taken your ship, is why."

"Dammit, no, I won't."

"Then, the chair, Captain Allen. If you would be so good." I point to the chair in which I was so recently a helpless, hopeless prisoner.

"Move it, soldier boy," says Lightfoot, gesturing with his rifle barrel.

Allen goes to the chair, sits down, and stares straight ahead. He puts his hands behind him and I, taking the same pieces of rope that bound me, bind him. Securely, but not too tight. I am a sailor, after all, and an expert at knots. When I am done, I stand back, fists on hips, and regard him.

"Poor Lord Richard. It has been a day of reversals, hasn't it? The world turned upside down, as it were." I ruffle his hair, run my finger along his cheek, and bend down to put a kiss on his brow. He does not look at me.

"You are a pretty one, Captain Allen, but I shall not abuse a bound captive, as you, most nobly, did not abuse me."

I turn to Higgins and say, my voice hard, "But as for

Moseley and Flashby, for them I have other plans. Where are they?"

"They are in the trap, Miss, protesting quite vociferously, as you may imagine," says Higgins. "The Misses Honeysuckle Rose and Tupelo Honey took them directly to their chairs resting on the trapdoor. It was a simple matter."

"Good," I say. "Have they given up their weapons yet?"

"No, they have not. The snakes, Miss?"

"Not yet. I want to be there." I lift the hem of my skirt to show him the two angry burn marks on my left leg there.

Higgins averts his eyes. "I am sorry for your pain, Miss. I cannot bear the thought of you being tortured. I wish we could have gotten here sooner."

"You got here in very good time, Higgins, and I bless you for it. It would have been worse, Higgins, if Captain Allen here had not stopped them."

Higgins looks at Allen and gives him a slight bow. Allen, still staring straight ahead, does not respond.

Lightfoot, now that Allen is firmly secured, puts up his rifle and takes my shiv from his belt and tosses it to me. I catch it in midair and slip it back in my arm sheath. "Thanks, Lightfoot," I say. "I thought never to see it again."

"Thank Tepeki," says Lightfoot, and I do, and then get back to business.

"Higgins. That cabin there." I point to what I think is Moseley's room. "There's a money box in there, somewhere. It was money to be used to buy the scalps of settlers—men, women, and children. See if you can find it."

"And these men are British agents? I cannot believe it," says Higgins, incredulous at the news.

I notice Richard, also, stiffens at my revelation.

"It's true, Richard. I heard them offer that to Chief Blue Hand, as I listened by the tent. I heard Moseley say later that the renegade Half Red Face had already signed on. Higgins, I can't believe it, either, but it's true. Now, see if you can find the blood money. We will make sure it goes to a much better use. Katy, search the rooms for any weapons. We'll be putting the soldiers down here as soon as we can, to hold them, and I don't want them to be able to lay their hands on any guns."

Katy nods and goes about her job, as does Higgins.

Very quickly Higgins emerges, carrying a brass-bound chest, and he puts it on the table.

"Open it up," says the pirate Jacky Faber, "and let's see what we have." Higgins takes a knife from the sideboard next to the stove and does just that. He pries off the lid and there sits a gleaming pile of metal: silver dollars, ten-dollar gold pieces. No copper, no paper, just silver and gold.

"Take it back and stash it. We'll count it later."

Higgins hesitates. "However hateful, this *is* Crown money, Miss."

"Well, considering the purpose for which it was to be used, I don't feel bad at all," I say. "Besides, they've already got a noose set aside for me, and I might as well be hanged for a wolf as for a sheep."

Katy comes out of the last cabin, carrying an assortment of pistols and rifles. "That's it, Jacky. You can put them soldiers down here now."

I look around and spot the key that Richard had flung aside in his haste to get out of the cabin, and I go out the hatchway and into the light. *Oh, the sunlight never felt better on my face, and oh, the* Belle of the Golden West *on no occasion ever looked better.*

That's more than I can say about the miserable group of soldiers who are huddled aft, guarded by Matthew, Nathaniel, and Chee-a-quat. Some are moaning, some sit with faces in their hands. All are bloody, but thank God, none are dead. I only hope that none are blinded, as well.

"All right, lads, let's get them below," I say, pointing to the hatchway.

Prodded by the Hawkes boys' rifles, the soldiers make their way aft and down the hatchway as best they can, several having to be helped by their mates.

"Sorry, lads," I say as they pass me. "The fortunes of war and all."

When all are below, I go halfway down the ladder and announce, "We are going to lock you down in this cabin for the time being. There is plenty of food and drink to sustain you. Take wet cloths and apply them to your wounds, cleaning out the salt as best you can. I'll be back later with healing salve. You may untie your Captain after I lock the door. As soon as we have disposed of Moseley and Flashby, we'll see if we can make more comfortable arrangements for you. Don't worry, you're not going to be harmed further."

"What are you going to do to them?" asks the still-bound Captain Allen, looking at me for the first time since his capture. His gaze is hot with humiliation and rage.

"Have I not been branded a pirate, Richard? They are going to walk the plank, of course."

With that, I leave the hatchway, lock the door, and go over to the starboard side, where I leap aboard my beloved *Belle.*

433

After embracing each of my crew in turn and giving them my heartfelt thanks for my deliverance, I turn to the problem of Moseley and Flashby. Down in the cabin, I cautiously approach the edge of the open trap. Curses and threats are heard from below.

"Gentlemen. Your soldiers have been captured. Put your weapons on half cock and throw them out."

"Like hell we will! You will hang for this!" bellows Moseley.

"I may very well hang, Mr. Moseley, but it will not be for this," says I. "Crow Jane, the snakes, if you please. But be careful of that rattlesnake, he's mad as hell. Make sure he goes down into the trap and doesn't get loose up here."

"Right, Boss," says Crow Jane. She fetches the canvas bag containing the reptiles.

"One last chance, gents. Toss up the guns or shortly you will enjoy some very interesting company."

"You're bluffing, girl," yells Moseley, somewhat doubtfully.

"Am I?"

I have added a refinement since we first used the trapdoor to rid us of troublesome customers: I have obtained a child's rattle, which I now give a vigorous shake and then say, "Dump 'em, Janey," and she does it.

There is a satisfying shriek from Flashby. I think the tangle of snakes might have landed on his head. I nod to Nathaniel and Matthew, who upend the table over the hole, plunging those below into total darkness, and there is nothing like darkness to work on the nerves.

There is the sound of one pistol shot, then another.

"Goddammit, Flashby! Calm yourself, man, or you'll shoot me!"

"Get us out of here! For the love of God, let us out! We'll do what you say!"

I nod again at the Hawkes boys, and they set the table back up on its legs.

Two spent pistols come flying out of the hole, followed by a third, unfired and at half cock.

"Very good. Now take off all your clothing, ball it up in a bundle, and toss it out. You may keep your drawers, as there are ladies present and we don't wish to be disgusted."

There is the sound of rapid undressing. I suspect the snakes have wisely retreated to a far corner, but they would still look menacing, curled up and hissing.

Presently two bundles are thrown out, followed by two pairs of boots.

"Very well, Mr. Moseley, you may come out first. You will note as you come up the ladder that there will be at least six rifles and several pistols pointed at you. Should you not be fully undressed and weaponless, I'm afraid the catfish will dine upon your carcass. Is that clear? Good. You may come up."

He looks even more toadlike than usual, his big white belly flopping over the waist of his drawers, the rest of his skin looking gray and mottled and appearing never to have seen the light of the sun. He looks fearfully from one gun barrel to another, all of them pointed at his face. He clambers out of the hole.

"What do you mean to do?" he asks. "You cannot mean to kill us."

"I mean to have you tied to that chair. Sit down in it, please."

435

He crosses the room and lowers himself stiffly. "Tie him to it, Mr. Tanner, if you would. Hands at the back of the chair." Moseley is soon expertly fastened.

"Now, Lieutenant Flashby, you may come up. Slowly." Flashby's ashen face appears at the edge of the trap. His eyes take in the trussed-up Moseley. "Yes, brave Mr. Flashby, it is your turn. That chair there, please." He, too, looks at the guns pointed at him, then he sidles across to the chair and sits. He is quickly tied.

"There," says I, brushing my hands together as if dusting them off after a dirty job well—but thankfully—done. "That's that. Janey, if I could have a cup of tea, I would be grateful. Mr. Tanner, as Sailing Master, will you take the tiller of the prison ship, with Matty and Solomon on sweeps, and assign the *Belle* to Nathaniel on tiller, and Reverend Clawson and Higgins on sweeps? Mr. Cantrell, you will assist me when the time comes for the *interrogation* of the prisoners." Here I slide a glance at a very worried-looking Flashby. "I would like to be a good distance down-river before...*disposing* of these two."

"Aye, Captain," says Jim, playing this for all it is worth. "I'll see to it right away." He snaps off a salute.

"But before the boats separate, I want to go over and tend to the wounded soldiers. It's not their fault they are in this pickle, and I hate to see them hurt. Clementine, will you get the medical kit and assist me over there? And Chloe, too, if you would." There is nothing like delicate female hands laying on healing medicines to soothe the tormented soul of a wounded man, be he soldier or sailor. "Higgins, if you would lay out my uniform, and Crow Jane, if you'd whip up some dinner..."

Higgins nods, but Crow Jane says, "Yeah, Boss, I've got a real fine ham here..."

My eyes widen and I get a chill up my spine. "Oh, Janey, you didn't!" I cry as I charge out the gangway and look anxiously aft.

But no, Pretty Saro still regally reclines on her usual spot. She is genuinely glad to see me and gives me several delighted squeals and grunts as I come up to tickle her belly and to scratch her behind her ears. It's only been four days, but she seems *much* bigger than when last I enjoyed her company.

"I wouldn't let anything happen to her, Missy," reassures Daniel Prescott, giving Pretty Saro a pat of his own. "But I'm powerful glad to see you back."

"Me, too, Daniel, oh yes, me, too." I give Daniel another hug, lean down to plant a kiss on Saro's forehead, then head back to meet Clementine and Chloe, and together we cross over to the prison barge, to tend to my wounded countrymen.

Chapter 54

"Sergeant Bailey, you must swallow your stiff-necked Welsh pride and hold still! Right now I'm not your enemy, I am your nurse. Steady, now." For these men all hell had broken loose while they had been staring raptly at the girls strutting their stuff atop the *Belle*. Suddenly our cannons had fired upon them and a wall of stinging salt tore into them, painfully but superficially wounding all of them.

Sergeant Bailey's already florid face had been newly adorned with little red dots. His neck, too, and his hands. I dip my cloth into the basin of water and dab at the angry red spots.

"Just a poor little white girl captured by the redskins, they sez," grumbles the unfortunate sergeant. "Just a bit of a thing and so helpless, they sez. Worth a pile o' money, they sez. We'll just take 'er with us, they sez. Ha."

"Don't take it so hard, Sergeant. After all, you and all of your men are still alive after a major engagement and are being attended by the very finest of ladies." Clementine is finishing up on Quimby, while Chloe is working on Seamus McMann. The others have already been seen to—Bailey, like a proper sergeant, had insisted that his men be looked after first. Poor Archy MacDuff suffered the most, having gotten some flecks of salt in his now very bloodshot eyes, and I worked on him first, before turning to the sergeant. I think Archy's eyes will be all right, and I know my hands and words soothed him. *Poor laddie, ah, poor, poor laddie… Here, let me see, Archy, let me get this cool cloth on your poor face. There, isn't that better, now…?*

We had come over earlier with our cloths and our medicines, and I rapped on the cabin top of the prison boat and called out, "Ahoy, there! We have come to tend to your wounds! Stand away from the door as I open it!"

Jim and the Hawkes boys stood ready with cocked pistols to guard against a desperate escape attempt on the part of the soldiers, but none came. They are a dispirited bunch, having been sent on a mission which they found to be a foul one, and then being conquered by a mere girl and her motley crew.

I opened the door and looked into the gloom. "Captain Allen," I said. "Will you give me your parole, on your word of honor as an officer and a gentleman, that you and your men will attempt nothing against us during the time it takes to see to your men?"

There was a silence, then Richard Allen spoke. "Very well. But for that time only."

At that we had gone down and got to work.

"All right, Sergeant Bailey, we'll just dab on this healing ointment and soon you'll be your jolly, pink-cheeked self again… There!"

"Thankee, Miss," says the rough-and-tumble soldier. "We're obliged to ye."

"No thanks necessary, Sergeant. We all will do our duty, will we not?"

I stand and go over to confront Captain Allen, who has not uttered a single word the whole time. Smoking a cigar, he merely slouched in a chair, his booted legs crossed. Unsmiling, he watched me go about my business. "We are through here, Captain. I'll be back after we've disposed of Flashby and Moseley, and then maybe we'll talk about a more permanent parole for you and your men."

"You haven't killed them yet?" he asks with raised eyebrows. "I heard shots."

"That was the calm and steady Lieutenant Flashby, a credit to the Royal Navy, firing at shadows," I answer. "And no, I am not going to kill them—merely render them harmless. No matter what the world may say about me, I have never killed any man in cold blood, nor have I tortured anybody."

"I'm sure Flashby will be glad to find that out." A slight smile crosses his features. I'm certain *he* was glad, in a way, to find that I was not a murderess, just as I was relieved when I found out that he did not know what evil business Moseley and Flashby were up to.

"True, but he won't find it out for a while yet. A considerable while. Now, *adieu,* Captain Allen," I say as I pull out the chair from his crossed feet, which thump to the deck. "And next time, stand up when ladies enter a room. Come, girls, let us find less barbarous company."

"*Adieu,* Jacky," says the rogue, rising to his feet and sending a puff of smoke in my direction. He bows deeply. "Till later, Captain Faber."

———

Upon returning to my ship, I gave orders for both boats to weigh anchor and get under way. When we were well into the stream and moving smartly along, I went aft to my cabin, and, *Oh, how good it looks. I thought I'd never see it again!* Higgins helped me into my splendid Royal Navy lieutenant's gear—the blue jacket with gold lace running through the turned-out lapels, and the white lace at my throat, and the white britches tucked into my gleaming black riding boots. Pity I don't have my sword *Persephone* once more hanging by my side, she being at the bottom of the Atlantic, or, as I like to think, in her namesake's grasp, down there in Hades, but oh, well...

I leisurely dressed and took some refreshment, too, while Jim Tanner acted upon my orders to get us downstream for a good bit before dealing with Moseley and Flashby. *Let those two rotters cool their heels and sweat a bit,* I thought as I stuck my nose in a fine cup of tea and ate what Higgins put before me. After a while, I estimated we were a good four miles downriver from our last anchorage and figured it was far enough. I did not want Moseley and Flashby to be in any territory they might recognize.

"And now for these two," I say as I go back into the cabin of the *Belle* and gaze upon my two very worried-looking captives. They look at me in wonder, for not only do I have on the uniform of the Royal Naval Service, I also have my two new pistols stuck in the leather straps that cross my chest.

"You note with admiration my fine uniform, gentlemen? Oh yes, don't we military types just love to dress up for executions?" I purr. "Oh, Matthew, Nathaniel, will you be so good as to go set up the plank? And make sure it's a stout one, as Mr. Moseley here must go at least three hundred pounds, and we wouldn't want to botch things, would we? And Mr. Cantrell, would this not be an excellent time for you to fire up one of your fine cheroots and have a smoke?"

I look at Flashby as I say this, and he turns an even paler shade of white, but it is Moseley who asks, "Surely, you can't be serious? Walking the plank? Drowning us? In this day and age?"

"My dear Mr. Moseley. Haven't you seen the bulletin that names me as *La Belle Jeune Fille sans Merci*, 'the merciless female pirate'? That is the charge, after all, that you were taking me back to London to face, *hmmm*? And as a pirate, I can do none other than humbly request that you walk the plank. It would be a violation of the Pirate Code, Article Sixteen, paragraph eight, for me to fail to do so. If I were found out, I would be drummed out of the Pirate Brotherhood, forever. Nay, gentlemen, it is the plank for you." I poke my finger in the air. "After all, it's tradition!"

I do love a bit of dramatic theater.

"It's absurd!" shouts Moseley. I don't think Flashby is able to speak at all. His eyes are on Yancy, who is puffing up his cigar to a fine glow.

"As absurd as paying a bounty on the scalps of women?" I ask, no longer with the bantering tone. "The scalps of children, for God's sake?"

He ain't got no answer to that.

I sit myself in a chair next to Flashby and reach down and pull up the leg of my britches to show the burn marks. "Damn!" says Yancy. "Oh, you poor little thang," say Honeysuckle Rose and Tupelo Honey together. "They sure got it comin'," says Daniel. Yancy hands me the cigar, its end gleaming a fiery orange-red.

The legs of Flashby's drawers come down to just above his trembling knees. I delicately lift up the fabric of the left one to expose the same area on him that he had branded on me. I purse my lips and blow on the ash.

"Plank's ready, Skipper," calls Nathaniel down into the hold.

Heaving a sigh of regret, I look Flashby in the eyes and say, "Too bad, isn't it, that I can't repay kindness for kindness? But we must get on with things, mustn't we?"

I hand the cheroot back to Yancy Cantrell and stand up.

"Mr. Moseley first, if you please, Mr. Hawkes. Reverend Clawson, do you have your Bible?"

The Reverend nods sadly and takes his position at the head of the line that will be formed. Matthew and Nathaniel untie Moseley's feet and lift him from the chair, leaving his hands tied behind him, and all three take their place behind the Preacher. I fall in at the rear.

"All right, let's go," I say, as I bow my head and put my hands together in the aspect of prayer.

"Lo that I walk through the Valley of the Shadow of Death, I will fear not evil for Thou art with me...," intones Reverend Clawson, as he begins the long walk to the hatchway and thence to the plank. I sneak a look back at Flashby. His eyes are wildly staring, and he struggles vainly in his bonds. *Good for you, you bastard!*

Out in the light, we put Moseley up at the foot of the plank.

"Have you any last words, Sir?" I ask.

"Only that I'll see you in Hell, you monster!"

With that, the fiend Jacky whips a thin strip of rag about his face and into his mouth and ties the ends at the back of his head, so that he can no longer inform Flashby, who is back in the cabin with the door wide open, what is happening to him. I nod to Jim and he guides the *Belle* into the shallow water next to the bank.

"Reverend?"

"Ashes to ashes, dust to dust..."

I put my lips up to Moseley's ear. "Go and sin no more!" and with that, I cut his wrist bonds, place my booted foot on his ample arse, and push him into the shallow water.

We watch to see him hit the water with a satisfying splash, which is sure to be heard by Flashby below, and then we see him gain his feet, stumble and fall, and then finally make the bank.

As he tries to get the gag out of his mouth, I call softly to him, "Why not look up Half Red Face now and see how hospitable he might be? Now that you have no money or power."

I turn to Jim. "Let's steer over to the other bank. I don't want these two to have the comfort of each other's company." He nods and puts the tiller over. "Nathaniel," I call out to the other boat, "steady as you go. Keep steering south. We'll join up with you after we've sent Flashby off to his reward." He gives me the thumbs-up and the boats begin to part. Lightfoot, Katy, and Chee-a-quat are on the prison boat, armed to the teeth, to make sure there's no funny business from Allen and his men. On the *Belle* I put Solomon on port aft sweep and Clementine and me on the starboard one, and we all pull hard for the other bank.

"I think this will do. Up, sweeps," I say as we drift in close to the Arkansas shore. "Keep her parallel to the shore, Jim." For Flashby's benefit I call out, "Rig the plank on the starboard side! The water's deeper there! All right, bring up the prisoner!" In reality the water is only about four feet, but it's muddy and the bottom cannot be seen.

Higgins, Reverend Clawson, and Yancy Cantrell go below. There are sounds of struggle and desperate pleas for mercy...*No, no, I beg you, please*...but presently the Reverend reappears holding his Bible and reading a prayer, followed by Higgins and Yancy, supporting the condemned between them.

Flashby looks wildly about, sees me at the foot of the plank, and tries to wriggle away, all to no avail. He is placed on the plank and forced to the middle of it, with eternity, as I'm sure he thinks, waiting in the swirling waters below.

"Come, Lieutenant Flashby, let us do this thing in a proper military manner, eh, what? You don't want to make a bad show of it, do you? I thought not—the Honor of the Service and all. A little farther out now, Sir, if you please."

We shove him out to the end.

"Good. Oh my, Mr. Flashby, I fear you've gone and soiled your drawers. *Tsk, tsk.* Ah well, they'll soon be washed clean, as will your soul, I'm sure...after a few eternities in Hell, that is. Oh, but I do ramble on, and I'm sorry for it. I'm sure you want to get this done quickly, *hmm?* Very well, then. Do you have any last words, Mr. Flashby?"

He is unable to speak. I look in his face—his eyes have become glazed, unfocused.

"Well then, good-bye, Mr. Flashby. Give my regards to the Devil."

I take my shiv and quickly slice through the cords that bind his wrists, then give him a poke with the point of my blade in his left buttock.

He screams as he goes over, a scream that is cut short by the water that fills his open mouth. He goes under, but he bobs back up and stands looking in amazement at his unbound hands. Then he looks up at me, standing at the rail as the *Belle* pulls away from him.

"Burn me, will you?" I ask. I work up a gob of spit and send it down at him, and then I turn and see Lieutenant Flashby no more.

The prison barge has gained about a mile of downstream yardage on us, what with our crossing back and forth, but with all four sweeps going, we soon catch up and pull ahead. I'm going to have to come up with a name for the other boat.

"Good work, all!" I call out so both boats can hear. "We shall all have a fine dinner tonight in celebration!"

This is greeted with a cheer, from my crew, at least. We hear nothing from Captain Allen's.

Seeing everything shipshape, I go forward to seek out Higgins.

"Higgins, will you give me a bit of a brushup and comb, as I intend to go see Richard...er...Captain Allen about his parole?"

"Of course, Miss Faber," says Higgins, very formally.

Uh-oh. When Higgins addresses me so, it means I've stepped over the line on something and he means to correct me on it. He follows me to the aft cabin and I plop myself down in a chair and he gets to work on my unruly thatch.

"Out with it, Higgins, what have I done this time?"

After reflecting for a moment, he says, "It appears to me, Miss, that we have not been seeing you at your best during the past several hours."

"What? Because I threw a bit of a scare into those two rotters? They certainly had it coming, what they planned to do, what they did to me! You spend the night stuffed into a tiny box and see how charitable you feel about those who put you there!"

"I'm sorry, Miss. They should not have hurt you and they should not have been inciting the Indians to riot. However, if you begin adopting the practices of bad people, you run the danger of becoming one yourself. I'll say no more on it."

"Y'know, Higgins, it's sometimes hard traveling with your conscience right by your side, always ready to appeal to your better nature, a nature you might not even have."

"Please don't pout. It doesn't become you. I merely ask you to think about what I said."

"I'm not sorry. When I think of little kids being...no, I'm not sorry."

"Very well, Miss. There, I believe that's the best we can do with this. You are presentable, at least, and can now go and present yourself to Richard...er...Captain Allen," he says, putting up his comb.

Grrrrr. Why can you always see right through me, Higgins?

I stand and get a final brush off.

"Will you come with me, Higgins? As my protector?"

"Of course, Miss. Let us go."

I rap on the cabin top of the prison boat. "Truce! For a parley! Agreed?"

There is a pause, then Captain Allen growls, "Agreed."

I unlock the door and enter the hatchway and Higgins follows.

Allen is seated at the table, again with his booted feet up in a chair. He looks at me in my lieutenant's rig and I'm pleased to see that his eyebrows lift as far as they are able to do so. He gets up and bows, the ghost of a smile on his face.

"That's much better," I say. "May I present my First Mate, Mr. John Higgins? Mr. Higgins, Captain Lord Richard Allen, Royal Dragoons." The two exchange slight bows. "Mr. Higgins distinguished himself at the Battle of Trafalgar and is quite expert with those pistols you see." I had doffed my pistol belts back in the cabin, figuring them to be a bit too much. "Shall we be seated?"

We sit down and I continue. "We are here to discuss your parole. Will you give your solemn promise that you will not try to harm us if we let you out of here?" The other men are grouped in the rear, with some probably stretched out in the cabins. I'm sure they are listening avidly.

"And what will we get in return?"

"The freedom of this boat. You will be allowed to steer and row it and remain in our company. You not having weapons, I would advise you to stay close to us in this wild land so that we might protect you."

"That's not much."

"I think it is all you could hope for. After all, this is *my* boat now. It is a prize. Do you have a name for it, Captain?"

"No."

"Then I name it *Britannia,* since it contains eight fine, valiant servants of the King." I hear a snort or two from the rear. "You will not offer us a glass of wine? Our throats are dry from today's sport."

He barks out a laugh. "We drank it all up during our courtship, don't you remember, Princess Pretty-Bottom?" More snickers from the back.

"Ah, well," replies this princess, "we have ample stores of

good food and drink, and we shall share. There is that to consider. I assume your stores are both low and mean." Grunts from the rear.

"All right," says Allen to his soldiers, "that's enough out of you!" There is silence aft. "Will you give the money back?"

"Why? So you can use it to buy the scalps of innocent women and children?"

"I am not in the market for any scalps. Except perhaps yours."

"You shan't get it."

"We'll see. I should be most honored and pleased to add your scalp—your figurative, metaphorical scalp, of course— to my belt." He looks at me with a merry impudence. *Just who is the conquered one here?*

"I think you have had too much education, Lord Allen, and I suspect it was all wasted on you."

"Too true. I am educated, but in any exchanges I have had with you, I must confess I feel myself an educated fool."

"This will further your education, then. I am promised in marriage to Lieutenant James Emerson Fletcher, Royal Navy, and I intend to honor that pledge." I stick my nose in the air and assume the Lawson Peabody Look.

"And just where is this fine lieutenant who has brought the formidable Jacky Faber to heel? Is he hereabouts, so that I might run him through quickly and cleanly and so relieve you of the onerous burden of your pledge of maidenly fidelity, which I'm sure was a hasty one?"

My face is beginning to burn, as I feel I am losing in this exchange. "Well, will you give your parole?"

"Will you give us back our weapons, if I do?"

"No."

"Then I will not. We are soldiers and we do not like being defenseless."

"Then good day to you, Sir. Suffer your confinement for your stubbornness. Higgins, let us go."

"*Adieu,* my little woodland sprite." He does not get up as we exit.

I stomp out of the *Britannia* in total retreat. *Fine, Mr. Captain Richard Lord Allen! Sit down there in the gloom with your sullen men and listen to the revels that will resound from the* Belle of the Golden West *this night. Oh, yes, I will make sure the music is loud and the laughter is wild and joyous, oh yes, and it will continue far, far into the night. Count on it!*

Chapter 55

"Katy, did Lightfoot give you anything when he got back from the Indian village?" I ask. It's morning and we're down in our cabin getting ready for the day. Katy is washing up and I'm combing out Clementine's hair and getting ready to put it in braids. We're all a bit groggy from last night's celebration, which went on far into the night. We had pulled the *Britannia* up next to us when we anchored for the night and grappled her tight to our side so that the soldiers therein could fully appreciate what they were missing. I made sure the fiddling, harpsichording, singing, and general carousing were as loud as I could possibly make them. I also made a point of singing "As We Marched Down to Fennario" loud and clear, especially to gall Richard Lord Allen. Or so I fondly hoped.

"No. Why would Lightfoot want to give me something?"

Why, that bashful dolt! He'd fight ten men, wrestle a mountain lion, and kill a bear with his bare hands, yet he can't give a present to a girl!

"Oh, nothing, Katy. Just asking, is all. There, Clementine, you are done." I pat her on both shoulders. "I think

Jim Tanner could use a nice strong cup of tea." She hops up and darts out of the cabin.

"Could you stay here a moment, Katy? I'll be right back. Thanks."

I leave the cabin barefoot, dressed in my Indian skirt and light cotton shirt, my intended costume for the rest of this voyage, as it is the coolest possible outfit I have that still stays within the admittedly loose bounds of propriety that manage to exist on board the *Belle*. Hell, in this heat I'd go starkers, but for sure *that* wouldn't wash, not even here.

I find Lightfoot up forward, crouched with Chee-a-quat, sharpening knives. They have done their own and are now honing Crow Jane's.

"Lightfoot, how come you didn't give Katy Deere those presents you got for her when you got back to the boat?"

Lightfoot rises to his feet and towers over me. Could he be blushing?

"Uh...didn't seem right. We hadn't gotten you back yet."

"I've been back almost a full day now."

"Well...uh...I..."

"Do you want me to give 'em to her?"

"Yup."

"All right, hand 'em over."

Lightfoot ducks into the open hatchway to the main cabin and shortly returns with the quiver and the buckskin dress. He thrusts them at me and then returns to sit with Chee-a-quat.

I go see Katy Deere.

She is done washing and sits looking expectantly at me when I come into the cabin bearing gifts. "These are from Lightfoot," I say, handing her the quiver of arrows and laying the beaded skirt and shirt on her bed, spread out so she can see them. "He asked me to tell you that he's willin'. Those were his words."

She smiles slightly as she draws one of the finely crafted arrows from the quiver and then chuckles, "Well, I'll be durned."

I turn and leave Katy Deere with her new treasures and, undoubtedly, some very new things to ponder.

"She didn't say anything," I report to Lightfoot. "But she took 'em."

When he doesn't say anything, I say, "You've got to give a girl time, Lightfoot, especially a girl like Katy."

"*Wah,*" he replies, and turns back to his knives.

I give Pretty Saro a bit of an ear scratch and then climb up on the cabin top and take a seat at my table. I am thankful for the canopy overhead, shielding me from the fierce sun, and I am ever so grateful to be back here at my usual station, free once again.

Seeing Higgins emerge from the main cabin, I catch his eye and he comes to my side.

"Good morning, Miss. I trust you slept well."

"Like a baby, secure in the company of my dearest friends. Please have a seat, Higgins, as we've got to talk."

He sits, folds his hands on the table, and waits for me to begin.

"We're stretched too thin, having to manage four, sometimes eight, sweeps with our little crew. We've got to do something about it."

Higgins nods, looking over both the *Belle* and the *Britannia.*

"You could release the other boat and let them make their own way downriver."

"I could, but I don't want to leave them unarmed and helpless in this wilderness. But on the other hand, I don't want to give them back their guns—Captain Allen might feel honor bound to try to capture me. After all, I am a wanted fugitive. I know he wouldn't do it for the reward, but he might do it out of a sense of duty. No, I must have his parole."

"Do you think he would stand by his word, if he gave it?"

"He could have ravished me when I was a bound captive and he didn't, though I know he very much wanted to."

"*Hmm.* Well, that's commendable. Is he really a lord? I heard you call him that."

"Aye. He portrays himself as the black sheep of the family."

"*Umm.*"

We both sit and mull over the problem for a while, then Higgins says, "You'll remember, Miss, that during yesterday's discussion with Captain Allen, he asked if you would return the money and you refused."

"Right. It goes against my nature to return plunder."

"I know. But consider this: I have counted the money and it is not much—only eight hundred and ninety American dollars. We have been making steady money on our way down these rivers. What with the Cave-in-Rock loot, the income from the performances, the house percentage from Mr. Cantrell's games, and the tavern sales, we are quite well-fixed. We shall be able to pay off everybody when we get to New Orleans and book quite comfortable ship passage to anywhere you might like to go."

"We'll be even better off if we keep that money."

"Yes, but I will say again that this is Crown money. If you are ever taken by the British government, you could make a strong case against the piracy charge, since you had the Letter of Marque. Your seizing of the *Emerald* could be justified, too, because as commander of the *Wolverine,* you felt it was your fair share of the prizes. But if you keep the scalp money, you would not be able to argue against a charge of common theft of the King's treasure. There would never be a hope of acquittal or of pardon. I say it's not worth it."

I give out a low grumble of dissatisfaction, but I say, "Oh, very well, then. We'll give it back. But if any of our pirate acquaintances from last summer's Caribbean cruise get wind of this, I shall be mortified. Drummed out of the Brotherhood, as it were."

"If any of them remain yet unhanged, Miss, we shall certainly endeavor to keep it from them."

"Good, then let's set up another parley with Captain Allen. Go see him, please, and take a bottle of wine and present it with my compliments and request that he join me for lunch at my table here. If you could whip up something special from our stores, Higgins, I would greatly appreciate it. Oh, and my blue dress, if you would."

The arrangements are made, Captain Allen's temporary parole is taken, the two boats are brought together, and he hops over onto the *Belle* and is escorted up to my table by First Mate Higgins.

I, of course, am not there to see it. When I am told he has been seated, I give my chest one more dab with the powder puff, I assume the Lawson Peabody Look—eyes hooded, chin up as if balancing an invisible book on my head, lips together, teeth apart—and I go up to join him. He has seen me as Wah-chinga, Indian Maiden, and then as Lieutenant Faber, Naval Officer, but now he shall see me as Jacky Faber, Fine Lady, or at least the best I can manage in that regard.

I am taken up to the table on Higgins's arm, and Captain Allen, resplendent in his regimental jacket of scarlet, rises. He looks me over and pulls out my chair. I smooth the back of my dress and sit down.

"Thank you for inviting me, Miss Faber. You could not look lovelier."

"It is my pleasure, Captain Allen. However, before I take refreshment, I must insist that you take off your fine coat, as it is much too warm today. You can see that I, myself, am dressed in a manner quite cool."

My blue dress, which I had first tailored on the mizzen top of HMS *Dolphin* and which has since gone through many alterations by female hands much more expert than mine, does not cover much of my upper body. It leaves my shoulders bare, while it pushes up certain parts of me in a hopefully appealing way. Higgins has arranged my hair in an upswept French fashion, which, I think, makes me look older than my years.

Nodding, Allen, whose gaze is fixed on my bodice, strips off his jacket, drapes it over the back of his chair, and sits back down.

"Thank you, Higgins," I say, as he fills my glass. When he is done, I lift it and say, "A glass of wine with you, Sir. Shall we not toast to love and friendship?"

"Aye, that we most certainly shall," he says, clinking his

glass to mine and looking into my eyes with a good deal of heat. "But I cannot think that you invited me over just for that."

"Oh, no, Captain, I do not take you for a fool. We shall parley, you and I, to seek a solution to your unfortunate situation, but we will do that after we dine. Higgins has prepared some very special treats."

"Very well, Jacky, you may try to soften me up with some wine and then we shall talk—oh, and may I call you Jacky? I once did, you know. What was it, all of…yesterday?"

"Yes, you may, Richard, as we are of similar rank."

"What? A captain surely outranks a mere lieutenant?"

"He does in the Army, Sir, where there is the rank of major, and lieutenant colonel to which a mere lieutenant can aspire before he reaches the Flag rank of colonel. But in the Navy there is only lieutenant and captain, as in captain of a ship. Many have spent long, honorable careers as lieutenants. I am proud to have been named one."

He gazes at me without expression. "You know, when you told me of your past life yesterday, I didn't believe half of it. Now I am starting to change my mind."

"Put thoughts of any kind out of your mind, Richard, and enjoy what Higgins is setting before us. See, those are rare mushrooms that Katy Deere has gathered—oh, no, they are quite safe, as we have already eaten many of them. And that is the finest of sturgeon roe over there—caviar, and right here in the American wilderness! Can you imagine? And Crow Jane tells me that soon we shall be in the land of the crawdads, little creatures that look like miniature lobsters and taste divine." I clasp my hands together in rapture. "Is not the world a place of wonder, Richard?"

"Oh, indeed, Jacky," he says, his eyes never leaving either me or my own eyes. "It is that."

The dinner finished and the table cleared, we turn to business.

"Captain Allen, we cannot have your men suffering confinement any longer. It is cruel, and I won't have it. I must have your parole."

"What you mean is you don't want your crew rowing us downriver while we sit at our leisure. Do you mind if I smoke?" He pulls out a cheroot and holds it up for Higgins to light. "Thank you, Higgins. If you ever lack for employment, please look me up."

"What I mean is, we must come to an agreement." I lean forward, over the table. "In return for your parole, your promise not to harm us, I will give you back the money, provided you do not use it to buy scalps."

"Very nice move there, my dear, that bit with your chest," he says, lifting his eyes from my chest and puffing on his cigar. "But we'll need a little more than that. Will you give us back our weapons?"

"That would be hard for me to do. You could take me captive again, and carry me back to England, where I would surely be hanged," I say, dropping the eyelashes over the eyes and squeezing out a tear.

"I know that you plan to stop in the towns that lie below us, to put on your shows. We would be with you, but we cannot be seen without guns. It would shame the men beyond all endurance. They wouldn't stand for it."

"Suppose we give you back the weapons, but without powder and shot?"

"*Hmmm.* That might be acceptable. I assume we'll be allowed to leave when we wish?"

"If you want to leave us now, I won't prevent you, but unarmed in these hostile territories, well, you might reconsider..."

"Our sabers. They will be returned?"

"Yes."

"I think we are close to agreement, my dear."

"That is very good, Richard. What do you plan to do with the money?"

He takes another long drag on his cigar and then brings his attention back to me. "I plan to acquire horses when we reach a place called Baton Rouge, which is in Louisiana, and it is there that we will leave you. We'll travel overland to the south and thereby find our way back to our base in Jamaica. According to maps left behind by former agents Moseley and Flashby, we'll be getting into flatter, more open country, and much more suited to horses, and at Baton Rouge we should be able to get outfitted properly. I must tell you that, however charming the company, these leaky, damp, and altogether wretched boats do not suit Heavy Cavalry. I can tell you the lads will be much relieved."

"We have agreement, then?"

"*Umm.* And just what *did* you do with Moseley and Flashby?"

"I marooned them on separate sides of the river, many miles upriver, and several miles apart, dressed only in their drawers."

Richard Allen throws back his head and roars with laughter. "Serves the buggers right! Oh Lord, the picture of Flashbutt scurrying around in the bush with only his knickers to protect him from mosquitoes, gnats, and hostiles! It is just too, too rich!"

I rise from the table. "All right, Richard. Recite to me your oath."

He rises and holds out his half-full glass to me. "I, Richard Allen, Captain of Royal Dragoons, give my pledge that I will not cause harm to you, Lieutenant Jacky Faber, nor to any of your crew of the…what?"—he pauses to look over the side to read—"the *Belle of the Golden West,* in return for the terms agreed upon."

He drains the glass and continues. "I do, however, reserve the right to continue to pursue the aforementioned Jacky Faber, Wah-chinga, and Princess Pretty-Bottom, for purposes amorous!"

I lift my own glass and say, "It is so agreed. You may release your men and tell them of the terms. Please station your own men on the tiller and sweeps as soon as possible. Have them take position behind us until we stop for the night. Since you have already dined here, we will have Sergeant Bailey and Privates McMann and Merrick over for dinner tonight. As for assaults on my virtue, you, Lord Allen, are confined to the *Britannia* unless specifically invited over to my ship."

Richard Allen prepares to leave. "So you do not trust me, then?"

I down my glass and say, so that others cannot hear, "Nay, Richard, it is myself that I do not trust."

He smiles, bows, looks at me from under lowered brows, and then crosses over to the *Britannia.*

Hmmm…

———

The three soldiers are shy at first, but they are soon relaxed by the food, the drink, and the general merriment of our little tavern, to say nothing of the presence of Clementine, Chloe, Honeysuckle Rose, Tupelo Honey, and my own cheeky self. In no time at all, the stiff-collared red jackets are cast aside and the dragoons are bellowing right along with us as we sing every song we know.

As I crawl into bed, thankful for the bits of canvas that we'd rigged to scoop any errant breeze directly into our cabins, I gaze up at my picture of you, Jaimy, and pray once more for your health and safety. I have no idea where you are and I'm sure you couldn't possibly guess my whereabouts, either. We are just two little specks on the surface of this great big old world, aren't we?

G'night, Clementine. G'night, Chloe. G'night, Katy...
G'night, Jaimy.

Chapter 56

And so my fleet, such as it is, rolls on down the Big River. Higgins has taken to calling me Commodore again, Solomon is teaching me the guitar, Pretty Saro grows bigger by the day, and what I'm going to do about that, I do not know.

Memphis is a pretty large settlement, compared to what we have seen lately, so we set up for the full show there, and do well. We haven't had to use the trapdoor since Moseley and Flashby—it doesn't hurt to have a fully armed squad of red-coats ready to dampen the spirits of any would-be trouble-maker, does it? Even if the guns are not loaded, they are in plain sight, and there are those cavalry sabers hanging by the soldiers' sides. There had been a few small settlements on the way here, so tiny that Sergeant Bailey and his men made up a large part of the audience, but they were appreciative of the shows and applauded loudly—especially when my dress comes off in the last act of *The Villain Pursues Constant Maiden*. Captain Allen had insisted that he be given a part in the play, and so he was given the role of Captain Strongheart, which he played with great gusto. He was much better at it than poor Jim, who was glad to get out of the part, and at the end, I would fall into Richard's arms, which was fun. No kiss, though, oh no. I must be good. And careful.

When we leave Memphis, it is not long till it is no longer Tennessee, but the Louisiana Territory, that we have on our left.

"No, Miss Jacky, you've got to get your pinky finger all the way down here, and you got to hold the string down hard, so's it won't buzz when you pluck it with your other hand."

We are at my table on the cabin top, under the canopy.

"But, Solomon," I wail, "it won't stretch that far. My hands are half the size of yours!"

"It'll stretch. I seen littler girls than you make that chord. There, see, you got it, Miss Jacky. Now with your right hand do thumb, first finger, thumb, middle, and now do it again till you got a nice roll goin', like that. Good. Now keep up that roll and change to the G chord. Good! Now you rollin'! You a fast learner, Miss Jacky."

Solomon had not known the names of the fingerings, but he did know how to do them. So after we matched up the chords to the notes on Chloe's harpsichord, we were able to name them, which made it easier for me to learn.

Although I glow under his praise, I grumble, "You don't have to butter me up, Solomon. No one else around here does. And you must stop calling me Miss Jacky. It sounds too slavey, and you're a free man now. You may call me Jacky."

"*Huh,* I'll count myself a free man when I step on the dirt of a free state, not before, and as for callin' you by your

463

name, *huh!* See this neck that my head sits on, Miss Jacky? Well, I'm right fond of it and don't want no rope gettin' around it, just 'cause some cracker in one of these towns hears me slip up and call you Jacky, all familiar-like. Uh-uh, no, Ma'am."

"Then how about Miss, like Higgins does, or Skipper, like the Hawkes boys do, or Missy, like Jim?"

"All right, Missy, but if we ever in the hearin' of any crackers, then you'll hear me fallin' right back into Miss Jacky right quick. Now, whyn't you try that Frenchy thing again?"

I finger the C chord and start the roll with my right hand, and then I start to sing that song I had learned from our rich French captive on board the *Emerald.* What was his name? Oh, yes, the Marquis de Mont Blanc, the man with many jewels, half of which he left with us, much to his sorrow.

> *Plaisir d'amour*
> *Ne dure qu'un moment.*
> *Chagrin d'amour*
> *Dure toute la vie.*

I run through the three chords used in this song, keeping up the roll, and then I sing the translation.

> *Joys of love*
> *Are but a moment long.*
> *Pain of love endures*
> *The whole life long.*

A final strum across all strings and I'm done. It does sound so much better than with the fiddle. I shall learn to do all my slow, sad songs on the guitar, I think, and save the fast, raucous stuff for Lady Gay.

"Bravo, Jacky! Bravo!" I look over to see Richard Allen, seated at his table on the cabin top of the *Britannia,* in open white shirt, white britches, and black boots. He has taken to setting his table up there in a mockery, I think, of mine. He has a glass of wine in front of him, no doubt from the case he bought from us, paid for, I'm sure, from the scalp money that I returned to him. It seems he means to be quite free with it.

"I thought I told you to stay behind us. You are blocking my view of the shore."

"The better to hear your sweet voice, my dear, raised in joyous song!" he taunts. "Perhaps you'll join me in this one. I'm sure you know it." He stands up and, completely unabashedly, begins to sing.

> *There once was a troop of British dragoons,*
> *Went marching down to Fennario,*
> *And their captain fell in love,*
> *With a lady like a dove,*
> *And they called her by name, pretty Jacky-o.*

This could be fun, I'm thinking. *Why not?* I rise and go over to the edge of the cabin top, opposite him, as he does the second verse.

> *Oh, I will give you ribbons, love,*
> *And I will give you rings,*
> *And a necklace of pure amber-o,*
> *And a silken petticoat with flounces to the knee,*
> *If you'll take me into your chamber-o.*

Solomon takes the guitar from my hand and begins to strum along with the tune. On the other boat, Archy Mac-Duff has taken up a small snare drum and begins a soft *rum-tum-tum* in march time, so I know this is a set-up thing. No matter. I lift my voice and and give the song back to him.

> *Oh, I'll not go with you, sweet Richard-o,*
> *And I'll not take you into my chamber-o.*
> *No, I'll not marry you, for your guineas are too few,*
> *And I fear it would anger my poor mama-o.*

Striding to the edge of his cabin top, Allen, cigar in hand, sends it back to me.

> *What will your mother think, pretty Jacky-o?*
> *What will your mother think, my sweetheart-o?*
> *What will your mother think*
> *When she hears the guineas clink,*
> *And my soldiers all marching before you-o?*

The man on *Britannia*'s tiller thinks it would be in his captain's interest to bring the boats even closer together, so that Captain Allen and I are a mere six feet apart. I puff out my chest and trade another verse.

> *I never did intend a soldier's wife to be,*
> *No, a soldier shall never enjoy me-o.*
> *I never will go into a foreign land,*
> *And I never will marry you, sweet Richard-o.*

Captain Allen tosses his cheroot into the narrow gap of water that flows between us, fixes me with his gaze, and launches into his last verse.

Come tripping down the stairs, pretty Jacky-o,
Come tripping down the stairs, oh, my lovely-o,
Come tripping down the stairs, combing back your yellow
    hair,
You're the prettiest damn thing I ever seen... Oh.

Richard bows to me and acknowledges the cheers of his men, but I pipe up and say, "Surely you've forgotten the last verse, Sir? Perhaps I should sing it for you." And I do.

Sweet Richard he is dead, we must mourn him-o,
Sweet Richard he is dead, oh, my comrades-o,
Sweet Richard he is dead and he died for a maid,
The fairest of the maidens in Fenn-ar-i-o.

Applause from my boat, but my partner in this duet is not yet done.

If ever I return, pretty Jacky-o,
If ever I return, oh, my lovely-o,
If ever I return, all your cities I will burn,
Destroying all the ladies in Fenn-ar-i-o.

I give him a deep Lawson Peabody curtsy on that one, which must look a bit foolish, with me wearing my Indian buckskin rig, but so what. There are cheers from both boats.

"Now, about that bit concerning you inviting me down into your chambers," says Captain Allen, "shall we discuss that?"

"No, Captain Allen, we shall not. I have invited a much more cultured man than you, a common soldier, to grace my table today. Ah, here you are, Mr. Cantrell. Please have a seat. Our food and drink will be up directly. If you'll excuse us, Captain Allen?"

Yancy and I sit down at my table. I sneak a glance sideways and find that Richard is again seated at his table, but his boat does not return to its position behind us. Well, so be it. It's not important. I turn to Yancy to make small talk and I find him much amused.

"That was quite the performance, Miss. I enjoyed it thoroughly." He looks over at Captain Allen, who has lit yet another cigar and continues to gaze upon me. I pretend not to notice.

"I'm glad you did, Yancy. Ah, here is our dinner. Thank you, Higgins. A glass of wine with you, Mr. Cantrell?" Higgins draws the cork, pours out two glasses, and then puts the cork back in the bottle.

"Thank you, Mr. Higgins, but could you have my Chloe bring me up a glass of water? I fear my throat is dry and I don't want to waste this fine wine on mere thirst."

Higgins nods and goes below, and presently Chloe appears with the glass of water. She places it on the table and Yancy takes a sip of it. "Thank you, Daughter."

She murmurs, "You're welcome, Father," and steps off the cabin top.

I take a mouthful of my wine, swallow, and look at my guest. "It must be hard on you, Yancy, not to have had a game of chance to play since Memphis. I do hope you haven't completely cleaned out the Reverend and the Hawkes boys?"

He laughs. "No, we pass the time playing pinochle and whist for mere worthless chips. They are becoming quite expert." He looks at me in an appraising way. "We could, however, play a game of chance between ourselves, Miss. A harmless game that will cost you nothing."

"And that game would be?"

"I will bet you that I can make fifty dollars without moving from this spot."

"Don't think, Yancy, that I would ever think to best you in a game of cards. I have gotten quite skilled, but I'm not stupid enough to take you on in that regard."

"No, Miss, it will not be a card game, but it does involve a wager."

"Go on," I say, all suspicious.

"I bet you that I can take a drink out of that bottle right there, without taking out the cork."

I look at the bottle. It is about half full. As I look at it, Yancy reaches over and with his thumb, pushes the cork down even further into the bottle's neck.

"And what will be my part of the wager?"

"A mere kiss, Miss Faber. On the lips, and shall we say of a thirty-second duration?"

Hmmm… I didn't know that Yancy thought of me in that way—*men, I swear!* But what the hell, it's only a kiss, although Yancy *is* a somewhat older, handsome man.

"Very well. I take the bet, provided your part of the wager is giving up those foul cigars for a full week, should you fail."

"Done."

"So let's see you try to do it."

Yancy smiles at me with a look that says, "I have done this as part of your continuing education, Miss, and the title of today's lesson is: Never Bet on a Sure Thing. Or, at least what looks like a sure thing."

"*Regardez-vous, Mademoiselle,*" Yancy says.

He takes the wine bottle and turns it over. Like all wine bottles, it has a depression in the bottom—something to do with how the glass is blown—a depression about an inch deep. Yancy takes his water glass and fills the concave depression with water. He lifts it to his lips and drinks.

"Ah. That was most refreshing," he says, smiling like the cat who has just swallowed the bird, "and you see, I *did* take a drink out of that bottle without removing the cork. And, furthermore, I believe I have won the wager."

"I believe you have, and I'm certain I have learned a great lesson here, but still, all you have won is a kiss, one that I will readily give you, but you have not won fifty dollars."

"That is true, Miss, but the kiss is not for me. The wager was for a kiss, not necessarily a kiss for me. You must learn to read the fine print in a contract. That is your second lesson today."

I feel a slow burn working up my neck and into my face. "So what will you do with this promise of a kiss?"

"Why, auction it off, of course! To the highest bidder!"

He stands and addresses all on both boats. "Gentlemen, listen to me! I am the bearer of a note promising one kiss, one most extraordinary kiss, one kiss on the lips of Miss Jacky Faber, the Lily of the West, the duration of said kiss being a slow count of thirty! What am I bid?"

Every man, every boy, every girl on both these boats is

standing and looking at me with great glee. *I have been had, but good!*

On the *Britannia,* Archy MacDuff fishes in his pants pocket. "I got half a crown, and I bids it!"

"We have a bid of half a crown. But please, gentlemen, this is the fair Jacky Faber we are talking about here, and we can do better than that, surely. The winner will be able to tell his grandchildren that he once placed his lips on those of the famous riverboat queen, and they will look on him with awe and admiration. Do I hear more?"

"Two dollars," calls out a hugely grinning Jim Tanner, which gets him a glare and a poke in the ribs from Clementine.

"I have two dollars! Who will say more?"

"Two-fifty!" says Private William Quimby, followed quickly by "Three dollars!" from Seamus McMann.

"Gentlemen, gentlemen," says my former friend Yancy Cantrell, shaking his head. "I'm afraid we're going to have to up the ante, or we'll be at this all day. No, I must say that the minimum bid will have to be fifty dollars. Do I hear fifty?"

"Fifty dollars." All heads turn to look upon the bidder, who now stands at the edge of his cabin top, with his thumbs hooked into his belt, his cigar at a rakish tilt, and his eyes burning into mine.

"I have fifty dollars! Do I hear sixty?" Yancy looks around, but finds no other bidders. "No? Then, going once, going twice—sold!—to the gallant and dashing Captain Richard Allen!" shouts the auctioneer. "Daniel, please hop across and collect the money from the victorious winner!"

Daniel Prescott jumps up on the rail, and as Nathaniel, on tiller, brings the two boats together, he hops over. Allen turns and says something to Sergeant Bailey, who goes down into the *Britannia's* cabin, and then Allen returns his smug, arrogant gaze to me. *The cheek of that man!*

I leap to my feet and go to the edge of my own cabin top and face him.

"Is that a proper use of the King's money, *Mr.* Allen? I regret giving it back to you," I say with the best glower I can manage.

"Of course it is. The expenditure will be put down as 'Morale-Building Entertainment.' It will certainly boost my morale, Princess," says the cocky wretch. "And I'm sure King George would approve. So run that cunning little tongue over those lips to moisten them up and prepare to deliver!"

Out of the corner of my eye, I see Daniel hop back aboard.

"You have wasted your money, Captain," I say, tight-lipped and stern. "For by the terms of your parole, you are forbidden to set foot on this boat, and I am certainly *not* going to go over on that one!"

With that, I stomp back to my table and sit down, preparing to treat Mr. Yancy Turncoat Cantrell to a very frosty meal.

"That's all right, Jacky. I can wait," says the still-grinning rogue. "The anticipation will make the final calling of the note all the more sweet. But count on it, I *will* collect and you *will* deliver."

I take my eyes off of him and lift my glass in a mock toast to Yancy Cantrell. "My congratulations, Sir, for—"

I hear a *pop* and the glass shatters in my hand, shards and red wine flying over the tabletop. Shocked and dumbfounded, I look over at Captain Allen, who I am thinking to blame for this outrage, and I shriek, "Richard! Look out!" for behind him at the far rail of the *Britannia* has appeared a face, the hideously painted face of an Indian brave. More snarling faces appear, then shoulders, and then paint-streaked hands holding knives and tomahawks. There is a great howling of war cries.

"To arms! To arms! We're under attack!" I scream. "Get the guns! Higgins, go below and get the troops' powder and balls and get it over to them! Daniel, tie the boats' rails together! Yancy, get the girls below!" Over on the other boat, the soldiers are desperately trying to fight off the boarders as best they can, using their unloaded rifles as clubs, while Richard slashes at the attackers with his saber, but it's not gonna serve, there's just too many of them. They're swarming all over us *and it's all my fault! I wasn't prepared! I let things get slack! Stupid! Stupid!*

I vault down into my cabin, grab my pistols, dash back out, jump over the rail, and land on the deck of the *Britannia* at the side of Captain Allen. He curses mightily as he swings his bloody saber back and forth like a scythe, reaping great gouts of blood and wounded flesh. The Indian in front of him falls back into the water. Many of the savage howls are now cries of pain.

"Richard! Higgins is bringin' over the powder and shot! Have your men get ready!"

He looks down at me. "They should already have been prepared and you know it!" He still has his cigar clamped between his teeth.

I know, I know, I'm sorry...

An Indian has gotten over the bow and runs toward us screaming, his tomahawk raised. I lift my pistol and fire, hitting him squarely in the chest. He staggers and then falls face-first at my feet. I spin around, pick another target, and aim at him, too. At this close range, it is hard to miss, even though my hand shakes as I fire.

I'm beginning to hear the rapid *pop* of musketry behind me, which means my own men are firing. Lightfoot and Chee-a-quat are never far from their weapons, and I know they are exacting a toll on the enemy. Another brute tries to hoist himself aboard near me and I pull out my shiv, but an arrow that I recognize as one of Katy's thuds into his chest, and he, too, falls back.

There is a sound behind me and I whirl about, expecting an ax in my brain, but it is only Higgins, bearing powder and shot for the soldiers.

"Richard! It's here!"

"Get it up to Bailey!"

I flip my pistols over to Clementine, who sits at Jim's feet, reloading each gun as he fires. "Reload those! They're faster!" She hears me over the din and runs down into the cabin to get my special percussion caps and balls. I see that the Honeys are reloading for their men, too.

"Higgins! Give me those!" I grab the sacks of ammunition from him. "Go back and uncover the swivel gun!"

I run up to Sergeant Bailey, who is aft on the *Britannia*. On his shoulder is a darker stain of red, around a tear in the fabric of his jacket. "Sergeant! Powder! Shot!"

"'Bout time, girl," he growls. He sheathes his saber and begins stuffing the cylindrical paper-powder shells into the slots on his belt. "Quimby, Luce, Merrick, fall back and reload." He picks up his own rifle, to which a bayonet is now fixed, and proceeds to load. Before I can get back to the *Belle,* he has already fired it.

I leap back over the joined rails of the two boats and then up onto the cabin top, where I find that Higgins has thrown over my table and pulled the cover off the gun. I get up behind it and survey the battlefield. If this is Half Red Face's bunch, he sure got a lot of new recruits since last we ran into him. In addition to the Indians who had attacked the *Britannia* from the shore, to which I had so foolishly allowed us to drift too close, there are a number of canoes full of warriors coming up from the south and a veritable flotilla of them coming from upriver. I train the gun on these and pull the lanyard. There is a sizzle, then a *crack!* as the gun fires. Several of the canoes are hit, and I can see the pattern of the grapeshot as it hits the water. Several of our would-be attackers pitch over the side, and one canoe is swamped.

"Reload with cannonball this time, Higgins! I'm going forward to see about the other gun!" I run up to the bow, where Chee-a-quat, Lightfoot, and Katy are calmly dealing out death. I yank off the cover of the forward gun and sight along it, but no enemy is in range. *Damn! Why didn't I get two swivel guns!*

I see Chloe lying next to the rail, reloading her father's small pistols, as he kneels beside her and peppers the screaming horde. "Chloe! If any of the enemy get in front of that barrel, tell everyone here on deck to step aside, then pull that lanyard!" She nods.

I turn to go back to the swivel gun, but first I say, "Lightfoot, if you see one of 'em with his face painted half red, shoot him."

He chuckles. "Oh, we seen him. He's lurkin' back in those bushes there, prolly thinkin' he's actin' like a general or somethin'. *Huh!*" Lightfoot rams a ball home, primes, aims, then dispatches yet another hostile.

In a moment I'm back up behind the swivel gun. Higgins has reloaded, with the help of the Reverend, and he has set the matchlock. I grab it, aim the gun, dog it down, and fire. *Crack!* The cannonball hits the water about ten feet in front of the canoes, skips, and crashes through one and into another, sinking them both. That's two more, but it ain't enough, not yet, anyway.

Little Daniel comes up on deck bearing another bag of powder and hands it to the Preacher. "Grape again, Higgins! They're all getting too close for ball!" I go forward again.

The savage attack continues. Sergeant Bailey has gotten his men into a good disciplined rotation of standing, firing, crouching, reloading, and standing to fire again, such that there is a constant stream of fire at the enemy. Richard makes murderous work with his pistols, loading, firing, and reloading at great speed. I see that the forward gun still will not bear, and we are much too close to the bank and getting closer. I see Solomon down below, Crow Jane's wood-chopping ax in his hand, standing by, ready to do damage to any who might manage to get on board.

"Solly!" I cry. "Go over to the other boat and man the port forward sweep! Try to row away from the shore! Matthew! Get on the starboard forward sweep here! Jim, man the tiller! Steer away from the shore as soon as the sweepers give you steerageway! If we go into the bank we are lost!" Even as my mind rages in the heat of battle, I realize we have been very lucky. After the first weak volley of shots from the Indians, one bullet of which shattered the wineglass I held in my hand, there were no others. This means they are out of powder. Had it been otherwise, the decks of both the *Belle* and the *Britannia* would be strewn with the bodies of the dead and dying.

They all leap to their stations. Solomon leaps over to the other boat and picks up the sweep, pausing only to sink his ax into the wood by his feet, close at hand should he need it. He pulls on the sweep, muscles straining with the mighty effort, while Matty backs with his oar. Jim grabs the tiller and throws it over to the left, while at his feet, Pretty Saro's squeals of terror add to the din of battle. A tomahawk sails through the air by Jim's ear and clatters harmlessly to the deck, but he sticks to the steering oar. Clementine keeps on loading and firing on her own.

Good girl!

Slowly, slowly the heads of the two boats turn out to the center of the river.

"Good boys!" I shout, as we gain even more fighting room.

"Gun ready, Miss!" shouts Higgins, and I bound back over to it. I see that the boats upriver are hanging back a bit, perhaps cowed by the cannonball that ripped through two of their boats to such good effect. So I undog the swivel, swing it around, and point it forward over the bow of the *Britannia*.

"Everybody down! I'm gonna fire. Solly, get down!" When everybody has hit the deck, I give one more squint over the barrel, dog it down, and pull the lanyard. *Crack!* and the hail of grapeshot tears into the enemy, and then, suddenly, as if that were the final straw, it is over. Half Red Face must have called off the attack. In a moment, not an Indian is to be seen. Not a live one, anyway, but there are plenty who float, facedown in the river, all about the *Belle* and the *Britannia*.

I lean against the warm barrel of the swivel gun and let my breathing get back to normal. Then I stand and address all on both decks.

"What is the damage?"

Aside from Sergeant Bailey's cut shoulder, there is surprisingly little. Private Alfie Jackson caught a ball in his lower leg on the first Indian volley, but it went clear through his calf, so he should be all right if the infection doesn't set in. Thank God we don't have to dig out the bullet. Private Fred Luce got a slash on the back of his hand from a boarder's knife, as did Private MacDuff. The soldiers took the brunt of the punishment since they were the closest to the shore, but Matthew Hawkes took a nasty gash on the upper chest from a thrown tomahawk. He is being seen to by a very tearful and adoring Honeysuckle Rose.

I nod and say, "Before we tend to our wounded, let me say that I am profoundly sorry for what happened this day. I was unprepared and I let you down. You have every reason to feel nothing but contempt for me, but if you continue to follow my lead, I promise you it will never happen again." There is silence all around. I know it is due to the aftermath of battle, when the blood sings in the veins long after the danger is past, and then, after it subsides, a great tiredness ensues. "Chloe, Clementine, will you get the needles, thread, and alcohol, as well as the tincture of opium? Thank you. Higgins, will you please reload this gun in case they are so bold as to come back at us?"

He goes to do it, and then I hear Richard Allen say, "Sergeant, have the men reload and stand at Port Arms facing the *Belle of the Golden West*."

Uh-oh...

I turn to face him. "Do the terms of your parole still stand?"

He smiles, hand on the hilt of his now-sheathed sword. His cigar, miraculously, is not only still in his mouth, but still lit. He sends a puff of smoke in my direction. "My parole? Why, yes, it still stands—did I not give you my word? But, Princess, my men *will* keep their powder and shot."

"Very well, Captain Allen. You and your men acquitted themselves bravely and honorably today. You have our heartfelt thanks. And you, Sir, showed yourself to be a much better leader than I."

"Ah, Princess, not so. You were unprepared, true. You let your guard down, also true. 'Tis true also that you should have trusted my word and let us keep our powder, but when it came to the fight, well, you were every inch a general!"

There is a weary but generous cheer to that, and for that, I am grateful.

After tincture of opium is swallowed, teeth are gritted, and torn flesh is sewn up, we have a conference on the top decks.

"Did you notice anything about the attack?" I ask, as Higgins brings me a wet towel to wipe the blood from my hands.

"That they had no powder, else half of us would be dead?" asks Captain Allen.

"Right. They probably wanted that as much as they wanted our scalps for the bounty."

"Ha! The scalps! The money for which to pay for them lies right down below me! Oh, how I do love a bit of delicious irony," says Richard from his cabin top. "But you know, of course, they will be at us again."

"Yes, I know, but perhaps we can prevent that. Nathaniel, Jim, Solly…could you make us up a little raft, say about six feet square?"

Mystified, those named nod assent.

"Good. Then let's get on it. How many hostiles do you think are left, Sergeant? About sixty, you think? All right. Reverend Clawson, how much elixir do we have left? You've just made up a new batch? Good. Mr. Higgins, when the raft is complete, will you put on it twenty one-gallon jugs of our fine Kentucky bourbon, with as many bottles of the elixir as will fit neatly between those jugs? Also, Mr. Lightfoot, do you think our tormentors will find our little gifts?"

The frontiersman leans on his rifle and laughs. "'Course they'll find 'em. They're watchin' us right now. They'll be on that hooch 'fore we rounds the next corner!"

Good.

Chapter 57

We haven't seen signs of any Indians for several days now, so we're starting to relax a bit—not too much, though, as we have learned our lesson well. We now have armed men on each boat scanning the shore during the daylight hours, and at night we anchor out as far as we can with night watches set.

But it is not only Indians that we fear, for now a new threat has arisen to worry us—we are being watched by slave hunters.

It was at a town called Thomasville on the Arkansas side, not much more than a salt lick and a hog wallow, but we decided to set up the show, anyway, just to keep our hand in and maybe spread a little joy.

We had sold a few bottles of Captain Jack's Elixir and were halfway through our little playlet when we heard the sound of hoofbeats and saw five men pull up behind our small crowd. They did not dismount.

So what, I think, *all are welcome to the show. Gather round.*

So the play goes on, the dress comes off, there is the final curtain, and when we go to take our bows, there is no applause—the five men have rudely spurred their horses through the audience and are directly in front of us. They are dressed in long, dirty white dusters, buttoned to the neck, and have wide-brimmed hats on their heads. There are rifles stuck in leather boots on each saddle, and it's plain that each man wears a belt with two holstered pistols under his coat. Manacles and chains lie across the saddles of several. All of the men have long, stringy hair hanging down to their shoulders; four of them are dark-haired, but the old one in the middle has only wispy strands of gray, blowing about his face in the light breeze.

The formerly festive mood of the audience is gone, and the families fearfully melt away.

"Sergeant," says Captain Allen quietly, "form your men. Port Arms." The *Britannia* is moored alongside of us, and I hear the soldiers' boots scrape on the cabin top as they line up, their rifles held diagonally across their chests, at the ready.

"What do you want?" I ask of the men.

"We'uns think you stole those nigras," says the old man, looking at Chloe up top, seated at her harpsichord, and Solomon to the left of the stage, with the guitar. "And we'uns aims to get 'em back to their rightful owners."

"You are wrong, Suh," says I, thinking it wise to sound a bit southern. "These here are my nigras."

The old man smiles a sly smile and looks to the men on either side of him. "Ah think that buck's name is Solomon and you stole him from a plantation up in Tennessee. The wanted poster said some people saw him climbin' on a boat. A boat painted up like a whore, just like this one." The old man whips back the tails of his duster to show the butts of his pistols, and the other men do the same. Several of them chuckle at the old man's wit. "Is that your name, boy? It is, ain't it, Solomon?"

"No, it ain't," says I. "It's Bill, if it's any of your business, which it ain't. And speakin' of business, what gives you the right to come bustin' in here and wreckin' our show?"

"Yer show didn't look like much to us, just a whore show with you takin' off yer clothes and prancin' around like that."

"Pick your targets, men," orders Captain Allen. "Full cock. Shoot the first man who goes for his gun."

"Ah think yer not only a whore, but a goddamned Abolitionist as well," says the old man lazily. "You know what we do with goddamned Abolitionists around here? You tell her, Ezekiel."

The man next to him giggles and says, "We hangs 'em, is what."

"I think you have said just about enough, old man. Take yourself off," says Allen. "If you'd like to try us, just reach for a weapon."

"Calm yerself, General. We're a-goin'."

Fearing for his safety, I go over to Solomon and put my hand on his shoulder and say, "Get back on the boat, Bill." I feel his muscles tense under my hand.

"Yes, Miss Jacky, I'm goin'," he answers as he steps back on the *Belle*. "I'm goin'."

"You see that, Pap?" says the man named Ezekiel. "She touched that dirty nigra. On his skin."

"I seen it, boy. Don't you worry, I seen it good and plain," replies the old man, looking at me through narrowed eyes. "Makes me sick to my stomach." He takes his gaze off me and slowly looks over my crew. He then leans over to spit a brown stream of tobacco juice on the stage in front of me. "Let's go, boys, and leave this goddamned bunch o' nigra lovers. For now..."

And with that, the horsemen wheel about and gallop off, their white dusters flying out behind them.

"Wrap it up," I say. "There'll be no tavern tonight. Let's get on over to the other side. Don't like it here, much, no, I don't."

I don't hear anyone argue with that.

Chapter 58

The confrontation with the slave hunters cast a pall on things for a few days, but gradually our good humor returned. All of the wounds encountered during the battle with Half Red Face and his bunch healed nicely, though we had worried about Alfie's leg. But that, too, eventually cleared up, and soon he was up and about.

And as for the slave hunters, what did we have to worry about when we were in the company of a squad of fine British Regulars?

This afternoon I'm feeling extremely lazy and indolent. The sun is shining, but it is not too hot as I amble back to the quarterdeck looking for a likely spot for a bit of a snooze. I spot Pretty Saro lying there on her side, snoring fitfully away, and take a notion to lie down next to her, my head on her fat, soft belly and my straw hat pulled down over my eyes.

Ahhh...I sigh as I contentedly drift off to dream, my head rising and falling with Saro's deep breathing.

And I'm back on the quarterdeck of my lovely Emerald *and the wind is fair and in my face and hair, and oh, this time*

Jaimy is with me, by my side, and we are sailing off to far Cathay to see what riches might lie in store for us there, and then I see the door of my cabin is open and I take Jaimy by the hand and we go down below and he puts his arm around my waist and then, oh my, all my clothes have disappeared, and his, too, and then... and then Constance Howell, of all people— Connie Howell?—has me by the foot and is saying, "Naughty Jacky, naughty Jacky, naughty, naughty Jacky..."

I awaken to find Higgins gently nudging together my two ankles as I lie sprawled on the deck.

"It is to be devoutly hoped, Miss, that you will not take up other disgusting habits like chewing tobacco and spitting or saying things like *pshaw!*"

I lift my straw hat to glare at him. "Higgins, you have just ruined the most wonderful dream."

"I am sorry, Miss. Did it concern your Mr. Fletcher, or was it about Captain Allen?"

"You wound me, Higgins. Of *course* it featured Jaimy Fletcher," I growl, pulling my hat back over my eyes.

"Your pardon, then, Miss. I must be off."

I close my eyes, hoping to slip back into the same dream again, but then that never happens, does it?

All of a sudden, I'm noticing a strange sweetish odor. I sit up and sniff. "Saro, you stink, and Daniel has just given you your bath." I smack her lightly on her belly and she lets out a small grunt.

Clementine, sitting over next to Jim, who is on helm, hears me saying this and raises her own nose and sniffs. Then she comes over on hands and knees and lifts Pretty Saro's curly tail and peers under.

"Yup. Thought so. Your Pretty Saro is of a mind to have

486

herself some little piggies," says the farm girl Clementine Jukes, releasing Saro's tail and going back to Jim, to twine her arms about his calf and rest her head against his leg.

"Why, you hussy, you!" I say, giving her another little smack.

"It's prolly hearin' all those wild porkers in the woods is what set her off," says Clementine.

Hmmm...We have been hearing a lot of oinks and grunts from the woods lately. Crow Jane says they're pigs who've descended from the hogs that escaped from farms and went wild. *Real* wild, according to Janey—"They've gotten big and lean and mean, and they've got big tusks, so you got to watch 'em, as they can hurt you. Good eatin', though."

I think about this and go over to the port rail, the one closest to the shore. I sit there and listen, and in about a half hour I am rewarded by the sound of thrashing and loud grunting in the woods.

"Jim, swing in close to the bank, if you would."

"Sure, Missy."

I look back at the *Britannia*, on station behind us, with Private Luce on helm. "Fred!" I shout. "We'll anchor here for just a bit!"

Richard, sitting at his table topside, looks up from his book. The cur has books over there, but that swine won't lend me any unless I come over there to get them, which I won't do. I know he has Izaak Walton's *The Compleat Angler*, a book about fishing, and I really want to get my hands on that book, but...oh, well.

Jim tosses out the *Belle*'s anchor without having to be told and we come to a halt, close to the Louisiana shore.

Higgins comes up with a questioning look, and I say, "Will you please get me two silver dollars from our cache? Thanks. Place them right there on the cabin top. Good."

I take one of the coils of rope that we always have positioned in various spots on the deck and I kneel down next to Pretty Saro. I lift her trusting head and tie a noose about her neck, just behind her ears. I've got to pull it pretty tight, 'cause her neck is wider than her head, and she squeals a little bit in protest.

Then I stand and say, "Anyone who wants to look away may do so, as I'm about to take off my skirt." I slip my buckskin skirt down and flip it into my cabin, leaving me in my light cotton top and my cutoff drawers. I notice out of the corner of my eye that Captain Allen has forsaken his book and now stands in the bow of the *Britannia*, taking this all in.

Taking the other end of the line that I tied to Pretty Saro, I jump into the water. My feet hit the sandy bottom and I am able to stand.

"All right, shove her in!" I shout, and it takes Jim and Clementine and the Hawkes boys to move her, but presently about two hundred pounds of squealing pig hits the water.

She goes under, but her snout pops right back up. Most animals know how to swim and this pig is no exception. Her cleft hooves churning, she makes for the shore, with me trailing after her. We make the bank and we both climb up.

I give her ears a rub, 'cause I know she likes it. "You hear them out there, Saro?" She seems to cock her head at the sounds of rooting and grunting not far off in the forest. "That's right, Saro, listen up good. Y'think any of them gentleman piggies might strike your fancy?"

Grunt?

I swear she grunted in a questioning way—interested, yet a bit doubtful.

There's a high-pitched squeal from the woods off to the left. Her head jerks up.

Grunt?

"Ah, so maybe he's the one, Saro. Here, let me get that off." I loosen the rope from around her neck and set her free, but she does not run off. "You ain't got much choice, my girl, either a dangerous life of freedom, or Crow Jane's knives."

She starts forward, making a few tentative steps in the direction of that last squeal. Then she looks back at me and I give her a last scratch on her bristly head and slap her on the butt. She lets out a high, trumpeting squeal of her own and goes charging off into the woods. The last I see of my little piglet is her little curly tail.

Fare thee well, Pretty Saro. May you wed with the fiercest of all the tuskers out there in those deep, dark woods. May you live long and have many fine babies and may none of them ever end up in a cook pot. Amen.

I coil the rope over my arm and swim back to the *Belle*, climb the ladder, and confront a furious Crow Jane. Before going down into my cabin to change, I pick up the silver dollars that Higgins had placed on the cabin top and put them in her hands.

"Here, Janey. In the next town we hit, go off and buy some meat. Some meat we don't even know the name of."

With that, I dive down into the cabin.

That evening, just before we are to anchor for the night, we come to a fork in the river.

489

"You're gonna find that happenin' a lot as we get farther into the delta," says Lightfoot. "The river takes off into all sorts of directions."

"Which one, Missy?" asks Jim.

"Let's take the one on the right, Jim. It looks to give us a bit more sea room."

He moves the tiller over and down the right course we glide.

Chapter 59

James Fletcher, Riverman
Somewhere on the Mississippi River
Somewhere in the USA

Jacky Faber, Showgirl
On the Belle of the Golden West
Somewhere downriver

Dear Jacky,

I sit here with my paddle across my knees, trying to decide which fork of the damned Mississippi to take.

I did not expect the river to separate like this, but I tell myself that surely the two branches will rejoin up ahead and, besides, the land between the forks is but a very large island. But what would happen if I took the wrong branch and got ahead of you? To be sure, it would be highly ironic if I were to beat you to New Orleans.

Of course, all I will have to do, after the waters converge, is to inquire in the next town whether or not your boat has passed, and from what I have heard of your boat and your shows, the townspeople could hardly have missed you.

And yes, Jacky, I have heard of your torn-away-dress routine—you know, Miss, the second thing I am going to do when I catch you is to sit you down on my knee for a stern lecture on behavior.

Aside from the various reports I have heard about you from the towns where I have stopped, I believe I might have other evidence of your passage: Several days ago, as I rounded a bend in the river, I was shocked to see a man, an Indian with a half-red face, dangling from an overhanging tree and staring right down at me! I furiously back-paddled away from the shore, but then I discovered that I did not need to, for it was then I saw the tomahawk thrust in the back of his head and realized he was quite dead.

As I cautiously proceeded, I found several more bodies lying facedown in the water, their toes still stuck on the bank. Many other Indians were sprawled about nearby, most of them not dead, but moaning and groaning mightily, as if unable to rise. When I spotted the empty casks and bottles strewn about, I understood the reason. It's plain they'd gotten into the whiskey and then turned to fighting among themselves. A bottle floated by my canoe. I reached over and picked it up to read the label that still clung to it: Captain Jack's All Season Tonic and Elixir. I don't know if you had a hand in this, Jacky, but it certainly has your mark on it. If you did, then my thanks, for I certainly won't have to worry about this bunch any longer.

I have also heard that you have somehow picked up an escort of British soldiers and that gives me cheer, knowing you have that extra protection. Reports portray your demeanor as happy and cheerful, so I must assume the soldiers did not know of your status as a wanted fugitive. May that remain the case until I can join you and spirit you away.

I put my paddle back in the water and dig it in. I move forward again, having made up my mind—the water on that side is calmer, and for that reason, I think you would have chosen that branch.

I take the left fork.

Oh, Jacky, you are so close, I can just feel it!

Yours,

Jaimy

Chapter 60

"When Old Man River takes it into his mind to cut him a new course, he does it," says Crow Jane. "Next summer someone comes by here, that island could be gone, or else all the water moved over to this side. Who knows?"

We can see the river widening up ahead so we know that the land to our left is indeed an island, a huge island that we have been passing for a couple of days now.

"Private Merrick!" I sing out to the *Britannia* following in our wake. "Toss out the anchor! We're stopping here! I want to check around the bend before we go any farther!"

"Thanks, Nathaniel," I say to my own tillerman, as he puts up his steering oar and tosses in the anchor.

We have come to a stop about fifty yards from the end of the island and I want to make damned sure that there's nothing lurking on the other side. I have learned my lesson.

"Jim, take the *Star* and have a peek around the corner. Make sure that pack of rascally Indians ain't fixin' to jump on us again. But be careful."

"Yes, Missy," he says, and in a moment he is in the *Evening Star*, oars in the water, and off.

He disappears from sight around the bend, and in a few minutes we are surprised to see him walk out of the bushes that line the bank on this side. He's not but twenty yards away.

"All clear," he calls out. "Island's real narrow right here, as you can see. Nice little cove on the other side, with a sandy beach. Water's pretty clear, too. Well, I'm headin' back," and he ducks into the bushes.

Nice sandy little beach, eh?

It's been a while since I've had a swim, what with all these men being around and all. It's about four o'clock and this is as good a place as any to stop for the night. And the island end with its thick growth of bushes makes a good privacy screen. *Why not?*

"Anyone care to join me in a dip? Katy? Chloe? No? Honeysuckle Rose? Tupelo? Clementine? 'Snakes'? What snakes? Ah, what a bunch of cowards you are. Fine, I'll go by myself. Higgins, a bit of soap if you would."

There's a thump as the *Evening Star* comes back alongside.

"Don't bother tying up, Jim, just jump aboard and let me get down in the *Star*." In a moment Jim is on deck and I am rowing for the end of the island, and when I am around the bend, I pull into the cove.

Jim was right, it is a lovely spot. There is a gently sloping, almost golden sand beach, and the water runs clear next to the bank. Trees, thick with summer leaves, lean over and shade the pool. I hop out into the ankle-deep water, pull up the bow of the boat, and go along the soft sand to the nearest tree. I shed my shirt, skirt, and drawers, and hang them on a branch and then go back to wade into the water. I get maybe six yards from the shore when suddenly I'm completely underwater—*the current must have carved out a deep trench during some mighty flood!*

I kick and come sputtering back to the surface—I certainly didn't expect that! I swim a little farther out and my feet hit sand again so I am able to stand, the water now waist-deep. It is wondrously cool and refreshing after the heat of the day and I splash about for a while, diving like a porpoise, floating on my back, then flopping over to look underwater, all the usual things I do when in the water.

After a bit of this, I swim back across to get my bar of soap from the *Evening Star*, wash myself, and then begin lathering my hair. From across the narrow island, I hear Solomon strike a chord on the guitar, then he begins his three-finger rolls, this time heavy on the bass strings to give the sound a driving, throbbing, pulsing beat. He begins to sing.

> *Black snake, black snake, lyin' in a persimmon tree,*
> *Yes, black snake, black snake, lyin' in that 'simmon tree.*
> *You mean old black snake,*
> *Don't you flop down on top of me!*

"Very funny, Solly!" I shout, and look more closely at the branches and vines that trail in the water. *Could that be a… no, of course, it is only a black stick.* He sings on.

> *Now Sister Cottonmouth, don't you come out to play, no,*
> *And Mr. Water Moccasin, you just slither on your way.*
> *And Brother Rattler, you just stay there sunnin' on the clay,*
> *'Cause Miss Jacky's gone a-swimmin' in your water today!*

"You stop that now, or I'll get you, Solly! I mean it!" I yell, scanning the bank on either side of me for reptiles that might be sneakin' up on a poor girl.

Solomon laughs his deep, booming laugh and hits an ending chord. "Yes, Missy."

I flip the piece of soap back into the *Star*, my hair now a mass of lather, and decide to put some distance between me and the shore. I dive down into the trench and run my fingers through my hair to rinse it. When I resurface and stand on the sandbar, facing the shore, my hair hangs in my eyes and as I pull it clear, I see that it is not a black snake that I must beware of, but a white one.

"Richard!" I gasp, clasping my hands to my chest. Richard Allen stands on the bank, shirtless and barefoot, in his dripping wet drawers. It is plain that the scoundrel had slipped over the side of the *Britannia* on the *Belle*'s blind side, and then had waded over to the shore, through the bushes, and here, to stand in front of me.

"I believe you missed a spot, behind your left knee," says the grinning rogue. "Shall I come over and scrub your back?"

"You are not allowed here, Mr. Allen!"

"You may own the boats, Princess, but you do not own the river. I don't believe that was part of my parole."

"If you touch me I'll scream for Lightfoot and he'll put a bullet in you!"

"I'm not going to touch you, Jacky, unless you touch me first. How's that for a bargain? You couldn't be safer," he says, his hands going to the drawstring of his drawers. "But I do think this would be an excellent time to pay off on that kiss you owe me. On neutral territory, as it were."

I whip around and face away, fuming, so as not to see whether he drops the drawers or not. *The cheek of the rascal!* I hear his feet splash as he enters the shallow water.

"You know, Princess, one time when I was on tour in Italy, I saw this painting called *The Birth of Venus,* and seeing you just now reminded me so much of that picture. All we'd need to complete the tableau is a big seashell for you to step out of and...*urk!*"

There is a bigger splash as he steps off the ledge and into the trench.

Ha! Take that, you dog!

I turn around and crouch down so the covering water is up to my neck, not that it matters much now, considering the show I've already given him. I wait for him to come back up to scold him further.

He doesn't come back up.

Uh-oh...another damned Englishman who can't swim?

His face, terrified now, breaks the surface for a moment. "Help! Help me, I can't...*glub!*" He goes down again, with only his hand above the water, then that, too, goes down.

Damn!

I spring out of my crouch and arch my body forward in a surface dive and look below. Sure enough, there he is down there, arms thrashing, his long hair floating about his fool head. I kick down and grab a handful of that hair and kick again to pull us to the surface.

I needn't have bothered. His arm goes around my waist and his own two strong legs kick and bring us up to stand on the sandbar. He holds me tight to him.

"You touched me first, Princess. The bargain is made," says he.

"I thought you were drowning! That you couldn't swim!" says I, furious. Our chests are pressed tight together. I struggle, but I can't get out of his grip.

"Can't swim? My dear little woodland elf, I am a British *soldier,* not a sailor. Of course I can swim, my saucy, frisky river nymph. I can't tell you how many rivers I have forded, swimming next to my noble steed."

The ever so smart and clever Jacky Faber, scammed again!

I calm myself down. "So you'd keep to the letter of your word, you rascal, I will give you that. But now you must let me go." I can tell that the randy hound did *not* leave his drawers on.

"I have heard you say that Jacky Faber also keeps her word. That you honor your bargains. Could it be that you will not pay your bet, when it would be so easy to do it right now, just a slow count of thirty?"

I think about this. *I've got to do it sometime. Why not now? I could always yell for help and it would be here in an instant.*

"The kiss and nothing more?" I ask, doubtfully.

"The kiss and nothing more, on my sacred honor," answers he, whose blue eyes are a scant three inches from my brown ones.

My hands are free, so I reach up and take the strands of wet hair, hair very much the color of mine, that hang down in his eyes and I pull them to the side. I cant my head and say, "Very well, Captain Allen, you may commence the slow count."

I keep my lips pursed tight, unyielding, and I intend to keep them that way for the duration of this thing, and he brings his mouth down on mine and tightens his grip about my waist. I keep my lips firm.

Then he takes his free hand, the one not around my waist, and puts it to the back of my head and leaves it there, the better to hold my face to his. I let my lips relax a bit and then, *Oh, Richard!* I relax them even more, and then I let them open and—and then I pull back, starting to breathe hard, and look into his eyes, which are as feverish as mine, and he says, "That's only fifteen, Princess...fifteen more, now," and then I clamp my open mouth back on his and run my hands up into his hair and moan and move myself against him and then...

...And then I hear what sounds like a paddle being run along the gunwale of a boat... *What?... Who?...* And I pull back from Captain Richard Allen to look up into the astonished eyes of none other than James Emerson Fletcher.

Chapter 61

I am not usually at a loss for words, but the sight of Jaimy Fletcher, dressed in fringed buckskin, sitting alone in a canoe in the middle of the American wilderness, with a look of total amazement on his face, robs me of all power of speech. My mouth hangs open in absolute, stunned shock, unable to utter a word as his canoe drifts by not six feet away.

It's when the astonished look on his face changes to one of dejected disappointment that I remember that I'm standing stark naked in waist-deep water with my hands on the shoulders of a man I have just been kissing. Then the ability to speak returns to me.

"J-J-Jaimy!" I wade toward him, my arms outstretched. "Oh, Jaimy! Oh, I'm so glad! I'm...Jaimy, wait!"

He dispiritedly shakes his head and directs his gaze downriver, his mouth set in a grim line, as he digs in his paddle and pulls away.

"No, Jaimy, it's not what you think! I can explain!" Desperately, I try to swim after him, but it's no use—he pulls steadily away. I cross the trench to stand and slap the surface water in an agony of frustration and dismay. "Jaimy, you come back here right now!"

He rounds a bend and I can't see him anymore, so I let out a long *waaaaaaaa* of despair. *Jaimy, please come back!*

I lunge out of the water—*maybe I can catch him in the Star!*—and feel the wind. With a sob I realize it is blowing from the south, directly against me. The *Star* is useless, for as a rowboat she could never catch that canoe.

Maybe Higgins can still see him from...

I tear across the sandy beach and through the narrow strip of woods to stand behind the bushes on the other shore and shout to the *Belle*. "Higgins! That's Jaimy Fletcher up there in that canoe! Call him back! Oh, please, Higgins, get him to come back!" and I start bawlin' for real now.

Through my tears I see Higgins jump up on the cabin top and peer forward. Then he cups his hands around his mouth and bellows, "Mr. Fletcher! Come back!"

Higgins continues to look south, and then he shakes his head and turns to me. "It's no use, Miss. If that was indeed Mr. Fletcher, he is gone."

Waaaaaaaaaaaa...

"Come back to the boats, Miss, and we'll discuss what can be done."

I stumble back to the other side, wailing, my chest wracked with sobs. Through a fog of misery, I find my clothes and tearfully pull on my shirt.

"I fear the rare mood of the day has vanished, along with that fellow there," remarks Captain Allen, who stands regarding me, his thumbs hooked in the waistband of the drawers he has put back on. "Eh, what?"

"You sh-sh-shut up, you," I blubber. "This is all your fault."

"*Hmmm*…that would have been your ex-betrothed, then. Pity, that."

I pull on my drawers, cinch up the waistband, and throw my balled-up skirt into the *Star*. "Find your own way back to the b-b-boat, you…you brute!"

"I am sorry, you know. I really don't like to see you cry."

I shove off the boat, get in, and row back to the *Belle*, returning so much sadder than when I left.

"Please, Miss! Please calm down!" begs Higgins, but I won't calm down, I won't. I won't.

"You back there! MacDuff! Haul in your anchor and set some men on the sweeps! We're moving on!" I yell as soon as my foot is back on the *Belle*. "Jim! Up anchor! Hawkes on sweeps! Move it, dammit!"

Nobody on these boats has seen me in full rage before, but they're sure seeing it now. I jump up on the cabin top and go forward and look intently downriver. Nothing.

"Lightfoot, Chee-a-quat," I say to the two of them standing below me. "The next canoe we see, we buy it, and you go track him down and bring him back. Will you do it? *Please*."

"We'll try, Wah-chinga," says Lightfoot, shaking his head doubtfully. "But this river's gonna divide and split again up ahead, and we'll just have to guess which way he might have gone. We could track him in the woods, but we can't on water. But we'll give it a try."

I nod my thanks and go to my table and flop myself down in my chair, a quivering ball of misery. I steam and I glower, but I have managed to stop crying. We are moving again, so we'll at least get in a few more hours of travel before dark. Maybe we'll find a canoe, maybe...

"Perhaps you are ready to talk now?" asks Higgins.

Heavy sigh. "Yes, please sit down."

Higgins pulls out a chair and seats himself. "Do you mind telling me what happened?"

"I was paying off the bet to Captain Allen when Jaimy pulled up next to us in a canoe."

"Um. I notice that the clothes you have on are dry. Can I assume that you were..."

"Yes."

"And Captain Allen?"

"The same."

"Ah. Did Mr. Fletcher say anything to you?"

"No. He...he just looked at me and shook his head and p-p-paddled off." The tears come again.

"Here, Miss, take my handkerchief and blow your nose. That's better. Now, how was he dressed?"

"Jaimy? In buckskins, of all things..."

"*Hmmm...,*" says Higgins, and then goes quiet, plainly mulling over all this.

"Is there reason to hope?" I ask, ready to grasp at any straw.

"I think there is, Miss," he says. "You know he can only go to New Orleans, don't you? You'll surely be able to catch up with him there and explain things. I'm sure Captain Allen will be happy to write out a statement detailing the extent of your relationship with him."

"But what if he gets there and is able to book passage back to London, where he surely would be wantin' to go?"

"You said he was dressed in buckskins, so I can only assume he met with unfortunate circumstances on his journey and had to work his way downriver as best he could. I don't believe he would have the money to book passage."

I think on that for a moment, then say, "Thank you, Higgins, for trying to make me feel more hopeful, but that won't wash. Jaimy could ship out as a mate or, if he couldn't manage that, then as a common seaman. Anything to get as far away as possible from m-m-me."

"*Hmm.* Well, maybe a ship won't be available. Maybe Lightfoot and Chee-a-quat will be able to find him. You must not give up hope, Miss."

Another heavy sigh. "I know, Higgins, I know. Oh, why must I always mess up everything?"

"Your impulsive nature is part of your character, part of what made you so charming to Mr. Fletcher in the past, and what, I am quite sure, will make you charming to him in the future as well."

"I hope so, Higgins," I say, putting my hand on his. "You are so good to try to cheer me, but, oh, if you could just imagine my shock at seeing him, just coming out of the blue like that. I am shaken to my core and I still cannot fathom just how he got here."

"Well, I'm guessing that Ezra Pickering figured a way for him to be freed from HMS *Juno,* or maybe it was a handsome bribe paid to Captain Rutherford—we do remember him as a greedy sort, don't we? And then Mr. Fletcher took off after you. You will recall that Mr. Pickering knew where you intended to go."

"You're probably right. And if I hadn't decided on a

swim, we'd be preparing for a wedding right now. We even have a preacher to say the words."

"Yes," says Higgins, "I imagine he was right behind us the whole way and"—Higgins stops and I look over and notice his upper teeth bite his lower lip as if he had suddenly realized that he had just said something he regretted—"and could I get you a glass of wine, Miss, for your nerves? And perhaps you might think of putting your skirt back on?"

I frown. *What is he trying to gloss over?* From the corner of my eye I see Clementine start to edge away. She must have been listening, she...

Then it comes to me, as seconds ago it had come to Higgins, but it hits me a lot harder. That time, outside the jail in Pittsburgh...Mike Fink taunting me: *I know a secret thing... and I ain't gonna tell you what it is...* and then later...Oh, my God...

My name is Missus Clementine Fletcher!

Slowly I rise from my chair and turn to face her. As soon as she sees the look on my face, she cuts and runs aft.

"Why, you scheming little bitch!" I snarl and take after her, hands hooked into claws.

"Miss, don't!" I hear Higgins shout behind me, but I will, oh, yes I will. *You're gonna get it, you sneaking, two-faced—*

Clementine runs to the stern, turns, and sees me still comin'. Her eyes are wild, tears stream down her face. She hooks her leg over the rail and turns to Jim, standing openmouthed at the tiller. "Good-bye, Jimmy! Always remember that I loved you more than anything else in the world!"

And she launches herself off into the deep water on our starboard side.

"You ain't gettin' off that easy, damn you!" I screech and dive in after her. *No, you ain't!*

I resurface just as her head breaks water, and I am on her in an instant, putting my hands about her throat.

"What a fool I was! I took you in, I cared for you, I loved you as a sister, and then I find I have clasped a snake to my bosom! I'm gonna *kill* you!"

But I ain't gonna do that at all, 'cause while I'm expectin' her to squall and thrash and fight back, she doesn't do that at all. All she does is hang there all limp in my grip, sobbing, her yellow hair plastered to her head, her face contorted, with tears pouring from her eyes.

"Go ahead and kill me, I don't care! I don't! Jimmy ain't gonna want me no more and I'd rather be dead! Just let me go. I don't know how to swim, so you just let me go, if'n you want to kill me!" Her bawling redoubles, her mouth opens, and her lower lip goes back over her bottom teeth, her eyes still squeezed tight shut. "God, you give me Jaimy, then you give me Jimmy, then you take 'em both away! Oh, Lord, how could you do that to me?"

I release my grip on her neck and put my arm around her waist, and my other arm under her legs, behind her knees and tread water, holding her there.

"Nobody's gonna kill you, Clementine. Just hush, now, hush. Everything's gonna be all right, you'll see."

What *I* see is a very concerned Jim Tanner rowing toward us in the *Evening Star*. In a moment he is alongside us and I hand him Clementine's trembling form.

"Take her off for a spell, Jim. You'll need to talk. I can swim back to the *Belle*. And I'm sorry, Jim, for how I acted."

He nods, but he ain't lookin' at me. I swim back to the boat and climb the ladder.

Higgins insists that I change into decent clothing and I do it and go back to my table up top. Jim and the other boat had thrown out their anchors when Clementine and I hit the water. *So be it,* I think, *let us stay here for the night. To hell with it. To hell with everything.*

Higgins brings me up food and drink, for I certainly don't feel like being sociable with my crew this evening. Captain Allen, I notice, has the good grace not to sit at his table and taunt me with his smirk, and I am glad of it.

As I sit and force myself to eat, I steal glances over at Clementine and Jim, still sitting in the *Evening Star.* I can see her shoulders shake as she sits apart from him, telling her story. This goes on for a while, then I see him put his arm around her and he draws her to him, and she lays her head on his shoulder. They remain that way for a while and then Jim picks up the oars and rows back to the *Belle.*

Higgins notices me still glowering as he sets down a glass of wine.

"Do you know the meaning of the word *hypocrisy,* Miss?"

"Of course I know what it means, Higgins, and I take your point. I have been a complete hypocrite, and I know it."

I have smooched, sparked, and wriggled my way halfway around this world—Randall, Robin, Jared, Padraic, Arthur McBride, and finally Richard Allen, and I should expect Jaimy to be an angel? No, it's not fair.

Jim hands Clementine up the ladder and Chloe takes her by the hand and leads her into our cabin, to get her dry and presentable. Jim comes up to me and looks me square in the eye, unsmiling. He says, "Clementine and me are going to get married. Today. I'm gonna go tell the Reverend now."

He ain't askin' my permission, but I nod anyway.

So we do have a wedding aboard the *Belle of the Golden West* on this day. It just so happens that it is not *my* wedding, which should have been the one so happily celebrated, had not cruel fate and my own headstrong stupidity intervened.

"Dearly Beloved, we are gathered together here in the sight of Almighty God," intones the Very Reverend Jeremiah Clawson, "to join in Holy Matrimony Mr. James McNeil Tanner and Clementine Amaryllis Jukes..."

We are assembled below, bathed in soft candlelight. Matthew Hawkes is Best Man, and Yancy Cantrell will give the bride away. Crow Jane is Matron of Honor, and the rest of us girls are bridesmaids. Jim is dressed in a clean white shirt with a bit of lace at the throat that I'd insisted he wear for this special occasion, while Clementine is decked out in a stitched-together white gown we hastily made from the play's tearaway dress, to which we'd added some flounces. While we were doing this, I sent Daniel over to pick some flowers I had spotted earlier on the bank, and with them I made a posy chain for her hair. When I placed the floral crown upon her head, I said, "May you have a happy life, Sister. Jim Tanner is one of the finest persons, man or boy, that I have ever met." She nodded and squeezed my hand.

With that, I kissed her on the forehead, and we led her up to her wedding.

"If there is any here among us who object to this marriage, let him speak up now, or forever hold his peace..."

No one objects, and the thing is done.

"Very well. Do you, James McNeil Tanner, take Clementine Amaryllis Jukes to be your lawful wedded wife..."

We hold the party out on deck, under the moonlight, so as to give the newlyweds a place to flee to, a cabin of their own having been set up below. All are dressed in their finest. Toasts are drunk all around, coarse jests traded, and eventually the bridal couple goes below. A delighted Clementine tosses her flower crown before going down and a surprised Katy Deere catches it.

The party continues above for an hour or so, to give them some private time below. I sit with Higgins, Yancy, and the Reverend at my table, while the Hawkes and the Honeys carouse down on the deck. After a bit, I call out to Richard Allen, "Get over here, you complete rascal, and have a glass of wine with us." And he bounds over.

"Is it not a crazy world?" I say to the party at large.

"Indeed it is, Princess," agrees Richard Allen.

"And I hope you'll soon be able to pronounce it a wonderful world as well, Miss," says Higgins.

"Oh, yes, Higgins, I do, after all is said and all is done." I lift my glass in the light of the full moon. "On to New Orleans."

"Hear, hear," says my dear company.

PART VI

Chapter 62

"'My Dear Mr. Fletcher: Your former fiancée, Miss Jacky Faber, has requested that I relate to you the particulars of our relationship. I am happy to do so'..."

We are seated at my cabin-top table, and Captain Allen, dressed in full uniform down to the spurs on his boots, is reading from a letter that he holds in his hand. My small fleet has arrived in Baton Rouge, and he and his men are preparing to leave us for good. The *Britannia* has been sold and horses hired to take the soldiers directly down to the coast to where a cutter awaits to transport them back to their base in Jamaica. Richard was of the mind that with New Orleans having only recently become American, a boatload of fully armed British redcoats might not be received too kindly by the largely French populace, and so he made the decision to go overland from here and thus avoid that city.

"...*Ahem*. I am happy to say I galloped your pretty little dollop of trollop from St. Louis down to Baton Rouge and she proved a *most* spirited mount, as we—"

"Give me that, you!" I snatch the paper from his hand and read what he had actually written there.

To Lieutenant James Fletcher,

Greetings from a fellow officer and admirer of Miss Jacky Faber. Here is a brief history of my time in her company: She was captured by our party far upriver, she escaped, and she took us prisoner in return. I gave my parole and we traveled downriver together, my mission having been aborted by her actions. We bore each other no ill will and soon became friends.

On the day you arrived on the scene, Miss Faber had decided to take a swim in a private, secluded area, and I, unbidden, decided to join her, and, surprising her there, demanded the settlement of a silly bet she had made and lost, the wager being for a kiss. A long kiss. She acquiesced, being a girl of her word, and I was collecting my winnings, as it were, when you showed up.

I swear to you, Mr. Fletcher, that what you saw then was the entire extent of our intimacy. She has often spoken of you in the most glowing terms, declaring that she was promised in marriage to you only.

I know what you must have surmised when you saw us together in that pool, and I regret that you beheld that, but I further regret that your suspicions were in fact not true, for I found her a most neat and beguiling piece of work and I would have been delighted to say that I enjoyed all of her charms. But I cannot in all honesty say that, for, alas, it would not be true. More's the pity.

If you object to my saying these things, you may find me at my barracks in Kingston, Jamaica, and you may have satisfaction.

I congratulate you on winning the favor of such a lovely and spirited young woman and I am,

Your Humble and Most Obedient Servant,

Captain Richard Lord Allen

P.S. I offered to make her Lady Allen, but she demurred. Pity, that.

I fold the letter and put it aside. "Thank you, Richard. That was kind of you. I don't, however, recall the great Lord Allen asking the very common commoner Jacky Faber to marry him."

"Ah, I just threw that in for good measure."

"So it's a lie then, my lord?"

"All right, will you marry me and become Lady Allen?"

I laugh. "I can't tell whether you're joking or not, you rascal. But the answer is 'no,' either way."

"Pity, that," he says in mock seriousness. "Wouldn't that just put the Old Man's nose in a vise, though, my bringing home something like you as his daughter-in-law? 'Father, may I present my wife, the extraordinary showgirl and actress Miss Jacky Faber, the Toast of the Mississippi and the Lily of the West? Lift your dress to show Father your fine knees, dear, if you would.' The Old Prune would drop dead on the instant. Ha! It's damned tempting. Are you sure you won't reconsider?"

"No." I laugh. "But I will thank you for your kind protection on our journey here."

"My pleasure, Princess," he says, looking out on the preparations for his departure that are taking place on the dock. Sergeant Bailey is having a fine time ordering the privates about as packs are being loaded and horses are being bridled, saddled, and cinched up. It is plain that these cavalrymen will be glad to get back in the saddle again.

"I think you should be all right, as regards safety, from here on down. The land is quite settled and there are no reports of hostile Indians about. And we haven't seen those slavers for a while."

I nod and reflect that no, we have not. We spotted them a few times, lurking around the edges of our crowds, but they made no move against us. We had found out, by asking about, that they were the Beam family, Pap Beam and his five grown sons. They were supposed to have a farm of some sort on the river and from there ranged up and down in search of escaped slaves to sell back to their owners. The Beams were much feared in this region, by both blacks and whites, and all gave them a wide berth.

"I'm sure we'll be all right, Richard. We're going to stay well out in the river, and that should be protection enough."

"You'll not set up for a performance today?"

"No, we'll get under way as soon as you take your leave. We're all anxious to get to New Orleans as soon as possible, me to see if I can find Mr. Fletcher, the others to enjoy the charms of a real city after this long journey." I shake my head. "No, I think the showboat *Belle of the Golden West* has had its final curtain call. Besides, how could poor Prudence Goodlove ever manage without her Captain Noble Strongheart?" I say, smiling and putting my hand on his.

He laughs. "I did enjoy that bit of nonsense, though."

"As did I, and I did enjoy your company, you arrant knave, even though you did mess things up." I see Sergeant Bailey come to the edge of the landing, leading a saddled horse. "I think the sergeant wants to speak to you."

He turns to look.

"All packed and ready, Sir," says Sergeant Bailey, saluting with his open hand held up to his hat, his shako, as they call it.

"Very well, Sergeant," says Captain Allen, rising from his chair.

I, too, rise and go over to the edge of the cabin top and look down at the men, each standing by a horse. "Goodbye, Sergeant Bailey, it was very good to know you. Goodbye, Willie, good-bye, Freddy, give my regards to Kingston. Good-bye, Seamus, I hope you see Ireland again soon, and may you, Archy, once again roam the heaths of Scotland. Alfie and Walter, good-bye and the best of luck. All of you give my regards to Mother England should you get back to the home ground—she may not love me, but I still do love her. Farewell all and Godspeed."

Each of the men touched their hands to their shakos as I said their names. As with all the leave-takings and departures of my life, my eyes start to mist up.

I turn to Captain Allen and extend my hand. "Good-bye, Richard. Fare thee well."

He takes my hand and bows over it, and I dip down in a deep, formal curtsy. When I come back up, he says, "I once heard you use the saying 'Might as well be hanged for a wolf as for a sheep,' and I agree, Jacky, I might as well." And with that he puts his arm around me, bends me back, and puts a real kiss on my mouth.

He releases me, and I say, "Good-bye, you rogue. Go now, your men are waiting." *Go now, before I start really crying.*

He plants another kiss on the back of my hand, steps down to the lower deck, and then off the *Belle of the Golden West,* his saber hanging by his side, his spurs jangling. He goes to his mount, puts foot in stirrup, and swings up into the saddle, and all his men follow suit.

Wheeling the horse about, he takes one last look back at me and calls out, "Good-bye, Princess, I will remember you, and you can count on that!"

He puts the spurs to the horse's flanks and gallops off and away.

I stand and wave till I can see him no more.

And I will remember you, Lord Richard Allen, oh yes, I will, and you, too, can count on that.

I shook all thoughts of dashing young captains of cavalry from my head and wasted no time in getting under way again.

"Jim. Get us out farther into the stream. Matty, 'Thaniel, on the sweeps. There'll be time for rest in New Orleans, and it's only sixty or so miles away." They leap to it, as I'm sure Honeysuckle Rose and Tupelo Honey have told them many tales of the delights that wait for them in New Orleans.

I scan the bank as we move along. The shores have changed a great deal as we have moved farther south into the delta of Louisiana. Before, the banks held trees that could easily have grown in England, or at least looked like they could have grown there. Now there are deep, dark shaded inlets where trees trail long beards of moss down into the black water, bayous they are called, and it don't look like England anymore, no, it don't...

"Good God, what's that?" shouts Clementine Tanner, pointing with shaking finger at something on the bank. It looks like a huge black and bumpy log, about twelve feet long, but it is not that, oh no, for it has a tail and it swings it back and forth as it slips its bulk into the water.

Crow Jane, alerted by Clementine's cry, comes up on deck, holding a ladle. She looks over at where the girl is pointing and squints. The beast lies in the water, just its two eyes showin'.

"It's a 'gator," she says. "They eat up little girls like you. Everybody be careful 'bout fallin' overboard." She points the ladle at me. "And no more swimmin' for you!"

I nod in agreement to that.

I watch the bank slip by, looking for more alligators and finding them, and seeing snakes on branches, raccoons coming down onshore to catch crayfish, and big, squawking birds with flapping doomed fishes in their long beaks, with swarms of bugs flying about, and I wish myself back in merry old England, or at least in good old staid, starched-drawers Boston.

I shake off these thoughts, too. Upriver we had found and bought a canoe, and Lightfoot and Chee-a-quat had gone off in it several times to see if they could run down Jaimy, but no luck—there were just too many tributaries in this fickle and maddening river.

I decide on one more try. "Lightfoot. Will you and Chee-a-quat take the canoe and search again?"

Lightfoot is sitting up with Katy, watching her fish. She has a stringer of fresh-caught fish trailing in the water beside her, species we have not seen before. He looks at Chee-a-quat, on the opposite side, they both say *wah,* then get up, take their rifles, and climb into the canoe.

"We'll try this one last time, Wah-chinga, but you gotta know that soon this river widens out into a big, *big* old lake called Pont-char-train, and if'n he's on that, we ain't gonna find him, ever. We'll be back tomorrow, with him or without him." He nods at Katy and then pushes off.

I watch them go, wondering if it was wise to send them, we now having no protection, save the river and the few left aboard.

No, no...everything is all right. We'll get dinner and then anchor for the night. Everything is all right. We'll get some sleep...

Jaimy, I know you hate me now, and think me false and deceiving and of very low character, but still I long to see you and I pray for your health and safety, I do. Amen.

Chapter 63

"Fire's out, Boss," Crow Jane is saying as I gaze southward looking for Lightfoot and Chee-a-quat to return. "That wood we bought up in Natchez must've been green. Damn crackers, you just can't trust 'em."

"Can you start it up again?"

"Sure, Boss, but I'm gonna need an armload o' kindling to get it going."

"*Hmm*...I would like the crew to have a hot breakfast and I could use a cup of tea, myself." I scan the near bank, which is heavily wooded and looks like a likely place to find some wood. It's pretty high land, not swampy like where the 'gators tend to hang out. We haven't seen anyone on the shore since we left Baton Rouge yesterday, so it should be safe enough.

"All right, I'll hop over and gather some." After I decide this, I call back to Jim, "Pull her over next to that low bank there. I'm going ashore to get some firewood."

As the *Belle* slips over to the shore, I go down into my cabin and take off my buckskin skirt and pull on my white duck trousers, 'cause I know the bugs'll be bad onshore.

When I come back out, we are alongside. "Solly, come

help me if you would." I hop over and he follows. I go off to the left, picking up sticks as I go while he forages straight ahead. *Sticks are plentiful and dry, so this shouldn't take long,* I'm thinking.

"Hey, Missy, there's a road back here!" says Solomon, out of my sight to the right. "And there's— Missy, run! Get back to the boat!"

"Make a move and yer one dead nigra!"

Oh no!

I drop my load of kindling and charge off toward Solly, but I don't get ten feet before a hand comes across my mouth and my arms are pinned to my side. Desperately I kick and squirm but to no avail, I am held fast and forced to do nothing but listen as disaster falls upon us.

I don't hear nothin' from Solly so I guess they've got guns pointin' at him, but I do hear somethin' from the direction of the *Belle,* somethin' that chills me to the core.

"Hands in the air, all of you! Anyone goes for a gun, I kill this here girl!"

"Get your hands off her, you bastard!" *Jim's voice! They must have pulled Clementine off the boat and now have a pistol to her head!*

"Shut up, boy! Absalom, git the nigress!"

"Got her, Pap! Git down there, you!"

"Stop! You can't—"

A shot rings out and then a scream.

"Can't, can't I? Shadrach, Moab, you keep these ones covered while we truss up the three we're taking. You there! Cast this boat off and take it to the middle of the river or we'll blow her brains out. Do it now!"

"What possible use do you have for the white girl?" *That's Higgins…*

"Oh, we got a use for her all right, big man, bein' she's the leader of yer gang of low-down slave stealers. A real good use."

There is a thrashing of the bushes and then they are parted and my horrified eyes behold the grinning face of one of the Beam boys. He holds a length of rope.

"Turn the little nigra-lover around, Mordecai, so's I kin tie her hands."

I'm roughly spun around, and as my wrists are crossed and bound, the grimy hand is taken from my mouth and I scream out, "Higgins! Jim! Wait for Lightfoot!" My mind may be shocked, but it's still working. *"Ow!"*

I'm backhanded hard across the face and then a rope is shoved between my teeth and tied at the back of my head. "That'll keep her quiet, Ezekiel," says the one named Mordecai.

Ezekiel turns me again to look me in the eye. "Got yer little Abolitionist ass now, don't we? And we got it good. Hee-hee, oh, yeah."

They push me back through the bushes where there waits an open buckboard hitched to two mules. Solomon slumps in the back, his head shaking as if he was slowly returning to consciousness. They must have hit him pretty hard, the bastards. There are strong ropes wrapped all about him. Next to him is Chloe, her face a mask of complete horror. I'm thrown into the wagon and made to lie down behind the seat. My ankles are tied together.

Pap Beam comes out of the woods, climbs up, and sits

down. He grabs the reins and shouts, "Moab! Are they out in the river?"

"Yeah, they are, Pap! 'Bout in the middle!"

"Good! Throw the girl in the water and let's go!"

There is a shriek and a splash and then the two men come charging out of the woods, and all mount their horses.

Solomon looks at Chloe and says, "This here's a free Colored girl. You should be lettin' her go, Suh."

Pap Beam looks back at him. "If that don't beat all, a nigra tellin' Hezekiah Beam what he should or shouldn't do. What's this world comin' to?" And with that he picks up the buggy whip from its holder and swings it, catching Solomon across the back with it. Solly stiffens and groans. "You say another word, boy, and the black bitch gets the next one, y'hear? Good. All right, let's go, boys." He slaps the reins on the backs of the mules and we move off.

"What we gonna do, Pap?" asks one of the riders.

"Wal, Shadrach, we're gonna get back to the farm, lock up the two nigras, and then as soon as we can dig a grave, we're gonna hang the Abolitionist whore from the sweet gum tree."

We rumble along for about a half hour, then pull up next to a field. "Let's take down those rails, boys, and cross over here, so that in case anyone follows us, they'll think we went straight along the road."

"Good thinkin', Pap."

Think, dammit! You've got to think of something or else you're dead! If only I could leave something here as a marker for Lightfoot, but I can't, I can't. Oh, Lord!

"Say, Pappy, kin we have some fun with her, afore we hangs her?" Ezekiel Beam giggles. "You know…"

"You would sully the purity of your body by cleaving unto this Jezebel, this whore of Babylon, Ezekiel? You saw yourself how she tore off her dress and exposed herself to inflame the lusts of men, how she danced like wicked Salome, herself! Nay!" roars the old man. "Never, never in my house or on my land!"

"Sorry I axed, Pap," says Ezekiel, smarting under the rebuff, but the crazy old man is not yet done.

"Scripture says the Great God Jehovah gave us dominion over the beasts of the field, and the nigra is a beast of the fields and any damned Abolitionist who says any different is goin' against the Will of Almighty God and needs hangin' and that's what she's gonna git!"

"Wal, Pap, nobody know the rules of Scripture like you do, that's for sure. Pity, though…she ain't half bad-lookin'…"

He may be a crazy, God-struck, and twisted man, but he has given me a ray of hope. It's a slim chance, but it's the only chance I got.

We clatter ever onward.

The buckboard pulls in to a farmyard early in the afternoon. Chloe and Solomon are dragged out and taken into a barn, where I am sure cruel shackles await them. Poor Chloe is stunned with grief—I found out on the way that Yancy Cantrell had been shot by Pap Beam as Yancy tried to prevent the abduction of his daughter. I am left in the wagon.

The Beams dismount and tie up their horses, then two of

them take up shovels and go to a bare spot of ground and begin to dig what might very well turn out to be my grave. Pap and the others go into the house that sits next to the barn. I don't see anyone else around—no wives, no children, just a few chickens pecking in the yard. I see a big, smooth-bark tree at the edge of the yard and a shiver runs up my spine—that can only be the sweet gum tree.

The two digging Beams, Shadrach and Absalom, I think, labor at their grim task for a while, and when they are knee-deep into the dirt, Shadrach calls out, "Pap! Come out here! Is this deep enough?"

Pap Beam comes out onto the porch of his house, his duster now shed, his gray beard resting on a dirty gray shirt over which a pair of suspenders lie, holding up his stained black trousers. He looks upon the work of his sons and shakes his head.

"Nah, it should be about waist deep, else the hogs might root up her corpse."

"Then, hell, Pap, git the other boys to help," whines Absalom, dusting off his hands, "I think I'm a-gettin' a blister."

"Moab! Ezekiel! Mordecai! Git on out here!" His sons come out of the house, dressed exactly like their father. "You two spell Shadrach and Absalom. Moab, you pick her up and stretch her out there next to the hole and see if they got it long enough."

Moab leans over the buckboard and picks me up and hauls me over to the edge of the pit and drops me hard on the ground. I try to speak around the rope, but all I can get out is a garbled mumble.

"You'll git yer chance to say a few last words, slut, so just be quiet now," says Pap. He looks down, appraising the measurements. "Yeah, it's long enough. Just git it waist deep. Shadrach, you go set up the rope there on that limb, and then bring over a horse. We'll do it that way. And get them nigras out here to watch it—teach 'em a good lesson."

"Yes, Pap."

Another half hour later and the job is done. I am lifted up and the bonds are taken from my ankles. I struggle and try to wriggle and make a run for it, but I am held too tight. I am placed on the horse and the noose is put around my neck and drawn tight. I know that the rope goes up over that limb and then is brought down, wrapped around the trunk of the tree, and tightly knotted. The Beams gather in a circle about me.

"All right, then, let Divine Justice be done," says Pap Beam. "Mordecai, take the rope from her mouth." The man pulls out a knife from his belt and reaches up and places the blade between my cheek and the rope gag and pulls back, cutting it clean. It falls from my mouth.

"Any last words before you go to stand before the Great God Jehovah?" says Pap, his hand upraised, ready to slap the flank of the horse that sits beneath me.

"I pleads my belly!" I gasp out.

"What?" says Pap.

"You may hang me for being an Abolitionist, for I fully confess that, but you cannot kill the innocent unborn child that lies within my womb, if you are, as you say, a man of God!"

I puff out my belly and make it as hard as I can, ready to receive the hand I know is coming.

"See if it's true, Pap," says Mordecai. "You musta felt

Mama's belly, God rest her poor soul, when we was all in there."

Pap Beam runs his hand up under my shirt and runs his hand over my stomach.

"Her belly's round and tight," he reports, "but I can't tell for sure. Damn."

"It's true, I swear," says I.

"It's true," says Chloe from across the yard. "She bin gettin' sick and throwin' up ever' mornin' for a month now!" *Oh, thank you, Chloe!*

"Damn, damn, and double damn!" sputters Pap. "Was it that nigra what put it there?" He points across at Solomon.

"No, Suh, it was a fine southern gentleman, a man of high degree. It was Colonel William Howe of the Virginia Howes, who's sure to be the next guv'nor of the state, a false fine gentleman who left me alone to fend for myself and my poor baby to come!" I babble along for all I'm worth, hopin' to keep this horse under me for just a little while yet.

"We could keep her till she has the baby and then hang her. Maybe have a little fun with her till then." Ezekiel giggles. "She could even clean up a bit around here. Hoe corn and pick cotton and such. But what does Scripture say, Pap?"

"Scripture says we'd have to keep her alive till the child was off the tit. Scripture also says we should stone her for the adultery, but that don't solve the unborn-brat problem. Dammit all to Hell and back! Boys, I got to talk to God about this!" and he strides off into the woods at the edge of the farmstead.

"Pap's gone to his prayin' place. You comfortable up there, girly?"

The horse under me is gettin' skittish and is liable to solve this problem for everybody by runnin' off and leavin' me danglin' while Pap and his God argue the fine points of this thing. *Nice horsie...nice horsie...*

"Let's move this nag just a little bit forward," says Eze-kiel. "Just a little bit. Hee-hee, look at her neck stretch, listen to her choke."

Oh please, God, I can't breathe...it hurts...I can't...

"Take her down and put her in the shed. The Great God Jehovah has spoken to me and shown me the way," says Pap Beam, coming out of the woods, his face all aglow with spiritual rapture.

Oh, thank you, God!

I am wrapped in my own rapture of thankfulness and relief as the hateful rope is taken from my neck and I am taken down and tossed into a rough woodshed. Very roughly am I thrown—they were probably trying to cause a miscarriage. I hit the earthen floor and hear a bolt being thrown.

My hands still bound, I wriggle about the floor, searching desperately for some way out, but find none. Then, on the breeze that blows in through the cracks in the door, I smell a wood fire being started. *Could they mean to burn me?* I wonder with renewed dread.

Then I hear the squawks of chickens being chased and then the thump of ax on chopping block and then I hear the squawks no more. *Could it be that they are preparing dinner and have forgotten about me for the moment?*

Oh, no, that is not it at all.

For then I breathe in the unmistakable smell of hot tar.

Chapter 64

The door of the shed is pulled open and I am dragged out by Ezekiel and Moab and taken back to the sweet gum tree, where the noose still dangles. The rest of the Beams stand there, waiting. Solomon and Chloe are off to the side, bound back-to-back to a post. The grave is still open.

Have they decided to hang me after all? Oh please, God, no!

"Be careful how you handle me, you're gonna hurt my baby!" I wail.

"We ain't gonna hurt your baby none, heh-heh," chuckles Moab, "but we're sure gonna hurt you, girly. You git over here, now."

I'm pulled till I'm under the noose and then I am stood up. Mordecai goes to where it's bound and lowers it till it hits the top of my head.

"String her up," says Pap Beam.

They are, they're really gonna do me! My knees tremble and my legs begin to give out, but the two Beams have their hands under my armpits, so they hold me up.

"No, please don't!" I burst into tears as the rough rope of the noose brushes against my face. But instead of putting it around my neck, they untie my hands and stick my crossed wrists into it and pull it up tight. Mordecai goes back to the other end of the rope and pulls on it till my arms are stretched above me and I'm standing on my tiptoes.

"Can I take off her clothes, Pap?" begs Ezekiel.

"Just the shirt, son. I don't want you boys' innocent eyes sullied by gazin' upon the sex of a whore."

Are they gonna whip me to death?

Ezekiel puts his hand on the neckline of my shirt and yanks down hard, ripping it from me. Bits of my sleeves still remain and he tears them off as well. "There," he says. "Ah, yes, ain't that some fine?"

"What are you gonna do to me? Please, I beg of you..."

Pap Beam shows me his yellowed teeth in a grisly smile. "You love them nigras so much, we gonna make you just like 'em. We gonna make you a tar baby."

"Hee-hee, good one, Pap."

"Go git it, boy."

Moab goes around the shed and comes back bearing a large bucket, which, when it is brought close enough for me, I see is filled with the tar I had smelled before. *Hot* tar. It ain't bubblin' but it still looks pretty warm.

"Oh, how could you be so cruel to me? Oh why, oh why?" I blubber. "I ain't never done nothin' to you!"

"You bin stealin' niggers and that's a capital crime round these parts," says Pap. "If'n you weren't with child, yer dead ass'd be hangin' from that limb right now. Do 'er, Moab."

The handle of a brush sticks out of the tar bucket and Moab brings it out, dripping with tar. I try to swing out of the way, but I can't, I can't. "No, no, no, please," as he runs the brush from my shoulder to my stomach. "Yeeeeeooowww! No more! It's hot! Please, no more!"

But my pleas fall on deaf, uncaring ears, and Moab keeps on painting me. When he's done covering my front, he goes around and does my back. "Lord, help me! Oh, you monsters, stop! Yeeeooooww!"

Then I hear one of them say, "Hey, Pap, that belly looks pretty damn flat to me."

My crazed mind is taken off my pain and jerked back to reality. *I can't puff out my belly when I'm stretched out like this, I can't...*

"I do believe you are right, Ezekiel, and if that don't beat all," says Pap, and then he bursts out laughing. By the time the wretched Moab has tarred my once-white trousers, Pap trails off to a rueful chuckle. "Boys, boys, I reckon you just now saw how the Lord works His will. When I talked to Him before, He didn't come right out and tell me that she was lyin' about havin' a child in her womb, lyin' to save her wicked neck, no. He tells me to tar 'n' feather the strumpet and I does, and behold! I see that her belly's flat as a board! Oh, boys, the Lord works in mighty and mysterious and wonderful ways, Amen!"

Moab is done doing the Lord's work on my pants and feet and then turns to my arms. There ain't no more screams left in me, just tears and sobbing.

"Git 'er done, Moab. Lord tol' me to tar her, so we gotta do it first, 'fore we do anythin' else with her."

"Yes, Pap," says Moab. He stands in front of me grinning. "My face is prolly the last thing yer evah gonna see on this here earth. Ain't that somethin'?" With that he upends the bucket over my head and the rest of the tar pours over my hair and face, and he finishes the job by running the brush down over my eyes, sealing them shut.

I hang limp in the bonds, my mind numb. I am totally without hope now, knowing that the rope that binds my wrist will soon be around my neck yet again, and that will be it for me. *Good-bye, Jaimy, I loved you...Good-bye to all my friends in this world. You always did your best for me, you did...*

"All right, git the feathers on 'er now," says Pap, and I suppose that is being done, but I can't feel the feathers, not through the tar. I am beyond caring. "Good. Now, Absalom, go loosen up the rope."

In a moment I feel the rope give way and I crumple to the ground, and then the rope is taken from my hands and then...

...and then I hear a thud and then a scream, then... "Pap! I...I got an arrow in my gut! Help me, Pap!"

And then all is confusion, and in my case, blind confusion. There's a rattle of gunfire and more grunts and screams.

"Git in the house, boys! Git the guns!"

"God, it hurts, Pap! I think I'm gonna die! Don't leave me out here, Pap, don't..."

I hear a sound like an ax splitting a melon and I know a tomahawk has ended Ezekiel Beam's concern over what must be Katy Deere's arrow and over his own miserable life, as well.

I hear a Shawnee battle cry as well as some *yeeee-haw*s that have to be coming from the Hawkes boys. *Oh, my friends, my friends...*

"Solomon! Pick her up and get her back to the boat. Katy, show 'em the way," shouts Lightfoot. "We'll clean up here and meet you a little ways down the river! Go!" There's the sound of more shots, some now coming from the direction of the house. There's another scream of pain.

I feel myself being lifted and held to Solomon's broad chest, and then my tortured mind gives out and I know nothing for a while.

"Oh, my God, look what they've done to her! Tupelo, come help. Chloe, you'd best go down and see your father."

"Is she still alive, Solly?"

"I think so, Mr. Higgins."

I prove that I am by pulling apart my tar-caked lips and commencing to bawl.

"Thank God."

"Oh, poor Jacky! I just can't bear to look!" wails Tupelo. "Those horrid men! Crow Jane, what can we do?"

"The tar's still warm. Let's git her in the water, cool her off. When the tar gets cold, it'll git stiffer and we should be able to peel some of it off. Honeysuckle, run to the paint locker and git the turpentine. Clementine, go git some rags. Lots of 'em. Mr. Higgins, we'll git this stuff off her, but it'll take some time. Best find some shears, though, 'cause there won't be any savin' of her hair."

I hear the sound of Solomon wading in the water, and then I am lowered down into the river. *Ahhhhhh...* It slowly enters my mind that I am going to live, after all, and I begin to leave off on the crying. *Thank you, God.*

I'm held there in the stream for a while, and then I hear Higgins say, "Bring her up, Solly," and I am taken up, then put down faceup on what I suspect is the big tavern table.

"Let's get to work, girls," says Crow Jane. "Pick a spot and start scrapin' with them knives. Careful not to cut her, though. Gimme those shears."

"Mr. Higgins," says Katy, "Lightfoot said we should get going, that he and the others'll meet us downriver a piece."

"All right. Solomon, on tiller; Reverend, you and I on sweeps. Let's go." I hear them leave as I feel the edge of the shears slip over my belly to cut the drawstring of my tarred pants, which are then slid down off of me. My wet drawers are pulled off, too, and I am shamed to admit that it is not only the waters of the Mississippi that they are wet with. A towel is thrown over my midsection and upper thighs, the only parts of me that are still white. The knives begin their work.

"Katy. When you left, was Jim all right?" asks Clementine to my right.

"Yeah. None of ours got hurt," answers Katy on my left. "We caught 'em by surprise and left three of 'em lyin' dead in the dirt, 'fore the others could get in the house. They got 'em trapped in there. Only a matter of time till it's over."

"Eyes're gonna be tricky. Can't just slosh turpentine there. Let's use spoons to scrape out what we can," says Crow Jane. "But first the hair."

She works the shears in close to my scalp and begins to cut away the thick, clotted mass of ruined hair. She works from the front to the back and soon I am shorn.

"You okay, Boss?"

"Yes, Janey, and thanks. Thanks, all of you."

They work on me all through the rest of that day—scraping away to get down to my skin, then wiping with a turpentine-soaked rag to get up the residue, then strong soap and hot water and bristly brush, and then more turpentine, and then back to more soap and water. After about an hour, Crow Jane manages to clear out my eyes and I am able to open them and look about. Several hours after that, my front being done, I am made to sit up so Katy and Clementine can work on my back, while a Honey works on each foot, and Crow Jane finishes up my face, neck, and head.

Finally, it's done.

"All right, into the tub with you," and I gratefully crawl in. *Ahhhhhh…*

Later, when the water in the tub has cooled, I get out, dry off, and put on the white shirt, drawers, and skirt that Clementine has laid out for me, and I go up on deck. Higgins is on the starboard sweep.

"Hello, Higgins."

"Good day, Miss. I am very glad to see you. I must admit I feared the worst this time."

"It was a close thing, Higgins. I have much new food for my nightmares. How's Yancy?"

Higgins doesn't say anything for a moment and then shakes his head. "He is dying, Miss. The bullet took him in the abdomen, in the vicinity of his liver. The bullet is still in there and there is no way to get it out."

Oh, no…

I go down to his cabin, knock lightly, and am told to enter. I find him lying in bed, Chloe sitting in a chair beside him, holding his hand in one of hers, a handkerchief in the other. He is ashen but awake, and I go to his side.

"I'm so sorry, Yancy," I say, the tears coming on. "It's all my fault. If I hadn't stopped for firewood, we—"

"Now, Jacky, you couldn't know those varmints were

lurking about, so don't go blaming yourself. We were all in this together, sharing the joys, sharing the risks. As you said yourself, it's the old pirate ethic, 'We stood on board as brothers,' and we did." A slight smile crosses his lips. "And I did enjoy this last trip down the river, perhaps the most of all that I have made."

"Don't say 'last,' Father. You don't know."

"No, dear, I'm afraid Yancy Cantrell has knocked down his last game, but he's not complaining. Maybe I didn't get the full three-score-and-ten years that the Bible promised a man, but I got most of it, and I had a good time of it, too."

The slight smile turns to a grimace of pain. Chloe squeezes her father's hand and puts the handkerchief to her eyes.

Yancy reaches over and takes my hand. "I will ask one thing of you, Jacky, and that is to do everything in your power to get my girl here back to her people in New York."

"Of course, Yancy. Of course."

He looks up at me and lets go of my hand. He reaches up and ruffles the stubble on my head and chuckles, "You look just like a dandelion, Jacky. A pretty, wild, little dandelion."

I lean over and put a kiss on his forehead. "Good-bye, Yancy Cantrell," I manage to say without dropping too many tears on his face, and I leave father and daughter to have their last bit of time together.

"There they are!" shouts Clementine from the bow. She points off to starboard and I see them, my recent saviors, standing together on a spit of land that juts out into the water. Behind them I make out the shapes of horses, six of them.

"Steer for 'em, Solly."

"Aye, aye, Skipper."

We anchor there for the night. When Lightfoot comes aboard, he dangles a tangle of scalps—five of them dark and one gray. He hangs the grisly trophies over the rail and says, "We picked off two more of 'em when they stood up in the windows to fire at us, and then the old man came roarin' out, shoutin' somethin' about the Great God Jehovah, and each of us put a bullet in him and still he stood till Chee-a-quat parted his hair for him with his tomahawk. He didn't have nothin' to say after that."

Clementine embraces a very subdued Jim Tanner, and the Hawkeses are welcomed back by their Honeys.

"Will anyone be looking for us, you think?" I ask.

"Naw, Wah-chinga, ain't gonna be no one comin' after us. Naw. We got 'em all. Warn't no wimmen nor kids there. We just put 'em all in their beds and lit the place on fire— ain't no one gonna be probin' their bodies for bullets and fer sure they ain't gonna know they was scalped. Ain't gonna be nuthin' but ashes. We set the livestock loose and brung along these six horses."

"You're sure they were dead when you did that?" I ask.

Lightfoot looks slyly at his Shawnee brother. "Wal, some of 'em said they weren't...but you know how them Louisiana people lie."

That gets a laugh out of the Hawkeses, and even a deep chuckle out of Chee-a-quat.

Then Chloe comes quietly onto the deck. She folds her hands together and looks out over the water.

"My father, Mr. Yancy Beauregard Cantrell, has passed on to his reward."

Chapter 65

Let six young showgirls follow my coffin,
Let six young rounders carry my pall.
Put bunches of roses all over my coffin,
Roses, to muffle the clods as they fall.

We have the funeral for Yancy Cantrell first thing in the morning. Nathaniel and Matty had spent some time last night and some more time this morning making his coffin out of wood taken from the performance boards for which we have no more use. The merry showboat is a thing of the past.

Yancy is laid in the box with his hands crossed on his chest. With Chloe's permission I have placed his deck of cards in his pocket, all the cards except for five. In his hand I put a full house, aces over kings, so when he gets up there, they'll know he died standing pat. I put my hand on his hands, those hands that were so skillful and adroit and will now be forever still, and then I step back.

Nathaniel picks up the coffin top and looks at Chloe. She says, "God be with you, Father. May you sit at His right hand."

The lid is put on and nailed shut. Matthew has nailed six leather handles to the coffin, three on each side, and the pallbearers—Higgins, Jim, Matthew, Nathaniel, Solomon, and Lightfoot—pick up the coffin and carry it out of the hatchway and over the gangway to the shore. We all fall in behind: Chloe first, with one hand on the coffin and the other on my arm for support. Then Reverend Clawson, open Bible in hand, then Katy, Clementine, Honeysuckle Rose, and Tupelo Honey. Crow Jane and Daniel stay back, guarding the *Belle*.

While the Hawkeses were building the coffin, Solomon was digging the grave, up on a piece of high ground about fifty yards from the shore, and it is to that open grave we sadly tread.

Reverend Clawson begins a hymn, one that we all know and so join in the singing of it.

> *I'm just a poor, wayfaring stranger,*
> *Traveling through this wearisome land,*
> *And there's no sickness, no toil or danger,*
> *In that bright world to which I go.*

Chloe stumbles, but I catch her and the cortege toils on.

> *I'm going there to see my father,*
> *I'm going there, no more to roam.*
> *I'm just a-going over Jordan,*
> *I'm just a-going over home.*

We arrive at the open grave, and as the pallbearers lower down the coffin, the Preacher gives us the last verse.

I'm going there to meet my mother,
She said she'd greet me when I come.
I'm just a-going over Jordan,
I'm just a-going over home.

The song ends and Chloe reaches down and picks up a handful of dirt and tosses it down onto the coffin, and Preacher Clawson reads, *"Ashes to ashes, dust to dust…"*

When the words are said and done, I put my arm around Chloe's shoulders and together we walk away. The Hawkeses begin covering the grave. We don't have roses, so the clods ain't muffled as they fall, but make a sad, hollow, thudding sound.

Chapter 66

⚓ And later today I lose yet another member of my company.

When I go to breakfast with the rest of my crew, I am greeted with the news that Chee-a-quat is leaving us.

"Nee-ah-hanta is with child and her time is soon," explains Lightfoot. "And we're now headin' into territory where he might not be welcome. Chickasaw land, if you get my drift. He will take three of the horses, one for himself and two as presents for our father. It will bring him much honor."

Nodding, I sigh, then say, "Well, that is as it should be. But we will miss his presence, if not his conversation. Jim, we'll not be weighing anchor just yet. Stand by." I go below to collect some things.

Chee-a-quat prepares to leave with very little ceremony, just some manly grasping of upper arms and thumping of chests with his Shawnee brother, but I won't let it go at that.

"Chee-a-quat, hold for a moment," I say, as he seems about to hook a leg over the rail and go. He pauses and looks at me. "For our brave and noble warrior Chee-a-quat, we give this pistol and money in return for his valiant service." I hand the pistol and a bag of coins to him and he takes them. "There is a necklace in there for Nee-ah-hanta, too. Please send my regards, for she was kind to a stranger when that stranger was in your town."

I sign *thank you* and *good-bye.*

And then, for the first time, Chee-a-quat speaks directly to me.

"*Wah-ho-tay,* Wah-chinga-sote-caweena-que-tonk. May you find a brave man for your husband and bear him many strong children. Good-bye, Jah-kee."

The mouth of She-Who-Dances-Like-Crazy-Rabbit drops open at the sound of English coming from the lips of the Shawnee warrior Chee-a-quat. He smiles, nods once more at Lightfoot, and then is over the side, across the sandbar, and into the woods and gone.

Yes, this morning I lost two of my company, and sadly, I find that I will lose two more this afternoon.

She appears on the quarterdeck, dressed for the first time in the buckskins that Lightfoot had gotten for her those weeks ago in the Shawnee village, and I know what that means.

"I'm goin' off with Lightfoot," says Katy Deere. "I talked to the Preacher. He's gonna say the words. My mama was a church lady and she'd have liked to see it done proper with a preacher and all."

I nod, having expected this. "Sit down, Katy, and tell me what you plan to do."

She thinks for a while and then says, "Y'know, Jacky, I really liked bein' on this run down the river with you—seein' new things at every bend in the river, huntin', fishin', pokin' around in pools and streams, explorin', like...But I know it's comin' to an end and you're gonna go off into those cities and towns and I just don't do good there. I tried it and it don't work."

She pauses and takes a breath. I know this is one of the longest speeches Katy Deere will ever deliver.

"You'll go back to Lightfoot's Shawnee village?"

"No, we're gonna go out West, see what's there. Listenin' to that Injun girl that time, Crow Jane's niece, you remember, the one who'd been on that expedition, about all those things out there—spouts of hot water that shoot a hundred feet in the air, streams full o' fish, deer with horns that curl back over their heads, big, *big* mountains, herds of buffalo so vast y'can't see across 'em, and another ocean over at the other edge. Well, we want to see it. Me and him."

Just a different version of me wanting to get the Bombay Rat, the Cathay Cat, and see the Kangaroo, but the same old thing...

"And when you and me was on that *Bloodhound*? Right, it was awful, but...up till then, I'd never felt so...I don't know what..."

I nod at the recollection of that time, when we were both sisters-in-arms against evil.

"And come winter, well, we might go back to my farm and hole up there. He could hunt and trap, and in the spring we'd hire a man and get a crop in. Huh! Don't worry, I know that I'll never get that man Lightfoot to ever hold a hoe. And I know I'd never be able to hold him on the farm when the weather warms up, so I'd go with him again. Get someone else to tend the crop and bring it in."

She looks out to the west, over the treetops, and fondly I look upon her face in profile, with its high cheekbones, strong nose, and thin lips, knowing I'll soon not be seeing it. "Or maybe we'll go down into Mexico to winter over. Hell, you've given us enough money to get by for a coupl'a winters."

"Money you earned ten times over, Katy. How many times have you saved my life? Once, twice, at least three."

"Lightfoot don't think you'll have any more trouble in gettin' to the city—the Beams is dead, the Indians is peaceable around here. So since we've got the ponies, we figured this was a good spot to go."

She rises and so do I.

"I'll miss you, Katy Deere."

"Me, too, Jacky. Miss you."

Katy's things are packed and thrown across the back of the packhorse and secured, along with some provisions we have raided from Crow Jane's stores. Her bow is slung from the pommel of the horse she will ride. I make up another posy crown and I reflect that the Reverend's been real busy lately.

"Dearly Beloved, we are gathered here in the sight of Almighty God to join in Holy Matrimony Katherine Deere and Lightfoot...er, Lightfoot, do you have a last name?"

"Back when I was a young'un, it was Bumpus."

"Ah. Very well...and Lightfoot Bumpus. If any here among you..."

Crow Jane whips up a fine bridal luncheon and we toast the bride and groom, both of them in their buckskins, seated at the head of the long table. The only thing to show that a wedding has happened is the posy crown that I braided up for her. I am getting quite good at that.

I give each of them a pistol, with powder and ball, and a bag of coins, which is their final share of the spoils of this journey. Of Lightfoot I ask, "Will she ride beside you or behind?"

He thinks for a moment, and then says, "Beside me, Wah-chinga, just the way you'd want it."

"I'm glad, Lightfoot. Thank you for everything you've done. Fare thee well."

Katy goes down the gangplank and gets on her horse.

"*Wah-ho-tay,* Wah-chinga. It was good knowin' you," says Lightfoot, and he, too, goes off the *Belle* and mounts up.

"*Wah-ho-tay,* Lightfoot."

When I have said good-bye to dear friends in the past, they have usually been of the seagoing class, and as there are only so many ports of call in this world, there was always the chance that I would meet up with them again, sometime—and that possibility would dull the pain of parting. After all, didn't I see Davy Jones and Hugh the Grand again? And sometimes Jaimy Fletcher?

Yes, but when I think of the vastness of this American continent, with its forests and rivers and hills and mountains and prairies that roll on forever, I know that I will never see this girl again.

"Fare thee well, Katy Deere."

She nods and we lock eyes for a moment, and then she and Lightfoot turn their horses and are gone.

The *Belle of the Golden West* gets under way once again, this time with a much diminished crew—we now have only myself, Higgins, Jim and Clementine, Reverend Clawson, the Hawkes boys and their wives Honeysuckle Rose and Tupelo Honey, Crow Jane, Solomon, young Daniel Prescott, and a very much saddened Chloe Abyssinia Cantrell.

We are fairly close to New Orleans now, and we settle back into our usual routines to pass the time on the last part of our long journey. Jim takes the tiller, with Clementine beside him, and I perch on my chair at my table under the canopy.

I notice that Solomon sits up forward on the cabin top, near, but not too near, to Chloe, who has forsaken our cabin to sit out in the air. Grief or not, it's just too damned hot down there. He has the guitar and plays some of the happy, spirited songs he knows, like "Hop High, Ladies," and "Sourwood Mountain," and "Sail Away, Ladies," and it seems to have a good effect on her spirits—I even saw her crack a wan smile, once.

Later, I take a lesson on guitar from Solomon, and as we toil away over a difficult fingering, I ask him, "Solly, you told me once that you didn't have a last name. Is that true?"

"Yes...uh...Jacky, most slaves take their owner's last name...or are forced to take 'em. I don't want to do that."

I knew it took an effort to say my name without the "Miss," but he did it.

"*Hmmm*. Well, you are a free man now, so you are equally free to choose a last name. Tell me, Solomon No-Name, what will you be known as from now on?"

He puts up the guitar for a while and thinks. Then he says, "Since I am to be a free man, I will take the name *Freeman*." He pauses again, plainly mulling this over. "Yes, I like the sound of that. *Solomon J. Freeman*. And the J, Miss Faber, stands for *Jack!*"

We go on with the lesson.

Last night I was so exhausted by all the events in what was probably the most horrific day of my life that I fell into a deep, dreamless sleep. But not tonight, oh no, not tonight, for tonight he comes, as I knew he would—old Pap Beam with a rope in his hand and a tomahawk in his head, grinning at me through the blood that runs down over his face and reachin' out for me...

I wake up just when I'm into the babbling-pleas-for-mercy stage of the nightmare and not yet into full-scale howling, and I rise up on my elbow and collect my scattered wits. And then I hear Chloe weeping in her bunk across the room.

"Come over here, Chloe," I softly say. "We could both do with a bit of comfort."

And she does.

Chapter 67

We first noticed it as a worrisome bank of low black clouds lying off on the southern horizon, when we were about a day's travel outside of New Orleans. With increasing worry, we watched it grow higher and higher.

"We'd best batten down for a blow, Jim. Get everything below that's likely to be carried away," I say. "It'd sure be nice if we'd find a nice quiet cove to anchor in."

"Sure would, Missy," says Jim. "I ain't never seen clouds that dark before."

But we found no such luck. The banks of the river remained straight and featureless, with nothing even suggesting shelter, and unlike Jim, I *have* seen clouds this black before—last summer in the Caribbean, on the *Emerald*. We were lucky; we managed to get her into safe harbor at St. Maarten before the storm was upon us. I hope we'll be lucky again, but I worry, for I well remember the fury of a hurricane.

My table and canopy are taken down to be stowed below. Windows are closed and tightened down, and everything breakable is taken off shelves and secured. I have Crow Jane make up the big meal of the day at noon, for there probably won't be any cooking tonight. We all eat together at the big tavern table, mostly in silence.

There is a strange, oppressive stillness in the air. It is dead calm, and seabirds, gulls and such, are overhead, flying inland.

We have done all we can. Now we wait.

In the early evening, the storm hits. It starts as a sudden strong breeze, and within minutes it is a howling gale. Minutes after that, a full-blown hurricane. Like a dog on a leash, the *Belle* thrashes about on its anchor line, and I am glad we secured the boat with backup lines tied to trees on the shore, should the anchor drag.

We all sit at the tavern table throughout the long night and try to give one another cheer, as sleep would be impossible in this maelstrom. There is only the light of a single candle set in the middle of the table, for we don't want to take a chance with a lamp, which might overturn and spread fire in the hold.

We try a few songs, hymns mostly, and Reverend Clawson offers up a prayer for our deliverance, to which we all add a fervent *amen*. We fall silent after an especially fierce squall that sets the *Belle* rocking in a very alarming way. Young Daniel sits by my side, and I can feel him shudder. I reach over and take his hand and hold it.

"Tell me a story, Missy," he whispers. "Please."

I have to smile, thinking of other stories I have told in other places in other times. "All right, Daniel," I say, and collect my thoughts. Then I begin.

"Any old port in a storm. That's what I was thinking as I wove my little boat through the ships in the crowded harbor..."

At about midnight, the wind suddenly lessened and then died out completely. Many heads, which had been resting on arms, popped up to listen.

"Is it over?" wondered Honeysuckle Rose. "Lord, I hope so. This has been the worst night of my life."

"Maybe not," I say. "I was in St. Maarten down in the Caribbean last year when a hurricane struck the island, and the wind died down all of a sudden just like this, so we went out and saw that the storm was swirling all around us. People told us it was the eye of the hurricane and we'd better get back inside or we'd be sorry. And they were right— the storm came back, fiercer than ever. But maybe..."

And then again, maybe not. It starts as a low whistle, then a long whine, and then it slams into us again, twice as hard and from the exact opposite direction—where before the wind was trying to drive us into the bank, now it's trying to force us to the middle of the river.

Sometimes I hate being right.

Oh well, where was I? Oh, yes...

"*'Take her up and tie her to the mast!' roared Captain Blodgett, and heavy hands are put on me...*"

In the morning, well before dawn, we are granted relief. The wind subsides to a mere gale and then tapers off to nothing more than a strong breeze. I conclude my tale and find that my telling of the exciting story has put young Daniel fast asleep. Ah, well, that is for the good. A young boy needs his sleep and I shan't take offense.

I stand up to stretch and say, "I think we're through it, mates, and—"

And I am knocked off my feet as there is a terrific shock and a great splintering, grinding noise aft and then along the *Belle*'s port side.

Damn! Something hit us hard!

"Nathaniel! Open the hatch! We've got to see!"

He unlocks the door and I rush past him and look aft.

A house! A goddamn whole house has crashed into us, splintering the steering oar!

The building, which must have been unwisely placed on a bank near the river and was washed away by the storm's floodwaters, slowly turns in the current, then grinds down the *Belle*'s port side, and then floats off, rocking wildly in the madly roiling water.

I run aft to look at the damage.

"Jim! The tiller is gone! We'll have to rig another! And it looks like there's a crack in the hull, down by the waterline, see it? Get some girls on the pump below and report if we're taking on any water!"

I look out over the river. There is all manner of flotsam, whole trees uprooted—there's a giant oak, its roots washed clean by the flood, turning over and over as it floats down the river.

"We've got water down here, but I think we can stay ahead of it!" shouts Clementine from below.

"'Thaniel! Matty! Get some boards and nails! We've got to—"

"We've got to get below!" hollers Jim, pointing up to the sky. "Look! It's a tornado!"

I look up and see the thing, its black funnel twisting out of the edge of the retreating storm, and scream, "Everybody back below! Move it!"

The Hawkes boys pound across the deck and down the hatch, with Jim and me close behind.

"Hurry, Jim!" I shout, pushing my hand on the small of his back, as we round the edge of the cabin top and head for the open hatch. He tumbles down in and I go to follow, but it is too late. The twister is upon us, howling out its natural fury.

It lifts me up and I grab for the hatchway top and manage to catch it, but my fingers soon start to slip. Jim's hands grasp my wrists, but they, too, cannot hold on.

"Close it up and dog it down!" I shout. This might be the last order I ever will issue on the *Belle of the Golden West*.

Jim's hands slip and I am lifted into the air.

I am aloft in the sky over Louisiana for what seems an impossibly long time, but is, in fact, probably only five seconds or so, and then I am dashed back into the waters of the Mississippi.

I go way under and then kick myself back to the surface and look about—'least I ain't got no hair to get in my eyes—and see only darkness. But then out of it approaches this many-tentacled monster and I scream in terror and flail about—only to see that it is merely the roots of that huge tree I had seen float by earlier. The tree seems to have steadied itself, so I swim out beyond the roots to the trunk and climb aboard.

I see the first glimmers of dawn in the east, but still can see nothing of the *Belle*, or much of anything else, for that matter.

Oh well, I say to myself as I wrap my legs around the trunk beneath me. *Let's just see where this ship takes us, shall we?*

That ship, HMS *Log,* takes us to a sandbar on the western bank of the river and there runs aground, its sailing days forever over. It is full light and I look upriver to see plenty of other stuff floating by—sheds; fence poles; chicken coops with the hens still sitting, clucking on the roof; many more big trees; the carcass of a poor drowned cow; dogs and cats, and sometimes people sitting up on the rooftops of their washed-away homes, but I see nothing of the *Belle of the Golden West,* nor any of her gallant crew.

I decide to follow the bar to the shore and then find a tree to climb, to see if that gives me a better vantage point.

I unwrap my legs from the HMS *Log* and walk along the sandbar to the shore, and I pick out a good tall tree to climb. As I put my foot on a lower limb, I see a movement out of the corner of my eye. It is but a small alligator, no more than four feet long, but still it sends a shiver up my spine. I climb up and look about, but again I see nothing welcoming to my eye—still nothing upriver. *Damn!*

I worry about my crew, of course, but not too much. I have the sense that the tornado only skirted us; otherwise, I would be quite dead and no more a bother to anyone.

Should I try to go back upriver, overland? It would seem to be the thing to do, after all...

No, that is not *the thing to do at all,* I think as I look below. My four-foot alligator has been joined by numerous relatives, many of whom exceed his length by ten feet or more. Some lie on the bank, some lie in the shallows just under the surface, with their two inquiring, *very* interested eyes poking through the top of the water.

Damn!

Looking out on the river, I see something new slipping by. It is a crude raft, maybe fourteen feet square, made up of logs bound together with rope, upon which sits a cabin of sorts, a rude hut, really. *Perfect!* If I can make it to that raft, I'll make it to New Orleans! I start my journey out on a long, overhanging limb. The eyes look up at me, one of my stranger, more hostile audiences, I reflect.

I run to the end of the limb, to the place where the branch will no more support my weight, and I leap off.

I hit the sandbar running, and I hear the monsters behind me bellowing and lunging out of the water and comin' after me, and *Lord, help me!*

I get to the end of the sandbar and dive in, arms and legs churnin' for all I'm worth, and I pull for the raft, which is slippin' on down the river, and I hope nothin' comes up from the horrid depths below and grabs one o' me legs and drags me down. *Oh please, please, God, don't let that happen. I'll be good from now on. I promise!*

Nothing grabs me and I am allowed to keep my feet, my legs, my life. *Thank you, Lord, oh thank you!* and I clamber aboard the raft.

I take more than several deep breaths and then look around me. The cabin is such that it could barely keep off even a light rain, and it contains only a pile of rags for bedding, but it sure looks like home to me. There are long poles laid out on the deck and I take one up to keep us off the shore, and I realize that this is how it will be from now on....

I will float and pole myself down to the city of New Orleans, and, if all goes well, as it very seldom does, I will be there tomorrow.

Chapter 68

I keep hoping that my friends on the *Belle* are all right after yesterday's blow. *They must be safe,* I pray, *'cause everyone but me got down below and the tornado only struck us a glancing blow, I'm sure, for if had it hit us full on, I'd be lyin' dead somewhere far away.*

I keep telling myself that.

Yesterday, after I had gotten on the raft, which I promptly named the *Deliverance,* I tried to think of a way to signal the others that I was all right and heading downriver for New Orleans. I knew that they would be delayed by making repairs, but as soon as they were able, they'd push on, and I didn't want them wasting any time looking for me. What to do? I'd only three things to my name: my shirt, my skirt, and my cutoff drawers. *Ha! That's it,* I thought, and poled my way over to the shore where I had spotted a likely looking overhanging tree. The sun was up over the horizon and it was now full day.

I maneuvered under the branch, then reached up under my skirt and pulled off my drawers. Then I hung them by the drawstring so that they'd be spread out to flap in the breeze. Anyone on the *Belle* would certainly recognize the underpants as being mine, all being quite familiar with their shortened condition, as I had pranced about on board on many an occasion, wearing only them as my lower garment. I know, I know…I wasn't raised up proper.

There being a clear open bank of fairly hard sand next to the tree, I hopped over and, keeping a wary eye out for 'gators, scrounged up a long stick and two short ones and laid them on the sand in such a way as to form an arrow pointing downstream. Then I scatched a *J* in the sand and got back on *Deliverance* and poled as far out toward the middle as I could, and when the pole could no longer find bottom to push on, I let the current take me.

There being no one in sight, I shed my shirt and skirt and hung them on the shack to dry. I sat down and leaned my back against the wall of the shady side of that cabin of sorts, and then as the day warmed up, I dozed off. I had, after all, been awake for over twenty-four hours.

I awake with a start as the raft bumps against something.

Oh, no! How long was I asleep? Damn! Just like Jacky Faber, Fine Lady, to arrive in New Orleans spread out on a raft, starkers!

But I see it is only another floating trunk of a tree and there is still no one close around. There are, however, boats in the distance, and if anyone's got a long glass…I jump up and throw on my now quite dry shirt and skirt. The skirt, being of leather, has shrunk up considerably and stretches tight across my tail and only goes down to mid thigh now. *Lord, I must present a sight.*

I scan the horizon and realize it was lucky I awoke when

557

I did, for there, to the southwest, rise the spires of the city of New Orleans.

I find the bottom again when the raft floats near to the levee, and I pole over to an empty spot on the dock and tie up. It is, indeed, a bustling harbor—barges and flatboats clustered around, bales of cotton piled high on the docks, workmen all over the place, noise and confusion, and the masts of tall ships poking up into the sky.

Ah, yes, my kind of place!

I nip into the raft's shack and find the cleanest of the dirty rags and wrap it around my head as a shawl to hide my shorn hair and dart out into the town. I hurry, so that no one can come up and demand of me a dockage fee for my *Deliverance*.

Oh, I could have a good time here, I'm thinkin', looking around at the profusion of taverns and bars. There is the smell of good food everywhere and my belly is growling, but I don't even have a pennywhistle to play upon to earn some coin with which to buy the food. Nobody's gonna put a penny in my cup if I just stand on a street corner and sing. I don't even have a cup. *Shall I beg?* The idea fills me with revulsion. No, never again will I beg. There is another way, and I start asking passersby for information.

I try, but I don't get the answers I'm looking for. I think maybe I've been asking my questions of people who are a mite bit too respectable looking. Ah, here's two that look like they might be of the sportin' class.

"Excuse me, Sirs, but might you know of a woman—"

"Comment?" says one of the men, clearly taken aback by my appearance. *Ah, he is French. Well, then…*

"Pardon, messieurs, mais…," and I ask the same question in French.

They look at each other and smile what they think are secret smiles, but I know what they're smiling at, the dogs.

"Oui," says the other man. *"À la Maison de le Soleil Levant. La rue Conti,"* and he points up a street leading into the town. *"Là."*

I say, *"Merci, Monsieur. Au revoir,"* then head up Conti Street, wrapping my shawl tighter about my head.

The street is narrow, as all the streets here seem to be, and long balconies hang overhead, with people sitting on them and laughing and talking back and forth. There seems to be a good deal of gaiety in this town, and I like it.

I pass Decatur Street, then Chartres, then Royal, and… there it is, just as he said. There is a sign above the doorway, made of carved wood, showing a semicircle sitting on a horizon, with rays coming out of it, all painted in bright golds and oranges and red.

It is the sign of the House of the Rising Sun.

A man in livery stands at the entrance and greets men as they enter. I know that welcoming customers *in* is not his main duty, though, that being keeping scum like me *out.* So I lurk and await my chance.

It comes when a carriage drawn by two fine horses pulls up in front and the doorman goes to it to help the occupants out. He goes down the six or so steps to the street, and I dash up them and through the door.

It takes a moment for my eyes to adjust to the dim light. I make out a small trim woman standing before me.

"Please leave," she says. "We don't take on Indian girls here."

I'm astounded. "Missus *Bodeen*? How could—"

"My name is Mrs. Babineau. Mrs. Bodeen is my sister. How do you know of her?"

"Uh, she got me out of a scrape one time. In Boston." I let the rag slip back from my head, exposing my sandy blond stubble.

"*Hmmm*. It is obvious that you are not an Indian, but just what do you want here, child? Employment?"

"No, Ma'am, but I'm told a friend of mine lives here and I'd really like to see her. Her name's Mam'selle Claudelle de Bourbon, and—"

"Precious! Dear, dear, Precious!" A burst of vivid yellow comes out of the next room, arms extended. "You've come to see your Mam'selle, just as I *knew* you someday would. Oh, come here, Precious, and give your auntie a big ol' hug!"

"Oh, Mam'selle, I'm in so much trouble!" I wail, letting the tears come and falling into her embrace. "I'm all alone and I ain't got a dime! Can I stay with you for a few days till my friends catch up with me? I'd be ever so grateful!"

"Everybody in this house pays their way," says Mrs. Babineau, in warning.

"Oh, she will," says Mam'selle, brightly, "she will. But first we've got to get this poor little thing into a bath."

"There now, Precious, you shed your darlin' little Indian-girl outfit—I declare you arrive in our midst at the forefront of fashion—and slip into that tub. That's it. Now, isn't that some fine?"

Ahhhhhhhh…oh, yes, it is.

"I must say your choice of hairstyle had me quite astounded when first I gazed upon it," she says, running her hand over my fuzzy head, "but now I must say I find it… curiously charming. Perhaps, someday, you'll tell me how you came by it?"

"A long story, Mam'selle, involvin' some crazy men and a whole lot of tar and feathers."

"Ah yes, I see some black smudges, here and there. Have you been a bad girl, again? I certainly hope so," she says, giving me a broad wink. "But don't worry, Precious, I've got an emollient right here that'll take that tar right on off. Here, lean forward. Let me work it in. That's it."

Ahhhhhhhh…

"You shall sleep next to me tonight, Precious, safe and protected, so shut your lovely eyes and relax, free of all cares and woe."

I crack open one of those lovely eyes and say, "I gotta tell you, Mam'selle, that I am promised to another person, body and soul…and that person is a young man."

"That's all right, Precious, and that is how it should be. I just want to feel the warmth of your dear body close to mine as we lie in sweet slumber. That's all," Mam'selle says.

She picks up a towel from a hook on the bathhouse wall and spreads it open. "Stand up, dear, and let's dry you off. Then we'll see about some proper clothing for you. That's it, step over here."

I stand and climb out of the tub.

"Oh, Precious, you are just the most *exquisite* little thing."

Chapter 69

"Yes, Precious, the Lafitte brothers do, indeed, frequent this establishment, mostly for the gambling. They were here not two days ago. Why do you ask?"

"Because, Mam'selle, if they get their hands on me, they'll kill me. Jean Lafitte bears me a special grudge 'cause we stopped one of his ships last summer, and when we found it was full of slaves, we liberated the poor wretches on the coast of South America and gave them all the ship's stores of food, tools, and weapons, to get them started in their new life. I marooned the slavers' crew on an island after several days' sailing and then burned their ship to the waterline right before their eyes. Told 'em to give Jean Lafitte the regards of Jacky Faber, *La Belle Jeune Fille sans Merci*."

"That was very gallant of you, *chérie*. Here, turn around, we must adjust the sash. There."

A dress, a red one with a very low-cut bodice, has been found for me and I am being put in it, on this, the morning after my arrival in the city. I spent last night in Mam'selle's yellow room, in one of her flimsier yellow nightgowns, she having taken the night off in order to tend to me. She had dinner brought up to us—it was hot, spicy, and good.

Tonight, however, we know we must work—she at her trade, me at mine.

"Stupid of me, really. The taunting—not the liberation—I mean. The slavers were picked up by a passing ship and they got back to Lafitte and reported what had happened, and he, of course, was furious and swore eternal vengeance. I saw him once after that, when our ships passed close going in opposite directions in the harbor at San Juan. He stood on his quarterdeck and shook his fist at me and cursed great French oaths, but we had the wind behind us and he did not, so he could not make good on his threats. I thought of bending over and giving him a look at my backside, but instead I merely gave him a deep curtsy and laughed. Prolly shouldn't have laughed at him, male pride and all that, but I did, long and loud. One of these days I will learn when to keep my mouth shut."

"You were not afraid he might chase you?"

"Chase and catch my *Emerald*? It never happened. Well, except for the last time, that is," I say wistfully. "She was one fine, fast ship."

"And she is now...?"

"At the bottom of the sea, off the coast of France."

"Ah, I am sorry...But you know, don't you, Precious, that he's a respected citizen of New Orleans?"

Which tells you something of the nature of this town, I'm thinking.

"Lots of people think Jean Lafitte is a bold pirate, Mam'selle, but really, he's just a dealer in stolen goods and a slaver. He buys things off of real pirates and then sells them in this town. That's why people here like him. They like the price of those stolen goods."

"*Eh bien, chérie.* But since he has many friends here, we must put you in disguise. This will help. Mam'selle Colette was kind enough to lend it to you till your own lovely locks grow back out." Mam'selle takes this huge wig from its stand and puts it on my head. "My! Look at you now, child!"

I stand in front of Mam'selle's full-length mirror and I am amazed at what I see. Long, thick black ringlets hang by my face and tumble off my shoulders and back. My chest swells out of the lace that lines the bodice of the dress, which goes in tight at the waist and then flares out the back, over my rump, and down to my ankles. There are gossamer white, puffy sleeves, for coolness, and white cotton gloves for my hands. I am speechless with wonder.

Mam'selle is not, however. "Precious, you are the very picture of a Marie Antoinette of Color! Why, with that tan, you look every bit a very pretty high-yellow gal, just like me. I declare you could pass for mulatto, or at least quadroon."

She pats things in place and takes a powder puff and dusts my upper chest and then my nose.

"You're lucky, child, that you have those big brown eyes—were they blue, we might have trouble, but they aren't, are they? They're just the loveliest shade of deep amber. Now, let's get some color on that cunning little white eyebrow and a little rouge on your cheeks, uh-huh…and a little red on your lips. Pucker up now, darlin', that's it. Oh, that's so cute, I can't resist. A little kiss, Precious? Just a peck? Oh, thank you, dear, and be still, my heart! And now a little beauty mark right…there. Done! Even your dear old mother wouldn't know you!"

She sure wouldn't, I think to myself, *and if she did, she'd be aghast. Painted up like a three-dollar—*

"We shall have to choose another name for you, Precious, for purposes of concealin' your identity and keepin' you from further harm. How about...Jasmine?"

I consider this and continue to regard myself in the mirror and a wicked smile comes over the lips of the person reflected. *Oh, if only I could appear to Miss Amy Trevelyne like this, why I declare she'd just faint dead away, yes, she would...*

"That's very nice, Mam'selle, but I've always been partial to Tondalayo. I could be your sister, Mam'selle Tondalayo *day* Bourbon, of the New Orleans Bourbons, and none of that Baton Rouge trash," I say, recalling Mam'selle's first introduction of herself to me in Constable Wiggins's jail in Boston.

She clasps her hands together and exults, "Oh, that's just perfect! My own dear little sister Tonda lay o, come in from our country estate to visit with her big sister Claudelle! Oh, we will have such fun together! Here, let's put this hat on you, and off we go into the town, to see the sights and search for your lost friends! Take your parasol, now, for you must keep the sun off your face."

Shortly, we are off in the town, heading in the direction of the levee, Mam'selle pointing out things of interest as we go.

"...And we are now crossing Bourbon Street, which, as you must know, was named after my family, and over there's the graveyard—see how all of 'em's aboveground like that? That's 'cause the water level is about a foot under the surface, so they can't put 'em below. They've got to put 'em up..."

I nod, noting with fondness that Mam'selle's speech sometimes lapses back into that which she learned as a girl, just like mine does sometimes.

"...there's the Convent and the Church and there's..."

We meet many people, some of whom know Mam'selle and bow politely, and she introduces me as her sister and some ask me if I am a new resident of the House of the Rising Sun and I answer that yes, I am. I'll be performing musical numbers tonight as well as dealing faro, three-card monte, and blackjack, and would they please be so good as to drop by? It is in my nature to always drum up business for whatever establishment I happen to be playing in.

Finally, we come down to the docks, where I had arrived only yesterday.

I look anxiously around for the *Belle*, but find nothing. *Was I too optimistic to think that they had got through the tornado all right? Oh, I hope not...*

I see that my raft *Deliverance* is still there, tied alongside the dock. It's got a little bit of paper tacked to the shack, probably a demand for dockage. I ignore it and move on.

"Your pardon, Sir," I ask of a man who looks like he's in charge of things on the dock, "but have you seen this boy— this man—recently? His name is James Emerson Fletcher, and I'd be ever so grateful if you'd search your memory for any sign of him. He probably tried to gain a berth on an outbound ship as either mate or seaman. He is an experienced sailor. He was dressed in buckskins, last I saw him..."

The man shakes his head, looking at the drawing I had done of Jaimy only this morning. It was, of course, from memory, and memory is fading.

"Nay. Could be any of a hundred men I've seen today. And ships come in here and go, they don't sign in with no harbormaster, no, and don't post no manifests, neither.

Three left just this mornin'—one to gather sugarcane in the Caribbean, one to Boston with a load o' molasses, and the other to the South Seas. Bor-nee-o, and all that."

"Well, thank you for your time, Sir, and if you hear of anything…"

"Say, sweetie, where're you berthin' right now?" asks the man, lookin' me up and down. "Yer a right good-lookin' little Colored gal."

"At the House of the Rising Sun, Sir," I simper.

"Wal, I'll sure be there later tonight," says the man, with a big grin.

"That's fine, Sir. All true gentlemen are welcome at our *maison*."

"Come, Precious, let us take a table at the Café Dauphin, right over there. We shall take refreshment and you'll be able to keep an eye on the levee," says Mam'selle, as she drags me over to a table on an open patio over which canopies have been spread.

"Ah, that's much better," says she, sitting and folding her parasol. I do the same. "*Garçon*, two dry sherries, please. And a plate of crawdads, too."

"Is this the only place the big ships dock?" I ask, still scanning the harbor area.

"Oh, no, sugah. They dock all the way down the river from here. All the way to Lafitte's slave pens on Grand Terre Island, out on Barataria Bay. Then the Gulf opens up and it's all salt water from there on."

Hmmm…when the Belle *gets here, we'll have to search even farther on down. If the* Belle *gets here…*

I lift the glass of amber-colored wine to my lips and take a mouthful and swirl it around on my tongue and then swallow. *Ahhhhh...* There is always something to be said for the riches of a seaport town.

"Slave pens. Slavery everywhere you turn in this world, it seems," I say, disgusted.

"So it seems, Tonda-*lay*-o. Will you not try a crayfish? They are very good here."

"Thank you, Sister," says I, taking the tiny red lobsterlike thing from her. "How do I eat it?"

"Why, you bite off the tail and chew it with your dear little teeth and then you suck out the head and then you swallow."

It sounds disgusting, but then I've eaten some pretty strange things in my life and so I do it and find it quite delicious.

"Um, that's very good," I say, reaching for another. "But tell me, Mam'selle, how did you manage to remain free in this world of slavery?"

"*Free?*" Mam'selle asks, incredulous. Then she begins to laugh. "Free? Why, child, Missus Babineau owns my high-yellow ass from the top of my yellow hair down to my yellow-painted toenails! Didn't you know that?"

Shocked, I shake my head.

"Oh, yes, she bought me when I was a little girl and raised me up right there in the Rising Sun, and when I was old enough and ready to enter the Sportin' Life, I did it."

Aghast, I say, "But when you were up at Missus Bodeen's in Boston, you could have run away..."

"And done what, Precious? Scrubbed floors, washed

clothes? No, not for Mam'selle Claudelle *day* Bour-bon. Come right down to it, I wanted the Life. I wanted the clothes, the music, the money, the fine wines, the high times, the well-dressed gentlemen, and the pretty, pretty girls. After all, I met you, didn't I, *chérie*? *Non, je ne regrette rien. Non.*"

But, dear Sister, the Life leads only to disease, disgrace, and death! I think that, but I don't say it, for I know it will do absolutely no good.

We sit the whole afternoon, sipping at the wine, snacking at food, and talking, but nothing comes in sight to bring me cheer. No *Belle of the Golden West,* no Jaimy. In late afternoon we rise and go back to the Rising Sun to prepare for the evening.

I had begun the evening's set by doing "The Willow Garden," followed by "Scarborough Fair," and then I turned to "The Young Girl's Lament," a sad song I recently learned from Solomon Freeman. It seemed appropriate, seeing the kind of place I was in.

> *When I was a young girl, I used to seek pleasure,*
> *When I was a young girl, I used to drink ale,*
> *Out of the alehouse, and down to the jailhouse,*
> *Right out of a barroom, and down to my grave.*

Mrs. Babineau had me placed in a chair, a guitar on lap, on a small stage off the main entrance and between two arched doorways, where I can be seen and heard but not be in the way.

If he had but told me, before he shamed me,
If he had but told me about it in time,
I could have had potions, and salts of white mercury,
But now I'm a young girl, cut down in her prime.

The doorway to my left is where the girls meet with their customers, and the one on the right leads to the gaming rooms. I am to play softly, just loud enough to lend some atmosphere to the place, some class. Mam'selle has fitted me with a filmy black veil that sits on the bridge of my nose and covers my lower face, should Jean Lafitte enter and recognize me. After my musical set, I am to go into the gaming room and deal blackjack. I will thus pay for my keep and make some money for myself in the form of tips, half of which I get to keep. Seems fair, considering.

When I was a young girl, I used to seek pleasure,
When I was a young girl, used to drink ale,
Out of the alehouse and down to the cathouse,
My body is ru-ined ... they left me to ... die.

I wind up the "Lament," not singing the lyrics very loud nor very plain, so as not to upset anybody, and figure I'll go next to some French tunes, and start up on "Plaisir d'amour ..."

Plaisir d'amour
Ne dure qu'un moment.
Chagrin d'amour
Dure toute la vie.

I'm well into it when I notice this gent standing off to the side, looking intently at me. He nods, smiling, then he chuckles at some secret joke.

I look away from him, and when I finish the song, he comes up to me and says, "Very nice, Mademoiselle. *Très charmante.*" He bows. He is middle-aged, well-dressed, bearded, and strangely familiar. *Who is he? Think, girl! Imagine him without the beard. No, perhaps I was mistaken...*

"*Merci, Monsieur,*" I softly say, looking into his deep, penetrating gaze. He reaches into a pocket and pulls out two silver coins and places them on my tip tray. "*Merci, encore.*"

"*Il ne fait rien,*" he says. "It is nothing, as they are nothing but coins, when they should be diamonds for one who has eyes as beautiful as yours, *chérie.* But, alas, they are all that I can afford at the moment. *Au revoir, Mademoiselle.*"

He bows again and then turns and goes into the gaming room.

What a strange thing to say...

The place is beginning to fill up and Mrs. Babineau nods at me and I put the guitar aside and rise. I go into the gambling room, sit down at the blackjack table, and shuffle the cards.

"*Bonsoir, mesdames et messieurs,*" I say. "Please place your bets."

Chapter 70

I learned a lot last night about the House of the Rising Sun, as I dealt out hand after hand of the game of twenty-one, sometimes called blackjack. *You are showing a four, Monsieur, do you wish a hit? Ah, a mighty king...are you still in the game? Busted, ah, what a pity, Sir. Madame, what is your pleasure? Hit you? But, of course. A five and a six showing...if you have a face card under, you will beat me. Too bad, you do not, but I do. I'm sure your luck will change. Place your bets, mesdames et messieurs, the cards are being dealt... Ohhh, double down on aces, Sir. Formidable!*

When I first arrived, I was made to show my skill with guitar, voice, and cards to Mrs. Babineau, so she could see what I might do to pay for my shelter. While she was pleased with my musical ability, she was most taken with my skill with the deck of fifty-two. *I want the house to win,* she had said, looking at me hard, *not too much and not too obvious, but win all the same. Do you understand, Tondalayo?*

I do. The players I liked, those who were kind and courteous, they walked away winners. Those I didn't like walked away considerably lighter in the purse than when they had first sat down. But, by and large, the house always came out ahead at my table. Cheating? Hey, cast the first stone, you. Those men shouldn't have been in a place like this, anyway, is what I say.

I learned that while the blackjack and faro and three-card monte tables were popular, it was at the poker table where the serious money was being wagered, bet by hard-eyed men with stacks of coins and bills in front of them. I further learned there was seldom trouble with sore losers because guns are checked at the front door by Mrs. Babineau, herself, and anyone who is found to have violated that hard-and-fast rule by sneaking in a handgun is forever banned from the Rising Sun. As it is the finest establishment of its kind in the city, that is severe punishment indeed. Herbert, the doorman, is expert at spotting suspicious bulges under gentlemen's coats and is not at all shy in giving a customer a quick frisk. Anyone found with a weapon of any kind is thrown over the wrought-iron railing to the hard cobbles below, no matter what his status or standing in the town.

And yes, I found that all feuds and disagreements among men, gangs, families, or even pirate crews, Lafitte and his bunch included, are left at the door, else they would be denied admittance forevermore, and everyone, *everyone*, comes to the House of the Rising Sun.

I discovered, too, that both men *and* women were welcome at the gaming tables, whether the game be faro, blackjack, dice, or poker, which sets New Orleans off from a lot of towns I know, Boston and London being two.

And I learned that Mam'selle was as good as her word in regards to sleeping with me—aside from sleeping with her nose pressed up against the back of my neck with her arm thrown across me, she was good. Mostly.

I step out of the House of the Rising Sun in late morning and stand blinking in the light of the actual sun, already well risen in the cloudless sky. Mam'selle has several...uh...appointments today, so I will strike out on my own.

"Good morning, Herbert," I say while putting up my parasol.

"*Bonjour, Mademoiselle de Bourbon.*" He offers his arm and I lay my hand upon it and together we go down the steps, then I am off down Conti Street, intending to check out the docks again to see if the new day has brought me anything in the way of good news of my friends. My picture of Jaimy is rolled up in my hand, too, for I will not give up on that.

As I walk away from the Rising Sun, I get several glares from ladies dressed more somberly than I, who had plainly seen me come out of the place. "The wages of sin are death, slut!" says one of them, unable to contain herself. I stick my nose higher in the air and walk on. I swear, there are biddies, always biddies, everywhere in this world, who are more concerned with the morals of others than they are with their own.

A group of nuns approaches me, as I near Royal Street, to tell me they can help me get out of the Life if I would just come with them and let them take care of me, but I say, "Thank you, Sisters, but not just yet," and press on. At least *they* were nice about it.

As I cross Royal and see Chartres Street up ahead, I become aware of three men walking behind me.

Uh-oh...Am I being followed?

I speed up my pace, but they stay right behind me. We

cross Decatur and then Peters Street and we're about to get out into the open area around the docks, and I'm about to break into a dead run, when, from the last alleyway to the left, step three more men. These men have swords, and they are drawn, and... *What?*... and at the front of them is the man who last night tipped me with two coins, saying he wished they were diamonds. *Diamonds! Of course, you idiot! It is the Marquis de Mont Blanc, the Frenchman you captured off the coast of France, the one who was fleeing the wrath of Napoléon and who had converted all of his family's wealth into diamonds! Damn! You charged him half his fortune to get him safely to England! Damn, damn, and double damn!*

"I am but a defenseless girl. Why are swords drawn against me?" I ask, the Lawson Peabody Look in place, determined to bluff it out, if I can. The end of this street widens out onto the levee, and I can see the river shining up ahead. If I can make it there, I might yet be safe.

"You do not recognize me, my dear?" he asks, bowing low. "Why, I was the one who once taught you the song you sang last night, 'Plaisir d'amour,' when I was a guest upon your ship, *L'Emeraude*. Ah, I see that memory serves you well now. Will your memory also recall that you fleeced me of a fortune in diamonds, rubies, and emeralds?"

"Ah, the Marquis de Mont Blanc, of course, I remember you, and most fondly, I might add. And I recall you saying, when you last dined with me, that you would make for New Orleans after we reunited you with your family, and here you are. Imagine that." *Stupid, stupid, not to remember that, you!*

"It is true you brought me to the bosom of my family, but for that you charged me half the ancestral fortune of the

575

family Mont Blanc. Would not even *La Belle Jeune Fille sans Merci* find that fee a trifle exorbitant?"

"You might like to know, Monsieur, that your fine jewels went to build an even finer thing, an orphanage, the London Home for Little Wanderers, where many a woeful waif has found warmth and refuge and much kindness and love," I say, with a full curtsy. "There is even a bronze plaque in the dining room, telling of your generosity. Daily the children sing your praises."

"You cannot know how that gladdens my heart, Miss Faber," replies the Marquis de Mont Blanc. "But for now, on to other matters. May I present, Mademoiselle, my cousins Jean and Pierre?"

I gasp as a sword point is put to my throat. I look down the length of the blade and behold the smiling face of Jean Lafitte, who holds the hilt at the other end.

"*Bonjour, ma petite*. I see that you have grown some since our last encounter and that is good. The exacting of my revenge is going to be very, very pleasant for me...But as for you? Ah, well, we will see if you enjoy it as much as others have. You will place your person in that carriage there, yes, and—"

"She isn't going anywhere, Froggy, 'cept into a ship bound for England and the gallows at Newgate! Now stand back!"

All heads, including mine, jerk up to see in the alleyway to the right, a group of men holding guns, both rifles and pistols, all cocked and pointed at my captors. Lafitte's men, thinking only to capture a helpless female, did not carry any guns, and must therefore drop the points of their swords.

"*Qu'est-ce que c'est?*" exclaims Jean Lafitte, enraged at the intrusion. "Who dares—"

Flashby? How—

"*I* dare, Frenchy," snarls Lieutenant Harry Flashby, his face covered with what must be a thousand insect bites. He is surrounded by a crew of grim-looking thugs. "I have here with me heavily armed agents of the British Embassy in this town, and if you do not wish an international incident, or to have a bullet put in your snail-eating guts, you will stand back and you will stand back *now, Mon-soo-wer!*"

Jean Lafitte's sword point does not drop from my throat.

"Stand back? *Stand back?*" he cries, ready to thrust the blade into my throat. "I will not stand back, dog of an Englishman! I laugh at your threats! I spit in—"

"OOOOWEEEE! STAND BACK! STAND BACK! I'M A REAL STRAIGHT-OUT RING-TAILED ROARER AND I GOT 'ER NOW, AND I GOT 'ER GOOD, BY GAWD, AND I'M A-GONNA KILL 'ER. YESSIR, GONNA SNAP 'ER SKINNY LITTLE NECK, RIGHT HERE, RIGHT NOW! YES, LORD, IT'S JUDGEMENT DAY! OOOOOWEEEEE!"

All heads, both English and French now, turn to look at the shaggily bearded three-hundred-and-fifty-pound apparition pounding up the levee on tree-trunk-sized legs, hands outstretched and reaching for my neck.

Good God, it's Fink!

I look at my options—Lafitte, Flashby, and Fink—and decide on the lesser of three evils.

I duck under Jean Lafitte's sword point and run to Mike Fink and throw myself upon him, my arms about his thick neck, my face buried in his bushy beard.

"Oh, Mikey, save me! Those men, they wanna hurt me!"

"Hurt you? Hell, I'm a-gonna *kill* you! Hurtin' ain't even in it!"

"You can kill me later, Mikey, but right now you gotta

577

stop those men, 'cause they wanna deny you the pleasure of killin' me!"

"They do, do they? Wal, we'll see about that!"

With me still clinging to his front, Mike Fink picks up a medium-sized anchor from inside a dory that's drawn up on the levee and commences to swing it on its rope, around and around, letting the line play out till the anchor describes a fifteen-foot arc in the air, whistling around and keepin' my would-be captors back and at bay, at least for the moment.

But it ain't gonna serve! Soon they'll start pepperin' Mike with their pistols and he'll go down, no matter what he says about his invincibility! What to do, what—?

"Jacky! Get down! Now!"

I pull my face from Mike's bristly beard and look over his shoulder and peer right down the five-inch barrel of the bow gun of the blessed *Belle of the Golden West.* Jim Tanner stands to the side of it, firing lanyard in hand.

"Mike! Get down! They're gonna fire! Get down!"

He jerks his head around and stares at the *Belle* drawn up to the levee bow first. He lets fly the anchor, which I see with some satisfaction lands on the foot of Lieutenant Flashby, who grabs his wounded part and hops about, bellowing in pain, and then all three hundred and fifty pounds, more or less, of Mike Fink hits the deck—right on top of me.

"Oooofff!" I gasp, unable to draw breath.

Crrrrrack! barks out the bow gun.

"Omigawd!" scream out the English, clawing at the red-hot chunks of rock salt imbedded in their faces and hands.

"Mon Dieu! Diable!" echo their fellow victims, the French, similarly afflicted with the painful condition of salt under the skin.

Mike starts to rise, but I reach up and grab his ears and pull his massive face to mine. "Not yet, Mike! They're gonna fire the other gun next, they'll—"

Crrrrack! The swivel gun fires and I hear the salt whistling overhead on its way to sting the flesh of any who might have escaped the first blast. There are more screams and now there is the sound of running feet, feet running away.

"Now, Mike! Now while they're reloading! Let's go, let's get in the boat!"

Fink jumps to his feet, picks up my gasping self, and runs for the *Belle*. I peek back over his shoulder as I suck some breaths of air noisily back into my grateful lungs. Most of my would-be nabbers have fled, as well as any amazed by-standers, but I note with some satisfaction that Flashby is on his knees, his hands to his face. The dock area, just lately a hive of activity, is mainly deserted, only some very cautious eyes peeking up over cotton bales are to be seen.

"OOOOOOWEEEEE! LOOK OUT BELOW! HERE COMES MIKE FINK, KING OF THE RIVER! STAND BACK OR BE SMASHED LIKE THE LITTLE PISSANTS YOU ARE! WOOOOOOEEEEE!"

And with a leap, the King of the River's mighty boots hit the deck of the *Belle of the Golden West.*

"Put me down, Mikey! You can deal with me later!"

He does it, seeing that the *Belle* has pulled away from the dock, such that I cannot escape my impending execution by his hand, and I run to the swivel gun, which has been freshly reloaded by Matthew Hawkes.

"Good to see you again, Skipper," says Matty, handing me the firing lanyard.

"Oh, Jacky, we were so worried!" cries Clementine Tanner.

"If I ever see you attired in such a way again," warns

John Higgins, "I believe I shall have to terminate my employment."

I sight across the barrel and what should I see but Lieutenant Flashby clambering to his feet, his hands still to his face, but yet another part of him presenting an excellent target.

I aim, I dog down the gun, and pull the lanyard.

Crrrracck!

I am rewarded with the sight of Lieutenant Harry Flashby shooting straight up, grabbing his buttocks with both hands, and running back down Conti Street, howling.

Burn me, will you?

"Jim, take us off into the river! There ain't much law in this city, but what there is of it will want to know why the hell we're bombardin' their town!"

Jim Tanner pulls on the tiller and we head out into the river, to safety.

Safety, that is, of sorts. There is still another matter to deal with...

"OOOOOOWWEEEEE! I THINK IT'S RECKONIN' TIME NOW, GIRLY! TIME TO MEET YOUR MAKER! TIME FOR OL' MIKE FINK TO SETTLE A SCORE! TIME TO WRING YOUR NECK FOR GOOD AND EVER! OOOOOOWWEEEEE!"

I go back to the quarterdeck area where the shouting Fink—a colossus of muscle, bone, and hair—is standing. On the way, I shake my head and wink at Higgins, Jim, and the Hawkes boys, and then I kneel in front of Mike Fink.

"All right, Mike, it's time to do me, but I hope you will be as gentle as you can, so I don't suffer too much. It would be easy for you, since I am but a frail thing and you are so very, very strong." I yank off the wig with its long tumbling ringlets and put on the Full Waif Look, all trembling with big teary eyes. "After all, I've been treated most cruelly on my journey to this place—I have been almost hanged and then tarred and feathered, and the most awful of all, I've lost the respect, admiration, and affection of my own true love."

I pull the bodice of my red Rising Sun dress down over my shoulders, exposing my neck. I lift my chin and say, "Go ahead and do me, Mike. Wrap your hands about my poor throat and exact your revenge, but first...first, please, my last prayer."

He places his hands about my neck and I lift my own hands under his and put them together in an attitude of prayer, and I pray:

"Lord, please take this poor girl to Your saintly bosom, this girl who really meant no harm to anybody but just tried to make her way in this world as best she could, and sometimes she done wrong, yes, but mostly she tried to do right, at least in the way she saw it. And please take care of my grandpapa and the poor little orphans at the Home for Little Wanderers and find them another benefactor, one who will be more constant than I have been. Amen." I pause here for some sobs and sniffles. "And Reverend...Clementine...could you please sing me on my heavenly way with a sacred hymn? It would be a balm to my troubled soul, it would, indeed."

Reverend Clawson and Clementine Tanner look at each other and immediately raise their voices in song:

> *Oh come, Angel Band,*
> *Come and around me stand,*
> *Bear me away on your snow-white wings,*
> *To my eternal ho-o-o-o-ome.*

Mike Fink places his two thumbs on the pit of my throat and grins. "Tarred and feathered, eh? Shore'd like to have been there to see that!" He tightens his grip. "All right, girly, you're goin' home to Jesus..."

But I don't go there, not just yet. He lowers his head and drops his hands and wails, "I can't do it! I just can't do it! I've killed a thousand men, but I just can't do a cryin' little girl!"

And I knew you couldn't do it, Mike!

It is possible that he fell prey to my charms, but it is also possible he sensed the four cocked pistols that were pointed at the back of his head from behind, where he could not see them. I prefer to believe the former.

I stand and lay my hand upon his shoulder. "I will give you your boat back, Mike. And look what we've done with it! Ain't you pleased?"

His head looks about and says, "Yeah, sure. You've turned it inta somethin' I can't use. And hell, there's nothin' more useless than a flatboat or a keelboat down at this end of the river—have to hire a crew to git it back on up. Nope, t'ain't worth it."

"Got whiskey, Mike," I says. "Two full kegs."

Mike lifts his head and smiles. "Whiskey, hey..." He looks off up the river. "All right, Mike Fink thinks maybe you've suffered enough for your crimes agains' him, what with the tar and featherin' and all, so...gimme two hundred dollars and that two kegs of whiskey and we'll call it even."

Done and done!

We nose the *Belle* into the bank and Nathaniel hops off to go back up to the levee to get my raft *Deliverance*, and he poles it down shortly thereafter and the two kegs of whiskey are put on it.

Mike Fink puts the two hundred dollars into his vest and says, with a sly look on his face, "You think you're smart, girl, but I got two hundred dollars in my shirt and I didn't really own that boat."

"I had a strong suspicion in my head that you did not, Mr. Fink," says I, "but does it really matter?"

"No, it don't, girly," says Mike Fink, stepping onto the raft. "But I gotta tell you, I know somethin' you don't know." And an even slyer look comes over his broad face.

"You're gonna tell me, Mike, that my friend Jaimy Fletcher was in the jail in Pittsburgh with you," I say, with a glance at Clementine. "But I already knew that."

Mike Fink sticks his pole in the water and starts back upriver, and then he says, "But what you don't know, Miss Know-it-all, is that I saw yer pretty boy Jaimy not two days ago, down in Chalmette, intendin' to take passage for Jamaica. Now, how's that for somethin' you didn't know?"

Mike Fink roars out, "WEEEEEOOOOOOOP! I'M A RING-TAILED WALLOPER AND READY TO DO DAMAGE! LOOK OUT, I'M A-COMIN'! HOLD ME BACK! HOLD ME BACK!"

And he disappears around a corner of the river and, I think, out of my life forever.

I, on the other hand, roar out, *"All hands to the sweeps! We gotta get down to Chalmette before he gets away again!"*

Chapter 71

Lt. James Emerson Fletcher
Chalmette, St. Bernard Parish
Louisiana Territory
USA
1806

Mr. Ezra Pickering, Esquire
Union Street
Boston, Massachusetts
USA

My dear Ezra,

It is my greatest hope that this letter finds you well. Please convey my felicitations to the many friends I made during my last visit to your fine city.

I have had a long journey down through this country on the Allegheny, Ohio, and Mississippi rivers, and though the travel was hard, I do not regret the trip, for I learned much about myself in the process. I do, however, regret to say that the much anticipated joyous reunion with Miss Faber did not take place as planned, for I found to my sorrow that I am no longer in her heart, as it is apparent that she has taken another in that regard. However, you and her other New England friends will be glad to know that when I last laid eyes on Miss Faber, she appeared to be in the pink of health and in extremely high spirits.

As for my own fortunes, when I finally reached New Orleans, destitute and clad only in rough buckskins, I immediately took myself to the British Consul in that city and was treated most courteously. I told the story of my problem with Captain Rutherford of HMS *Juno,* and asked the question: Can an officer of the Royal Navy be pressed like a common seaman?

On the consulate staff was a lawyer expert in military law and it was his opinion that such an impressment was highly improper and that I had nothing to worry about, which relieved me greatly—as did the news that Captain Rutherford had been cashiered from the service for letting Miss Faber escape from custody and was no longer in a position to do me harm. I could continue to pursue my naval career without concern.

The Consulate graciously accepted my note on my family's bank in London and soon I was dressed again in a proper uniform.

A ship is leaving for Jamaica in two days, so I shall go there, for English warships are sure to be there, it being a British holding, and I shall try to find a berth. I am anxious to do so as I intend to live a solitary life, taking the ocean as my only mistress. I do not seem to do well on land.

Again, regards to all my friends and may you all prosper. I remain,

Yr Humble and Obedient Servant,

James Fletcher

Chapter 72

We get the *Belle* down to the docks in Chalmette in late afternoon and I leap off as soon as we touch the landing, to search for a shipping agent if such a one exists, and it turns out he does.

"Yep, the *Jefferson Hayes*, left coupl'a hours ago, on the outgoin' tide, bound for Kingston. What? Who? Well, let me just check the passenger manifest...Let's see...Yep, right there, Lieutenant James Fletcher. He was on her, all right."

Damn!

"When's the next ship leave?"

"For where?"

"For Kingston, for Chris'sakes! Where the hell do you think I meant!"

"Now, you mind your manners, little lady, or I'm closing this hatch and you'll be travelin' nowhere."

The officious fool sits behind a barred window with a small counter in front of him. *Grrrrr.*

"I am sorry, Sir. Yes, for Kingston."

He scratches his head and looks off. "Well, the *Jefferson Hayes* generally gets back in a fortnight..."

"*Two weeks?* Where're all these other ships goin'?" I wave my hand at the forest of masts clustered at the docks.

"Other places, not to Jamaica."

I stand there and fume. *I can't wait two weeks! I've got to figure some other way, maybe we could...well, first things first...*

"Is there a ship for Boston?"

"Yes, as a matter of fact, there is. The *Hélène Marie*. Leaves tomorrow mornin' ten o'clock."

Well, that's a relief, anyway. I've been worried about Chloe and Solomon getting nabbed again, down here in the very heart of the slavery world.

"Good. I'd like to book a party of four—one cabin for a man and wife, Mr. and Mrs. Tanner, and a cabin each for Miss Chloe Cantrell and Mr. Solomon Freeman, both of them persons of color."

The ticket agent, who had been vigorously writing, puts down his pen.

"No, girl, these ships don't haul no coal. Mr. Lafitte's orders—only way blacks travel is if they're chained up down in the bilges."

I'm not believin' this!

I fume some more and then the agent gives a snide little laugh and says, "'Course you could *buy* a boat. Then you could haul your nigras around wherever you wanted to."

"Well, what's for sale, then?"

"Serious?"

"Yes, of course, I am."

"Well, wait a second, then."

He closes the hatch and, in a moment, comes out a side door and commences pointing out boats. "That's the *Hiram*

Johnson, two hundred feet, carries forty ton of cargo, and... what's your price range, girl?"

"Maybe a thousand."

"Ha! You can forget about the *Hiram Johnson,* that's for sure. 'Bout the only thing we got that's even close to that price and could make an ocean voyage is that one over there, the *Amelia Klump.*"

He points to a two-masted schooner lying alongside the next wharf over.

Ohhhhh... she's pretty!

"It's a schooner, come down from Boston..."

I know what she is—she's a Gloucester Schooner! I'd seen others like her up in New England, boats famous for being able to sail with a very small crew. It's said that if you set the sails and tie down the wheel, you could go down to bed, secure in the knowledge that she'll sail all night long in a tight, two-mile circle. *Just the thing!*

"...sixty-five feet long, twenty-five feet at the beam..."

"How much?"

"Two thousand, and no bickerin'. It's a good price considerin' she's got a full cargo of molasses in her hold, ready to sell to the rum distilleries up north."

"Why is she for sale?"

"Owner got drunk up in New Orleans and lost her at a gamblin' table. New owner don't know nothin' about ships and wants his money out fast."

"How soon could the new owner get here to sign the papers, should I be able to get up the money?"

"I could get him here in twenty minutes."

"Good. Let's go aboard. I want to check her timbers."

———

"She's sound, she's beautiful, and I want her. I want her so very, very much. Higgins, an account of our finances, if you would. How much has Faber Shipping, Worldwide got?"

"Well, Miss," says Higgins, his fingers running over the bills and coin in our strongbox, "it appears that, after paying off your crew, we have about a thousand dollars, American."

Damn!

"A thousand short," I say, with a dispirited sigh.

"It seems so, Miss," says Higgins, "but you are welcome to my share."

My entire crew, or what is left of it, is gathered at the big table in the main cabin of the *Belle.* I have explained the situation with Chloe and Solomon and how the *Amelia Klump* would solve many of our problems, and all think hard on what to do.

On the way down from New Orleans, Nathaniel Hawkes and his wife, Tupelo Honey, and Matthew and *his* wife, Honeysuckle Rose, had come up to me with a proposition: that they, in partnership with the Reverend Clawson, would take the *Belle of the Golden West,* herself, as the greater part of their share of the profits from the voyage, along with the rest of the whiskey and provisions on board. Crow Jane would be an equal partner and stay on as cook. It was their intention to continue to operate her as a tavern, on the New Orleans levee, with the Reverend as greeter and host, the Honeys as bartenders, barmaids, and local color, as it were. The Reverend had opined that there were surely many, *many* souls that needed saving in the city of New Orleans, and of that there can be no doubt. Plus, there were more bottles of Captain Jack's Elixir to sell. I liked the idea that my *Belle* would continue as a showboat, as I believe she was born to be, and since she would be of no further use to me and was of little real value down at this end of the river, I agreed.

It was further agreed that Jim and Clementine would go on to Boston, and Jim would resume his duties at Faber Shipping, Worldwide, while a place for Clementine would surely be found. I had thought to myself that place would be a nice cozy set of rooms, for a baby is certain to be in the offing.

Solomon and Chloe would also go to Boston.

Chloe explained, "Were I to go back to New York, I would fall under the protection of my grandparents, and I am sure, though I know that they love me, I would find it unbearably suffocating. No, it's Boston for me, as I have played the risky game for far too long to fall back into propriety."

I had assured her that, with her talents, we would certainly find her gainful employment, if not at the New England Abolitionist Society, then at least as a harpsichord instructor at the Lawson Peabody School for Young Girls.

Solomon, for his part, said, "I will go to Boston and I will enjoy being a free man for the first time in my life. I will hold my head high and I will sing and I will pull traps with Jim Tanner to earn my keep and I will take upon myself some wealth and some education, and when I have done all of those things, then we will see about Miss Chloe Abyssinia Cantrell. Ha!"

I would write out a letter of introduction for him to Messrs. Fennel and Bean, as they would certainly find the talented Mr. Freeman quite useful in their productions.

Daniel Prescott would go to Boston, as well. He would be ship's boy to Jim Tanner, which I thought he would like.

Nathaniel looks at Matthew, then they both look at their brides. All nod in silent agreement. "You can have the *Belle* back, Skipper. We don't mind, if'n it'll help out."

"My share, too," says Reverend Clawson. "There's always another collection plate out there."

"And mine, too," says Chloe, echoing Solomon's pledge a moment before. "As well as the money Father left me when he died."

My eyes mist up as I hear these words from my loyal crew, but my cold mind does the arithmetic—it is still not nearly enough.

"We could pull the little-slave-girl-who-knows-how-to-run scam one more time," says Chloe, pulling out the ring of lock picks that she still wears tucked in her bosom.

"No, no, not that, ever again, Chloe. That might work up in the woods, but not down here where they know how to chain up a person real tight," says I, rising and pulling my black-haired wig on again. "No, there is only one thing to do. Jim, will you get the *Evening Star* ready to carry me back up to New Orleans?"

"What do you mean to do, Miss?" asks Higgins.

"I'm going back to the House of the Rising Sun. I *will* get that money; I *will* have that boat."

"Surely, you don't mean to…"

I laugh. "Come on, Higgins, surely you couldn't think that? I mean, who's gonna pay a thousand dollars for one night with my scrawny self?"

"Forgive me, Miss, but I have noticed in the past that there have been some who have expressed strong interest in that very commodity."

"Well, that ain't it this time, Higgins." I rise from my chair. "Will you get my seabag, as I need some things from it? And Chloe, if I could borrow your lock picks, please?"

Preparations are made and Jim and I are into the *Star* and off into the warm Louisiana night.

"Mademoiselle de Bourbon," says Herbert, upon recognizing me running up the steps of the Rising Sun, "everyone was missing you and wondering…"

"It's a long story, Herbert," I say, puffing from my dash up from the dock where Jim had left me off. "Just let me in, all right?"

"*Oui, mademoiselle.* We are glad to see you back."

I enter, catch a glare from Missus Babineau for my lateness, go to my spot, and pick up my guitar. Once again I launch into "Plaisir d'amour," and when I am finished, I get the nod from the madam, and I go into the gaming room and take my seat at the blackjack table, and again I pick up the deck.

"*Bonsoir, mesdames et messieurs. Je m'appelle Mademoiselle Tondalayo de Bourbon.* Place your bets, *s'il vous plaît.*"

And I deal the whole night long, and while I am doing it, I never cease to watch the big table, where the serious gamblers play at poker, dealer's choice. I watch what they do, what they say, how much is bet, and what games are played.

Oh, yes, I watch.

"Precious, where you been?" asks an anxious Mam'selle Claudelle when I slip back into her room when the night is done. "I was so worried about you. Did you have somethin' to do with all that shootin' down at the docks today?"

"Yes, Mam'selle, there was a bit of trouble…"

"Well now, you just tell your dear sister Claudelle all about it as we prepare for bed."

Later, long after Mam'selle has fallen asleep, I slide out of bed and put on a nightdress and slip out of the room, for I have some business to attend to in the now silent House of the Rising Sun. In the morning I shall sleep late and spend the day resting, as I'll need to be sharp tomorrow night, *very* sharp.

Chapter 73

Tonight I wear a different wig, a reddish-blond one, and I don my filmy veil. I do my musical set and when I get the nod, I go into the gaming room and take my place at the blackjack table and begin to deal.

"Place your bets, ladies and gentlemen," I say. "My name is Mademoiselle Tondalayo de Bourbon and the game is blackjack. Your cards then...There we are. A hit, Sir? A nine. Another? No? Then you, Mademoiselle..."

It is around eleven o'clock when I see Jean and Pierre Lafitte enter and take chairs at the poker table. I notice that both men have little red speckles on their faces, and on the backs of their hands, too.

Hmmmm. I hadn't counted on this...but it shouldn't really matter.

At midnight there are five men at the poker table, and at twelve thirty, two of them get up to leave and I know it is time to make my move.

I signal a girl named Marie and she comes over to take my place at the blackjack table, as we had previously arranged. I walk over to the poker table and the three men glance up at me. The one man I do not know has gathered up the cards in order to shuffle them and deal out the next game. I put my hand in the purse that hangs by my side and pull out the entire assets of Faber Shipping, Worldwide and put it on the table.

"May I join you, gentlemen?"

"But, of course, Mademoiselle," says that man, rising to pull out my chair and trying not to look too greedily at my money. "Are you playing for yourself or for the house?"

"For myself, Sir," I say, placing that self in the offered chair. I reach up and take off the veil.

The Lafittes also begin to rise as a courtesy to a lady being seated, but Jean, upon seeing my uncovered face, abruptly sits back down.

"So it's you again," he says, recovering from the shock of seeing me there and smiling. "Good."

He leans back in his chair and whispers something to a man standing behind him, who nods and leaves the room—his bodyguard, no doubt, sent out to set up a watch on the front door, to nab me whenever I leave.

The other gent passes me the deck of cards. "It is dealer's choice, Miss, and it's your deal."

"Thank you, Sir," says I, taking the cards and giving them a purposely not-very-expert shuffle. "The game will be five-card draw, nothing wild, three-card limit on the draw. Shall we ante up, gentlemen?"

It is now two in the morning and we are playing the last hand. The other gent has long since left, broke and unhappy, leaving only the Lafittes and me. The pot is huge, probably the biggest one of the night, and the game is five-card stud, one card dealt down to each of us, and then in succession, four cards up, with betting after each round.

I am the dealer and all the cards have been dealt. Jean Lafitte has a pair of kings, a ten, and a deuce showing. Pierre Lafitte folded in disgust after seeing the second king appear. I have a pair of fours, a jack, and an ace up.

"One hundred dollars is the bet," says Jean Lafitte, looking me square in the eye and shoving in his money.

"Very well, Monsieur, I will see you the hundred dollars and call."

He turns over his hole card. It is a ten of diamonds. "Two pair, kings and tens," he says.

I turn over my hole card. It is the ace of spades. "Two pair, aces over fours. I'm afraid I win, Sir...," I say and rake in the sweet pot. "And I'm afraid I must say good night. I must also say that it's been a most enjoyable evening." I stuff the money into my purse and rise.

The two Lafittes do not give me the courtesy of getting up as I do.

"Congratulations on your winnings," says Jean, "but I cannot see what possible good it will do you. You have surmised, of course, that I have armed men stationed at the door to take you when you leave?"

"Do what you will, Jean Lafitte," I say coldly. "Others may think you a bold buccaneer, but I know you for nothing but a filthy slaver, and I wish only the worse for you."

"We shall see who comes out the worse in this encounter, Jacky Faber," he says as he and his brother finally rise. "You see, we have the back door covered, as well..."

I let my face fall a bit at this.

"...and the alleyways all about. And, if you think to stay

597

inside the Rising Sun indefinitely, then think again, you per-
fidious little bandit, for tomorrow morning I shall go see a
magistrate who owes me a great many favors. He will issue a
warrant for your arrest on a charge of slave-stealing, and the
police will come in here to nab you and hand you over to
me. Ah, I see by your face you do not like the sound of that."

Smirking, he and Pierre take their hats from the rack, put
them on, and head for the door.

"*Au revoir, ma petite salope,*" Jean Lafitte says with a
mock bow. "I go now to my bed, a bed you will shortly find
very familiar, if not all that restful. I look forward to the occasion." And the Lafittes leave.

It is closing time, so I help the others put away the gear in
the gaming room and then go up to Mam'selle's room.

"So did it work, Precious?" she asks upon seeing me.

"Like a charm, Mam'selle. Unbutton me, if you would."

I pull off the wig and toss it onto the bed, as I feel
Mam'selle's fingers working the buttons on the back of
my dress.

"Oh, Precious, I'm gonna hate to see you go! You are *always* such fun to have around."

The dress is unbuttoned and I slip out of it, making sure
Chloe's ring of lock picks still hangs about my neck.

"Oh, Lord, look at you standin' there like that! I'm really
gonna miss you, child. You sure can put Mam'selle's heart
all aflutter."

"You've seen how I always seem to pop back up like that
bad penny, Sister Claudelle. Maybe someday you'll do another Boston tour and we'll meet again. You know you'll always be in my heart and in my fondest thoughts."

I take the money from the purse and pack it into my money belt, which I cinch tightly around my waist. Then I pull on my burglar's rig, which has been laid out across the bed—first the tight black trousers, then the black jersey, then the black skintight gloves.

I go over to the open window, ready to go out.

"Give us a last kiss, Precious, please."

"Will you thank the rest of the girls for their help, and Missus Babineau, too?"

"Yes, dear child, I will."

"Good-bye, Mam'selle," I say, and plant a kiss on her forehead.

"On the lips, Precious, for this is good-bye," she says, and I pucker up and do it. Then I pull on my black hood and climb up onto the windowsill and look out into the alleyway, two stories below. There is a man down there, but he is facing the other way. Time to go.

"Good-bye, Precious," says Mam'selle Claudelle de Bourbon, giving my tail a last squeeze as I jump out the window and grab on to the rope hanging there and start climbing up to the roof.

I go up hand over hand till I gain the edge of the roof, and then, by hooking my foot in the rain gutter, I am able to pull myself onto the top. I crouch and look down all four sides, and sure enough, Lafitte's men are all about. I untie the rope from around the chimney, where I had tied it the night before, and coil it about my arm for use later.

The House of the Rising Sun is a freestanding building, but the houses next to it are connected, sharing two walls each, all the way down Conti Street to Bourbon Street, and it is a mere five-foot gap that I will have to jump.

I back up and then run for all I'm worth and leap out over the edge...

"Hey, there's something up there!" I hear someone shout when I'm in midair. *"It's her!"*

It's her, indeed, and she hits the neighboring rooftop, and slips, recovers, then commences running over the uneven roofs, down toward the river.

"Where the hell did she go?"

Well, you can't know that, can you, scum? 'Cause I'm up here and you're down there and I could go down anywhere I want, and I choose to go down here, at the back of the last building that faces on Bienville Street, well out of sight of those racing down Conti.

I loop the rope around a convenient chimney and climb down to the street, and when my feet hit the cobblestones, I'm racin' off to the levee.

"Cast off, Jim, and let's get outta here!" I order as I jump down into the waiting *Evening Star,* and he tightens the sail and puts over the rudder.

We can hear sounds of commotion back on the levee as we pull away, but nothing comes out of it that could do us any harm.

The thing is done.

Chapter 74

"Is she not just the finest thing, Higgins?"

"She is, indeed, Miss."

We are slipping through the long, smooth swells of the Caribbean Sea, off the mouth of Kingston Harbor, on the *Nancy B. Alsop*. Although I have always felt that a ship, once named, should stick with the name it is given, I just couldn't keep the *Amelia Klump* as the name for this sleek, elegant ship, and so I have named her after my mother. It is a fine day, with a good stiff breeze filling our sails—we have main- and topsails set, as well as a fore-and-aft sail up forward. A schooner does not have square sails like a frigate or other big ship, but instead its mainsails are gaff rigged with the sails' forward edges attached to hoops that encircle the masts. That makes it very easy to raise, trim, and lower the sails, and it also makes her a very sweet sailer.

Jim Tanner is proudly at the wheel, squinting up at the set of the canvas, while his wife, Clementine, sits beside him on the hatch top, sewing a Faber Shipping, Worldwide flag, complete with white anchor, fouled, on blue background. Both she and Chloe Cantrell suffered a touch of seasickness, but both are better now. Solomon Freeman is on deck, adjusting the sail trim when needed, and young Daniel Prescott is up in the rigging, deliriously happy, whooping with each foaming dive of the *Nancy's* nose into the swells.

Ah, but it is good to feel the salty breeze in my hair once again, what there is of it, anyway. My hair, that is...

"Missy!" cries Daniel from above. "Look there!"

I follow the point of his finger and see that a ship is standing out of the harbor. It is a frigate and from her masthead flies the Union Jack.

Eight days before, when Jim and I had got back to the *Belle of the Golden West*, dawn was breaking and all on board were roused and preparations begun for departure. The *Belle* would return to New Orleans with her new owners, Reverend Clawson, the Hawkeses, and Crow Jane; and the soon-to-be-named *Nancy B. Alsop* would be purchased to carry the rest of us to Kingston, Jamaica.

I plunged down into my cabin to change, followed closely by Higgins.

"I trust all went well?" he asked.

"It went very well, Higgins. Not only did I win the money, but I won most of it from the Brothers Lafitte."

"Their love for you must grow by the day. How did you manage to evade their clutches after the gambling was done? I am quite sure Jean Lafitte was not of a mind to send you merrily on your way with his best wishes."

"They expected me to come out through a door but I went out a window and up a rope I had tied to a chimney. I gained the roof, and from there it was an easy thing to run across the other rooftops and escape."

"Easy for you, Miss," observed Higgins. "And what will you wear today?"

"The blue dress. It would be the coolest, I think."

I peeled off my black burglar's pants and Higgins said, "Ah-ha. So that is how it was done," when he spied the yellow garter that rode above my right knee, which had two aces still tucked into it. I took off the black jersey, too, revealing my shiv's leather sheath similarly adorned with cards.

"That, and the fact that I was able to get into the Rising Sun's gambling room and open the locked cabinet, where I knew they kept the cards, and so was able to mark them—your luck improves when you know where all the high cards are and who's got what."

And did I feel your spirit hands on mine, Mr. Cantrell, guiding them during the actual play? I'd like to think that I did. Thank you, Yancy Beauregard, I learned from the very, very best.

Higgins got me into the dress and we went off and bought the schooner *Nancy B. Alsop*, while the others packed and made ready to leave. When Higgins and I got back with the paperwork done and ownership transferred, we pulled the *Belle* up next to the *Nancy B.* and put our things on board and stowed them in our new cabins.

The tide was incoming when we were done, which would help them get the *Belle* back up to New Orleans, and so it was time to part.

There was much manly hand-shaking and backslapping among the males, much hugging on the part of the females, and much blubbering, of course, from me.

Good-bye, Matty; good-bye, Nathaniel, oh you, my brave and stalwart oarsmen, farewell! Good-bye, Honeysuckle, Tupelo, didn't we have some times, then? Fare thee well, Reverend, you're one of the best men of God I've ever known. And Janey, my good Crow Jane, how I will miss you! Oh, I just know you're all gonna prosper on the Belle...

Good-bye, Miss... Good-bye, Skipper... Good-bye, Missy... Good-bye, Jacky... Wah-ho-tay, *Wah-chinga...*

They put their sweeps in the water, wave, and in a very little while, the *Belle of the Golden West* was gone.

Eight days later, I am on the deck of the *Nancy B.*, with my long glass to my eye, and I leave it there, scanning the deck of the thirty-six-gun British frigate that Daniel had spotted coming out of Kingston Harbor. *No, nothing yet... that has to be the Captain, there on the quarterdeck... and that must be the Sailing Master, beside him...*

We have been lying off Kingston for two days now, watching the British ships that leave the harbor. That thing the ticket agent said last week when he examined the manifest of the *Jefferson Hayes* for Jaimy's name has stayed with me: He said *Lieutenant* James Fletcher, not Mr. James Fletcher. So I've got to figure that Jaimy's gonna try to get back in the Royal Navy again if he can.

We've checked each ship, warship or merchant, that has come out since we've been here, scanning them with the telescope and even coming up alongside and asking them if he's aboard or if they've seen him, but nothing yet.... Well, almost nothing yet—one young midshipman on HMS *Courage*, which went out yesterday, thought maybe he'd met someone of that name and description at the officers' club on the base, but he couldn't be sure. Of course, I can't bring the *Nancy B.* into the harbor itself, for I'd be nabbed for sure, as it is a British port, after all. I was thinking of sending Jim Tanner in on the lifeboat to scout around, but then this ship comes out. We'll see...

I see the back of another blue-uniformed officer approach the Captain and salute, and I think he says something, then turns...and *yes! It's Jaimy! Oh my God! Oh, thank you, Lord!*

"Jim! Bring her alongside that ship, port side!"

"Aye, Missy. All on deck...ready to come about...Hard a'lee!"

And he puts the rudder over and we swing around. The sails loosen and then flap wildly—*in irons,* it's called—and then firm up again when the *Nancy B.* comes back up on the other tack and slips in next to the warship. *Oh, what a sweet, sweet sailer you are,* Nancy!

The wind, for once, is perfect—right behind both schooner and frigate, so neither of us can go afoul or be caught on a lee shore.

"What is it you want?" calls a man over the side of the ship, which I now know is called the HMS *Mercury,* from the painted name on her stern.

"I want to speak with Lieutenant James Fletcher! I know he is aboard, and it is very important that I talk to him!"

The man looks back over his shoulder and says something, and presently the Captain himself looks over the side.

He looks down and smiles a raffish smile. "Well, I had thought we'd left the fleshy pleasures behind in Kingston, but perhaps I was wrong. I am Captain Henry Blackstone of HMS *Mercury,* and who, may I ask, are you?" He casts an eye over Clementine, who, because of the heat, is dressed in the light dress we first found her in, and then Chloe, who has on the shift we first found *her* in for reasons of both heat and disguise, and myself, wearing my loose cotton top, buckskin skirt, and scant else.

Thank God, a rascal and not a prude!

"I am but a poor girl who just wants to speak a few words to her own true love, Mr. James Fletcher, who is aboard your ship as a Royal Naval Officer."

"Well then, we certainly cannot stand in the way of young love, can we, Mr. Bennett? Where is Mr. Fletcher, our new Second Mate?"

"He just went below, to the gun room, Sir."

"Well, go get the young hound up here, then, if you would, Mr. Bennett," says Captain Blackstone, still appreciating what lies below him in the way of female form.

"I'm grateful, Sir," says I, and my eye spies a loose line hanging over the side—probably a line that held a supply boat to the side, but no matter what it was, it's a way up for me. I leap for it, and when I have my hands and legs wrapped around it, I say, "Jim! Take her off about twenty-five yards!" And he does it, the *Nancy B.* swinging swiftly away and maintaining her station.

I clamber up the line, get my hands on the rail, and pull myself over quickly, if not elegantly, onto the deck of the *Mercury,* just as James Emerson Fletcher appears before me.

"Jacky! What…?"

Oh, Jaimy, it is so good to see you!

"Jaimy," I gasp, pulling Richard Allen's letter out of my waistband and thrusting it at him. "Please read this. What you saw back on the Mississippi with me and him was not a true thing...I have been good, mostly, and I am still your girl if you still want me."

He takes the letter and flings it to the side.

"I don't care what the letter says...," he says.

And my heart dies within my chest...Oh, no!

"I still want you no matter what it says or what you've done, and that's the truth, Jacky."

"Oh, Jaimy!" I cry and rush at him and wrap my arms about him and press my tearful face against his chest. "How I have longed for you, and worried about you, and prayed for you, and—"

"Now, hush, hush, it's all right," he says, running his hand over the stubble of my hair. "I'm not even going to ask how *this* happened, not just yet, oh, no...I love you, Jacky, no matter what."

"I love you, too, Jaimy, and I try to be good, but things always seem to work out different somehow, I just...Oh, just kiss me, Jaimy, if you really love me!"

And he does, oh, yes, he does. I place my mouth on his, and all the troubles of the past few years just melt away. *Ooooohhhhh...*

I hear cheers behind me as we come apart, and I say, "So much to say, Jaimy, and so little time..."

"I know, I know..."

"Where are you bound, Jaimy?" I ask, my arms still tight about him.

"To China, to escort a fleet of merchantmen plying the silk-and-spice trade."

"You must go?"

"Aye. I am back in the Service again. I have given my word."

Ah well, I know what that means.

"When will you be back?"

"We should be back in London in a year, maybe less, depending on the winds."

"I'll be there, Jaimy, waiting for you."

"Will you not fear capture in England?"

"Nay, I know my way around the streets of Cheapside better than anyone. I could hide out there forever. Huh, look at the trouble I've had there in the wilderness of America, for God's sake—if I couldn't hide there, I can't hide anywhere. No, I'll meet you in London, Jaimy, count on it."

"I look forward to that, Jacky, with all my heart," he says, clutching me close to him again. "I'll be back within the year and we'll be married and have you settled, and all will be well," says Jaimy. He takes a deep breath. "If you could just go back to the Lawson Peabody and...just...be good for a while...till we can meet again."

Be good?

Oh, no, sorry, but I can't let that go. I step back and give him a poke in the ribs and say, "Look over there." And I hook my thumb over to the *Nancy B.*, which races alongside.

Jaimy looks over the side and sees Clementine standing by the after mast, her flaxen hair blowing in the wind.

"Oh. My. God," says Lieutenant James Emerson Fletcher, astounded.

"Missus Clementine Fletcher, as you will recall," says I.

Jaimy stiffens, comes to full Attention, and nods. "I will not deny her," he says.

I put my hand on his arm. "As well you shouldn't. She is a fine girl and I love her as a sister. I hope you will be glad to know that she is now married to Jim Tanner and is looking forward to a better life in Boston."

Putting my hands on his shoulders, I look into his eyes. "I want you to know that I have been as good as I could be, considering my nature, and I know that you have been the same," I say. "I will meet you in London. Now give me a last kiss, Jaimy, a kiss to last a year."

We come together again, and as we part, I hear, from high up in the rigging, "Hey! It's Puss! Puss-in-Boots, herself!"

Uh-oh...

Though Captain Blackstone has so far been most accommodating of young love, I know the prospect of a three-hundred-and-fifty-pound reward for my capture would sway almost any man, so...

"Good-bye, Jaimy," I say, planting one more kiss on his face, and then I hop up on the rail. "Gotta run."

I dive over the side and into the warm water of the Caribbean. I hit clean and open my eyes in the clear, azure underwater blue. I see the sleek hull of the *Nancy B.* up ahead and I kick my way toward her.

My long American journey is over.

Epilogue

"Three fathoms," says Solomon Freeman from the bow. He coils up the line and throws the lead again. "Mark twain," he says, measuring out the two-fathom distance on the line.

"Drop anchor," I say, and Jim Tanner lets it go. We back the sails and wait. The anchor holds and the *Nancy B. Alsop* is back in Massachusetts, the place where her keel was laid, the place of her birth. The anchor flag of Faber Shipping, Worldwide flies proudly from her masthead.

We are moored at the mouth of the Neponset River, off the town of Quincy, wherein lies Dovecote, the estate of the Family Trevelyne.

I felt it best to land here, where I would feel safe from capture. Jim Tanner will get the *Morning Star* in the water and so convey himself, his wife, and Chloe to Boston, and he will also see Ezra Pickering so as to find lodging for all and to dispose of our cargo.

I climb down into the *Evening Star*—yes, we were able to

bring her aboard the *Nancy B.* as lifeboat—and then I am rowed to the shore. I then begin the walk up to the great house at Dovecote. I get halfway there, when I see a very familiar figure, her black dress swirling about, her arms outstretched, come running down to me.